"Romance, mystery, folkways, flawless dialog, humor, true love . . . guaranteed to linger in the mind."
—*The Milwaukee Journal*

IT WAS VERY CLOSE NOW, directly above Mr. Clayton's cotton patch about a hundred yards from where she stood, and at the height of a tall tree. It must be some kind of airplane, but it wasn't like any she'd ever seen; it looked more like a gigantic saucer with a cup turned down on top of it. It was hovering over the field, but she didn't think it was a helicopter. She had seen them only in the movies, but she remembered that they were oblong and had big propellers on top. There were no propellers of any kind on this craft. There was no noise either except a smooth hum that sounded like a tremendous swarm of bees.

THE VISITATION

Elna Stone

FAWCETT POPULAR LIBRARY • NEW YORK

THE VISITATION

This book contains the complete text of the original hardcover edition.

Published by Fawcett Popular Library Books, CBS Educational and Professional Publishing, a division of CBS Inc., by arrangement with St. Martin's Press, Inc.

ISBN: 0-445-04696-1

Printed in the United States of America

First Fawcett Popular Library printing: January 1982

10 9 8 7 6 5 4 3 2 1

To
Jeffrey Daniel

1

Stella Lidell hurried down the frozen graveled road to get to the Clayton's before dark. Night fell early in January, and in Lanier, Alabama, in this year of 1947 women did not walk alone at night. Usually she started out at three-thirty, soon after school was dismissed, but today Mr. Dennis had unexpectedly called a faculty meeting which lasted until four-thirty. She had left immediately afterward, but it was a good mile and a half from the high school to the Clayton farm.

She had come about a mile already, because there just ahead was the Granger house, sitting high on a hill above the road. It was a large brick house in the Georgian style, with a formal garden on one side, unusual for this part of the country, where one was accustomed to houses with many porches and shrubbery that grew riotously free. It was an expensive house too; Stella had heard it cost thirty-five thousand dollars, and she wouldn't be at all surprised the way prices had risen since the war. But she supposed Mr. Granger, who owned the only Coca-Cola bottling plant in this part of the state, could afford it.

As she passed, Stella looked up at the blank face of the house and wondered what went on inside it. She saw Mr. Granger at church sometimes; he was a gray little man with a quiet, sad face, always alone. She had never seen Mrs. Granger, and when she inquired about her, Mrs. Overly, Stella's landlady, said vaguely that Mrs. Granger didn't get out much. It was not until considerably later that she learned about Maureen. Some people, Mrs. Overly said, lived in Lanier for years without knowing Maureen existed.

"The Grangers don't want it talked about," Mrs. Overly said, "and folks try to oblige them. They've got burdens enough without us adding to them."

Stella's first reaction had been an instinctive anger. It was criminal, she thought, to hide a handicapped person, keep her locked away from the world, refuse to let her achieve whatever semblance of normality she could. But then she realized that Maureen was probably retarded, like many cerebral palsy victims, and it was probably far kinder to keep her in a protected environment.

She sighed, shifted her books to her other arm, and walked faster. The cold air numbed her face, but otherwise she felt quite warm and comfortable. However, darkness was beginning to fall, and she still had half a mile to go. She really shouldn't have offered to teach Wilma Jean Clayton to read. Her days were already too full. She taught five fifty-minute English classes, organized the library work and assigned it to student volunteers, sponsored the Honor Society and the Senior Class, and produced all the plays and entertainments. All the teachers at Lanier High School had heavy schedules, because the Boone County school system did not provide such frills as librarians, physical education teachers, or school secretaries. Stella did not resent the heavy load and extra hours, as some teachers did, but she deserved no credit for that. She knew very well that she was only using her work to sublimate her sex drive.

At twenty-three Stella was still trying to come to terms with her own sexuality, a problem she had been struggling with since the age of ten, when she fell in love for the first time with the sixteen-year-old boy next door. Naturally nothing came of it then, but some six years later, she lost her virginity to that same young man.

"Lost" was a euphemism, she admitted to herself with her usual honesty—"gave" was more accurate, and "forced upon" more accurate still. When she got into his car that night, she had already determined to satisfy her curiosity as to what was missing in the petting sessions with boys her own age. That something was missing she knew from her feelings of dissatisfaction, but her ideas as to specifics were hazy.

She had no source of information about sex. Her mother, free with vague advice about not letting boys go too far, balked at any request for exact details. Her girl friends knew no more than she. Books and movies always ended at the wedding, before the bedding. Stella's only information came from a book called *The Art of Love*, which was surreptitiously passed around at school but which was so flowery in style that one could glean few facts from it.

The actuality was a shock. She had not expected the pain or the blood or the impossibility of changing her mind. She was outraged at his ruthlessness and startled by his anger afterward. "You should have told me you were a virgin," he said. "I thought you'd take precautions. I hope to God I didn't get you pregnant."

By the time *that* worry was over, she had promised God that if he'd let her off this time, she wouldn't do it again, and for over a year she didn't. Then at college she fell in love with Jim Winthrop, and after some weeks of verbal sparring consented to go to bed with him.

She approached the occasion in a frame of mind appropriate for a visit to the dentist—and found a pleasure she had not known existed. Love, she decided, made all the difference. Had there not been a war, she might never have had occasion to change her mind.

But Jim was drafted and insisted on delaying their marriage until his return. Desolate, she settled down to the meager rewards of V-mail—and was soon appalled at her lascivious thoughts about other men—4-F civilians, soldiers on leave, other women's husbands. But she resolutely resisted temptation.

The fraternity houses on campus were taken over by the military for a short-lived training program called STAR, and the flight-training field nearby also set up classes at the college. All day long she saw orderly ranks of uniformed men marching to classes, and even in her dreams she heard the cadence of their marching feet. Inevitably she met some of them, and soon she was dating again, dating men named Kowalski and Lamartine and Greenberg, men with backgrounds foreign and strangely exciting to one whose previous acquaintances comprised only Anglo-Saxons and Negroes. Yet she was still resistant, still determined to be faithful.

But when she got the news that Jim was killed, she went that same night to a motel with a young lieutenant. She could not remember his name now, nor any detail of the time they spent together. His face had long since blended with the three others who followed him. She did remember, however, that even in the desolation of her grief her body had responded to those nameless, faceless men.

For that she could never forgive herself. It was a betrayal of all decent emotion; it made the love she had believed she felt for Jim worthless, put it on a level of mere animal passion that could be satisfied by any passing male. It taught her that she was as out of place in the world of love she knew from literature as a hog would have been in a drawing

9

room. The marriage of true minds was not for her; she could not rise above the coupling of bodies.

But with that realization she had come back to herself. If that was the case, she would have none of it. She supposed she would continue to date, because that was the framework within which social life was carried on in small towns, and also because she enjoyed the conversation of men better than that of women, but she would not allow any relationship to progress too far.

However, at last she thought she had found someone she could love without any fear that it was based on sex. She admired Grant tremendously. He was intelligent, courteous, and handsome enough to make her feel proud of being seen with him and a bit awed that he had chosen her. Except that Grant's family had been somewhat wealthier than hers, they had similar backgrounds. Thus they understood each other's values and ethics, and felt at ease together. Their relationship was one of quiet affection, thus far uncomplicated by those purely physical urgencies that had always troubled her so much. She wasn't in love yet—at least she didn't think she was—but she was ready to be in love.

She would not think about that now. She must think about the reading lesson. She had assumed that because she knew how to read and also how to teach, she could teach reading. Now with Wilma Jean she was finding out that this was not necessarily true. She could teach Shakespeare and Milton, but "The Little Red Hen" seemed beyond her. After three lessons she still hadn't found a successful way to begin. In desperation she went yesterday to Miss Pauline Howle, the first grade teacher, but Miss Pauline fixed Stella with cold eyes and said, "You're asking me to teach you in one afternoon what it took me five years in college to learn. Besides, you're wasting your time. Wilma Jean is dull just like all her brothers and sisters, only more so, because she's in pain all the time. Sometimes it's better to leave things the way they are. But of course you haven't lived long enough yet to find that out." She made youth sound like a crime. It had been a long time since Miss Pauline was young.

Yet perhaps Miss Pauline was right, Stella thought with her usual habit of looking at all sides of a question. Learning to read might be a too heavy burden for a sick child. The day she had found out about Wilma Jean, she hadn't thought of that. She had thought only of what a restricted life Wilma

Jean led and how reading could open up the world for her. It might even give her intermittent release from pain.

Wilma Jean was nine years old, and she had rheumatoid arthritis. She was a small child, not much taller than a six-year-old, thin and pale with swollen knees and elbows. The slightest movement caused her pain, and she spent most of her time lying on a couch in the big farm kitchen where Mrs. Clayton, who had four other children, spent her days. Stella had seen her there when she went to see Mrs. Clayton about Bobby, the second Clayton boy, who was failing ninth-grade English. Before she left, she had offered to teach Wilma Jean to read.

"That's mighty nice of you," Mrs. Clayton said. "It would be a big help to me. Wilma Jean don't have much to do, only talk to me, and I'm so busy I can't keep my mind on what she is saying half the time. I've heard folks say reading is a good way to pass the time. I've never had a chance to do much reading myself. My problem is not passing the time; it's finding enough time to do all I've got to do ... Will I have to buy schoolbooks for Wilma Jean, or have you got some?"

"I'll get some," Stella said, and watched a relieved expression come into Mrs. Clayton's face. The Claytons owned their farm, and Mr. Clayton worked on construction jobs too, but with Wilma Jean's doctor bills and four other children to support, they were constantly short of cash.

Wilma Jean had seemed eager to learn, pathetically eager. A light turned on in her face when Stella walked into the room. But so far she hadn't made much progress. Stella sighed. Then she immediately began to scold herself out of her discouragement. It was too soon to expect results. Today might be different. Tonight, she corrected herself, noticing how quickly the darkness was growing.

She looked up at the sky. Off to the east she saw a star ... No, it wasn't a star, because it was moving too fast. It seemed to be coming lower, too fast for an airplane, but not fast enough for a shooting star. It wasn't the right color for a star either. Now that it was closer, it seemed to give off a bluish glow. She remembered scary stories from her childhood about fiery blue balls floating around in swamps at night. Swamp gas, they called it. But this wasn't floating; it was moving purposefully. It couldn't be swamp gas anyway, because the closest swamp was ten miles away. She didn't know what it was, but she stood still in the road and watched it.

It was very close now, directly above Mr. Clayton's cotton patch about a hundred yards from where she stood, and at the height of a tall tree. It must be some kind of airplane, but it wasn't like any she'd ever seen; it looked more like a gigantic saucer with a cup turned down on top of it. It was hovering over the field, but she didn't think it was a helicopter. She had seen them only in the movies, but she remembered that they were oblong and had big propellers on top. There were no propellers of any kind on this craft. There was no noise either except a smooth hum that sounded like a tremendous swarm of bees.

Interested and curious, Stella was not conscious of any fear. She watched while the strange flying craft hung motionless over the cotton patch. Then it came straight down and landed with a soft plop.

Suddenly Stella felt nervous. She had been so absorbed in watching the strange object that she had momentarily forgotten where she was or what she was doing there. Now she realized her situation—the darkness, the deserted road, her aloneness. However, she did not suppose that she was in any danger—unless the plane was in trouble and crashed or exploded. Obviously it was a new kind of craft, possibly still in the experimental stage. That was why it looked so strange to her.

Suddenly a new thought flashed into her mind. What if it looked strange not because it was new but because it was from a foreign country? Pearl Harbor was only six years past. There was no reason to think it could not happen again. She started to run.

And found she couldn't. She was standing in a pool of red light. She couldn't see anything else, and she was paralyzed, unable to move. The light seemed to be coming from a giant flashlight which was moving across the field toward her. She could not see what was behind the light. She could not move.

She didn't want to move. She was no longer afraid. Something in her mind told her to be calm. It was as if a voice were speaking to her, except that she heard nothing. "Come here," it said. And she went. She was pleased to find that she could move again. It was a strange kind of movement though. Curiously weightless. As if she were gliding inches above the ground.

12

But she went nowhere after all. She was still standing on the road, and the red light was gone. The flying machine was going too. It rose straight up in the air with that humming sound and then zipped away very fast toward the east. In a few seconds it was out of sight.

"Tell no man," she whispered to herself. Now why had she said that? She thought it was from the Bible, but she couldn't remember where, and she had no idea why the words had come to her now. Of course she was going to tell. She must report this; she couldn't keep it a secret, because it might affect the security of the country. She supposed Sheriff Perry was the one to tell. He should know what it was all about. If the army or navy was conducting tests in this area, they would have told the officials. If not, Sheriff Perry would know to whom a report should be made.

Yes, she'd have to call off the reading lesson tonight and ask Mr. Clayton to take her straight back to town in his old pickup. She hurried toward the Clayton house.

Mrs. Clayton came to the door. "Why, here you are, Miss Lidell. My husband was just getting ready to set out looking for you. We was afraid something might have happened to you on the way. But you're here, so everything is all right. Everything *is* all right?" she asked, looking closely at Stella.

"Yes, I didn't get started until four-thirty because we had a faculty meeting. I thought I'd make it before dark, but I didn't."

"You started out at four-thirty?" Mrs. Clayton asked, with a note of surprise in her voice.

"About that."

"But it's six-thirty now."

"No, it can't be. It's only—oh, my watch has stopped." She glanced toward the pendulum clock on the mantel. The hands stood at six-thirty.

"That clock can't be right," she protested.

"Yes, it was right on the button when they announced the time on the radio a few minutes ago. You look funny, Miss Lidell. What's the matter?"

Stella hastily wiped the expression of consternation off her face. "Nothing," she said. "My watch must have been stopped all afternoon, so I've been confused about the time. I'll set it now."

The business of setting the watch gave her time to consider. It was four-thirty when she left the school, and it never took more than thirty or forty minutes to walk to the Clay-

13

ton's. Even allowing for the short time she had watched the aircraft, it couldn't possibly have taken more than an hour. It should have been not later than five-thirty when she arrived. But it was six-thirty. She had lost an hour, and she had no idea what had happened in that time.

Until now Stella had accepted her experience calmly. Strange as it was, she had been able to think about it clearly and logically and plan what to do. Now she was in a panic. Her heart was beating too fast; her palms were wet; and she had a queer, breathless feeling. Everything looked strange and unreal. She wondered if she were going crazy. She had always thought that those people who said they blacked out and didn't remember what they had done were lying. Now it had happened to her. She had lost control of her mind. She did not know where or how she had spent that lost hour. Except for Mrs. Clayton and her clock she wouldn't even have known the time had passed. For all she knew, something dreadful could have happened during that time. She might have been injured or drugged. She could even have committed a crime.

She had fiddled with her watch long enough. Mrs. Clayton was watching her curiously. She couldn't spend any more time trying to figure out what had happened. But she couldn't tell the sheriff anything until she *had* thought it through. She would have to give Wilma Jean a reading lesson. She would have to behave just as usual until she had a chance to figure this out. Mrs. Clayton had accepted her explanation of the stopped watch. She couldn't know that the watch had run perfectly all day. The important thing was to act natural, avoid arousing suspicion. She did not want anyone asking her questions until she'd had time to find the answers.

As soon as she got home, she would mentally retrace her steps and go over everything that had happened from the time she left the school. That was what she always did when she had lost something. She wasn't sure it would work when it was time that was lost, but she would try.

She wished she could go home now. She didn't really feel like teaching Wilma Jean. She had a headache. It was not a bad headache as she had heard them described—she herself never had headaches—but it felt as if an iron band had been fastened tightly across her forehead from ear to ear. Her eyes were burning and watering too, and her legs and arms ached.

She started to hand Wilma Jean a book, but she changed

her mind and turned to Mrs. Clayton. "I think I'm catching the flu," she said. "I don't feel at all well."

"I thought you looked a little strange when you came in," Mrs. Clayton said. "There's lots of flu going around, and you're bound to have been exposed, being with kids all day."

"Maybe I shouldn't stay. I wouldn't want to give it to Wilma Jean. Could Mr. Clayton take me to town now?"

"Why, sure. If you're sick, you ought to go home and get right in bed. It don't pay to mess around with the flu this time of year. Better take care of yourself, so you won't get pneumonia. Best remedy I know of is a hot toddy. J.T. swears by it and always keeps a little whiskey around just in case. I'll make you one if you think you could drink it."

"No, thank you. I'm beginning to feel sick at my stomach."

"Better not then. I'll call J.T."

By the time Mr. Clayton parked his truck in front of the boarding house, Stella was feeling so nauseated that she could barely make the effort to say goodnight. She ran upstairs and just made it to the bathroom before the violent retching began.

2

J.T. Clayton turned his pickup away from the boarding house and headed home. He was stone cold sober, and he thought he'd stay that way for a good while. Fact was, he might never take another drink. He couldn't understand what had happened to him tonight. He'd been drinking whiskey since he was sixteen years old, and tonight was the first time he ever saw something that wasn't there.

He hadn't realized he was getting *that* drunk. He'd always had a good head for liquor, and he knew just how much he could drink without losing his wits. Admittedly it was a good bit, but he never exceeded it. Nobody could say he'd ever seen J.T. Clayton falling-down drunk.

Might as well face it though—he'd had the d.t.'s tonight. Nothing else could explain that glowing object he'd seen in the middle of his cotton patch, where there should have been nothing but dead cotton stalks with a few white bolls still clinging to them.

And the voices he'd heard—had he really heard them, or was that the whiskey too? He thought back. Yeah, he'd heard voices all right. And the gunshot. That's why he'd left the still and started down there. Probably the whiskey hadn't yet started to take effect when he heard the fracas, but, by the time he got in sight of the road, where he thought the noise was coming from, he was sure good and drunk. Without enough cause to be.

There must've been something wrong with the whiskey, like that Jamaica ginger that had given so many men in Mississippi the jake leg a few years back. He didn't see what could be wrong with it though. He'd made it just like he always did, the way he'd learned from his daddy, and him from his daddy, and so on way back to the beginning of time. Nobody had ever had any bad effects from it before.

Naw, there couldn't be anything wrong with the whiskey. He'd just drunk more than he thought.

But he remembered plainly that he'd taken only a few swallows out of the dipper when he heard the commotion and started toward it to see what was going on.

Well, the first thing in the morning he was going to pour out every bit of that whiskey. It would be a big loss to him, but he wouldn't sell anybody whiskey he wasn't willing to drink himself, and he sure Lord didn't mean to take another swallow of that run.

The whole thing was downright unnerving. He'd been mighty tempted to ask Miss Lidell what it was all about, but he couldn't hardly accuse her when she was being so good to learn Wilma Jean to read. Them lessons meant a lot to the young'un and to her mamma too.

J.T. Clayton was fond of his family, even, by his standards, indulgent. He'd never raised his hand to his wife in anger, and he whipped his kids only when their mother insisted. When he was away on a job, he sent half of his wages home nearly every payday, and when he was home, he made some money on the side by moonshining. After seventeen years of marriage he still thought his tall, plain wife pretty, and he hardly ever chased after other women.

He couldn't help it if they chased after him. At thirty-six J.T. was still a good-looking man. He had not lost any of his jet-black hair or white teeth, and he was as flat in the middle as he'd been at twenty, although his shoulders were wider and his whole body somewhat heavier. His outdoor life had tanned his dark complexion and made the bright blue eyes a startling contrast to the otherwise brunette coloring. His voice was a pleasant drawl, and his expression was good-natured and easy-going.

A farmer by inheritance and a crane operator by choice, J.T. liked both and divided his time between them. He would work several months on a construction job, and then as soon as he figured his wife had saved enough, he'd come home for a few months to spend his time hunting and fishing. He was a hard worker and a real artist with construction equipment; there was no machine he couldn't operate, and people said he could take a hundred-foot crane and move a dozen eggs without breaking one. On the farm he was slightly less diligent, tending to spend most of his time on the creek bank or at the still, but he was unfailingly good-natured about the little he could be persuaded to do and lavish in his praise of his wife and teenaged sons on whom most of the burden fell.

In short, J.T. was a happy man, satisfied with his work, in love with his wife, and fond of his kids. His conscience never bothered him, and he had no worries except Wilma Jean's sickness.

But he was disturbed by his experience tonight. Shocked into sobriety by his visions, he had been numb at first, but now the reaction had set in, and his hands were beginning to shake on the steering wheel. That unaccustomed manifestation of nervousness further upset him. What he needed was a drink, but he was afraid to take one. Maybe a cup of coffee would steady him. He turned around a block and headed toward the café.

He wondered if Billie Sue would be on duty tonight. Lately he had been trying to stay away from her. It didn't do to hang around any woman in Lanier too much. He sure wouldn't want Esther to find out he was stepping out on her. Once or twice with Billie Sue didn't make much difference, but carry it too far, and it would get back to the wife. Esther was a good woman, and he doubted if she'd put up with that kind of thing.

Well, it wouldn't make any difference if Billie Sue was there. He'd just tell her he had to get straight home. But when Billie Sue said, "I'll be off in fifteen minutes. You want to go to my house?" J.T. was astonished to hear himself say, "Yeah."

Two hours later he was even more astonished to hear himself answer Esther's inevitable question as to where he had been: "I went to Billie Sue Cook's house."

But the final staggering blow was yet to come.

"You had no business to go there," she said angrily. "You know what a bad reputation she's got. I've heard about some of them drunken brawls she throws. Who'd you go with?"

"With Billie Sue, and it wasn't no drunken brawl. I ain't had a drink since early this evening. You can smell my breath if you don't believe me."

She looked at him closely. Her brown eyes were flashing fire. "Well, if it wasn't a party, what *did* you do?" she asked.

And that was when he absolutely stupefied himself. "We had a roll in the hay," he answered.

J.T. never did get to sleep that night. He was frightened out of his wits, more scared than he'd been in his life, even in the bombing raids at the Seabee camps where he'd spent the war. He didn't know what was happening to him. He thought he must be losing his mind. First he saw things that couldn't be there; then he went home with Billie Sue when he'd made up his mind not to, and finally he admitted it to Esther, something he'd never done in his whole life and would've bet anybody five hundred dollars he never would. It was enough to strike a man dead with shock.

He didn't know what Esther would do; she didn't seem to know herself. But he knew mighty well what she *wouldn't* do, because she had made it plain to him in the course of her long and bitter harangue. She wouldn't let him touch her, not now, and maybe never again.

"I might've been able to get over that one time with Billie Sue," she said. "After all, anybody can make one mistake, and if they're sorry for it and don't do it again, they ought to be forgive. But to do it over and over like you've did—and not just with Billie Sue but with all them other women when you was away on the job—that's just too much. It proves your marriage vows didn't mean nothing to you."

He could've killed hisself for telling her about them women. But when she asked him, it seemed like he couldn't help telling her the truth. He just didn't have no control at all over his tongue; to save his life he couldn't lie like he ought to have. He *must* be going crazy.

He wondered if Esther was asleep now. He couldn't tell. She was lying way over at the other edge of the double bed with her back turned to him. He was afraid to touch her after all she'd said, and he didn't want to say anything that might get her started fussing at him again.

He hoped Esther wouldn't want to be separated. That would be just about the worst thing that could happen. As long as he could stay around, he had some hope of eventually getting back on the good side of her, but how could anybody make up a quarrel if they were separated from each other? If she'd just agree to live on in the same house with him, and sleep in the same bed, he'd promise not to touch her until she got ready. He knew that way she'd come around sooner or later, because Esther was a mighty loving woman, besides him being pretty good at sweet-talking her.

So maybe it would turn out all right, he thought finally with a return of his customary optimism. It would just take time and care.

But what in the world had made him do it?

3

Maureen Granger put down her book, a copy of Agatha Christie's newest mystery, *The Hollow*, with a sigh of regret. It was a good book, one of Miss Christie's best she thought, and she was sorry to have finished it so soon. Strange how she read as fast as she could to get to the end and then was sorry not to have more to read. But that was all of this one, and there were no more after it. Well, perhaps in this year of 1947, Miss Christie would write two books.

Maureen was a great reader. Every month a package of books was sent from Smith and Hardwick's in Birmingham, and she read all of them, selected the ones she wanted to keep, and donated the rest to the Lanier Public Library.

Maureen had never been in the library—or the school or the churches or any of the places of business in Lanier, Alabama, where she had lived all of her nineteen years. She knew where everything was, of course, because Daddy and Mother carried her for rides at night when other people were shut up in their houses and wouldn't see her. She knew most of the people in town too, because until Daddy built this house last year, they had lived three blocks from the business section, and Maureen had spent a lot of hours at her bedroom window watching the street below. She had learned to recognize people, and she knew a good deal about their lives from observing what they did and listening to Daddy as he relayed the news of the day to Mother. But she did not really *know* them, not the way Miss Christie knew the characters in her books. Only a few had she ever seen up close: Jeanne from the beauty shop, who came once a week to fix her hair; Dr. Taylor, who always came when she was sick and sometimes when she was not; and Miss Pauline Howle, the first grade teacher, who had taught her to read a long time ago. Maureen hadn't seen Miss Howle for several years now. Mother and Daddy discouraged unnecessary visits.

Maureen knew they were ashamed of her, and she couldn't blame them. Knowing how repulsive she was with her twisted limbs, erratic movements, and the disgusting drooling which seemed always to happen at the most embarrassing times, she often thought it was a wonder that even her parents could bear to look at her. Yet she had known nothing but kindness from them. In fact, she had been so well taken care of, so protected and petted and catered to, that except for having read about it, she would not have known there was any unkindness in the world.

Maureen fell into a familiar daydream. Someday she would be able to repay her parents for all they had given up for her. Her fairy godmother would wave a wand—or the doctors would learn how to repair her brain—and suddenly she would be normal; her parents would be proud of her, and she would spend the rest of her life being a companion to them instead of a burden. She imagined scenes in which she helped her mother to entertain, drove her to the church and club meetings she couldn't attend now, talked amusingly to Daddy when he came home from the plant. In those scenes she was still thin with her own narrow face, light-brown hair, and black-lashed green eyes, but her face had lost its grimaces and drooling, and her body was straight and still.

But the dreams would not last long before her common sense took over and reminded her of the truth: Cerebral palsy was a permanent impairment of motor functions; it had happened to her at birth or possibly even before, and there was no way to change that. Everything that could be done had been done. What she was now, she would always be.

20

With some difficulty she put her arms into the sleeves of the coat draped on the back of her chair; then she rose unsteadily and moved with her characteristically jerky steps to the French doors which led to her balcony. Here there was another delay while she tried ineffectually to get her hands on the doorknob and open the door. Maureen knew she had only to make a noise, and through the communication system it would be heard all over the house. Her mother or her maid Rose Ida or one of the other servants would come. But she liked to do things for herself, so she kept stubbornly silent and finally got the door open. She went onto the balcony and sat down in the chair in front of her telescope.

The telescope was one of the things her father had bought to make her happier about living in the new house. Maureen had not wanted to move, even though the new house was the finest in Boone County, and designed especially for her. The communication system, the elevator, the improved bathroom arrangements, all the things which were to make life easier for her, did not compensate for the loneliness of being in the country a mile from the edge of town with no people to watch and no chance to participate vicariously in the lives of others. When she saw her parents' disappointment, she could no longer protest the move, so she cast about in her mind for some substitute activity and came up with stargazing.

At first she was afraid she couldn't work the telescope with her jerky hands, but it turned out to be less a problem than she feared. Daddy set it up for her; so all she had to do was push the long tube toward whatever she wanted to see and occasionally turn a knob that was no harder to manage than a doorknob. She had learned quite a lot about the stars in the past year, but she had learned even more about her nearest neighbors, the Claytons, for she had found that the telescope could be set for viewing things on the ground as well as in the sky. Of course, that involved changing to a lower-powered lens, which had taken most of a day and the assistance of her maid.

But it was worth the trouble. The Clayton place was considerably lower than the hillside site of the expensive new Granger house, and she had a good view of the entire Clayton farm and the road which ran past it. She watched the children each morning as they left for school and in the afternoon when they returned. She watched Mr. Clayton fishing and hunting and Mrs. Clayton hanging out the wash,

21

feeding the chickens, and gathering vegetables from her garden. She knew where Mr. Clayton's whiskey still was and how often he ran off his moonshine.

Sometimes she saw other people too, for the road was a shortcut from town to the highway and was more traveled than other country roads. But on this cold January afternoon there was no one on it.

She had read the afternoon away, and now it was almost twilight. Soon the stars would begin to come out. In fact, there was one now, one she had never seen before, with a bluish light instead of bright yellow. Her heart began to beat faster. Perhaps she was seeing something no one had seen before; perhaps she was making a new discovery. She began to fumble jerkily with the telescope, but her hands would not work right, and she knew she would be too late, for the star was moving very fast. Too fast for a star. Now that it was closer, it seemed the wrong shape too. Round. Flat. But with a hump on top.

Her burgeoning hope withered and died. What she was seeing was an airplane. It was foolish to think she could find a star the astronomers had missed. She was only a useless cripple, and she would never be anything else. Better not to hope. Better to accept what she was and enjoy life as much as she could.

It was a strange airplane though . . . All the others she had seen flying over were roughly bird-shaped. This looked more like a soup plate turned upside down, so that the bowl part was on top. As she watched, it seemed to stop and hover over a field about a quarter of a mile away. Then very gently it floated downward.

Maureen had stopped trying to adjust the telescope; it was still set for ground viewing, and now she slanted it downward and peered through it. What she saw mesmerized her. She had never seen anything like this, no, nor read about it either. She doubted if anyone had ever seen such a thing before.

She watched for a long time, but she would not be able to tell anyone about it. Maureen could neither talk nor write, and gestures would not be enough for this. She was powerless to communicate what she had seen.

4

Miss Mattie Shepard wheeled into the driveway alongside the big white frame house where she lived with her spinster sister, Miss Eunice Hayes. A familiar pain was grinding away at Miss Mattie. She hadn't been able to take her last pain pill, because she was afraid she would fall asleep driving home, and now she was hurting so badly her lips were pressed together in a thin line, and her forehead had little drops of sweat on it even in this cold January weather. Every thought except one was temporarily pushed out of her mind. She couldn't even think about the tremendous thing that had happened to her not more than ten minutes ago.

She went in the house and hurried to the kitchen for a glass of water. There, the pill was down. Now she would go lie down and wait for it to take effect.

Miss Mattie was terribly ill. Everyone in town knew it and marveled at how she continued to carry on in spite of her illness. Of course, she wasn't quite as energetic as she used to be. She moved more slowly, and she had to rest during the day, but she still collected the rents on her property, ran the house with the aid of a maid-of-all-work, and ministered to the needs of her fellow townsmen.

Today she had been to Caleb's Point, a town eight miles from Lanier, to visit a first cousin who was sick. Usually she did not range quite so far, but kinship demanded extra effort, so in spite of Miss Eunice's objections, she had gone. She thought she had done some good too with her bracing talk, because she had noticed that when she got ready to go, her cousin looked relieved.

Miss Mattie Shepard was fifty-two years old and had been a widow for thirty years, having lost her husband to tuberculosis of the bone in the second year of their marriage. The unpleasant nursing duties forced upon her then had given Miss Mattie her first sweet taste of self-sacrifice, and she had thereafter devoted her life to others. Her penchant for doing good, coupled with an ingrained tactlessness, made

23

Miss Mattie one of the less popular people in Lanier. But now that everyone knew she was terminally ill and just carrying on by sheer strength of will, they accepted her advice and ministrations more tolerantly.

She awoke when Miss Eunice got home at six-fifteen. Miss Eunice worked at Bell's Dry Goods Store from eight to six for twenty dollars a week and a fifteen percent discount on whatever she bought. Her salary and the rents, plus frugal habits, enabled Miss Mattie and Miss Eunice to live as well as most people in Lanier and save a little toward their old age.

Miss Eunice came to the bedroom door and said, "I was afraid that trip to Caleb's Point would be too much for you. Would you like for me to bring your supper on a tray?"

"No, I feel fine," Miss Mattie answered. "I just lay down to rest while I was waiting for you."

"Will you feel like driving down to meet Cousin Edith's bus?" Miss Eunice asked anxiously.

"I forgot this was the night she was coming in," Miss Mattie said. "With everything that's happened, it went right out of my head. Yes, of course, I can go. The bus isn't due until nine, and I'll feel fine by then."

Both Miss Mattie and Miss Eunice were looking forward to the projected visit, which had resulted from a correspondence begun some two months ago. Edith Alexander was a second cousin, the granddaughter of their mother's older brother, who had moved to Texas in early manhood and married there. As the years passed, contacts between the two families dwindled, not by design but through the pressures of daily life, and although Miss Mattie and Miss Eunice were very family conscious and regretted that they knew so little of the surviving members of Uncle John's family, they felt powerless to do anything about it. They were therefore pleasurably excited when the first letter came from Cousin Edith and even more pleased when it developed that she wanted to visit them.

They talked about it as they ate supper, wondering if they would be able to notice any family resemblance, speculating about the length of her stay, as yet unannounced, and going over their plans for her entertainment, which would consist largely of visits to various cemeteries in the vicinity.

After they drained the last drop of nourishment from the talk about Cousin Edith's visit, they passed to other subjects. Miss Mattie gave the news she had garnered during her visit today, and Miss Eunice told what she had heard in town. They talked like this every night. There was always some event of birth, marriage, or death to be discussed. They did not talk much about their personal feelings, their affection for each other being taken for granted by both and so deeply felt that to talk about it would be embarrassing.

After supper they went back to Miss Mattie's bedroom, where there was a gas heater burning. This was the only fire they kept unless they had company, because the house was far too large and drafty to heat all of it, and there was no need anyway just for two people.

Miss Eunice started toward the radio, which sat on a table in front of the window, but Miss Mattie said, "Don't turn it on tonight, Eunice. I've got something to tell you. I waited through supper, because I wanted you to give all your attention to it, but I'd better tell you now before Cousin Edith comes. It's the most wonderful thing that ever happened to me, though I don't know what it means. Maybe you can help me figure that out . . . Eunice, I've had a vision!"

"Why, what do you mean?"

"I don't know exactly how to tell you, because I don't understand myself. All I know is that tonight as I was coming back from Caleb's Point, God sent me a vision. Let me tell you about it . . . It happened just after I passed the Clayton's house, before I got to the Granger's. I was just driving along, driving pretty fast the way I always do and maybe a little faster than usual because—well, because, to tell you the truth, I wasn't feeling any too well, and I wanted to get home and take a pill.

"Anyway, all of a sudden I happened to notice a light, sort of a bright, bluish-white glow that was hanging low in the sky not far from the road. You know what it put me in mind of? This may sound foolish, but the first thing I thought of was that verse in the bible that says, 'And, lo, the star, which they saw in the east, went before them, till it came and stood over where the young child was.'

"That's just what it looked like, Eunice, a big, blue-white star standing low in the sky. Only it started floating downward. There were a lot of trees cutting off my vision, so I couldn't tell what had happened to it until I rounded the curve. Then there it was, right before me, and it wasn't a star; it was a round, bluish-white light.

25

"I stopped the car and got out and knelt down right there in the middle of the road. I forgot all about my pain. I was too awed and scared to feel anything else. While I watched, the thing seemed to open up, and the white light changed to red, and . . ."

She paused, too overcome by a violent emotion to say any more. Her hands moved agitatedly, and her expression was exalted. "I saw our Lord, Eunice!" she burst out.

Again she paused, but after a moment she went on in a wondering voice, "He was clothed in light, shining from head to foot. And I—I swooned dead away. I couldn't help it. It was just too much for any mortal eye to behold. But I did behold it. I saw Jesus, just like Paul did on the road to Damascus.

"When I came to, I was lying in the road. I got up and looked about, and the light was still there, but the Lord had gone. Back inside the round thing, I guess, but I didn't have a chance to find out, because something seemed to be telling me to go. I got in the car and came home, but my pain came back as soon as I was away from the light; so I haven't had any time yet to think back over the experience and find out what it means. What do you think?"

"I don't know, Mattie," Miss Eunice said. Thoughts were whirling through her head, but she didn't want to speak too soon and say something discouraging. She was wondering exactly what had happened. Mattie tried to do too much, no doubt about that, and it could be that the pain got so bad she just passed out and then had the dream, or whatever it was.

Miss Mattie seemed to read her sister's mind. She said, "I know what people will say; they'll say I fainted and was out of my head. But I wasn't, Eunice, I swear, I was just as wide awake and as much myself as I am right now. It was only after I saw Jesus that I swooned. You believe me, don't you?"

"Well, I . . ." Miss Eunice paused. She was religious too. She went to church twice every Sunday and to the Wednesday night prayer service, and she read the Bible every night of her life. Yet she was aware that somehow she was not as spiritual as Mattie. She didn't know the Bible as well, and she didn't think as much as she should about serving God. In church her thoughts often wandered, and sometimes when she was reading the Bible, she was impatient to get through so she could read a chapter in one of Frances Parkinson Keyes's novels.

Maybe Mattie *had* seen a vision. If God had sent them during Biblical times, there was no reason he couldn't do the same thing now. Miss Eunice didn't know anybody more fitted to receive one than Mattie.

She said slowly, "Yes, I believe you. But I don't know what the purpose was, unless it was just to comfort you in this hour of trial."

"Or maybe to tell me that there's a new day coming," Miss Mattie said eagerly. For a moment her eyes were bright with hope. "You know I've always felt that God was going to heal me, and maybe this was an announcement of it."

But after considering that idea for a moment, she shook her head. "I didn't hear any announcement though," she said regretfully. "And I don't feel any different. I was in a good bit of pain when I got home. So I can't think I'm any better, no matter how much I'd like to. He must have had some other purpose. But what could it be?"

Miss Eunice said comfortingly, "Well, Sister, after all, Paul didn't find out the meaning until three days after Jesus appeared to him. In his own good time, God will doubtless reveal his purpose to you."

"You're right, Eunice, I must be patient."

"Meanwhile, maybe you oughtn't to mention this to anyone," Miss Eunice suggested.

Miss Mattie looked dissatisfied. She had meant to start telling it the first thing in the morning. Miss Mattie believed in giving her testimony on every suitable occasion, but she had never had such an experience as this to relate, and she was looking forward to sharing it with as many people as possible. However, she could see the sense in what Eunice said. She was obliged to wait to know God's will in the matter.

"Besides," Miss Eunice said, unaware that she had already gained her point, "it would be best not to have something else on hand while Cousin Edith is here."

"Yes, and it's time to get her," Miss Mattie said.

Had Cousin Edith not been the only passenger getting off the bus, Miss Mattie and Miss Eunice might not have recognized her. They had expected some family resemblance, but she did not look like either Miss Mattie, who was big-boned and hatchet-faced, nor Miss Eunice, who had patrician features and a gentle expression. Searching for some point of favor to their maternal grandparents, who were also Cousin Edith's ancestors, they had to content themselves with remarking that her nose might be slanted somewhat like Grandma's.

However, that was later. When Cousin Edith stepped out of the bus, they had time only to see that she was a plump, middle-aged woman, dressed plainly in a navy blue coat and hat, before they rushed forward to give her the welcoming hugs due a relative. Then they immediately began asking polite questions about her long bus trip from Texas.

"The trip was fine," Cousin Edith answered in a high, thin voice. "I slept most of last night; so I'm not as tired as I thought I'd be after riding two days. During daylight I enjoyed seeing the countryside. It's different here from my home."

"That's so," Miss Mattie, who had never traveled more than a hundred miles from Lanier, said. "You'll have to tell us all about Texas while you're here."

"Yes," Miss Eunice chimed in, "and we're anxious to hear about all the relatives there too."

By this time the bus driver had opened the baggage compartment underneath the bus and handed out Cousin Edith's large suitcase. Miss Mattie eyed it in dismay. She felt that politeness demanded her assistance, and once she could have carried the suitcase easily, but now she knew her strength wouldn't hold out. And it was far too big for Eunice, who had never been strong. Miss Mattie looked around for one of the Negro boys who hung around the bus station in daytime, waiting for just such opportunities, but they had all gone home.

The vexing little etiquette problem was settled quite easily, however, when Cousin Edith picked up the suitcase as if it weighed nothing at all and walked briskly toward the car. She's energetic, Miss Mattie thought approvingly. Strong, too. I don't know that I could have lifted such a big case with so little strain even in my best days.

In the car Miss Eunice asked again about the relatives. "It's been so long since we heard any news from Texas—not since Mamma died, I guess, and that was twenty years ago. Of course, Mattie and I never saw Uncle John or any of his family, but Mamma used to stay in touch and tell us about them. He had six children, I remember, but I doubt if I could even call all their names now. There was William, your daddy, and Johnny, named for Uncle John, and Ruby and Pearl—but I've forgotten the other two."

"Glen and Jane," Cousin Edith said. "They're all dead now. In fact, the whole family has died out. I'm the last one left, and I never had any children. That's the reason I wanted so much to visit you. There's nothing like family."

This was so exactly Miss Mattie and Miss Eunice's sentiment that they warmed toward Cousin Edith. She had seemed a little strange at first, but they were liking her better all the time.

"I'm real sorry to hear that your branch of the family is dying out," Miss Mattie said gruffly, "but you don't have to feel alone, because our branch has multiplied. Eunice and I didn't do our part, I guess, but our brother had eight children, and there are lots of cousins besides. We've got kin over three counties, and they're all anxious to see you."

"As to that, I don't know. I'd rather get acquainted with you first," Cousin Edith said.

"Of course. There'll be plenty of time to meet the others later. You're going to stay a week or two, aren't you?"

"Oh, yes, at least that, so I don't want you to make company of me. I'd just like to settle in and be part of your family for a while."

Neither Miss Mattie nor Miss Eunice betrayed by word or glance her dissatisfaction with this answer nor her anxiety to know the duration of the visit, knowledge that was vital in determining their plans for the care, feeding, and entertainment of their guest.

When they reached home, Cousin Edith once more picked up her own bag and carried it into the house.

"Eunice, you show Cousin Edith to her room, while I make some hot chocolate and slice the cake," Miss Mattie said.

The hot chocolate was made and grew cold, and still Eunice and Cousin Edith did not return. Miss Mattie poured it back into the saucepan and started toward the stairs to see what was keeping them. They were on their way down.

"Cousin Edith wanted the front bedroom instead of the middle one Arline had got ready for her," Miss Eunice said, "so I had to make the bed."

Miss Mattie was a little annoyed. She had decided on the middle bedroom for Cousin Edith, and she wasn't accustomed to having any interference with her housekeeping arrangements. "Why did you want to change?" she asked.

"I thought it would be better if I wasn't next door to Cousin Eunice," Cousin Edith said. "Living alone the way I do, I'm used to my privacy. Besides, I like to be on the front so I can see what's going on in the street."

Miss Mattie was a little puzzled. She didn't see that being next door to Eunice would interfere with Cousin Edith's privacy. But a guest was a guest, and she wouldn't be rude.

"Well, no matter," she said. "Come and have some cake and hot chocolate."

Later, after their visitor had retired to her room, Miss Eunice came into the downstairs bedroom Miss Mattie had used since her illness. "Anything you want before I go to bed?" she asked.

"No, I have everything I need. What do you think of Cousin Edith, Sister?"

Miss Eunice sat down. "I wanted to talk to you about that," she said, a troubled expression coming over her kind face. "She's nice and friendly, but—"

"Peculiar," Miss Mattie finished. "I can't imagine going to visit someone and insisting on having a different room from the one prepared for me. And she hardly ate enough of the cake to be polite."

"Maybe she doesn't like sweets," Miss Eunice said.

"You always try to find excuses for people, Sister. But that wasn't the only thing that seemed strange. Did you notice her eyes? They're yellow."

"I expect that was just the light," Miss Eunice said. "They'll probably look light brown in the daytime. Light-brown eyes often have a yellow cast to them."

"She's shifty-eyed too. Did you notice the way she kept looking everywhere but at you? I like a frank gaze. When somebody can't meet my eyes, I always wonder how honest he is."

"Sister! Of course she's honest. She's our own second cousin!"

"Any family can have a black sheep in it."

Miss Eunice looked even more troubled, but she said, "I expect we're just disappointed because she didn't seem like kin right away. We'll probably feel different after we get to know her better."

"I hope so. Anyway, she's company, and we'll have to be polite. Did she say anything else about how long she means to stay?"

Miss Eunice shook her head. "She brought a closet full of clothes though. In fact, big as that suitcase is, I don't see how she got them all into it. It looks as though she's going to pay us a nice, long visit."

They looked at each other. Somehow that prospect did not seem as appealing now as it had earlier. But, although each of them was aware of what the other was thinking, neither expressed it.

5

The first two days Stella was sick no one was much concerned. Flu was too common a winter illness to merit much attention when it occurred in a young and healthy person. Valerie Dixon, who was Stella's closest friend among the three other teachers who lived in the boarding house, took care of her at night, and Mrs. Overly, the landlady, looked after her as best she could while Valerie was at school. Undemanding as Stella was, the condition of her illness dictated considerable nursing. Stuporous with fever, racked by nausea, and plagued by nightmares, she hardly seemed aware of what was being done for her.

The afternoon of the second day Mrs. Overly was waiting for Valerie when she came home from school. "I'm going to call Dr. Taylor," she said.

Valerie looked startled. "Is Stella worse?"

"No, but she's no better that I can see."

"Well, it's only been two days," Valerie said. "Flu frequently lasts a week or more, doesn't it?"

Valerie was older than Stella, almost thirty now, and she looked it, even though her skin was still unlined and her raven's-wing hair had no gray. With her plump little body, quick movements, and soft, fluttery voice, she reminded one of nothing so much as a mother hen, especially when her second-graders were gathered around her. Mrs. Overly respected Valerie's opinions, partly because she offered them in such a soft, apologetic manner that one felt they must be valid or she wouldn't have bothered to offer them at all.

Mrs. Overly listened carefully to what Valerie had to say,

31

but after considering a few moments, she said, "I'm not sure Stella's got flu. I've seen a lot of sick folks in my time, but I don't know as I ever saw anybody vomit as much as Stella has. I get her to take a little juice or a sip of water, and as soon as she swallows it, she throws it up. I'd feel a lot better if the doctor saw her. After all, she's living in my house, and, in a way, that makes me responsible. Her mother is probably depending on me to look after her. So I've got to do what I'd want someone to do for a daughter of mine."

"Well, of course, if you think it's necessary . . . I'll go up and get her bathed and changed before the doctor comes."

Gaynell Moore, Dr. Taylor's office girl, said he was out of the office but she would find him and give him the message. Gaynell was only nineteen, but she understood enough about human nature to know that a person calling for the doctor did not like to hear that he was drinking coffee or talking with a friend. That was exactly what Dr. Taylor was doing, and as soon as Mrs. Overly hung up, Gaynell rang the drugstore downstairs where he was.

Dr. Samuel Taylor and Grantland Meadows, the pharmacist-owner of Meadows Drug Store, had been friends since their army days and were as close as brothers should be but often aren't. Yet they would have been hard put to explain their affection. It had no sexual overtones, because both of them, although bachelors, were unalterably heterosexual. On the surface they had nothing in common, Sam being five years older, thousands of dollars poorer, and only about half as handsome.

Grant was a tall man with sparkling blue eyes and even white teeth. Having been blessed with a rugged constitution, a well-to-do-father, and a kind mother, he had never known sickness, poverty, or ill-treatment in childhood and by virtue of his occupation had escaped many of the horrors of the war. His manners were as impeccable as several generations of Southern aristocracy could make them, yet underneath his outward courtesy he often felt a little unsure of himself, especially with women, many of whom he found too aggressive. Because of his looks and his social position in Lanier, he was considered "a good catch" by both mothers and daughters, and the bachelorhood he still retained at age twenty-eight was a hard-won accomplishment. Someday he would marry but not until he found exactly the right girl—attractive, intelligent, soft-spoken, and high-principled. Without being conceited, Grant knew his worth—and did not intend to throw it away on an unsuitable marriage.

Unlike Grant, Sam had never been called handsome and wouldn't have known what to do with the compliment if he'd heard it. He had none of Grant's grace and polish; he was reticent and frequently irritable, with a disconcerting habit of ignoring most of the trite comments which were so much a part of the social interaction of the town. His brusque speech fell strangely on the ears of people accustomed to expanding a statement about the weather into a fifteen-minute conversation. At first they had resented his taciturn, almost ill-natured manner. But on perceiving that his rudeness did not hamper his medical skill, they shrugged tolerantly and said that was Dr. Taylor's way, and if you wanted something different, you could go to Dr. Marvin, who was affable and optimistic but might let you die while he was cheering you up.

Sam had a square, muscular figure just above medium height and a square, uncompromising face topped by thick, black hair. The expression on his mouth was stern and unyielding, that of a strong-willed man who could face life without flinching and beat it down if necessary. One would have expected such a dark-visaged man to have cold blue eyes or stone-hard black ones. His were a soft gray flecked with brown and green, changeable eyes which softened the relentlessness of his face.

To get where he was, he'd had to be tenacious. The son of a carpenter who was frequently out of work during the depression years, Sam worked his way through college and medical school, a feat he now looked back on with amazement and disbelief. He'd got through those years with a dogged concentration on his goal, which permitted no frivolities such as football games, concerts, or dances. Love was out of the question; he had no time for the conventional chase and capture, and sex was merely a necessary tension-reliever, lifted out of its animal basis by his innate kindness and the determination that what he did would be done well.

By the time he went into the army, he was so in the habit of making work his whole existence that he was nonplussed at finding himself with some spare hours. It was into this void that Grant stepped. Soon they were spending their off-time together—playing in the same poker games, reading the same tattered paperback books, and talking about home.

Grant did most of the talking; he was by nature and training an easy conversationalist, and his memories were pleasant. He described the drowsy Alabama town of Lanier with its two-street business section and shady residential streets so often and told so many stories about the activities and people in the town that in the end Sam felt he knew Lanier better than any of the temporary stopovers of his nomadic childhood. When Grant asked him about taking over the office left vacant by the death of old Dr. Nichols, he agreed at once. He was looking for a home, and he thought he had found one.

Sam had been in the drug store ten minutes, but beyond a word of greeting when he came in, he had said nothing. He was drinking his coffee at the counter. Most Lanier residents drank coffee at meals only, and Dr. Taylor's habit of drinking innumerable cups during the day was a subject for comment. People knew he must have been brought up to drink Coca-Colas like other Alabama boys, and they could only suppose he'd picked up the odd habit from Yankees, either at medical school or during the war.

Suddenly Sam looked at Grant and asked, "Did you hear about Warner Fox?"

Warner Fox, who had graduated from high school with Grant, was a salesman for a wholesale drug company in Birmingham. Since Lanier was in his territory, he was often in town combining business with a visit to his folks.

Grant looked up from the prescription he was filling. "No, what about him?"

"He's disappeared."

"What do you mean, disappeared? He was here two days ago."

"I know, but he never got back to Birmingham."

"And they're just now missing him?" Grant asked in a surprised voice.

"Well, with all his traveling, his landlady is used to having him gone, and the drug company took it for granted that he was sick when he didn't show up for work yesterday. But when he didn't come again today, they called his landlady, and she called his mother here. It turns out that nobody has seen him since he left here day before yesterday."

Grant asked, "Where did you hear about this?"

"I was on a call next door to Warner's mother's, and when

I came out, the sheriff stopped me and asked when was the last time I saw Warner and if I knew what time he had left town."

"What did you tell him?"

"I couldn't be of much help. I told him that Warner came to see me about two o'clock Monday afternoon, and we talked for maybe an hour. There wasn't anybody in the office, so I had plenty of time to spend with him for a change. He showed me a couple of new products and gave me some samples, and then we got to talking about vitamins, which he thinks are a coming thing in the drug business. But when he left, he didn't say anything about where he was going."

"Well, he came here after he left you, but I was busy, so he said he'd come back later. He got back about four, and I was still busy, but between customers I managed to give him an order. When business finally slacked off, we talked ten or fifteen minutes—nothing of any importance, just about the way the town is growing and things like that—and he said he'd better get on the road to Birmingham, because he had to be back in the office the next day. As far as I know, he meant to drive straight to Birmingham."

At that point the phone rang, and Grant handed it to Sam. "For you."

Sam listened a minute and then said, "Okay, I'll be there shortly." He hung up and said, "Mrs. Overly wants me to see Stella Lidell."

"So she was sick after all," Grant said.

"What do you mean?"

"I had a date with her Monday night, but when I went by, Valerie said she was sick. I thought maybe she just wanted to break the date, but I guess I was wrong."

Sam didn't say anything. He was surprised to learn that Grant's interest in Stella had lasted so long—it must be three or four months now. Stella was very pretty, of course; she had the most beautiful body of any woman he'd ever seen, and her natural blonde hair was spectacular, almost white with a faint overlay of gold like pale winter sunshine. She had eyes so dark a blue as to look gray or brown in certain lights, and her slightly protruding teeth only added fullness to her lips and a provocative look to otherwise undistinguished features. Yes, Sam thought, Grant might very well be attracted by her appearance. He was attracted too the first time he saw her, before he got to know her—or rather found that there was nothing to know. Still waters run deep, they said, but in Stella's case Sam thought the still waters were those of a shallow, stagnant pond. He had never heard her say anything one could think about for two minutes. Still, there was no accounting for taste. Maybe Grant didn't care that she was a bore. Perhaps he was looking for a wife, someone who would be a good housekeeper and a conscientious mother. He might not mind if her conversation was dull or her sexual compliance merely dutiful, as Sam imagined it would be.

After he had taken Stella's temperature and listened to a recital of her symptoms from Mrs. Overly and Valerie Dixon, Sam told them, "I'll have the drug store send you some Coca-Cola syrup. Give her a teaspoonful every hour. Sometimes it will stop the nausea. Keep giving her as much liquid nourishment as you can get her to take. Some of it may stay down. I'll send a couple of prescriptions too."

Mrs. Overly followed him out of the room. "What has she got, Doctor?" she asked. "I thought it was flu at first, but then I got to worrying and wondering if maybe she'd got hold of some kind of poison by mistake. She doesn't have any cold or cough, just the sick stomach. And those red bumps you saw on her arms are all over her. It's different from any flu I ever saw, and I've seen many a case."

"People react differently to it," Sam said evasively "The main thing is to get her well. Just do what I told you. I'll come by again tomorrow."

This conversation took place just outside Stella's room, and she overheard it. Poisoned? Could I have been poisoned? I don't remember . . . If only my head didn't ache so. My mind won't work when I hurt so much. I don't even know what day this is. I was worried about losing an hour, and now I don't know how many days have passed. It was Monday when I went to the Clayton's, and I got sick while I was there. But before I got sick . . . I meant to tell the sheriff about that strange plane. Or did I dream it? I've had so many nightmares, perhaps that was a nightmare too. No, it was real. But what could it have been? Trying to think makes my head ache worse. I'll think about it later, after I'm well. I don't have the energy now. I can barely move my hand. But tomorrow . . .

When Sheriff Owen Perry got back from talking to Warner Fox's mother, he had already decided how to conduct the search. Sheriff Perry appeared easygoing and somewhat lethargic; he talked in a slow drawl and walked in a languid amble. He never made two moves when one would do and, indeed, did not move at all if he could avoid it. But the voters of Boone County had long since noticed that Boone had the least crime of any county in the state, and they delightedly told an anecdote to explain why:

The sheriff of a neighboring county had asked Sheriff Perry how he managed with only two deputies in such a large territory. "You don't even have enough men to bring in the lawbreakers," he said.

Sheriff Perry looked at him in a puzzled way. "We don't spend much time going out after folks," he said. "If somebody is breaking the law, I just send word for him to come in, and he knows he'd better come."

The sheriff walked into his office and hung his hat on the rack. He was tall—six-foot-two—and thin, with large ears and sparse sandy hair that barely covered his skull. The brown suit he wore seemed at once too large and too small; his bony wrists and ankles were not quite covered, yet the coat flapped around him like an oversized tent. His pale blue eyes were too small for his face, and his mouth was too large, stretching from ear to ear when he smiled. He smiled often, and even when he wasn't smiling, the blue eyes had a good-humored look. People liked him, and he liked them—until they broke the law. Then his resentment at having his easy routine broken made him a ruthless adversary.

He sighed and looked at his deputies, Jack Hall and Lake Matthews. "We've got a job to do," he said. "Warner Fox has disappeared."

The front door opened, letting in a blast of cold air. Sheriff Perry turned toward it. "Morning, J.T. What are you doing in town this time of week? Did you come to tell us where your still is located?"

The question was one of those half-jokes people use when they want to get across a serious point without offense. Owen was reminding J.T. that he knew about the still, even though he'd never found it or caught him selling whiskey, and he was saying too, "Don't let your whiskey business cause any trouble, or I *will* find the still."

Normally J.T. would have replied, "Aw, Sheriff, you know I ain't gonna get myself in no trouble by making whiskey," thus telling Owen that if J.T. did have a still, Owen couldn't prove it and that if he tried to, Judge Penbury, who had acquired a taste for moonshine in his youth and was one of

J.T.'s regular customers, would find some technicality in the law or evidence to let him off.

But today J.T. was staggered to hear himself replying to Owen's bantering question in quite an unusual manner. Instead of a good-natured retort, he said, "The still is on a little rise about three-quarters of a mile from that slue in Bear Creek. If you angle in to the northeast, you'll see a grove of hardwoods, and—"

"Aw, cut it out," Jack Hall said.

And Owen asked, "What did you really come for?"

J.T. was vastly relieved. He couldn't believe his own ears when he heard himself pinpointing the exact location of his still. Good God, he must be losing his mind. He'd been so closemouthed about his still that even Esther didn't know where it was, not because he couldn't have trusted her, but because he didn't see no use in making her a party to something she hated so much. Because of her disapproval too he'd never took the boys with him to the still, though they could've been a right smart of help. But after all the trouble he'd took to keep the location a secret, here he was telling it in the sheriff's office. He just couldn't get over it.

But thank God nobody believed him.

"What can I do for you?" Sheriff Perry prodded in an impatient voice.

"Sheriff, somebody's left a car in the lane to my hayfield," J.T. Clayton said.

"When?"

J.T. scratched his head. "Durned if I know," he said. "First I knowed of it was this morning. When I saw it, I allowed somebody was hunting squirrels in the woods, and you know I've got my land posted. Ain't nobody s'posed to be on it without my permission, so I sat down to wait and warn whoever it was. I didn't want to cause them no trouble, but I didn't aim to have it happen again. But it seemed funny that I never did hear no shots. So I got to thinking about it and decided I better come tell you."

"What kind of car is it?" Sheriff Perry asked. But he knew even before J.T. answered that it would be Warner Fox's new Chevrolet.

When he and the deputies arrived at the lane, the key was still in the car, and the front door on the driver's side was hanging open.

"That's funny," Deputy Jack Hall said. "I wouldn't have

thought Warner would go off and leave the door hanging open thataway."

"Naw, Warner is as neat as an old maid," Sheriff Perry agreed. "Either somebody else left the door open, or Warner was prevented from closing it somehow. We'd better have a quick look around, and then if we don't find any sign of him, we'll go back to town and get Red Connors to bring his bloodhounds."

The dogs couldn't pick up Warner's trail from the car. They circled around sniffing at the ground and then came back and looked up at Red with pitiful expressions on their ugly faces.

Red looked embarrassed. "I can't understand it," he said. "This is Warner's car all right, and he ain't in it, so there's bound to be a trail away from it. But I'd swear there ain't. These dogs wouldn't miss it if there was. Tip and Sky might possibly make a mistake—they're young dogs—but Moke's got the best nose of any dog in Alabama, or most likely the whole South, and when he don't find a trail, you can bet your life there ain't one to be found."

Sheriff Perry snapped a twig off the blackgum tree he was standing under and chewed absently on it. "What do you reckon happened then?" he asked.

Red shrugged. "Blamed if I know. You right sure Warner was driving this car when it got here?"

"Naw, I'm not sure of anything. All I know right now is that Warner is missing, and we've found his car . . . Well, much obliged, Red. Sorry to have got you out here for nothing."

"That's all right," Red said. "Anything else I can do, let me know." He put his dogs in the back of his pickup and left.

"We gonna search the woods ourselves?" Jack asked.

Sheriff Perry chewed thoughtfully on the blackgum twig. "That would be an awful lot of trouble," he said. "It's most too big a job for the three of us. No, the best thing to do is go back to town and see what we can find out. Maybe somebody saw the car head out this way. There's not much happens in Lanier that *somebody* doesn't see."

"Want me to drive the car back?"

"No, we better leave it where it is right now. If this looks like a kidnapping, we'll have to call the FBI in Birmingham. They'll want fingerprints and stuff . . . Lake, you stay here and make sure nobody messes with the car while me and Jack go to town and ask some questions. We'll be back after while."

Sheriff Perry's first stop was to tell Warner's mother about the car. Her two married daughters, Bessie Faye Mobley and Ella Mae Rayford, were with her, presumably to give her support in this hour of trouble. The minute the sheriff stepped out of the car, he could hear their loud, cheerful voices. Of course, Mrs. Fox was deaf, so one could expect the voices to be loud, but they did seem a bit good-natured for women who had just heard their brother was missing. Still, he was not surprised to find them in such high spirits. The Fox women were unfailingly optimistic; they never believed anything bad was going to happen until they were confronted with the accomplished fact. Yet, once it had occured, death and disaster held a morbid fascination for them. They had attended every funeral in Lanier for the past fifteen years.

Except for their ages, the three women might have been triplets, being uniformly fat and untidy with sandy red hair and weathered complexions. None of them bore any resemblance to Warner, who had inherited his father's dark coloring and precise ways. Mr. Fox had died in his sleep five years ago, slipping away as neatly and unobtrusively as he had lived. One would have expected Warner to go the same way rather than causing all this hullabaloo, the sheriff thought. With a start he realized that he was already assuming Warner was dead.

Warner's mother and sisters could not explain why his car was in J.T. Clayton's lane, but the news did not seem to distress them.

"There's a good reason for it being left there, you can depend on that," his mother said confidently. "Warner never does anything without a good reason. He took that after his daddy. Me, now, I've always been kind of slapdash, and the girls are too. But Warner is real careful."

"That's right," Bessie Faye agreed. "When he turns up, he'll be able to explain it all."

Such determined optimism momentarily silenced the sheriff. Then he shouted a question at Mrs. Fox, a question he had already asked earlier today. "Are you sure he didn't say anything about where he was going when he left here?"

"I thought he was going back to Birmingham," Mrs. Fox said, "but I could've misunderstood. He travels so much I don't know where he is half the time."

"You think he's on a business trip then?"

"Probably so," Bessie Faye said. She looked at Ella Mae. "We might as well come out and say it." Ella Mae nodded, and Bessie Faye said, "We were wondering, Sheriff, if there could be a woman mixed up in this. Warner not being married—well, you know how it is for a man. He's had a good many girl friends off and on."

"The car being parked in that lane seems all the more reason to think so," Ella Mae said. "That's the best reason I know of to park on a cold night." She laughed coarsely. No one accused the Fox sisters of being over-refined. "The only thing is, if it is a woman, we can't think of who it could be. He might have a girl in Birmingham, but far as we know, he hasn't dated anyone here in a coon's age. Not since way back in the fall anyhow."

"Who did he date then?" Sheriff Perry asked.

"One of the new teachers. The blonde one. Miss Lidell."

6

Gaynell Moore finished typing up a new medical record and stuck a red tag on the folder to remind herself to get more information when Miss Lidell came into the office. She knew it would be useless to ask Dr. Taylor to fill out the form. Dr. Taylor was not a record-keeper; he was only a record-user. He expected to have all the relevant facts in the folder, but she continually had to keep after him to give them to her.

She opened the ledger, wrote "Lidell, Stella," at the top of the page, and entered a three-dollar charge for the house call. Miss Lidell would probably pay. But it would be up to her. Dr. Taylor never sent bills. "Everybody who can, will pay, and I'm not going to send bills to those who can't," he said.

It seemed to work out all right—to Gaynell, Dr. Taylor's income seemed astronomical—but somehow she still thought it would be better to send out bills. Neater, and more finished.

She put the ledger away and began to tidy her desk. When she finished, it was bare of everything except a blotter, a pen in its holder, a glass containing five sharpened pencils, and a hyacinth plant not yet in bloom, which had been given to Dr. Taylor by a grateful patient. She walked across the room to a bookcase and straightened a book Dr. Taylor had put back upside down. Then she looked around, satisfied now that everything was in its proper place. She took her coat from its hanger. When she put it on, it struck her at mid-calf. She thought, another month or two, and everybody in Lanier will be wearing long dresses, now that the New Look is here. The New Look was not new to her; she had been wearing it all her life. Gaynell belonged to the Church of the Heavenly Light, a small sect indigenous to Lanier and not affiliated with the larger and more liberal Holiness denominations from which it had broken off. The church, named for the vision of its founder, taught, among other things, that feminine adornment was a sin comparable to adultery. Its women members wore dull colors, black cotton stockings, and flat-heeled shoes. They braided their long hair and wound it around their heads, and they wore no makeup, perfume, or jewelry. With bright golden hair and pink and white skin Gaynell needed no makeup, but she had longed for nylons and high-heeled shoes since she was fourteen. Now she had them, but she could not wear them in Lanier.

The Heavenly Light people did not go to movies, listen to music, or read anything except the Bible. That they were not totally without recreation, however, was attested to by the size of their families. Gaynell was the oldest of ten children. She had managed to graduate from high school before she was sixteen, when her father would have made her quit, and somehow she talked Dr. Taylor into giving her a job in spite of her bizarre dress. Then she had persuaded her parents to let her take the job by pointing out that healing was Christian work and that she could help with the family finances. She had come a long way from where she started. She had even acquired a lover—and not one of the ignorant Heavenly Light boys either, but a man with some position in the town. Her parents didn't know that, of course, and they must not find out.

Gaynell went down the stairs and onto the street. As the frigid wind hit her, she tied her navy wool scarf close around her head. She had two miles to walk. Dr. Taylor would have taken her in his car if she had waited until he was finished with his last patient, but she purposely left as soon as the clock hands stood at five. In spite of the cold she wanted to walk. Between her work for Dr. Taylor and her chores at home, Gaynell had little time to herself. Today she needed some.

She still hadn't got over the shock of hearing about Warner. She only hoped she hadn't betrayed herself to Dr. Taylor. She didn't think she had. She had not fainted, or cried, or done any of the things she felt like. She had stared at him sightlessly and then after a moment collected her wits and said, "I hope they find him. Does the sheriff have any idea what might have happened?"

According to Dr. Taylor, the sheriff didn't.

But she did. From the moment she heard the news she knew that Warner had deliberately gone away. And she knew why. She wished she hadn't told him so soon; she should have led up to it gradually, so he'd have had time to get used to the idea. Maybe he thought she was anxious to get married and lying to him. Maybe he didn't want to marry her. But then, why had he reassured her so often? He didn't have to; surely he knew by now that she'd give him anything, up to and including her life.

Yet over and over during the past six months, he'd said, "Don't worry, Gaynell, nothing is going to happen. And if it does, I'll marry you."

So, when it did happen, she had thought it best to tell him as soon as she was certain, because if they married immediately, they could say the baby was premature. There would be some gossip, of course, even among Warner's friends, who were a lot more tolerant than hers, but after raising their eyebrows and saying, "The first baby can come any time, but all the others take nine months," people would shrug and ignore the matter. Marriage made it all right.

Only she and Warner weren't going to be married. Warner had gone away, leaving her to face it alone. She supposed she had been stupid to think that a man as good looking and successful as Warner could fall in love with a Heavenly Light girl. She knew the people in her church were looked down on. There was an immeasurable gulf between them and the ordinary people—the Baptists and Methodists and Presbyterians—and no one had ever tried to cross it.

She was stupid too not to understand Warner's reaction

when she told him she was going to have a baby. But how could she when he sounded so—well, not eager, that was too strong a word, but at least willing, to get married.

He said, "How late are you? . . . Six weeks. There's probably no doubt then . . . Yes, I do remember . . . Well, don't cry. It's not the end of the world. [A trifle impatiently.] Yes, of course I love you. Haven't I said so all along? . . . It's too late to do anything this trip. I have to work here all day tomorrow, and I'm due back in the office Tuesday. Let's see. I'll come home next Friday evening, and we'll go across the state line and get married. I suppose you'd better meet me here. Your daddy might shoot me if I go to your house. Can you manage to bring your things?"

"I don't own anything but a few clothes," she said, "and I'd just as soon leave them behind."

"So had I. I never want to see you in those black stockings again. Pretty legs like yours ought to be shown. I'll bring the clothes I bought for you so you'll have something decent to be married in. I wish this hadn't happened," he said in an angry voice. Then he looked at her, and his voice softened. "But don't worry; it will be all right. I do love you, Gaynell."

Remembering his words now, she still couldn't find anything that foretold his subsequent actions. She had believed him. Sitting at her desk this morning, she secretly practiced writing her new name: "Mrs. Warner Fox, Gaynell Fox, Gaynell Moore Fox." And then a few hours later she heard the news.

But it couldn't be true, or at least not in the way people thought. Warner would come back and be astonished that they had thought him missing. "Why, I was just on a business trip," he'd say.

But he had not expected to make a trip this week.

Still, he would have some explanation. They would be married on Friday.

They had to be.

It was already dark when Gaynell crossed the little wooden bridge over the ditch and started across the bare dirt yard toward the old unpainted house which had been home for the last five years.

The Moores had come up in the world. During the Depression they were sharecroppers; now they were renters. Perhaps when the boys were a little older, Papa could buy land of his own. It was bad luck that his first four children had been girls, so that Andy, the oldest boy, was just now twelve and not yet big enough to carry a man's load on the farm. Bad luck too that there were so many children, ten in all, although Gaynell always pushed that thought out of her mind, because she did not know which of her brothers or sisters she could have spared.

She walked down the dogtrot and pushed open the second door on the right, the one into the bedroom she shared with her sisters. From a nail on the back of the door, she took down an old sweater and an apron and hung up the sweater and coat she had worn to work. Then she crossed the hall to help her mother in the kitchen. All of the Moore children had work to do; even Baby Sally, who was only three, brought in two sticks of stove wood each night.

In the lamplit kitchen Mamma was already dishing up supper while two of the little girls set the table. Unlike some women, Annabel Moore always served a hot supper in wintertime. It made double work for her, but she thought the kids needed it after eating a cold lunch at school. Tonight's fare was fried sausage, collard greens, and dried butter beans. The smell of the food made Gaynell a little queasy, but she knew she would have to eat, or Mamma might notice. Thank goodness, she'd had no real nausea, only a slight squeamishness.

There was no conversation at supper. Papa liked quiet while he was eating, and even Baby Sally had already learned to eat quickly and silently to avoid the wrath of the blond giant at the end of the table. Everything was passed to Papa first, so he finished before the others, got up from the table immediately, as was his custom, and went into the front room, where he would read the Bible until the rest of the family joined him.

They were in no hurry to do so. As soon as he was gone, the kids began to talk and laugh. Mamma didn't seem to mind the noise. If it got loud enough for Papa to hear from the other room, she'd say, "Y'all hush," or swat somebody on the behind, but otherwise she seemed to enjoy listening and would even smile occasionally, which she rarely did at other times. Gaynell thought this period after supper was probably the most pleasant time in Mamma's day.

The talk and laughter rose and fell, but Gaynell's mind was not on it tonight. She could think of nothing but Warner.

Suddenly she realized that someone had called her name.

She looked around the table, and Lila laughed. "I declare, I believe Gaynell's got a fellow," she said in a teasing voice. "She hasn't heard a word we've said."

"I was thinking about something at work," Gaynell said hastily, hoping her fair skin, which was so prone to blushing, wouldn't betray her tonight.

But Lila did not pursue her teasing. Instead she said, "Betty Lee asked you if you knew when Miss Lidell was coming back to school. She's been absent nearly all week, and we're tired of old Mrs. Blaine. She doesn't know anything to teach, so she keeps us writing the answers to questions all the time."

Mamma said in a mild reproof, "That don't sound respectful."

"It's the truth though," Gaynell said. "I remember Mrs. Blaine from when I was in school, and she's pretty dumb."

Mamma's voice grew sterner. "That's enough talk about the teachers. Ain't many of them as God-fearing as they ought to be, but regardless of that, the Lord has put them in authority over you, and you've got to respect them."

A silence fell over the table. Mamma was indulgent up to a point, but when she got that note in her voice, everyone was suddenly mindful of the hickory switch standing in the corner of the room. Mamma used it only for the worst misdeeds, but when she took it up, she didn't put it down until the child's legs were crisscrossed with red marks and he was crying from pain. So although the children did not dread Annabel's punishments as they did Silas's, the memory of past encounters with the switch was sufficient to throw a pall over their high spirits. The talk was over for the night.

Before she got up, however, Gaynell answered the question. "Miss Lidell is pretty sick," she said. "Dr. Taylor goes to see her every day, but I haven't heard him say when he thinks she'll be well." Then she rose and said, "I think it's my turn to wash dishes."

Mamma said, "Lila, you and Betty Lee help Gaynell. I want her to have time to piece a square or two of that quilt I'm trying to finish. The rest of you get down to your studying. I don't want to have to hand out no whippings when report cards come home. You can keep the fire going in the stove a little while longer. It's turning colder."

She took the two youngest children by the hand and went out. There was no increase in the noise level after she left.

Except for Gaynell and Lila, none of the Moore children were studious by nature, but, aware of the unpleasantness that would follow failing grades, they worked hard during the one hour permitted for studying.

Gaynell sewed the bright-colored quilt scraps and followed her own thoughts. They were all of Warner. She was ashamed now of the doubts she'd had earlier. Of course Warner hadn't gone away to keep from having to marry her; it was wrong even to let such a thought cross her mind. She never would again. Because if she couldn't believe in Warner, what would be left for her?

She loved him, and she trusted him. She would have no more doubts.

Only, where could he be? And—she was ashamed of the thought because it seemed so selfish, but she couldn't get it out of her mind no matter how she tried—what would happen to her if he didn't come back?

She still hadn't found any answers to these questions when Mamma came to tell them Papa was ready for family worship.

About the same distance from town in the opposite direction another nineteen-year-old girl was also thinking of Warner Fox. Unlike Gaynell, Maureen Granger had no personal concern with his fate. She knew Warner Fox only by sight, but the emotional impact of what she had seen happen to him was nevertheless very great.

She thought now of how she had felt, of the shock piled on shock. At the time she had no reason to suppose that the event would remain unknown, because several persons had been present, and no doubt they would report it immediately. She only wished she could add her account to theirs, because she was sure she had seen more than any of the others. They were nearer by, but not one of them was in a position to watch the whole occurrence from beginning to end, as she had.

Each night when her father came home from the Coca-Cola plant, she waited for him to tell about the singular incident and grew more and more puzzled each night as he discussed Warner Fox's disappearance without once mentioning the queer craft that had been on the scene. Finally she decided that she must somehow be mistaken. Perhaps if she had been more experienced, if she had known as much of the world as normal people, she would not have thought the occurrences strange. Perhaps she would have been able to identify the flying object and would have interpreted differently what she had seen. There might be some perfectly commonplace reason for it. Miss Lidell might have had nothing to do with Warner's disappearance.

Maureen could understand why Mr. Clayton might not have told about the strange craft. He wouldn't want the law officers poking about and hindering his whiskey-making. But it was strange that Miss Mattie hadn't told. Maureen knew Miss Mattie's propensity for gossip, because she had often eavesdropped when Miss Mattie, presuming on girlhood friendship and insensitive to a cool welcome, visited Mrs. Granger.

So by today, Friday, Maureen had almost stopped thinking about the events of last Monday, since after all nothing had come of them. And then tonight at supper Daddy said he'd heard the sheriff wanted to question Miss Lidell as soon as she was able to talk to him.

Maureen began making agitated noises.

"I don't understand," Mr. Granger said, frowning. He looked at his wife. "What's she trying to say?"

But Mrs. Granger didn't know either. She watched Maureen a few minutes and then looked back at her husband, shaking her head.

"Are you trying to tell me something about Miss Lidell?" Mr. Granger asked Maureen.

She nodded her head jerkily, made some unintelligible sounds, and moved her hands in wide, uncoordinated sweeps.

"I can't make it out," Mrs. Granger said. "What could you have to say about Miss Lidell, Maureen? She's new this year, and you've never even seen her."

If maureen could have spoken understandable words, she would have said, "I've seen her pass on her way to the Clayton's, and I recognized her from Daddy's description." If she couldn't say such a simple thing, how could she possibly make them understand about the strange aircraft that had landed in Mr. Clayton's field and the people who had been there and the strange things that happened?

She redoubled her efforts, but her eyes filled with tears of frustration as she saw her parents' blank looks. Finally she stopped. It was no use. She could communicate with her parents well enough when the subject was familiar to them,

48

but she could not tell them something new or different. Which really meant she couldn't communicate at all, for what was the use in telling people something they already knew?

As Mr. and Mrs. Granger got ready for bed—early, because Mr. Granger would be at the Coca-Cola plant at six to see the trucks off—Mr. Granger said, "I wish we could have understood what Maureen was trying to tell us. It seemed to be something about Miss Lidell. But, as you said, she doesn't even know her. So what could it be?"

"I can't imagine," Mrs. Granger replied. "It probably wasn't important. She often gets frustrated over not being able to talk."

"I've never seen her so excited before though."

"You don't know her ways like I do, because you aren't here with her all day."

"I know," Mr. Granger replied. "I don't think I could do what you do. I don't know many mothers who would do it either. You're a saint, Inez."

Mrs. Granger flushed with pleasure. "I don't mind my burdens," she said. "When I get tired, I just remind myself how much harder it is for Maureen than for me."

Just before he went to sleep, Mr. Granger said, "Maybe it wasn't Miss Lidell Maureen wanted to talk about. Could she know something about Warner Fox's disappearance?"

Mrs. Granger didn't answer. She was already asleep.

No, Mr. Granger decided, if it were that, Maureen would have tried to tell us when the news about Warner's disappearance was fresh. She doesn't know anything. Even if she does, there's no way to find out what it is. It will only upset her if we try again. Best to let it go.

7

Dr. Taylor visited Stella morning and afternoon for the next three days, but he noted no improvement. She was growing weaker day by day. She lay in a stuporous half-sleep most of the time, not seeming to notice or care what went on around her.

"When is she going to get better, Doctor?" Mrs. Overly asked on Sunday afternoon.

Sam shook his head. "I don't know," he said.

"Well, it's been nearly a week since she took sick," Mrs. Overly said, "and Valerie and I are about worn out. We can't keep doing our own work and nursing Stella too. We'll have to make some other arrangements. If she's not better by tomorrow, I think I'll write to her mother and see if some of her family can come."

Sam nodded. He didn't care who took care of his patient as long as somebody did, but he would welcome the chance to get a fuller medical history than he had been able to get from Stella herself. He was more puzzled about what was wrong with her than he wanted to admit. She had no fever and no respiratory involvement, and those red nodules on her body were like nothing he'd ever seen before. He had spent hours vainly searching his medical books, and he didn't know what to do next. Consultation with another doctor was an avenue closed to him, since the only other doctor in town was Dr. Marvin, who could scarcely distinguish between the gall bladder and the appendix. If he couldn't come up with the answer soon, he'd have to send Stella to the hospital in Tuscaloosa. Too bad there wasn't one in Boone County. Even the most minimal laboratory facilities would be a help.

When Sam left Mrs. Overly's, he went to the drug store. The businesses in Lanier were closed on Sunday, but the two drug stores opened from two until six on alternate Sundays for medical emergencies and also—although this was never mentioned—to catch some soda fountain trade from the young folks, who had little else to do on Sunday afternoons.

Sam found Grant sitting at the desk behind the prescription counter with his feet propped on it. He was reading *Argosy Magazine*. As Sam came in, Grant straightened himself in the swivel chair and lowered his long legs to the floor. "Come in and take a seat," he said. "Have you seen Stella today?"

This had been his standard greeting ever since Stella got sick, and it told Sam that Grant's interest in her was more than a casual fancy. He answered, "I just came from there. She's about the same, still a mighty sick girl."

"You haven't decided what's wrong with her yet?"

Worry clouded Sam's gray eyes. "Not exactly. I'd like to make some tests, but with no lab . . ."

"Maybe you should send her to Druid City Hospital. I hear they test you for everything under the sun when you go there."

"That had occurred to me," Sam said dryly, "but on a salary of a hundred and twenty-five dollars a month, a hospital bill comes as quite a blow. I thought I'd wait another day or two . . . Any news about Warner yet?"

Grant shook his head. "Owen was in here about half an hour ago, and he's pretty worried. Said he'd talked to everybody and hadn't come up with anything to help. Seems like nobody saw Warner after he left town. Of course, it was Monday afternoon, so it's not surprising that there wasn't any traffic on that country road. He wouldn't pass any houses except the Grangers', and they're so far back from the road, they wouldn't notice. So there just wasn't anybody who could have seen him."

"Except Stella," Sam said.

"What do you mean?"

"She's been teaching Wilma Jean to read, and she went out to the Clayton's on Monday."

"I didn't know that. Who told you? Stella?"

"No, Mrs. Clayton. She said she felt responsible because Stella had got the flu from walking out there on such a cold day. I told her that probably didn't cause it, but I couldn't convince her. She said Stella was already delirious when she got there—didn't know what time it was or anything. Mrs. Clayton must have told the sheriff about it too, because he had me ask Stella if she'd seen Warner's car. Stella just shook her head. I told Owen I thought that's all he'd get out of her until she was better. He's anxious to talk to her again."

"He's doing all he can to find Warner. Owen's funny—too lazy to hit a snake, but put a job in his way, and he'll work like a house afire to get rid of it so he can laze around again. He's so desperate he had Red bring the dogs back out there, and they searched the woods. But they didn't find anything. Maybe Stella will be able to tell him something."

Shortly after Dr. Taylor left Mrs. Overly's boarding house, Miss Mattie Shepard was on her way there. Beside her on the seat was a jar of chicken soup, which Cousin Edith had made.

Cousin Edith had settled in as she had hoped to and made herself at home. There were both advantages and disadvantages to this. Cousin Edith was no trouble at all. She didn't seem to want to be entertained and had, in fact, insisted that Miss Eunice and Miss Mattie go on about their usual activities without considering her. She was satisfied, she said, just to be there and listen to them talk. She was a great help in the house. Arline, the vigorous, middle-aged black woman who had worked for Miss Mattie for twenty-two years, had been overworked since Miss Mattie got sick and was unable to help her. But now with Cousin Edith here, Arline was finding time to wash windows and clean out closets.

Arline, however, did not like Cousin Edith and made it plain by her tightened lips and silent demeanor. Once she had talked freely to Miss Mattie and had sung as she worked, but now the only sound that came from the kitchen was the angry banging of pots and pans. When Miss Mattie paid her on Friday, Arline asked, "Miss Mattie, how long is yo' cousin gonna stay with you?"

She hasn't said, but I expect it will be a week or two. Why?"

"I just wanted to know."

Miss Mattie looked at Arline a minute and then said, "You must be more polite to her, Arline. She's company."

"Yes'm. I reckon I can put up with her another week if I have to."

"Why don't you like her? It looks like you'd be glad to have some help."

Arline's hands twisted her apron. She said, "That woman don't work like other folks, Miss Mattie."

"Why, what do you mean?"

"When she comes down in the morning, she'll say, 'Arline, I'll do so and so today,' something that's a pretty big job maybe, but she don't get started with it, she goes out in the yard and plays with the birds or something. Then after while she comes in and does whatever it was in ten or fifteen minutes instead of in the two or three hours it ought to take."

"How does she manage to do that."

"You tell me, Miss Mattie. I tries to watch her sometimes, but when I'm around, it looks like she's doing it like I would. But if she is, how can she do it so fast?"

"She's probably just a fast worker," Miss Mattie said. She could see now why Arline didn't like Cousin Edith. She was jealous of Cousin Edith's efficiency.

"She sure is faster than me," Arline said. "She's even faster than you used to be, Miss Mattie, and I ain't never before seen anybody that could outwork you when you're feeling well."

But something else Arline said was puzzling Miss Mattie. "You said she played with *birds*?"

"Yes'm."

"How?"

But Arline looked away and said, "Just plays with them." She looked back at Miss Mattie and said, "She's been going through all yo' things too. I caught her in yo' bedroom this morning searching through the dresser drawers."

Miss Mattie was shocked, but she didn't want Arline to see. After a few minutes she said, "Well, that's all right. She probably wanted to borrow a handkerchief."

But it wasn't all right. She didn't like the thought of Cousin Edith's hands pawing through her belongings. Why would she do that? What was she looking for?

Miss Mattie frowned. She hated to have such thoughts about a member of her family, but in a way she would be glad when Cousin Edith's visit was over. It hadn't turned out to be the satisfaction she and Eunice had anticipated. Cousin Edith didn't care about meeting the relatives, or visiting the cemeteries, or doing any of the things they had planned for her entertainment. In fact, she didn't seem to consider herself a visitor at all. It was more as if she had moved in to stay.

Miss Mattie parked the car and went into the boarding house. She met Mrs. Overly in the hall and said, "Good evening, Blanche. I've come to see Miss Lidell."

"She's resting now," Mrs. Overly said. "I'll tell her you came by, and I know she'll appreciate it."

"I'll tell her myself," Miss Mattie said. "Which room is she in?"

"The one at the head of the stairs, but you shouldn't exert yourself to climb."

"Nonsense," Miss Mattie said. "You ought to know I don't spare myself in visiting the sick. As much as Miss Lidell has done for this town, it's our duty to do what we can for her."

"She may be asleep," Mrs. Overly protested.

53

"Well, it won't hurt her to wake up. I've got something to say to her."

Miss Mattie was white-faced and out of breath when she got to Stella's room. She sat down in the first chair she saw and rested a few moments, then she got up, walked to the side of Stella's bed, and said, "How are you feeling, Miss Lidell?"

Stella opened her eyes and looked up. It took a moment for her stuporous brain to register who was there and what had been said.

Then she answered in a thick voice, "I feel very bad." She wished Mrs. Shepard would go away. She probably meant well, but her visit was not welcome. Stella didn't feel like talking to anyone. Speaking made her head ache worse.

Miss Mattie's twangy voice didn't help either. "You do look bad, but I know you're not as sick as you think you are," she said with her own peculiar brand of cheer. "You just need to get up from there and make up your mind not to be sick."

Stella closed her eyes and didn't answer. She hoped Miss Mattie would go away.

Miss Mattie said, "You're important to this town, Miss Lidell. The children need you. Everybody has a duty in this world, and we have to do it no matter how we feel." She reached out and gave Stella's hand a brisk pat. "It's all a matter of making up your mind to carry on," she said. "If you decide you're sick, you will be. I could be in bed right now if I'd listened to Dr. Taylor. He told me I was going to die. 'You're not telling me anything I don't know, Doctor,' I said to him. 'We're all going to die. But the good Lord promised me threescore years and ten, and I aim to have them.'

"Well, he just looked at me and shook his head. But I'm still up and around, and I mean to go on that way."

Up and around, Mrs. Overly thought, but getting weaker every day. She supposed it was better for Mattie to keep her spirits up as long as she could, but she wasn't sure her advice was doing Stella any good.

Stella looked at Miss Mattie's knobby, brown-spotted hand, still absent-mindedly patting hers. Stella's hand was brown, too, but only because her summer tan never completely disappeared. Stella had little vanity—she knew nobody could consider her pretty with her protruding teeth—but she had always been proud of her hands. They were small and well-shaped with tapering fingers and no visible bones or veins. The one Miss Mattie was patting had a strange tingle in it, like little needles stabbing out the ends of her fingers. Perhaps it was about to go to sleep. She moved it and flexed her fingers. After a moment the tingling stopped.

Miss Mattie said, "Well, I'd better go. I just wanted to come by a minute or two and cheer you up. You remember what I said now and make up your mind to be well. It's all in your own power. The Lord helps those who help themselves."

As soon as she left, Stella closed her eyes to slide back into the half-conscious doze that seemed the only way she could get any relief from her pain. But she couldn't drift off. Miss Mattie's visit had left her curiously upset. "I just came by to cheer you up," she had said. Well, she hadn't. Her talk about illness being a matter of will was annoying. As if anyone would choose to be sick!

And yet . . . there had been a time when Stella didn't care whether she lived or died. Jim was killed in the last days of the war, and three months later when she came to herself and realized how thoroughly she had lost him, not only Jim himself but every memory that could have comforted her, every iota of love and respect and devotion she had ever felt or thought she felt, then she had not wanted to live, had indeed been in a panic that she could not die. Of course, she had eventually got over that; she hardly thought of it any more. She had learned to enjoy living in her mind—teaching and learning and thinking—and lately she had begun to think that gaining control over her treacherous body was going to bring an unexpected reward, because she had begun to feel again. Her attraction to Grant brought her no shame, for it was not centered in physical passion but in a mature affection and esteem. Whether the feeling was mutual was a question that had no urgency. She knew now that plants which grow too fast have shallow roots and wither quickly. She was willing to wait.

Stella moved restlessly. Somehow she felt as if she should obey Mrs. Shepard and get up, regardless of how she felt. If only she were a little stronger.

The door opened again, and Mrs. Overly came into the room with a tray. "I thought as long as you were awake, I'd go ahead and heat up the chicken soup Miss Mattie brought," she said. "Can you sit up to drink it?"

"Yes," Stella said. Then in a surprised voice she added, "I'm feeling better."

"Well, I'm glad of that. I was afraid Mattie's visit wouldn't do you any good. She can be right worrisome sometimes. . . . Of course, everybody tries to overlook it now that she's in such bad shape."

"Then it's true, what she said? I'd heard she was in bad health, but I didn't know it was that bad."

"Yes, Dr. Taylor sent her to Tuscaloosa for an operation, but when they got a look at her insides, they just sewed her up again without doing anything. Nobody thought she would last this long, but she's still here and still on her feet, at least most of the time. Dr. Taylor told the family they shouldn't get their hopes up, but I don't know, she may go on another year. I've seen it happen before."

"Well, if she's so near death, it's no wonder my illness seemed minor to her. But saying it was my fault—"

"Don't pay any attention to that. Of course it wasn't your fault. Nobody can help having flu—but you do look better now. I think you're finally on the mend."

At that moment Miss Mattie was expressing an opposite view to Miss Eunice and Cousin Edith Alexander.

"Miss Lidell looks real bad," Miss Mattie reported. "Even though I'd heard that Dr. Taylor was worried about her, it was a shock to me. I've never seen anybody go down so fast. She's as white as a sheet and just skin and bones. I've never seen flu work anybody that way, even back during World War I when so many died with it."

"Maybe it's not flu," Miss Eunice suggested. "Blanche Overly said Dr. Taylor expressed some doubt about that. Said he wasn't sure what it was."

"If you'd told me you were going to visit Miss Lidell, I'd have gone with you," Cousin Edith said reproachfully.

Miss Mattie flushed a dull, unbecoming red. The truth was that she had slipped out of the house on purpose. She had wanted to get off to herself for a little while, so she could think without the constant interruption of Cousin Edith's shrill voice. But she said, "I didn't want to take you somewhere you might catch a sickness. I'm used to it—Eunice can tell you I've never spared myself when it comes to visiting the sick—but I'm wondering if maybe I did the wrong thing in visiting Miss Lidell. I don't feel so good. Do you reckon I've caught whatever she has?"

Miss Eunice said worriedly, "In your condition you oughtn't to visit anybody with flu. But I've told you before, and still you keep going."

"This time I'm a little uneasy about it though," Miss Mattie said. "The queerest feeling came over me when I touched Miss Lidell's hand. It was kind of like an electrical shock, only not exactly. I can't describe it. But I still feel a little strange. I think I'll go lie down a while."

"I still wish you'd told me you were going," Cousin Edith complained. "I'd like to meet Miss Lidell."

"If she'd been kinfolks, I'm sure Mattie would've thought to ask you," Miss Eunice said in a conciliatory voice, "but under the circumstances it's probably better to wait until she's well."

"That ought to be real soon," Cousin Edith said and gave a giggle which, like her voice, was thin and pitched too high.

Miss Mattie looked at her curiously. "I don't see how you can know that—unless you've had some experience with nursing?"

It was a question, but Cousin Edith did not answer it. After a moment Miss Mattie looked at Miss Eunice and gave a barely perceptible shrug. Cousin Edith, it said, was one of God's odds.

8

Gaynell had, as usual, spent the weekend at church. The Heavenly Light congregation held services on Friday and Saturday nights and morning and afternoon on Sunday, both because those times fit in best with farm schedules and because, all other forms of social activity being forbidden, attending church provided something to do on weekends.

The church was the center of life for the Heavenly Light people. It was the place children saw their friends, young people selected their future mates, and adults exchanged news, talked business, and gossiped with their neighbors. It was there that lifelong friendships were made or severed, trades were sealed with a handshake, and marriage vows

57

were sealed with—presumably—the first kiss. It was also the last place one's body would lie before being consigned to the dust from which it came. For all these reasons each member, barring serious illness, attended every service.

Everyone arrived early, and for an hour before meeting time, the churchyard was a beehive of activity with children playing jacks, marbles, or mumbledy peg, adolescents carrying on courtship rituals as stylized as the mating dances of exotic birds, and older people moving about to greet the friends they had not seen all week. Finally two of the men lit the kerosene lamps in the church; the noise outside ceased, and everyone went in to sit, sweltering or shivering according to the season, through a two-hour service complete with jazzed-up gospel music and a rousing hell-fire sermon with ample references to the sins of the flesh.

There wasn't much lingering afterward. Sleepy children were carried to wagons or pickup trucks, and courting couples set off for the girls' homes, because every parent knew just how long the walk should take, and the only way to have time for a kiss or two was to get an early start. Someone put out the lights and the fire; the grownups called hasty goodbyes and set off too, their spiritual experiences having stimulated them to an urgency for the bodily contact of the marriage bed.

Gaynell disliked everything about church. It seemed to her that the jazzy music was as worldy—but less tuneful—than that she heard from the juke box when passing the café. The fiery sermons bored and irritated her, because under the shouted warnings she found nothing but a rambling ignorance. Sometimes she even caught herself feeling hostile to the people because they so willingly accepted the church's concept of a vengeful God and its stern and narrow teachings.

Not attending, however, was out of the question. She was not heartless enough to trouble Mamma with her rebellious thoughts nor courageous enough to defy Papa. Besides, she had an occasional flash of fear that the Heavenly Light doctrine might, after all, be true. It was hard for her to throw out completely the things she had been taught from earliest childhood, things that were unquestionably in the Bible. Sometimes at night she lay sleepless and cold with fear over how much she had thrown out already.

But those times came seldom, because when she was thinking rationally, she could not consider what she had done with Warner a sin. The Bible said that God was love (although that was seldom mentioned in church), and if he was, then he must understand how she felt about Warner. He must know that she had done everything out of love and that, even if it was a sin, she could not repent it. To repent of a sin is to turn away from it, and she was not going to turn away from Warner, not ever.

On Friday night the sermon was about David and Bathsheba; on Saturday night it was about Joseph and Potiphar's wife; on Sunday morning it was about the strange woman in Proverbs. Beyond listening to the text, which Papa might question her about, Gaynell resolutely shut her ears. She did not want to hear about women who lured men to their destruction or about men who fought against their wiles. It had not been like that with her and Warner.

And yet, remembering the clothes she had worn to please him, the pride she'd felt in displaying her body to him, and the way she'd learned to kiss and caress him, she wasn't sure. Perhaps all that had been a snare and a temptation to him. Perhaps in some way she didn't yet understand, it had driven him to—no, not destruction, she couldn't believe that— she *wouldn't* believe it. Still, he was undeniably gone.

On Sunday afternoon the preacher announced that after the first song he would give an opportunity for testimony. He was sure, he said, that this week's sermons had made many members of the congregation aware of their sins and that they would now want to follow the Biblical command to confess them to each other. After all who wished to had confessed, they were to come forward and kneel before the altar for prayer and forgiveness.

For a moment there was dead silence in the church. Testifying was a frequent and emotional occurrence, members often stood to relate their salvation experiences, to tell how they had wandered from God and then come back, or even sometimes to admit that they had sinned and to ask the other members to pray for them. But never before had they been requested to confess *specific* sins, and especially not those regarding matters so intimate.

Finally Mrs. Reed stood up and, with her plain, middle-aged face breaking out in nervous perspiration and her voice trembling, admitted that many years ago, before she married Mr. Reed, she had kissed another boy. Then Mrs. Johnson said that she had hiked up her skirts and gone wading in the creek in plain view of a crew working on the road. The young Widow Crandall confessed that she had taken in all her dresses to make them tighter fitting (which was no news to the other members) and stated her resolution to give up the sin (which statement received somewhat louder Amens from the female than the male portion of the congregation).

And so it went as woman after woman tearfully confessed such pathetic little sins as she could conjure up out of a life so limited by ignorance, poverty, and obedience to her husband. Gaynell sat through it with downcast eyes and blazing cheeks. She was embarrassed by the dreary little stories, and she pitied the women who were telling them. But, most of all, she was angry, angry at the preacher who had started this, the women who felt impelled to speak, and the men who listened so avidly. She herself could never enter into so degrading a performance. She'd rather die than stand up and confess her sin. She had too much pride.

But pride was a sin too, wasn't it? One had to humble himself to be forgiven. Yet what did she have to be forgiven for? Unless it was a too willing compliance with Warner's demands? It was the girl's duty to uphold the moral standards; she'd been taught that all her life. Warner had a right to expect her to be stronger than he was, but she hadn't been. So it was all her fault.

Still, she hadn't known in the beginning what it would lead to; she had done what he asked because she wanted to please him. Was that wrong? Had it led Warner down that path to destruction? Where *was* he?

When she realized that tears were running down her cheeks, she hastily wiped them away and glanced around fearfully. But it was all right. Most of the women and girls were crying, and no one had noticed her. Her mind resumed its restless quest.

She didn't think Warner's disappearance was her fault, and yet as the self-recriminations continued around her and the emotional fervor rose higher and higher, she was no longer sure of anything. If these women felt guilty for so little, shouldn't she, who had done so much more, be aware of her guilt? Maybe God had taken Warner away to punish her for being too proud to admit her guilt. If that was it, she'd do anything to bring him back, anything. She would rather die than confess, but she'd do it for Warner. Right now, before she lost her nerve.

As soon as Mrs. Hopewell finishes, I'll get up, Gaynell thought. Her heart was beating fast, and her mouth felt dry.

All the moisture in her body seemed to be flowing from her eyes.

With a final sob Mrs. Hopewell sat down, but before Gaynell could rise, Mrs. Lester stood up and began telling about inviting the Watkins salesman in one day when her husband was gone from home. "I was just lonesome for somebody to talk to and didn't mean no harm," she said. "Or at least I didn't think I meant none, but I reckon I must have, because I didn't never tell Jim about it. I'm sorry now though, and if the Lord will forgive me, I ain't never gonna do nothing like that again."

The Lester family was sitting on the bench across the aisle from Gaynell, and Gaynell glanced at Mr. Lester as his wife spoke. Why, his face is like thunder, she thought. He's angry, murderously angry. Because of what Mrs. Lester did, or because she is telling about it? Either way, it hardly seems enough to make him that angry. Gaynell shivered, realizing for the first time that these confessions might be dangerous.

She felt as if a bucket of ice water had been poured on her head, and it stopped her cold. She had forgotten Papa. She hadn't considered what he would do after she confessed. But she was thinking about it now, and it shocked her back to sanity.

To confess was out of the question. She would never have thought of it except that her frantic worry over Warner's absence made her half-crazy and vulnerable to the general hysteria. Now that she was sane again, she knew that what she and Warner did might have been unwise, but it was not evil. She felt no guilt. What she felt was fear, and no amount of "confessing" would get rid of that. She could only wait—and hope—for Warner's return.

Her heart jerked as she realized how close she had come to giving away her secret. She hadn't realized before that she was in danger not only from outside observation but also from her own inner impulses. It was frightening to find that she was a danger to herself.

9

By the time Sheriff Perry called, later Sunday afternoon, Stella was feeling a lot better, almost back to normal. She told Mrs. Overly she would be glad to talk with the sheriff, but she couldn't imagine what it was about.

"The same thing he's been talking to everybody else about—Warner Fox's disappearance," Mrs. Overly said. "You've been too sick to know, but Warner disappeared on Monday, the same day you got sick, and nobody has seen him since, though they found his car abandoned in a lane on the Clayton farm."

At Mrs. Overly's words Stella's heart suddenly began to beat very fast.

Monday afternoon! Then Warner's disappearance must have something to do with the strange plane—or whatever it was. There couldn't be two strange occurrences the same day in a town the size of Lanier unless they were connected. But how? She hadn't seen Warner, or his car. She remembered her fright after the thing landed when she realized how alone she was. No one else was in sight then or a few minutes later when it took off.

She frowned. She didn't actually know it was a few minutes later. Somewhere she had lost an hour, and she didn't know whether it was before, during, or after the landing. In that hour anything could have happened. Warner might have come down the road then and been so frightened he left his car and ran away. She had not been frightened—not until the thing had landed—but perhaps that was because she knew so little about planes. Warner was a former Air Corps pilot; perhaps he had recognized it as an enemy plane. It might have been more terrifying to Warner than it was to her. For all his heroic war record, Warner was a nervous person.

"In a way I got my medals for cowardice," he had told her once. "I joined the Air Corps because I couldn't stand the idea of hand-to-hand combat. In an airplane at least I didn't have to see the enemy, and it was impossible to run away."

But if Warner had run away from the strange plane, he would have come back. He wouldn't still be missing a week later.

Something must have happened to him, something to do with the strange plane. Wild thoughts of military secrets, foreign spies, surveillance by unknown enemies chased through her mind. She was not naive enough to think that what one read in the papers was all that went on. Perhaps Warner had stumbled on something dangerous. He might have been kidnapped—or killed—because of what he had seen.

But that was ridiculously farfetched. More than that; it was impossible. Because she had seen it too, and nothing had happened to her.

Except the worst sickness she'd ever had in her life. She began to shake. *Had* she been poisoned? And, if so, by whom? What had happened in that hour she couldn't remember? She would have to remember it, that was all. She would have to think about every step she had made from the time she left the school building. Even if she had been delirious when she reached the Claytons, the knowledge of how she spent that hour was buried somewhere in her mind, and she could dig it out if she thought long enough.

But until then she'd better keep quiet. After she had sorted things out in her own mind, she could think what to do, whether to tell the sheriff or maybe go to the FBI in Birmingham or the Army base in Anniston. She couldn't risk any of those things until she was sure. She didn't want people to say she was crazy like Mr. Wright back home, who had claimed to be receiving radio messages from Japan during the war. When he began to prepare for an imminent invasion by laying booby traps all over town, he had to be sent to the insane asylum.

No, she couldn't tell the sheriff anything until she remembered all of it.

She hoped she wouldn't let something slip. Jim used to say she wasn't a good liar, that her facial expression was a dead giveaway. Perhaps she should have refused to see the sheriff, but it was too late for that now. She'd have to be evasive and tell him only that she didn't remember seeing Warner that day, which was true. If he pressed her too much, she could always say she didn't feel like talking any longer.

When Mrs. Overly showed Sheriff Perry into her room, Stella's hands were sweating with nervousness, and her heart was thumping painfully. She wondered if she would be able to talk past the tightening in her throat. Her contacts with the sheriff had heretofore been limited to casual greetings and an occasional comment on the most recent high school football game. She wished she knew him better, so she'd know what to expect.

A glance at him reassured her. His homely face was as good-natured as when he tipped his hat to her on the street. He said, "How are you feeling, Miss Lidell?"

"Not too well yet, Sheriff, but I'm better."

"Glad to hear it. I've been wanting to talk with you, but Dr. Taylor said wait. Do you remember him asking you if you saw Warner Monday afternoon when you were going to the Clayton's?"

Stella nodded.

"And you shook your head, 'No.' But you were in a sort of daze then, so I wondered if you'd like to add something to that, now that you're feeling better."

"I don't know that I can," Stella said slowly. "I didn't see Warner at all Monday. In fact, I didn't see him all weekend except at church Sunday with his mother."

"Monday afternoon you went out to the Clayton's to give Wilma Jean a reading lesson. What time was that?"

Stella chose her words carefully. "It's hard to say. Those reading lessons were not a part of my regular schedule. I just went out there when I could, so I didn't try to get there at any particular hour or pay much attention to what time it was."

"You must have some idea," he persisted. "School is out at three-thirty. How long was it after that?"

"Quite a while. We had an unexpected faculty meeting, and then I had to straighten up my room and get my books and papers together. It was pretty late when I got started."

Sheriff Perry glanced around the room and brought his eyes back to her. "Mrs. Clayton said you left at four-thirty," he remarked.

Suddenly the feeling of ease and self-confidence she was beginning to feel evaporated. The sheriff had already talked with Mrs. Clayton. He knew all about that lost hour. She must think fast. He must not see that she was upset. She said, "I was mixed up about the time. I hadn't realized until

I got to the Clayton's that my watch had stopped. But the faculty meeting must have lasted an hour or an hour and a half. Then I spent a good while doing the other things I had to do. So it might have been as late as five-thirty when I started."

"And you got there at six-thirty, Mrs. Clayton said. That seems like pretty slow walking—an hour for a mile and a half."

"It was," Stella said. "I'm afraid I always dawdle a bit when I'm walking in the country. There are so many things to notice, even in the winter. The bare trees and the mistletoe, the crunchy feel of the frozen ground, the birds—it's surprising how many stay here all winter. It was a cold day, but I was quite warm in my coat and mittens, so I just enjoyed the walk and didn't hurry. Not as much as I should have, I guess, because it was dark before I got there. But that was all right, because I knew Mr. Clayton would bring me back."

"And with all this looking around you were doing, you didn't see Warner's car? We found it parked in the lane that comes out into the road about a quarter of a mile this side of the house. It was visible from the road through the bare trees."

"I didn't see it, but I guess it could have been there. When it started getting dark, I quit looking around and walked faster. I wasn't really noticing anything then. . . . I'm sorry I can't be of more help, Sheriff, but I just don't know anything to tell you. You don't suppose Warner went off deliberately?"

"Do you have any reason for thinking he might have?" the sheriff asked quickly. "You went with him some back in the fall, didn't you?"

"We had four or five dates."

"Mind telling me why you quit? Did anything happen to, uh, disenchant you?"

"No, we're still friends. As to why we quit dating, that's easier to understand if you know why we started. I think perhaps Warner had broken up with someone else—he didn't say so, but I had that impression—and he wanted to date someone new. He had known all the girls here since they were born, and they couldn't hold many surprises for him. With me he could hear some different conversation and—well, there's a certain excitement in getting to know someone, because he or she may turn out to be the one you've been looking for all your life. But it didn't turn out that way for us. We liked each other, but the vital spark wasn't there."

"For you or him?"

"Both. As I said, I think he was still half in love with someone else. As for me, I realized that I'd accepted those dates only because Warner reminded me of someone—someone who's dead. But of course he was a different man. He couldn't take the place of the other one. It seemed better to drop the whole thing. I told him that, and he agreed."

"Still, you got to know him pretty well. He probably told you things he wouldn't say to other people. Did you have any reason to think he was dissatisfied with his life? That he might want to go away and start over?"

She considered a moment and then said, "No. He seemed to like his job, and he was fond of his family, his mother and sisters. I can't think of any reason he would leave. I only suggested it because the other seems so incredible."

He looked at her sharply, but his voice when he spoke was still smooth and unhurried. "What other? What seems incredible?" he asked.

Too late she saw her mistake. She had been thinking of the strange plane, and the likelihood that it had something to do with Warner's disappearance.

She said quickly, "It's incredible that Warner could have come to any harm. Everyone liked him."

"Yeah, well, if you think of anything else, be sure to let me know," Sheriff Perry said, getting up to leave.

He hadn't missed her look of dismay, and he wondered what she had been thinking. He was pretty sure she knew something she wasn't telling.

10

As he drove away from Mrs. Overly's, Sheriff Owen Perry was still frowning. He didn't like anything to disrupt the even tenor of his life. When he was in the war, he had made up his mind that he would spend the rest of his life in peace, and until now he had. He and Adelaide got along fine, and he had been lucky enough to get elected sheriff, so he had no financial worries. He liked his job. He didn't have any trouble enforcing the law. People in Lanier respected it. He thought they respected him too. They knew he tried to be fair, and they also knew that he could take care of himself in a fist fight or a gun battle.

If anyone had asked him a few months ago what he wanted out of life, he'd have told them he had it. But now—all of a sudden, it seemed—he was in hot water both at work and at home. He had to solve the Warner Fox case; that went without saying. There had been no unsolved crimes since he had been sheriff, and he didn't mean to start with the one which had aroused more talk and curiosity than any event in the last ten years. The mystery, however, was nearly a week old, and so far he had got exactly nowhere.

And to top that off, Adelaide was angry with him, a happening as rare as hen's teeth. Of course, that had nothing to do with Warner, except that if he hadn't been so worried about the case, he wouldn't have slipped up and told Adelaide about talking with Doc Taylor.

She said, "But, Owen, you said I could have the doctor I wanted to deliver the baby."

"Of course you can, honey. I wasn't trying to get you to change. I was just worried about you, and I wanted to see what Doc Taylor would say."

"I don't see how he could say anything. I'm not his patient, and he doesn't know anything about me."

"That's what he said," Owen conceded. "Just forget it. I didn't mean to upset you."

"Well, you have. You told me everything would be all

right, and now you say you're worried. If that's the way you felt, it looks like you'd have been more careful. You knew *I* didn't want to have a baby. Sometimes I think you did it on purpose, determined to have your way no matter how I felt about it."

Adelaide had made it clear to Owen before they married that she didn't want a family. "I don't think I *could* have a baby," she said. "All the women in my family have a dreadful time at childbirth, and I'm smaller than any of the rest. I don't intend to take the chance. So if you want to marry me, you'll have to promise that we won't have any children."

Owen wanted a family, but he wanted Adelaide worse. Barely five feet tall, with big brown eyes and curly hair, she was as pretty and sweet as a spring flower, and he could hardly believe she was willing to marry anyone as homely as he was. She made him feel proud and protective and very much a man, and for that he was willing to let her have her way in almost anything. It was no time to have children, anyhow, since he would be going to the army any day, and later, after he came back, she'd probably change her mind.

Owen returned from the war and was elected sheriff, and Adelaide settled down to enjoy her position and her life. To her, settling down meant a whirlwind of activity. She had a new house, a maid to do the work in it, and a car to go wherever she liked, and she made full use of all of them. She was the only woman in Lanier who found it necessary to keep an engagement book, and it could have served as a social calendar for the town. She belonged to the Baptist Women's Missionary Society, the Eastern Star, the Tuesday Afternoon Study Club, the Wednesday Morning Bridge Club, the Thursday Afternoon Sewing Circle, and the Friday Night Dinner Club. She headed drives for the Red Cross, the March of Dimes, and the Lanier Library. The only organization in town which she did not belong to was the PTA.

Adelaide did not involve Owen in any of her many activities except the dinner club, which was for couples, and he enjoyed that as much as she did. She did not ask him to do any chores around the house. She was a pleasant companion and a responsive lover. So, as time marched by in measured tranquility, Owen did not miss fatherhood. He might have lived out his life childless except for Miss Eunice's cat. It was on the roof and would not come down. After two hours of fruitless cajoling, Miss Eunice called the sheriff. The bedside telephone rang at a moment of high intensity; Owen jumped—and was lost. Two months later Dr. Marvin informed Adelaide with a jolly smile that she was a little bit pregnant.

Owen worried about Adelaide. She was so tiny, and nearly thirty years old, two handicaps right at the start. The third one was that she insisted on going to Dr. Marvin instead of Dr. Taylor, because she said, she'd be embarrassed to go to someone so near her own age, and besides, Dr. Taylor seemed grouchy, and she was sure he'd keep her upset all the time.

It seemed to Owen that Adelaide did not get along well. Every day she had a new ailment. When the vomiting stopped, constipation set in. She had backache, leg ache, and side ache. She had burning indigestion and freezing feet. Through it all she continued her social activities over Owen's protests. Listening to her complaints, he thought longingly of the days when women in a delicate condition retired from the world and spent their afternoons taking long naps. He was sure all this running about wasn't good for Adelaide. As her time grew shorter, he got more and more nervous about her coming ordeal. Finally his concern and guilt feelings drove him out of his customary lethargy, and he went to see Doc Taylor.

Sam said brusquely that since Mrs. Perry wasn't his patient, he could hardly comment on the case. Then, seeing the worry in Owen's eyes, he softened and said, "A woman's size doesn't have much to do with it; it's the measurement of her pelvic bones that counts. Some of these small women deliver more easily than large ones. But if there's any doubt, Dr. Marvin will undoubtedly send her to Druid City Hospital where she can have a caesarean."

"What's that?"

"Taking the baby by surgery. Dr. Marvin wouldn't do it himself, but there are several good obstetricians in Tuscaloosa. Why don't you talk to him and mention that possibility? But for God's sake, don't tell him I suggested it."

Dr. Marvin made short shift of Owen's worries. "You're just suffering from new-father nerves, Owen, my boy," he said. "There's nothing much to having a baby. If there was, there wouldn't be so many of them. You just go on home, and let me do the worrying. Adelaide's going to be all right."

Owen parked the car in the side yard and walked toward the house. He hoped Adelaide had got over her mad spell. Pregnant women were always unreasonable. She would be her old sweet self after the baby came. Thank God, it wouldn't be much longer now. Less than a month. Meanwhile, he'd just have to leave the Warner Fox case at the office and concentrate on Adelaide when he was at home.

When Stella awoke the following morning, she felt completely well. Remembering how sick she had been this time yesterday, she was surprised at having recovered so quickly. She wasn't even weak or lethargic as one sometimes is after flu; she felt full of energy and eager to go back to school.

However, when she came downstairs dressed and ready to go, Mrs. Overly looked at her aghast. "Surely you aren't going to school today," she said. "I don't think you should. This time yesterday you were sick enough to die. Even if you did make a miraculous recovery, you'd better rest up a day or two, or you may have a relapse."

She looked toward Valerie for support, and Valerie said, "Yes, Stella, you should take another day off. You can't really tell how you feel until you've been up a while."

After a little hesitation Stella agreed. She was still sitting at the table luxuriously having a second cup of coffee when the phone rang.

"That will be Grant Meadows," Mrs. Overly said with a meaningful smile at Stella. "He's been calling every morning about this time to ask about you."

"I'll get it then," Stella said, flushing a little. It was plain that Mrs. Overly thought Grant was serious about her. It was too soon for that yet, but maybe in time. . . . She pulled back from the beginnings of urgency. Leave it alone, she warned herself; let it grow naturally.

He said he was delighted to hear her voice. He sounded delighted. He wanted to come by to see her now and satisfy himself that she was really well. She laughed, protested that it was too early in the morning, but finally agreed. She went into the living room to wait for him.

Mrs. Overly's living room was large, like all the other rooms in the two-story frame house, and furnished with an overstuffed, wine-colored living room suite bought when she opened the house to boarders, and innumerable chairs, tables, what-not shelves, and fringed lamps left over from the early days of her marriage. There was a wool rug patterned with large pink roses and an ornate fireplace with a coal grate, where a fire was burning. It was an old-fashioned room, and it carried Stella back to the virtues of a bygone day and made her feel like a prim and proper Victorian lady. She liked that. It was what she was trying to be.

When he came in, Grant took both her hands and looked at her. His blues eyes sparkled like the sunlit sea. "You don't know how glad I am to see you well again," he said. "I've been worried about you. But you look fine—just a little paler and thinner, but we'll soon get that fixed. Lord, how I've missed you. Is it all right if I kiss you—not too much exertion, or excitement, or whatever?"

She laughed and held up her face. How like Grant to ask. He always did, one way or another. She supposed it was a part of his courtesy, and he did it so gracefully that she didn't mind, even though she had always felt that lovemaking was one activity in which a man should take his chances. There was, of course, no possibility that the kiss would prove too much excitement. Grant's kisses were warm and pleasant enough that she was always ready for another, but they had never left her shaken and trembling, as Jim's had. But I don't want that now, she thought, as his mouth opened hers with gentle, practiced skill. This is as good, merely different.

After a few moments she moved away. "What would Mrs. Overly say if she came in?" she murmured.

"Nothing," he said promptly. "She must know by now how I feel about you. I've talked to her twice a day ever since you got sick."

"Yes, she told me. I was . . . surprised."

He smiled, showing perfect teeth, white and even. Self-conscious about her own occlusion problems, she always noticed teeth. Grant's were one of the reasons she thought him handsome. A little flush came up in his face. "To tell the truth, I was surprised too. Until you got sick, I didn't know how much I cared. Being away from you for a week has opened my eyes. I know now that I love you, Stella."

For a moment she didn't say anything. She knew what he wanted to hear, the proper response—"I love you too." It was the reply she wanted to make. It was true. But it seemed surprisingly difficult to say. She felt totally inexperienced, as shy as a young girl. She answered, stumbling over the words, "I care for you too, Grant. I've never felt quite like this before, and it's a little hard for me to tell you."

"You need more practice," he said gently. His blue eyes

71

looked at her tenderly. He started to speak, apparently changed his mind, and then said, as if to himself, "There may not be a better time . . . Stella, will you marry me?"

"Yes, I will. But not right away," she said hastily. "When school is out."

"Four months from now," he said with a note of disappointment in his voice. "However, I expect you're right. It will be better to wait. You'll want a church wedding, and we'll have to give people time for the parties and showers . . . I'll order your ring today."

She started to protest. She hadn't looked ahead to all this—the social activities, the vows in church, the virginal white—for a girl who hadn't been a virgin for seven years. But the protest died on her lips. She already knew the importance Grant put on doing things right, on living up to his position. Of course he would expect a church wedding. Even though it wouldn't take place here, it would be a full page spread in the local weekly.

Suddenly her mind skipped away. She wasn't thinking of Grant any longer. Thinking of the newspaper reminded her of something else, and as soon as he left, she found Mrs. Overly and asked, "Do you still have last week's papers? I missed all the news when I was sick, and I'd like to catch up on what's going on in the world."

"Yes, I always save them to use building fires. They're stacked in the pantry. Help yourself.

It wasn't what was going on in the world that Stella was concerned about; it was what had happened here in Lanier a week ago today. If anyone besides herself had seen the strange flying craft, it would surely be in the *Lanier Register*, and perhaps in the Birmingham papers as well.

But it wasn't. She searched every paper for the entire week but found no mention of any strange object either in the sky or on the ground. She put down the last paper and sat staring into space. Other people either hadn't seen it—or they had kept quiet too.

Once more she went over the entire occurrence step by step, but in the end she was no closer to an answer than in the beginning.

She would tell Grant about what she had seen, of course, and soon too. She wanted to share everything with him, to have no secrets, none of the little subterfuges and connivings that cheapened the relationship between a husband and wife.

72

Suddenly her heart slowed. There would have to be some secrets. She could not tell him what her life had once been. It was too humiliating, too shameful. She could face it inside herself, but she couldn't bear for anyone else to know. Not even Grant. He was so conventional, so much a product of the society he lived in, so inured to the double standard, that he would be shocked and hurt. He might not see that those things had been done by a different girl, one who didn't exist any more. He would think that what happened once might happen again. She wanted honesty and truth between them, and that could be established only by withholding the facts. She would not tell him.

But she would certainly tell him about the strange experience she'd had.

11

At seven-thirty Monday morning Miss Mattie briskly walked into the kitchen, which had been modernized ten years ago by the addition of a sink, an electric stove, and a towering kitchen cabinet ordered from Sears Roebuck. As Miss Mattie came in, Miss Eunice looked up from the breakfast table, where she was having a last cup of coffee before going to work at Bell's Dry Goods Store. "Why, Mattie," she said. "What are you doing up so early? Arline isn't even here to cook your breakfast." She looked at her watch. "I guess I'll have time to do it before I leave for work. Let me get you some coffee."

"I'll do it," Cousin Edith said as she came in. "I'll fix Cousin Mattie's breakfast too." She went to the stove and picked up the coffee pot.

Miss Mattie took it from her. Her voice sounded a little irritated as she said, "I can wait on myself this morning. Sit down, Eunice. And you too, Cousin Edith, since you're here." It would have been plain to a discerning listener that she'd hoped to see her sister alone, but Cousin Edith didn't seem to notice. Miss Mattie sat down at the table across from them and leaned forward. "I have something to tell you."

Her cousin's yellowish eyes darted to Miss Mattie's face

and then away. She never looked at anyone for long; her eyes seemed always in motion, a peculiarity which still annoyed Miss Mattie even though she was accustomed to it now.

Miss Mattie said, "Look at me, both of you." Her words were meant for Cousin Edith, but she didn't get the results she hoped for, so after a moment she went on. "I wanted to tell you that I'm well!"

Cousin Edith's eyes darted from Miss Mattie to Miss Eunice, then to the stove and sink and back to Miss Mattie again. She didn't say anything. Miss Eunice's face blanched, and she stared at Miss Mattie with a shocked expression. This must be the end, she thought. People often seemed to get better, to be free of pain, just before they died. She had not expected it so soon though. She had thought that in spite of Mattie's determination to keep going, she would be forced to bed before the end. The release from pain would not come while she was still up and around. Of course, Dr. Taylor had told the family last summer that Mattie couldn't last long, but Miss Eunice thought that even Dr. Taylor would be surprised to have it happen now. It *couldn't* happen now. Not while Mattie still wanted so much to live. "Dear God, not today," she prayed.

Mattie was looking at her as if she expected an answer, but Miss Eunice couldn't think of one. Finally she echoed Miss Mattie's words. "You're well?" she asked.

"Yes, I'm cured. The Lord has healed me. He sent me a vision to fortell it, to get me in the proper frame of mind to receive it. He made me *expect* something. And do you know how he did it? Remember yesterday when I told you how strange I felt when I touched Miss Lidell's hand? Well, that's when it happened."

"But . . ."

"No listen. I've been awake all night thinking about this and praying and praising God, and I'm sure I'm right. It came through the laying on of hands . . . you remember that the Bible speaks of that. When Miss Lidell touched me, God sent her power through her hands and made me well."

"That's good," Cousin Edith said. She said it in much the same manner a mother would use to a five-year-old who had learned to tie his shoelaces. Her eyes darted from Miss Mattie's face to the window.

But Miss Mattie wasn't paying any attention to her. She was looking at Miss Eunice.

74

Miss Eunice said, "But Mattie, you've got—"

"Not any more. The cancer is all gone, Eunice, taken away by the power of God, praise his name. I'm well! I know I am. I feel just like I used to before I got sick. Better, in fact. I can't even *remember* a time I felt so good."

Miss Eunice looked at her searchingly. She couldn't see much difference in Mattie's appearance. The illness had whittled her weight down so that her tall frame was gaunt and her face a series of sharp bones. Her skin was as gray and lifeless as an old barn door, and her mouth was usually thinned to a grim line against the pain. This morning though it looked more relaxed, and Miss Eunice thought her eyes might be a little brighter too. But that might be only wishful thinking.

She said, "Oh, Mattie, I'd give anything to believe you. I've prayed and prayed, knowing how much you wanted to get well . . ." She wiped her eyes with her napkin.

Miss Mattie patted her hand. She said briskly in her whangy voice, "Well, your prayers have been answered, praise the Lord. And now I've got to get to work. There's a lot to do today. First, I've got to go by and see Miss Lidell and tell her what's happened. I want to find out if she's had this God-given power right along, or if it's just come to her. I wonder too if it's going to stay with her, because if it is, just think of all the good she can do around here! And than after that I'll go to the WMU meeting and start spreading the word. Just think! A miracle right here in Lanier—and me the receiver of it!"

Miss Eunice said cautiously, "Maybe you ought to wait until tomorrow, though, to start telling people." As much as she wanted to, she still couldn't believe. And she thought if Mattie told everyone and then it turned out she was mistaken, it would be such a setback that it might be the end of her.

Miss Mattie said stubbornly, "No, I've got to give my testimony right away. Jesus said, 'Go home to thy friends, and tell them how great things the Lord hath done for thee,' and that's just what I mean to do."

"That's the best thing to do," Cousin Edith said. "Tell everybody about it so they can get healed too."

But Miss Eunice was more cautious. "Couldn't you at least go to see Dr. Taylor first? Then you could tell everyone he said you were well."

Miss Mattie considered. "That's a good point," she admitted, "but he might not believe me, and then I'd get to doubting too. No, I *know* I'm healed, and I've got to tell it."

Miss Eunice sighed. When Mattie made up her mind to do something, neither hell nor high water could keep her from it.

Cousin Edith was still encouraging her. "I'll fix your breakfast, so we can get started spreading the news immediately," she said to Miss Mattie. "I can't wait to see how people take this."

Mattie had great faith, much greater than hers, Miss Eunice thought humbly as she hurried to town. Mattie didn't need any reassurance, but she wanted to talk to Dr. Taylor. As soon as she reached town, she went to his office. No one else was there so early in the morning, so she got in to see him immediately. The fast two-block walk in the cold had put her so out of breath that for a moment she couldn't speak.

Seeing Miss Eunice's breathlessness, Sam said sharply, "What's the matter? Is Miss Mattie worse?"

Miss Eunice shook her head and finally found her voice. "That's what I wanted to talk to you about. She says she's well. Says she never felt better in her life. Do you think—"

He shook his head. "Impossible."

Then seeing the way her face fell, he knew that wasn't enough. He would have to explain to her. He hated this kind of talk; he often wished patients existed apart from any relatives, apart even from any concern about their own illnesses. He enjoyed the medical part of his job, liked diagnosing the illness and seeing the body respond to his treatment, and if he could do only that, his job would be perfect. But he hated trying to explain to patients what was wrong with them in terms someone without a basic knowledge of anatomy could understand, and he hated even worse having to go over the same ground with their relatives. But he reminded himself that Miss Eunice had already had a long ordeal, and there was more yet to come.

He said, "Now, Miss Eunice, Miss Mattie isn't going to get any better. I told you that last summer. She has got along a lot better than I expected her to, but her condition is deteriorating all the time. She may take to her bed any day, and once she does, she probably won't last long. The only thing we can do is keep her supplied with pain pills and let her do as she pleases as long as she can.

"Don't cry," he said awkwardly. "I know it's hard, but you've accepted it well up to now."

Miss Eunice wiped her eyes. "Don't worry, Doctor. I'm not going to pieces. I can take whatever the Lords send me. Only I hope he won't let Mattie die while she's so hopeful of getting well."

Sam didn't say anything. He never knew what to say to people facing what Miss Eunice was facing. There was a long silence. Miss Eunice was not looking at him now; she was staring into space, apparently lost in thought.

At last she straightened her slumped shoulders. She seemed to have made up her mind about something. She said, "Well, I'm not going to grieve before the time comes. Mattie thinks she's well, and I'm going to let her think so as long as she can. In fact, I'm going to think so too. There's no use crossing bridges until you come to them."

Again Sam remained silent. Nor did Miss Eunice speak for a long moment. Then she said, "It sure will strengthen my faith though if Miss Lidell says this has happened before."

Sam's head jerked toward her. "Miss Lidell?" he said sharply. "What does she have to do with it?"

Ten minutes later he was on his way to the boarding house, at somewhat of a loss to know what to expect when he got there. Coming second-hand, the story had not been clear. Miss Mattie apparently thought she had been healed by some mysterious power from God flowing through Stella, but whether the idea was originally Stella's or Miss Mattie's, he had been unable to determine. He hoped he was not going to find Stella's mental balance as unstable as her physical condition.

He was surprised to see her up and apparently well. She insisted she felt fine, and he could find nothing wrong with her. The red nodules had disappeared, and her temperature, blood pressure, and heart beat were normal.

As he put his medical paraphernalia back in his bag, she said, "What was wrong with me, Dr. Taylor?"

Without looking around he said brusquely, "Call me Sam."

"I thought doctors always liked to be addressed by their titles. Mrs. Marvin even calls her husband 'Doctor.' "

"There's no accounting for the wild vicissitudes of taste," he said.

"The wild vicissitudes of taste," she repeated in a surprised voice. "What a nice phrase. It sounds familiar, but I can't place it."

"Samuel Johnson," he said briefly. But as he said it, he felt like a twelve-year-old showing off on his bicycle for his girl friend.

"You're better read than I thought," she said.

Hearing the interest in her voice, he was tempted to say no more, but after a moment's reflection he decided to be frank, "No, I'm catching up a little now after a lifetime of ignorance, but I'll probably never be really knowledgeable about literature. I'm not meticulous about grammar either, so I suppose I should feel self-conscious with an English teacher."

"I'm sure you know more about English than I do about medicine. I never even took a physiology course. Anyway, my grammar isn't all that precise either; my Northern friends laugh at some of the idioms I use. The only kinds of errors that really bother me are pretentious ones, such as saying, 'I feel badly,' or using 'fortuitous' for 'fortunate.' Oh, and to me, anyone who says, 'I'm nauseous,' truly is."

He laughed, and the uncompromising lines of his square, rugged face were momentarily softened. "At least I can promise not to make those mistakes."

She was looking at him thoughtfully, but he couldn't tell what her thoughts were. After a moment she said, "You still haven't told me what was wrong with me."

He sighed. "I was hoping you would forget to ask again, because I don't know. Maybe it was flu after all, but some of the symptoms were not what I would expect. Anyway, there's no need to worry about it now, because obviously you're well. . . . And now I want to ask you something. What's this I hear about your healing Miss Mattie?"

"You probably know as much about that as I do. She came by a few minutes ago, telling me she was well and saying the Lord had healed her through me. Is there something wrong with her mind?"

"Not that I'm aware of. She's seemed all right until now. Of course, she has known for several months that her case is terminal, and it's hard to tell what that could do to a person."

"Well, I hope she doesn't tell anyone else that wild story about my having the power to heal," Stella said.

Sam hoped so too, but without much optimism. He himself didn't tell even Gaynell, from whom he had few secrets, although he had a good opportunity when on his return she followed him into the inner office and asked, "Is Miss Lidell worse?"

78

"No," he answered.

"Oh, I thought she might be, the way you were hurrying."

"As a matter of fact, I found her much better. She's up and around and seems to be feeling well."

"I'm glad," Gaynell said. "The kids are missing her at school. . . .Is it true what people are saying—that the sheriff questioned her about Warner Fox?"

Sam looked up sharply. "Where did you hear that?"

"They're talking about it in the waiting room. They say he was with her quite a while yesterday afternoon."

"He's questioning everyone," Sam said. "Even talked to me. It doesn't mean anything."

Gaynell's question seemed of so little importance to him that he forgot it as soon as she left and started sending in patients.

But Gaynell did not forget. Between the tasks she was efficiently performing, her mind kept harking back to the problem from which she was never free: Where was Warner, and when would he come back? She wished she could talk to Miss Lidell and find out what she knew. But she couldn't. She couldn't talk to anyone. Even when people brought up the subject to her, she couldn't show more than a casual interest in it. No one must guess how she felt. No one must know how urgent it was that Warner return.

Thank goodness, the subject hadn't been talked of much at home. Warner's name was familiar to Papa and Mama, but they didn't know him, so when Papa heard the news in town, their discussion was brief and casual.

"Warner Fox has disappeared," Papa said. "I reckon Gaynell didn't think to tell us, but he's been missing several days. They found his car on J.T. Clayton's land."

"Do they think Mr. Clayton had something to do with it?" Mamma asked absently. She was more concerned with the meat she was frying than with men she knew only by name.

"I don't know," Papa answered. "A man who is in league with the devil is subject to doing any kind of meanness, but, on the other hand, if Fox was buying whiskey from him, he was asking for trouble. . . .Well, it's got nothing to do with us."

So Gaynell knew Papa hadn't the least suspicion, and she must be careful not to start any speculation which might reach him. No, she couldn't ask questions. She could only keep her ears open for any news that might be dropped.

*   *   *

With Cousin Edith in tow Miss Mattie arrived at the meeting of the Women's Missionary Union just before ten o'clock, and five minutes after that she dropped her bombshell. Eyes met in startled pity, disbelief, and embarrassment. As she continued her story, however, incredulity faded to doubt on a few faces and doubt was replaced by hesitant conviction on one or two. In the ensuing babble of questions, answers, and stories of similar experiences, all hope of presenting the planned program about the missionary work of Miss Annie Armstrong was lost, but by the time the ladies went home, several of them were fully persuaded that the Lord had performed a miracle in their midst, and several others went so far as to say cautiously, "Well, I certainly *hope* it's true."

Mrs. Bennett, the pastor's wife, was not a member of either group. She had been dismayed by the occurrence and at a loss for what to do. Properly speaking, it was not her job to do anything, since she held no office in the WMU, but she was aware that as the pastor's wife she was the final authority in any difficult situation. The other women expected her to know the Bible better than they did. She didn't know when they thought she had time to read it with all the other things she had to do. But a preacher's wife couldn't say that.

Desperate to stop the hubbub, she finally stood up and said, "I know you all have many more questions to ask Miss Mattie, but if I could beg your indulgence, Brother Bennett will want to hear this right away, and he's in his study now. If everyone is agreeable, I'd like to take Miss Mattie to see him. Mrs. Dennis, would you dismiss us with a word of prayer?"

Let Clyde deal with this, she thought. He's the one who knows the theology, and this is one time he'll just have to take the burden on his own shoulders. For a burden it was going to be, she could see that. Today the sticky subject of faith healing would be discussed around the dinner tables of all the most prominent members of the Baptist Church, and by tomorrow people would be arguing hotly.

When they left Brother Bennett's study, Miss Mattie asked, "Do you think people believed me, Cousin Edith?"

Miss Mattie's feeling toward Cousin Edith had undergone a slight change since yesterday. Cousin Edith might have some peculiar ways, but she had stood by loyally this morn-

80

ing. Of course, she hadn't said much, but just having her present and knowing she believed had been a comfort.

Mrs. Alexander's eyes flicked away, and she answered in her high, thin voice, "It doesn't matter, does it? What they think can't change what's happened to you."

"I want them to believe though. This miracle should cause a great upsurge of faith in Lanier."

12

At ten o'clock Tuesday morning when the bells in both the elementary school and the high school rang for the fifteen-minute morning recess, Miss Pauline Howle shepherded her first-graders out of the room and walked briskly to the high school building next door. Her Cuban-heeled oxfords beat a sharp tattoo down the oiled wood floors of the hall to the English room.

"Miss Lidell, I've come to apologize for the short way I answered you the day you asked me for advice about how to teach Wilma Jean Clayton to read," Miss Pauline said in a rush of words. It was not easy for her to humble herself before this younger teacher, but she felt she owed it to her and Miss Pauline always did her duty, no matter how hard it was.

She went on, "I guess I felt an implied criticism. I'm the first-grade teacher, and I should have been the one to teach Wilma Jean to read. But—"

"Oh, no, I certainly didn't mean any criticism," Stella said. "I know you don't have any spare time."

"What I came to say is, if you still want some help, I'll be glad to give it to you, that is, if you're willing to come to my home. I always go straight home after school, because my maid leaves then, and I don't dare leave Charles alone with Mother. He isn't really able to wait on himself, much less anyone else."

"How is your mother?" Stella asked.

"About the same. Dr. Taylor says she may have another stroke any time, but meanwhile she seems happy enough in her own little world. She doesn't recognize either of us and sometimes thinks she's a child again and Charles and I are her parents."

"It's nice that she's happy," Stella said.

"Yes, it could be worse. Lots of senile people are grouchy and suspicious. At least we don't have that to put up with."

Although Stella had been aware of Miss Pauline's situation before, it had not seemed as real to her as it did now. She had never met old Mrs. Howle, and she recognized Miss Pauline's brother Charles only from seeing him occasionally at the movie theater. She knew he had some strange disease which affected his movements.

"I shouldn't have asked you for help," Stella said. "You have enough to worry about without doing anything extra."

Miss Pauline's pale-blue eyes blinked behind her rimless glasses. "No, it's all right. I have to go straight home after school, but once I get there, I don't really have much to do. It's just a matter of being on hand in case I'm needed. So if you want to go with me this afternoon, I'll show you what I can and lend you some books."

"Well, thank you, I'll be glad to. I'll come to your class-room as soon as the bell rings."

The Howle house was built of wood with its once-white paint peeling and mildewed to a tired gray. Standing high on its brick foundation pillars, it looked like an old bawd with her skirts up. Miss Pauline drove her eight-year-old Chevrolet into the garage at the side of the house and led Stella to the door on the side porch. They passed through an unheated dining room filled with massive dark oak furniture into the living room where a coal fire burned in a small fireplace. A stocky man of about forty neatly dressed in a gray business suit was sitting in a chair before the fire reading the newspaper.

"Miss Lidell, this is my brother, Charles," Miss Pauline said.

Charles Howle had Miss Pauline's pale-blue eyes and large nose, but, whereas on her they looked coarse and plain, on him they were not unattractive. Stella could see no signs of his illness, whatever it was.

He said, "Forgive me for not getting up, Miss Lidell. I'm not well. But I can at least shake hands."

She took his hand gingerly, thinking it might be sensitive, as arthritic hands are. As she touched him, she felt a strange tingling in her fingers. It was almost, but not quite, a pain; it felt something like a mild electrical shock and something like the jabbing of dozens of tiny needles, but not exactly like either. She could not equate it with anything she had ever felt before. Except ... yes, she remembered now. It was the same feeling she'd had when Miss Mattie was holding her hand while she was sick.

She let go of Charles Howle's hand and put hers in the pockets of her coat. The tingling was gone now. She wondered what had caused it, and for a moment uneasiness jabbed at her mind.

Miss Pauline said, "Shall I take your coat? We can sit over here on the sofa. Just let me look in on Mother first."

"She's all right," Charles said, but Miss Pauline left the room anyway. Stella thought his voice sounded irritable, but perhaps that was because he was in pain. He turned to her and said, "Pauline makes things harder for herself, fussing over us the way she does. I often wonder what her life would be like if it wasn't for being tied down to the care of sick folks. Maybe someday—"

Miss Pauline came back then and began immediately to talk about teaching reading. During the next hour she gave Stella a condensed but comprehensive lecture on methods and materials. By the time she stopped, Stella's opinion of Miss Pauline's competence as a teacher had undergone a radical change. She had expected that Miss Pauline could help her; after all, Stella knew virtually nothing to start with, so anything would be an improvement. But she was now convinced that Miss Pauline could have taught something to the best-trained reading teachers in the state.

"I can't begin to thank you for this," Stella said. "You've showed me how, and, not only that, you've given me new inspiration. I was getting pretty discouraged, but now I can't wait to get started again."

"I'm glad I was able to help," Miss Pauline said. Now that she was no longer talking about teaching, all her enthusiasm had disappeared, and she looked homely and dull.

As Stella got up to go, she heard the sound of a car outside. Miss Pauline glanced out the window and said, "Why, it's Miss Mattie. I almost didn't recognize her. She's moving like she used to before she got sick."

Again Stella felt a tiny stab of—was it alarm?

By noon the next day all the town knew that Miss Mattie was claiming to be well, although not even half of them believed it. Imagination, some of them said, shrugging their shoulders. Religious fanaticism, others maintained. Time would tell, they all said. But by nightfall even the disbelievers had to admit that something strange was afoot in Lanier, because now they had not just one miraculous healing but two. Charles Howle, whom few people thought imaginative and none thought religious, had walked through town as spryly as if he had never been touched by illness. Several people stopped him and asked what had happened, but Charles would say nothing except, "I feel better today."

He went straight to Dr. Taylor's office, waited quietly until Sam got through with the two patients ahead of him, and said as soon as he sat down, "Dr. Taylor, I want to know what's going on. If I didn't know that multiple sclerosis is incurable, I'd swear I was well. I feel like a twenty-year-old. For the first time in years my muscles are all coordinated. I tied my own shoes this morning, and I can walk as well as you can. So what has happened?"

Sam sighed—another explanation to give. But, unlike some of his patients, Charles Howle was intelligent enough to understand. He said, "You've probably gone into remission, Mr. Howle. I explained your disease to you when you first came to me. It's caused by a degeneration of the myelin sheath and its replacement by scar tissue. Sometimes for no known reason the process of degeneration stops, and it may stay stopped for a considerable period of time."

"Yes, but I wouldn't completely recover, would I? I mean, it stands to reason the degeneration that has already occurred would still be there."

"We don't know exactly how much *has* occurred," Sam said. "All we know is that when a patient is in remission, most of the worst symptoms disappear, and he is able to live a normal, fairly active life. Let me see you walk across the room."

When Sam completed his examination, Charles said in a challenging voice, "Well, what do you think?"

Sam replied briefly, "Just what I told you when you first came in. You seem to be in a period of remission."

"Dr. Taylor, maybe I didn't make things clear to you. I don't just feel better; I feel completely well. So I've been wondering all morning—is it possible you made a mistake in diagnosing my case? Could I have had something else all along, something that I've recovered from?"

"It's possible," Sam said shortly. "Anything is possible. But I don't think it's probable."

Charles flushed and said, "Why not?"

"Because your symptoms indicated multiple sclerosis, and the progress of the disease has been what I would expect. This sudden improvement is a frequent occurrence and doesn't change my mind in the slightest. Even your feeling that you are cured doesn't surprise me, because periods of buoyant optimism are an emotional concomitant of the disease."

Charles said, "But I know how I feel, and, no matter what you say, I think I'm well. So if you didn't make a mistake in the diagnosis, Miss Lidell must have performed a miracle for me too. Only she didn't do it through my faith, because I don't have any."

He told about shaking hands with Stella and how he'd felt a kind of sting in his hands and afterward a strange all-gone sensation. "I was still feeling queer when Miss Mattie came in," he said, "so at first I didn't pay much attention to what she said. She comes about once a month and preaches to me about going to church. If she was a man, I'd tell her to get the hell out of my house and leave me alone, but, of course I can't say that to a lady, so I just tune her out. But when she started telling about how she had been healed by Miss Lidell's touch, I listened because of the funny feeling I had.

"And it's happened the same way to me," he finished, "except that I know damned well it has nothing to do with faith. You know—everybody knows—that I'm an atheist. So what caused it?"

"If we knew what causes these spontaneous remissions, we'd be a lot further toward finding a cure for multiple sclerosis, Mr. Howle. No doctor could answer your question. Just be glad it happened."

After Charles left, Sam sat motionless at his desk for a good ten minutes. His gray eyes were staring into space, but there was nothing absentminded or dreamy in their expression. His square face looked grim. He hoped he had convinced Charles Howle of the truth of his condition. And he wished Miss Mattie would come to see him, so he could talk her into having some X-rays. Chances were a million to one they'd be the same as before. This cure was all in Miss Mattie's mind. But what incredible will power the woman had!

Still, it was strange about both Miss Mattie and Charles Howle thinking Stella had healed them. Stranger about Charles than about Miss Mattie, who was extremely religious and ready to believe anything she could link to faith. No one knew exactly what had caused Charles's loss of faith, because he didn't talk about it, but he had returned from the war adamantly set against God, thus refuting one of Brother Bennett's favorite remarks, that there were no atheists on battlefields. Charles had not set his foot in church since his return and seemed totally unmoved by the Baptists' opinion that his illness had been "sent on him" in retaliation.

No need to worry about Charles starting a faith healing furor. Miss Mattie was a different proposition. A faithful church member and an inveterate do-gooder, she would tell her experience far and wide and try to scold every sick person in town into being healed. She would cause controversy in the churches, a loss of confidence in medical treatment, and feelings of anxiety and guilt in the incurably ill. And she was creating an embarrassing situation for Stella Lidell. Miss Mattie could do a lot of damage.

Owen Perry had heard the news about Miss Mattie from his wife, who was at the missionary society meeting, and he had seen Charles Howle on the street and talked with him briefly, but he had no opinion on the miraculous healings which were the main subject of conversation in Lanier just now. He figured to leave all that up to the doctors—and to the Lord if he was interested. Owen had enough to do, trying to determine what had happened to Warner Fox. So far he had come up with only two additional facts.

Brother Ben Jones, the Holiness preacher, who lived next door to his small, white-framed church on the edge of town, had seen Warner's car pass his house about five-fifteen. That proved Warner was on the road to the Clayton's at the same time as Stella Lidell. She must have seen him. But she still wouldn't admit it. The best he could get from her in a second talk was that either she or Brother Jones must be mistaken about the time.

The other bit of information came from the Fox family. Mrs. Fox and her daughters had gone to Birmingham to get Warner's things, and among them was a suitcase filled with women's clothes. Bessie Faye remembered seeing the suitcase in the trunk of Warner's car several times when he was

86

at home, but she had thought it was a drug sample case. "It looks like we were right about there being a woman mixed up in this," she said.

Owen was puzzled as he examined the clothes: a blue silk dress, size 10; spike-heeled, black-suede pumps, size 6½; an assortment of nylon lingerie; and a black-lace nightgown. All expensive. Owen had bought one of those black nightgowns for Adelaide on her birthday, and it cost twelve dollars. What woman would leave such costly clothes packed up in a suitcase in her lover's apartment?

Owen judged by the size of the clothes that the woman was taller and larger than Adelaide but had a nice figure. Offhand he could think of four or five girls in Lanier who probably wore a size 10. One of them was Stella Lidell.

He continued to ask his unobtrusive questions, convinced that nothing could happen in town without someone knowing about it. But every day he was conscious that time was passing and the trail was growing colder.

Stella too was conscious of passing time and unanswered questions. Try as she would—and she had spent hours in the effort—she could not account for the hour she had lost on her way to Clayton's. It was plain to her that the sheriff thought she knew more than she was telling. Heaven knows, I'd like to answer his questions if I only could, she thought. But I didn't see Warner, or, if I did, I don't remember it. Yet that hour must be in my mind somewhere. I must have been conscious during it. I don't know what it's like to be unconscious, but surely I would remember the beginning of it, the fainting spell or the blow on the head, or whatever. I don't remember anything like that. Time moved along in an orderly sequence all afternoon until Mrs. Clayton told me it was six-thirty when it should have been only five-thirty. But Mrs. Clayton wasn't mistaken, because when I got back home, my clock was with hers.

Eager to try out the teaching methods Miss Pauline had given her, Stella went to the Clayton's the following afternoon. As she reached the edge of town, unease began to gnaw at her mind. She had not realized she would be nervous about coming out here again. But the road was as lonely and deserted as before. She walked between the same brown fields. The same bare trees stretched their skeleton limbs to the sky. The clouds overhead were the same cold gray. She expected to hear a humming sound any minute.

Her heart jumped in her chest when it came. But it was only the sound of a car behind her. As it drew even, Miss Mattie rolled down the window and stuck her head out. Stella could see that her cousin, Mrs. Alexander, was beside her on the front seat. Stella had met Mrs. Alexander yesterday and thought she was as eccentric as Miss Mattie, but in a different way.

Miss Mattie said, "I'm going to the Clayton's. Can I give you a lift?"

Stella hesitated only a moment before getting into the back seat. She was tired, and the ride was welcome, even though Miss Mattie and Mrs. Alexander made her a little uncomfortable.

"If I'd known you were coming out here today, I'd have come to school and picked you up," Miss Mattie continued, as she mashed the gas pedal and sent the car hurtling forward. "I'm on the church committee to visit the shut-ins, and Wilma Jean is on my list."

Stella thanked her and fell silent. She didn't know whether to bring up the subject of Miss Mattie's healing. She had told Miss Mattie—she had told everyone—that she had nothing to do with it. She wasn't even persuaded that Miss Mattie was healed. Like Grant, she thought the cure was probably in Miss Mattie's imagination.

"If you'd known Miss Mattie as long as I have," he said last night, "you'd know she can believe what she wants to believe. Sam assisted at her surgery; he *saw* what shape she was in, and he says her case can end only one way. So don't worry about being a faith healing freak, Stella. The whole hullabaloo will die down eventually."

Somehow, Grant's words were not as comforting as they should have been. He had rather missed the point. She wasn't worrying so much about what people were saying as about whether she really had some strange power of which she wasn't aware.

Miss Mattie's raspy voice broke into Stella's thoughts. "I wonder if a child could have enough faith to be healed," she said thoughtfully.

"I think children may have more faith than anyone else," Stella said. "They're willing to believe. Sometimes adults aren't." She had answered quickly, and only after she began speaking did she realize what Miss Mattie was getting at. She said hastily, "If you're thinking about Wilma Jean,

88

maybe she will be healed someday. Mrs. Clayton says the doctor holds out some hope. But I don't have any healing power, Miss Mattie, and I hope you won't upset the Claytons by telling them I do."

"You healed Cousin Mattie," Mrs. Alexander said in her high, strange voice.

Miss Mattie followed her immediately. "Miss Lidell—no, I'm going to call you Stella and give you some straight talk—you're kicking against the pricks, just like the Apostle Paul did. God has chosen you for a special service, and the sooner you accept it, the sooner you'll have peace in your heart. If it had just been me that was healed, I might have thought he meant to perform only one miracle, but there's Charles Howle too."

"Yes, I know. But Miss Pauline told me Dr. Taylor said Mr. Howle's improvement was temporary, and Mr. Howle himself doesn't attribute it to God."

"Sooner or later he will. Charles has more faith than he admits to," Miss Mattie said. "He was brought up in the Baptist Church, and deep down he still believes. Train up a child in the way he should go, and when he is old, he won't depart from it, the Bible says. So Charles was healed by faith, and even though he's hardened his heart against saying so, the Lord is working on him. Before it's over, he'll be brought to repent and confess, just mark my words."

Miss Mattie paused, but she was merely gathering her forces for another onslaught. "Yes sir, I guess we can leave it all in the Lord's hands," Miss Mattie said, with the air of one who means to help him every step of the way. "He'll do his part if we do ours. So after you get through teaching Wilma Jean her reading lesson, I'll just say a short prayer for her while you hold her hand, and we'll see how it works out."

Stella protested that it wouldn't work out and it was cruel to get the Claytons' hopes up and then disappoint them, but Miss Mattie was determined. "Even if it doesn't work, it won't hurt them any more than looking at that poor, afflicted child every day," she said. "It won't cost anything to try. And *I* know it will work. You've just got to have more faith, Stella."

I won't do it, Stella thought. It's wrong to create false hope. It's not honest. It makes me a charlatan. If Miss Mattie doesn't stop this, she'll cause me to lose my job, and

89

teaching is the one thing I *can* do. When she gets ready to do it, I'll refuse.

Wilma Jean's lesson went very well. It seemed as if the heretofore meaningless black marks on the book pages suddenly translated themselves into pictures in Wilma Jean's mind, and she began to read the story of Chicken Little with great excitement. Stella had never seen her so animated. She patted Wilma Jean's hand and said, "I'm going to leave the book with you, Wilma Jean, but don't wear yourself out reading it. Reading is fun, but it takes energy, and I don't want you to get too tired."

She stopped suddenly. Her hand, the one touching Wilma Jean's, was tingling again. Just as it had before. Quickly she looked at Wilma Jean, but Wilma Jean was looking at her book, seemingly oblivious. Miss Mattie came into the room with her cousin and Mrs. Clayton. They had been talking in the parlor while Stella taught Wilma Jean in the kitchen.

Miss Mattie said briskly, "I've told Mrs. Clayton what we mean to do. You stand over there, Stella, and when I start praying, just take Wilma Jean's hand with one of yours and lay the other one on her head."

Mrs. Alexander giggled. Startled, Stella turned toward her. But Mrs. Alexander's eyes were roaming about the room, and Stella decided it must have been something she saw that caused the giggle. In a moment her eyes lit on Stella's again, and she said, "You'll have to do what Cousin Mattie says, Miss Lidell." She giggled again.

Stella gave a sudden shiver. No, I won't, she thought. You're as crazy as she is.

But afterward Stella was surprised to realize that, in spite of her resolution, she had done exactly as Miss Mattie ordered without a single demur. She hadn't even told Mrs. Clayton it would do no good. She just followed Miss Mattie's commands. It had no results though. There was no change whatever in Wilma Jean, either during or after the prayer ceremony. Stella was miserably silent, but Miss Mattie said to Mrs. Clayton, in a comforting voice, "Don't worry about not seeing any change yet. It seems to work that way. She'll probably be well by morning."

13

Bright and early the next morning Miss Mattie headed her car toward the Clayton's with Cousin Edith again by her side. Miss Mattie hadn't invited her, but Cousin Edith followed her to the car and got in, so what could Miss Mattie say? She would have preferred to go alone; then in case things hadn't turned out as she hoped, she could delay the bad news. She felt a responsibility to help Cousin Edith keep her faith in the healings. All the same, she thought, the result of the little healing ceremony she had devised for Wilma Jean would be good.

She was overjoyed to find that it was—and a little surprised to notice that Cousin Edith accepted it so matter of factly.

The first place she went on her return to town was to the boarding house where she gave Stella the good news just in time to upset her before she left for school. Her second stop was Bell's Dry Goods Store, where her sister Eunice worked. Miss Mattie wanted to get the news circulating as soon as possible. About nine o'clock she reached the parsonage.

"You can wait in the car if you want to," Miss Mattie said to Cousin Edith. "I won't be long."

"No, I'll go in with you," Cousin Edith answered.

But, as at each of their previous stops, she took no part in the proceedings except that of an onlooker.

"Brother Bennett, you know that I've been healed," Miss Mattie began.

Brother Bennett did not know any such thing. The most he could have truthfully said was that he knew Miss Mattie was claiming to be healed. He had not heard what Dr. Taylor's opinion was—the doctor seemed to be keeping his thoughts to himself, as usual—and as far as Brother Bennett knew, no X-rays had been made. But Miss Mattie was a faithful member of his church, and, moreover, several other faithful members were relatives of hers, including the bank president, who was a first cousin. So Brother Bennett merely nodded.

Miss Mattie continued, "And Charles Howle was healed, too, and Wilma Jean Clayton."

Again Brother Bennett nodded. Charles could not have been called a faithful Baptist, but he was on the church roll, and Miss Pauline attended regularly and was a tither besides. Mrs. Clayton and her children were Baptists too and, although not such large contributors, they were a big family, and one had to look to the future. Therefore, Brother Bennett was not disposed to argue about the healings.

"And of course, you know that the power of God came through Miss Lidell, by the laying on of her hands. In my case, and in Charles's too I reckon, it happened sort of accidentally that Stella touched us when our faith was operating. But with Wilma Jean Clayton it was different. Stella and I planned it on the way out there; I would pray, and she would lay on her hands. That way we could have a controlled situation, a way to call up the healing power at a definite time and place. We could *create* the conditions of faith, as you might say, instead of waiting for them to happen accidentally. So I thought I'd better come by to see you right away, so we could get the plans made in time to announce it at church Sunday."

Brother Bennett was looking at her in confusion. Somewhere the conversation had got away from him. "Announce what?" he asked.

"Why, the healing service, of course. Isn't that what we were talking about?"

"Oh, Lord," Brother Bennett said in a voice of shocked dismay.

Misinterpreting his emotion, Miss Mattie beamed. "That's exactly how I felt, just overjoyed to think of what the Lord is doing right here in Lanier. Stella Lidell could have gone anywhere to teach school, but no, the Lord in his goodness sent her to us and put her in my hands to manage. It's enough to make a body stand in awe. So I thought we'd better get to work right away. There are a lot of sick folks in Lanier—as the Good Book says, the fields are white to harvest." Vision was in Miss Mattie's eyes and satisfaction in her voice.

"Uh . . . ah . . ." Brother Bennett was trying to think of some tactful way out. He looked out the window—and saw salvation approaching. Mrs. Bennett came up the walk and into the house.

"Oh, Alma," he called. "Would you come in here a minute? Miss Mattie is here."

Mrs. Bennett surmised that Miss Mattie's visit concerned the miracle she was proclaiming all over town. She was annoyed. Miracles were Clyde's business, not hers. She hadn't seen any miracles in the eighteen years she had been married to him. Unless you counted it a miracle that she had stayed married. But that was no miracle; it had taken a lot of hard work and forbearance.

She went into the living room and greeted Miss Mattie. Brother Bennett said, "Miss Mattie thinks we should have a healing service."

"Oh, I do hope we can," Mrs. Bennett said in a voice of ringing sincerity. "I've thanked God every day for the marvelous things that are happening. But of course you can't make any plans, Clyde, until the matter has been presented to the deacons. Any change or addition to the regular worship services would have to have their approval." She looked back at Miss Mattie. "That's inconvenient sometimes, but it's really a very good thing. I wouldn't want to belong to a church that wasn't democratic, would you?"

"Well, I don't know about that," Miss Mattie said. "I guess it's a good thing to take a vote once in a while. But the Lord's commands don't need voting on. 'Heal the sick, cleanse the lepers, raise the dead,' he said. We don't have any lepers in Lanier, and I don't reckon we've got the power to raise the dead, although . . ." She paused a moment with a faraway look in her eyes; then she snapped back and said, "Well, anyway, first things first. You call the other preachers and tell them to announce it in their pulpits too. And don't forget the Holiness preacher and those Heavenly Light people. 'Go ye to all the world,' the Good Book says, so we don't want to leave anybody out."

"When shall I say the meeting is to be?" Brother Bennett asked.

Mrs. Bennett said, "Clyde! The deacons will—"

Both Brother Bennett and Miss Mattie ignored her. Miss Mattie said, "Wednesday night during our regular prayer service. You read the Bible and say a few words if you like, and then Stella and I will conduct the healing service."

"All right," Brother Bennett said in a docile voice.

The minute Miss Mattie left, Mrs. Bennett turned on her husband. "I don't know what's got into you," she said. "You're fixing to open a Pandora's box. As I told you last night,

Clyde, if you want your church to fall apart under your eyes, just start healing or speaking in tongues. Baptists won't go for those outlandish practices. Leave them to the Holy Rollers."

"You're right, of course. But somehow when she told me what to do, I just felt like I had to do it."

"Well, you'd better call her up right now and tell her you've changed your mind."

His eyes clouded. "I guess I should. Yes, I'm sure you're right. But somehow I just can't do it. I've got to call the other ministers as she told me to."

"Clyde Bennett! I've never seen you act like this before. Anybody would think you were nothing but a milquetoast, to do what Miss Mattie orders instead of what your own wife tells you."

"Yes, dear. But you don't understand. I'd like to do as you say, because I know you're always right, but I have to follow Miss Mattie's orders. I can't explain why. She just seems to have some power . . . Maybe God is speaking through her."

He turned to the telephone, leaving Mrs. Bennett staring open-mouthed. What if it is the power of God? he thought. Once he had believed all kinds of impossible things. But Alma had showed him that pastoring a church took more than dreaming, as she called it. He had learned to be practical. It was better this way. Yes, it was better. But sometimes . . .

Just after Miss Mattie left Bell's Dry Goods Store that morning, Adelaide Perry and her neighbor, Fanny Sue Langford, came in and were told the news about Wilma Jean Clayton. Since Fanny Sue was one of the busiest gossips in town, this insured that everyone would know by afternoon.

Three miracles in one week! It was enough to turn a larger and more sophisticated town than Lanier topsy-turvy. Warner Fox's disappearance receded into the realm of past events and was temporarily dropped as a topic of conversation. The healings were on all tongues. For many, they were a basis for wonder, awe, and renewed faith. Others doubted, argued, or derided.

Grant disapproved vehemently.

He made his displeasure plain that night when he said, "Stella, I know none of this is your fault, but can't you get it stopped some way?"

He and Stella were seated on the sofa in the living room at the boarding house, and Sam Taylor and Valerie were in chairs across from them. The foursome had happened fortuitously. Grant and Stella gave Valerie a ride to the theater, where they saw Lawrence Olivier in *King Henry V*, and when they came out, Grant's car had a flat. Sam, exiting just behind them, offered to drive them home. Now he was drinking the coffee Valerie had made and giving every indication of being settled for a long stay. Stella was surprised. She had never thought Sam cared much for company.

He said to Grant, "Stella probably wouldn't have any more luck than I've had with stopping the talk. I've told everybody that all the cases can be explained reasonably, but they don't want to believe that. They prefer to believe in magic. At least, some of them believe, and the others are having a good time shooting holes in the belief with theological bullets, when all they'd have to do is look at the medical facts."

"What are the medical facts?" Stella asked.

"That Miss Mattie has no proof of a cure beyond her own statement because she won't have X-rays made. That Charles Howle's multiple sclerosis is in remission. That Wilma Jean Clayton has had a spontaneous recovery, which I've seen before in female children, although I'll admit it usually seems to happen at puberty."

Stella said slowly, "You say you've seen these—improvements—before. Have you ever seen three in one week?"

Sam's eyes flashed to her, but before he could answer, Grant said, "Stella! You sound as if you believe in the healings!"

"No, of course I don't believe in them."

Sam was still looking at her. "Because?" he said.

"I don't think my reasons would be particularly interesting," she said stiffly. She'd never been one to parade her beliefs as Miss Mattie did, and she certainly didn't want to express them to Sam, who would probably refute them with one brusque remark. He was looking at her now as if he were just waiting to pounce on whatever she said.

Grant said, "I think Stella feels as I do that faith healing is like witchcraft: its time has passed. Back in Biblical times there was no other recourse. If God wanted to heal somebody, he had to perform a miracle. But now he can do his healing through doctors and nurses and"—he grinned—"pharmacists."

"Yes, that's what I think too," Valerie said in her soft voice.

"And you, Stella?" Sam asked. "Do you agree?"

His eyes were still watching her, but she noticed that they weren't black and hard, as she'd always thought, but a soft gray—curious, interested eyes. Suddenly she thought, he has a right to know. Those three people are his patients; he's responsible for them, and he must wonder about my part in this.

She said, "No, not exactly. I doubt if God ever did a miracle in the way Grant said."

Valerie gave a small exclamation of surprise, but Stella hurried on, "It seems to me that everything works by plan, according to rules. I think a Supreme Intelligence, which we call God, laid down the rules, and I don't think they've ever been changed or ever will. Those miracles in the Bible were simply a matter of someone's understanding the rules better than we do now, certainly better than the person who told the story and reported it as a miracle. The healing that Jesus did, the loaves and fishes, even the walking on water—I think they were done through the use of natural law, rather than by nullifying it. He understood the rules better than we do. We understand them better than our grandparents did, and we do things they never dreamed of—ride in automobiles and airplanes, talk across vast distances, watch pictures that move. But those things aren't miracles; they're based on scientific principles. The possibility of doing them was there all the time. No new laws were made, and no old ones were suspended, and I can't think God has changed his plans now for the benefit of Lanier, Alabama."

She stopped, a little breathless, and saw that Grant was smiling, "You've agreed with me after all, honey," he said. "You've just gone all around the world to do it."

"No, as she said, not exactly," Sam said. "You believe in the miracles as they're reported in the Bible, so you're admitting the possibility. Stella isn't."

"But you have to believe in the Bible!" Grant said, looking from Sam to Stella with troubled eyes.

"You may, but I don't," Sam said. "Or rather I don't have to believe what Brother Bennett preaches about it." He turned to Stella. "I think I agree with you," he said, "except that for these healings to have occurred, it wouldn't be necessary to change or suspend any laws; it would only be necessary to use some we're not yet aware of."

"But you've just told us the medical facts," she protested. "As a doctor you know—"

"I'm glad you have so much faith in me," he said. Hearing the undertone of amusement in his voice, she realized he was teasing her, and it seemed so strange, so out of character, that she blushed.

She said, "I'm not totally naive. I know doctors make mistakes—teachers do too—but you have a body of knowledge that—"

"That's like the tip of an iceberg, seven-eighths underwater and still completely unknown to us. For all I know, these people may have been healed by some law medicine doesn't yet recognize."

"Now wait a minute," Grant said. "You are contradicting yourself. You've already said they weren't healed. Which is it going to be?"

"I don't think they were. But I was trying to find out what the rest of you think, particularly Stella, since she's supposed to be the healer. I wanted to know whether she believes in this and what we can expect from now on."

"Nothing," Grant said. "Stella hasn't done anything; it's just that Miss Mattie insists on seeing two or three accidents as miracles and attributing them to Stella. I guess Miss Mattie is sincere, but she's mistaken, and I don't want Stella to have anything else to do with her."

Grant's voice was vehement. Valerie's placid face looked a little startled. Sam raised his eyebrows and said, "That sounds pretty high-handed. What do you have to do with what Stella does?"

Grant said, "Shall we tell them, Stella?"

Stella nodded, and Grant said, "We didn't mean to tell anyone until we got Stella's engagement ring. We're going to get married when school is out."

Valerie squealed and ran to hug Stella. Sam looked surprised and—disconcerted? But after a moment he said, "Congratulations," to Grant and, "I hope you'll be very happy," to Stella. All very correct, but somehow Stella had a feeling he didn't approve. She felt a tiny flash of apprehension. It couldn't matter, of course. Grant loved them. But he and Sam had been friends for a long time, and she didn't want marriage to change that for Grant.

She must be especially nice to Sam and try to win him over. She dreaded it though. He made her feel uncomfortable sometimes. He was so gruff and unapproachable most of the time, and then suddenly he'd open up and be human, as he was tonight. It kept one off-balance. Right now he was making her uncomfortable with a speculative stare, as if he were measuring her for the position of Grant's wife and finding her wanting.

Looking at Grant, Sam said, "To get back to the subject . . . I guess you have the right to make a decision for Stella, if that's what you both want, but I don't see what good you think it will do. You can stop the praying and the laying on of hands, as Miss Mattie calls it, but there wasn't any of that anyway in Charles Howle's case."

"Not even any faith," Stella said, frowning. "Miss Mattie has an explanation for that, but it seems to me that Charles himself is the only one who knows whether he believes in God."

"How can anyone not believe in God?" Valerie said with a shiver.

"Charles can tell you how," Grant said, "and almost make you believe as he does. Stella's right. He has no faith at all."

"Not in God, maybe, but he had faith in getting well," Sam said, "and I'm not sure that isn't more important. An old reprobate who wants to live is a lot easier to cure than a religious man who has resigned himself to the will of God.

"It's true," he insisted to their shocked faces. "There's nothing as hindering to health as a certain type of religious faith. The kind that looks on illness as a cross to bear or a punishment for sin. So Charles Howle's faith in living may have been worth more to him than faith in God."

"You're only saying that to shock us," Valerie said with a nervous little laugh. "You know you don't believe like that. If you did, you wouldn't come to church."

"Sam likes to play devil's advocate," Grant said.

"It keeps a discussion going," Sam said with a smile. But Stella had a feeling that he believed what he had said.

She said, "I've told you I don't believe what Miss Mattie says, and I don't. But I keep coming back to one thing—three people who were invalids last week seem to be well now. So how can I just say I won't have anything else to do with it? If there's a possibility of helping people, I don't see how I can refuse."

All eyes were turned toward her. She looked from one face to another, seeking agreement, but she found none. Grant looked surprised and a little angry. There was a small frown between Valerie's eyes. Sam's face was expressionless.

She said, "It can't do any harm, can it, for me to touch people? To find out for sure whether there's anything in it?"

"And if there isn't, you'll be the laughing stock of the town," Grant said with an edge to his voice.

"Isn't it a little—well, cheap—to claim to be a healer?" Valerie asked. "It's like those evangelists who set up tents in the summer, or the fortune tellers at a carnival."

"Exactly," Grant said. "Stella, you don't want to be lumped with those kinds of people. You're cultured and refined: You've had no experience with this kind of thing, and I don't want you to get mixed up in it."

"You asked if it could do any harm," Sam said, "and the answer to that is yes. Grant and Valerie are right about how people will look on you. In fact, they probably haven't painted the picture black enough. Besides that, you'll probably do a lot of other damage—cause some not to seek medical treatment, others to stop taking their medicine, still others to feel guilty and depressed because they haven't enough faith to be healed. You ought to think all that over at length before you decide to go on with this. If you consider carefully, I think you'll see that *it just won't do*." His voice was emphatic.

Afterwards, it was Sam's words that rang in her ears rather than Grant's, for Grant was only thinking of her welfare, and she wasn't so much concerned about that. She wouldn't mind taking a chance on being criticized or laughed at, but the idea that she might harm people was abhorrent. She thought of the results Sam had mentioned and others he hadn't. It would be different if she knew she had healing power, but she didn't. People might think they were cured when they weren't; they might even seem to be cured for a while and then lapse back into a worse state than before. She didn't know what the results would be. Did she have the right to raise false hopes? "Hope deferred maketh the heart sick," the Bible said. She thought that might be the worst result of all.

14

J.T. Clayton threw the frayed hickory limb on the bed and said, "You can go now. But mind you behave yourself from now on, you hear me?"

"Yessir," J.T.,Jr., said. He was snuffling but trying to hide it, trying to be a man. Well, he was nearly a man, six feet tall and sixteen years old, plenty old enough to be sowing a few wild oats and too old to be whipped for it. J.T. felt sick as he watched Junior reach for his shirt and put it on, wincing as it touched his welted back.

J.T. hated to whip any of his kids. And this time it was so uncalled for. Why in hell hadn't the boy lied and said he was going to a Sunday school party or something like that? But no, he had to go and cause trouble just when everything was looking good.

They had found out this morning that Wilma Jean was cured, and the whole day was like Christmas. J.T. knew that Esther couldn't stay mad at him when she was so overjoyed about Wilma Jean. After supper when Wilma Jean was in bed tired out from the excitement and the other kids were gathered around the radio, he sat down to read the paper in a happier frame of mind than he'd been in lately. He felt like his troubles were over.

And then Junior came through the room wearing his jacket, and Esther asked him where he was going. "Out," he said, sort of sassy.

Esther's lips tightened, and without putting down her sewing she nudged J.T.'s leg with her foot. He looked up from his newspaper. "Tell your mamma where you're going, Son," he said mildly.

"Going to drink whiskey and shoot craps," the boy said as bold as brass.

He shoulda knowed what his mamma would say to that, J.T. thought resentfully. And of course after a shocked gasp she said it: "Junior Clayton, you go out and cut a long hickory switch. J.T., you've got to whip him. He's just too big for me to handle. And mind you give him a good one too."

Well, he had. Partly because he knew Esther was listening from the next room, but mostly because he was angry. Of course, his anger was more over the boy's lack of sense than his intention to drink and gamble, but he couldn't tell Junior that. He had to uphold right to his kids, and, even more, he had to uphold Esther. She'd had most of the burden of raising them, and it was nothing but fair to help her when he was home. But he sure wished Junior had used the sense God gave him and lied.

It looked like everybody in his family had lost what few wits they had, hisself included. Esther still hadn't spoke a word to him except the necessary ones in the course of the day. At night she lay on her side of the bed, as stiff as a board. One morning though she woke up curled against him in the old way, and since then she'd been putting a rolled-up quilt down the center of the bed every night to keep herself from doing that again.

He had thought maybe tonight, what with being so happy about Wilma Jean and all, she would leave the quilt out and move toward him. But now he didn't know. And even if she had that in mind, he thought dispiritedly, he'd probably ruin it before bedtime, just like he'd did so many times already.

One night after they went to bed, he'd spoken into the darkness telling Esther how much he loved her and how he felt about things in their married life—their wedding night and when the kids were born and every time he came home from a job. A lot of it he'd said before, but he'd never said so much all at one time. It wasn't as easy to speak toward the ceiling as it would've been to say it into her ear, but he knew she was listening by the way she lay so still.

"I hate myself for what I done the other night," he finished. "I ain't got no excuse excepting I didn't think it would make no difference in us, in our marriage. I just thought I'd have a little fun on the side and you'd never find out about it."

"If you didn't aim for me to find out, why did you tell me?"

"I wish I knowed. It just seemed like I couldn't lie when you asked me where I'd been."

"I wonder if the Lord is working on you," she said after a long moment of silence. "He works in mysterious ways, and could be he's taking this way of bringing you to repentance.

101

If I knowed it was that, I reckon I'd think the pain it caused me was worth it, because you not being a Christian and a church member is one of the greatest sorrows of my life."

J.T. didn't say anything to that. He knew Esther had always wanted him to join the church and attend the meetings with her and the kids, but he never had seen any sense in it. Church was good for women and kids, gave them somewhere to go and seemed to make them happy, but he was all right like he was and didn't feel no need to be saved. But he made up his mind right then that if it would get Esther over her mad spell, he'd do it.

So he went to sleep feeling pretty good. By this time next week everything ought to be back to normal again.

Then the very next day he had ruined it. It happened at dinner. They had round steak, and one of the older boys said, "Mamma, why don't you cook it with gravy the way Grandma used to?"

"Because your daddy likes it fried plain."

"I bet he likes it better with gravy, don't you, Daddy?"

"Yeah," J.T. answered.

Color came up in Esther's face. She said, "You always told me you liked it the way I cooked it better than the way your mamma cooked it," she said. "Now what's the truth?"

"I like it better with gravy," he said. "This way it's like eating shoe leather."

Esther got up from the table and busied herself at the stove. After a few minutes she left the room and did not return until everyone was out of the kitchen. J.T. could have kicked himself a mile down the road.

What's wrong with me? he thought, picking up the switch and breaking it up to throw into the cold fireplace. It seemed like every time somebody asked him a question, he had to tell them the plain, unvarnished truth. He said things he didn't mean to say, things he'd rather cut out his tongue than say, and he couldn't seem to help it.

He went back into the other room, his and Esther's bedroom, where the fire was. The minute he walked in the door, Esther said to the boys, "Y'all cut off the radio and go to your own rooms. It's bedtime."

J.T.'s heart jumped. It wasn't but eight o'clock, and she usually didn't make them go to bed till eight-thirty or nine. He looked at her and saw that she had a kind of half-smile on her face.

He said, "Where's Junior?"

"He took his books and went toward the kitchen. I reckon he was too ashamed to stay in here with the rest of us. Don't worry, J.T., I know how you hate to whip the kids, but Junior won't hold no grudge for this. He knows he deserved it."

"I guess so," J.T. muttered. But he turned and walked toward the kitchen. Junior looked up when he came in and then hastily dropped his eyes to his book. J.T. could see that he had been crying again.

He couldn't think of anything to say to the boy. Finally he said, "The kitchen has cooled off since supper. If you're gonna be here long, you better build up a fire in the stove."

"I'm about finished," Junior mumbled.

"Well . . ." J.T. started to go, but then suddenly he knew what ought to be said. "Son, I ain't never gonna whip you again no matter what you do. But you try to keep from upsetting your mamma, hear?"

"Yessir, I will."

J.T. went out and closed the door. He felt better.

When he got back to the bedroom, Esther was standing before the dresser mirror. "I just finished this dress. How does it look?"

"Like a circus tent," J.T. said.

Which it did, from the voluminous skirt to the snuff-brown color, but he knew immediately by Esther's stricken expression that he shouldn't have said so. Stiff and silent, she pulled the dress off and put it on a hanger.

He tried to make amends. "Sugar, don't pay no attention to me. I don't have no idy what women's clothes ought to look like. If it fits tight and is blue, I think it's pretty. But you can't wear blue all the time, and, anyway, you look pretty in anything."

She didn't answer. He knew she would wear the dress—she was too thrifty to waste it—but he doubted if she'd ever take much pleasure in it.

He sat down in a chair and put his head in his hands. He was in despair. He knew all the chances of making up with her tonight were gone. Why did he keep saying things he didn't mean to say? He didn't have no control at all over hisself. It was like a sickness. And Junior seemed to have caught it too, the way he acted tonight.

Yeah, that's exactly what it was like, a sickness. And the only thing to do when you got sick was to go to the doctor.

103

He'd do that the first thing in the morning. He hoped to hell Doc Taylor could help him.

The next morning J.T. was alarmed at Dr. Taylor's reactions. The doc had looked worried the minute he looked up and saw J.T. Immediately J.T. jumped to the conclusion that he *was* crazy and Doc Taylor had already noticed it.

He couldn't know that Sam's concern was caused by what he saw on J.T.'s face. He's got trouble, Sam thought, and it can't be Wilma Jean's health now. I hope to hell he hasn't come to ask me any questions about genetics.

Then as J.T. stated his case, the worry went out of the doctor's face, but it was replaced by shock. And Dr. Taylor never seemed shocked at anything.

"It must be something bad from the expression on your face," J.T. said anxiously. "What have I got, Doc? Am I losing my mind? You can tell me. I ain't no braver than the next guy, but I don't think nothing could be no worse than what I've been going through."

Sam said hastily, "No, you're not losing your mind. Maybe you've got religion, and your conscience won't let you lie."

J.T. shook his head. "I ain't right sure I've got a conscience, some of the things I've did. And if I have, it wouldn't make me say things to hurt Esther, would it? I guess it ain't right to lie, but Doc, sometimes it ain't right *not* to lie. Some lies are necessary if a man's to get along in this world and keep from hurting other folks."

Sam nodded.

J.T. said, "And something else—I'm scared the kids are catching this trouble, whatever it is. Last night with Junior and then again this morning with Bobby—well, anyhow, it seems like when I ask them a question, they've got to tell me the truth, even when a lie would do better."

He paused, considering. He was in thought for several minutes. Than he said, "Funny thing though, they can still lie to their mamma. So it must be just me. I can't lie to nobody, and can't nobody lie to me."

Sam said, "You say this started on Monday night two weeks ago. What did you do that night?"

"I've done told you that, about bringing Miss Lidell home and then going up to Billie Sue's house. That was the start of the whole trouble, me telling my old lady what I done."

"No, I mean before that." Sam was trying to find some explanation for the strange trouble J.T. was experiencing. Post-hypnotic suggestion? The well-publicized "truth serum"?

That might hold for J.T. but not for his entire family, and anyway, the effect wouldn't have lasted so long. Besides, they didn't work quite that way. Nothing Sam could think of seemed to fit the case.

J.T. said, "Before that, I was working at my whiskey still." He looked at Sam with a perplexed, half-angry expression. "You see—how it is? In my right mind I wouldn't admit I had a whiskey still, but here I am telling you about it, and that ain't the worst. I even told the sheriff where it is. Lucky he didn't believe me that time, but if I can't get this loose talk stopped, I'll be in trouble with the law as well as with my wife."

"I never tell what's said in this office, so you can feel free to talk. Did anything unusual happen at the still?"

"Naw, not at the still." J.T. was glad the doctor had put his question the way he had. If he'd asked it a little different, all J.T. knew about Miss Lidell and Warner Fox would've probably come pouring out, and he wasn't gonna tell anybody *that*. That's another reason he had to get this sickness cured. He'd die before he got Miss Lidell in trouble after what she had did for Wilma Jean. Having Wilma Jean well was the greatest thing that had ever happened, and if there was any little old thing he could do for Miss Lidell, he aimed to do it. He had a feeling this might not be so little.

He said, "I drunk some of the whiskey I'd just made. I guess maybe I had more than I thought, because I got the d.t.'s and saw things that wasn't there."

"Do you want to tell me about it?"

"I'd just as soon not. It was like a nightmare that once it's over you'd rather not think about. I did wonder though if there was something wrong with the whiskey that might've caused it. Do you reckon it could've caused this other trouble I'm having too?"

"I don't know, but if you'll bring me some, I can get it analyzed, and we'll see."

"I wish I hadn't poured it out. But I did, every last drop. . . . Ain't there anything you can do for me, Doc?"

Sam thought a minute. "I can write you a prescription for some pills to slow down your reactions and give you time to think before you speak," he said. "I don't guarantee it, but if you'll take a pill every morning and count to ten before you answer any questions, it will probably be some help."

"I can use all the help I can get," J.T. said gratefully.

What Sam gave him were placebos, but he thought they

105

might help by giving back J.T.'s lost confidence in his ability to lie.

After J.T. left, Sam couldn't help grinning. He had known when he decided to be a general practitioner that he'd be dealing with a variety of illnesses, but he couldn't have guessed he'd be called on to prescribe for a loss of the ability to lie.

It wasn't funny to J.T. though. And it was odd. A lot of queer things were happening lately.

It had not occurred to anyone that Stella would not be willing to participate in a healing service. Brother Bennett assumed Miss Mattie was speaking for both herself and Stella, and Miss Mattie made the same assumption. Seeing so plainly the fields white to harvest, she had no doubt that Stella was eager as she to labor in them.

But to her astonishment when she went by the boarding house to discuss the procedure they would follow, Stella said, "Miss Mattie, we've had two cases, three if you count yourself, of what might seem to be miraculous healing. But Dr. Taylor says they are explainable medically. If we had a healing service, there would be people present whose diseases wouldn't have the possibility of a remission or a spontaneous recovery. They would expect to be healed, and they would be disappointed. I don't want to be a party to that."

And in spite of all Miss Mattie's arguments she continued adamant. She had no healing power, and she would not perpetrate a fraud that would disappoint people and perhaps cause them to lose their faith.

Finally Miss Mattie ran out of arguments. She said, "Stella, it doesn't make any difference whether you believe you have any healing power or what you think the results will be. That's up to God. You just come to the church and lay your hands on people."

"All right," Stella said.

She couldn't believe she had said it. She certainly hadn't intended to give in. She tried to back up and take the words back, but instead she found herself listening to Miss Mattie's instructions and repeating them, as if to fix them firmly in her mind. She couldn't understand it.

From the expression on Miss Mattie's face, Stella thought she was astonished too. Nevertheless, the meeting was to be.

Once it was decided, it seemed to Stella that it had always

106

been inevitable. She still didn't want to do it, but she realized that she had to, because if it was true that she had the power to heal, it would be wrong not to use it. This was the best, perhaps the only, opportunity. In no other way could she see so many sick people in such a short period of time. At least, she thought, when this is over, I'll know.

Yet she knew instinctively that Grant would not like it.

Even so, the fierceness of his opposition dismayed her. What she hoped would be a reasonable discussion soon degenerated into a bitter quarrel, during which the kindest thing he said to her was that she would make a public spectacle of herself with her cheap exhibitionism.

"I don't want to embarrass you," she said reasonably. "But need you be embarrassed? This may be a mistake, but you aren't making it. Why must you feel it's your responsibility?"

"Because from now on everything you do will reflect on me."

"So I'm supposed to do what you tell me? To make no decisions of my own?"

His blue eyes were cold. "Don't be silly. Of course you'll make your own decisions. But I certainly don't expect them to be the kind that will humiliate me."

"Which is just another way of saying that I'll have to base them on what you think and feel, and that leaves me no freedom at all."

"If you loved me, you'd want to please me."

"And if you loved me, you wouldn't ask me to be no better than a slave." Hearing the hot sound of her voice, she was shocked back to her senses. Better stop this before it goes too far, she thought, before we've said something that can't be unsaid.

"We aren't getting anywhere except angrier," she said. "Let's leave it. Maybe things will look different tomorrow."

"Not to me," he said.

Nor to me, she thought. But she didn't say it aloud. There had to be some way to resolve the quarrel. Perhaps Grant would change his mind before the meeting. Surely he would see that the possibility of healing people was worth the risk of embarrassment.

15

Never in the history of the Baptist Church had so many people turned out for midweek prayer service. Baptists, Methodists, and Presbyterians packed the church. Solomon Greenbaum, the only Jew in town, was there, and so were the Holiness people. Even the members of the Church of the Heavenly Light came, the men in ill-fitting dark suits and the women in high-necked, long-sleeved dresses and black stockings.

Gaynell Moore was there with her family; they filled two pews. Gaynell was a little nervous. She wanted Miss Lidell to succeed. Actually it was nothing to her, as she kept reminding herself to quiet her pounding heart. But across the church she could see Dr. Taylor, and she thought it mattered a good deal to him, possibly more than he himself realized. Anything that was important to Dr. Taylor was important to Gaynell.

Across the church she saw Mrs. Fox and her two daughters with their husbands. She wished she could talk to them about Warner. They would know how the investigation was going and what the sheriff thought. They might even know something which would locate Warner if only she could help them dredge it up out of memory. But she couldn't do more than greet them lest someone wonder why she was so interested.

Or was she being too careful? Maybe her concern for her own safety was preventing her from doing something to help. Still, the sheriff knew better than she did how to get information. There was nothing she could do but wait. But waiting was so hard . . .

J.T. Clayton and his family had come in a little late and were sitting toward the back of the church. Wilma Jean was still thin, but she moved as easily as her older brothers, among whom she stood out like a white puppy in a litter of black ones. The four boys all had the dark good looks of their father, but Wilma Jean was tow-headed with light-brown eyes and a receding chin—not as good-looking as the boys, not even as attractive as her rather plain mother, from whom she must have inherited her blonde coloring, although Mrs. Clayton's eyes were blue instead of brown. All the Claytons were dressed in their Sunday best, and they were getting considerable attention from the congregation, many of whom turned around to see Wilma Jean.

Miss Eunice and her cousin, Edith Alexander, were sitting together near the front. Miss Eunice moved restlessly on her seat, and her hands were clasping and unclasping nervously. For Mattie's sake, she did hope the meeting would be a success.

One person who might have been expected to be at the healing service was absent. Maureen Granger had not come.

She had wanted to. The minute her father told her mother about the announcement at church Sunday, she began making gestures and noises to indicate her desire to go. She was sure they understood her, although at first her mother pretended not to. When Maureen's agitated grunts drowned out all hope of conversation, her mother turned to her and said, "Now, Maureen, you know there's nothing to this. It's just a crazy idea of Miss Mattie's. She's always been a religious fanatic, and I suppose in her present condition she's grasping at any straw. But I'm surprised she's been able to talk Miss Lidell into participating in such an undertaking. You'd think a teacher would have more sense . . . No, of course we aren't going. There's no use embarrassing ourselves for nothing."

Maureen turned to her father. He said, "Honey, I agree with Mother. If there was any hope of helping you, I'd take you to the meeting, but you know what your situation is. The best thing to do is accept it and get what pleasure you can out of life without exposing yourself to the curiosity and unkindness of the public."

And although Maureen grunted and gestured until tears of frustration ran down her face, her parents could not understand that she wouldn't mind people looking at her. She wouldn't care how much embarrassment it was to be in public; she wouldn't mind anything if only they would take her to the meeting. She wanted to tell them that any chance of improvement, no matter how slim, was worth taking. If she could have talked, she would have told them about the strange things she had seen two weeks ago and said if those

109

things had happened, other unbelieveable things could happen.

But Maureen's means of communication were too limited to permit her to advance arguments for her cause. She could only continue to plead. She became so upset that Mr. Granger finally suggested to his wife that they give in and take her. But Mrs. Granger said Maureen would be twice as upset if she went and was not healed, which, she said, was what would happen.

So Maureen was not present. Only a few people in the church wondered at her absence. Many of them did not know her, and those who did had other things on their minds. Dr. Taylor was looking at Stella and wishing she hadn't done this; Miss Pauline Howle was looking at Charles and Valerie Dixon and wondering if Charles was seriously interested in her; even Mrs. Bennett did not notice Mr. Granger's absence, although normally she checked at every church service to be sure the wealthier members were present.

Stella was sitting on the front bench with Miss Mattie. She felt extremely nervous. Maybe I am wrong to do this, she thought.

She had come in late, after the church was almost filled and Miss Mattie anxious for her arrival. She was late because she had refused both Miss Mattie's and Mrs. Overly's offers of a ride, thinking that Grant would surely change his mind even this late and come by for her. But he hadn't. He said last night that if she did this, she needn't expect any support from him, and he stuck to his decision. She was trying not to be angry. She told herself that if she demanded the freedom to choose for herself, she must grant him the freedom to disapprove. But she felt very alone.

None of the few people she considered her friends approved this meeting. Mrs. Overly said she was afraid Mattie Shepard was mistaken about the healing power. Mattie had some funny ideas, she said, and was inclined to push them too hard.

Sam Taylor had been cool when she met him in the post office yesterday. "I think you're making a mistake," he said.

Even Valerie, who seldom offered advice, said, "Stella, even if you've decided to do this, maybe you ought to wait a while. How do you know the cures will be permanent? Charles says his is, but I don't know—wouldn't it be better to wait and see?"

"If I can heal anyone, it seems better to do it as soon as possible," Stella answered. "But what's this about Charles Howle? I didn't know you knew him that well."

"I had a date with him last night," Valerie said. Her round face flushed a little. "We started talking in the drug store, and, well, he asked me. Maybe it seems strange to you—we've always spoken of him as if he were old—but he's just forty, and I'm nearly thirty myself. It was only because he was sick that he seemed so old." She sounded defensive.

"I wasn't criticizing," Stella said. "I'm delighted. He seems a nice man."

Valerie was with Charles tonight; they were sitting about three rows behind Stella in the pew with Grant. She saw them when she came in. Grant had not looked at her as she passed but stared straight ahead, his blue eyes expressionless and his handsome face set in lines of disapproval.

Sam was there too but not with Grant. She wondered why they didn't come together. It might have been some comfort to Grant to have Sam to talk with, since they were agreed that this was a mistake.

Was it a mistake? The next hour or two should show. She hardly knew what to hope for—no, that wasn't true; she had to hope for success, for people to be healed. But if they were, she would have to go on with it, wouldn't she? And that meant she would lose Grant. He might forgive her a mistake, but he would not want to be married to a healer.

Still, she had to hope for success. Those who had come to be healed must be as nervous as she was. She didn't want them to be disappointed. She didn't want them to go away hopeless. If only one were healed, the rest could still hope. Please let there be at least one.

Brother Bennett rose from his chair on the pulpit and walked to the lectern. Rustling and chattering ceased, and a few last coughs punctuated the sudden silence. Brother Bennett spoke briefly about the miracles of healing that had occurred and prayed a lengthy prayer for more. In his prayer, he did not forget to thank God for "these women who have been touched by God, that they may become greater channels of blessing." He was so hearty in his praise of Miss Mattie in particular that by the time the prayer ended, no one in the church could have guessed that fifteen minutes ago he had been saying, "Yes, Alma, I agree that she is probably insane, but what can I do? We're committed to

111

having this service, and if I show any reservations, everyone will say it was my lack of faith that prevented miracles."

After the prayer he read the ninth chapter of John and emphasized the fact that the blind man's healing had resulted in faith. He then preached such a powerful sermon that he felt compelled to open the doors of the church to new membership.

There was an audible gasp as J.T. Clayton rose and stepped into the aisle. J.T. was considered so unlikely a possibility for conversion that he was not even visited during the annual revival, when the drive for new membership was at its hottest.

He walked all the way to the front and shook Brother Bennett's proffered hand. No one could hear what was said, because the heretofore rather unenthusiastic singing swelled in volume at this unexpected evidence that miracles were already happening tonight. If the congregation could have heard the exchange between J.T. and Brother Bennett, the singing would have ceased at once, cut off by an even bigger shock than J.T.'s walk down the aisle.

Brother Bennett waited a moment for a declaration from J.T. and then, seeing that it was not forthcoming, he followed his usual procedure of eliciting it. "Do you repent of your sins and accept the Lord Jesus Christ as your personal Saviour?" he asked.

"No," J.T. said truthfully.

Brother Bennett was struck speechless. In all his years as a pastor this was a situation that had never occurred. After a moment he stuttered, "Uh, then why are you, ah, doing this?"

He still had hopes; he thought J.T. would probably say that the Lord was working on him and he wanted the prayers of the church. But the truth had J.T. in its grip, and he replied, "I thought it would be nice for my wife if I joined the church."

By now the congregation, although still singing lustily, were staring at the two men with puzzled looks on their faces. Brother Bennett wiped his forehead with his handkerchief and said, "You can't join the church unless you have been converted, Mr. Clayton. Perhaps I'd better come out to see you tomorrow, and we'll talk about what it means to be a church member. I think now it would be best if you just returned to your seat."

Which J.T. did, with lowered eyes and a face showing red

112

under his dark complexion. The Baptists watching him were a little surprised that he had not actually joined after making that difficult walk down the aisle, but they assumed that a decision was in the making; after all, one might expect it to take a little longer than usual with such a sinner as J.T. Besides, they were so eager for the healing to start that they couldn't spare any more thought for J.T. Most of them had been a little impatient with Brother Bennett for preaching a sermon at such a time and could forgive him only because it was the largest crowd he was ever likely to see in the Baptist Church.

At last Brother Bennett said, "And now we come to the part of our service that you have all been waiting for. Miss Mattie and Miss Lidell will stand at the front of the church; and those of you who wish to be healed of your afflictions, please approach in an orderly manner for the laying on of hands and a short prayer. Please bear in mind that we may not see any immediate miracles. Wait on the Lord, my friends, wait on the Lord."

Brother Bennett did not truly believe there would be any miracles later, either, but he was determined to delay and diffuse the disappointment as much as possible.

Stella was trembling as she followed Miss Mattie to the front of the church. Her face felt on fire. She wondered if everyone could see how nervous she was. The faces in front of her looked blurred and unrecognizable. They were like so many white onions lined up in rows, each indistinguishable from the next. Grant was out there somewhere, but she could not pick him out. She couldn't find Sam either. All these people she had lived among all year might have been strangers.

Ten or fifteen people lined up in the aisle. Some of them were alone; some were supported by friends or relatives. The silence was broken only by the shuffling feet. As each person in line reached Stella, she held his or her hands for a moment and then put her hand on each head, as Miss Mattie had directed, while Miss Mattie said a prayer of one or two sentences. Then the petitioners passed to the other aisle and went back to their seats. There was no evidence that anyone had been healed, although Stella had felt the familiar prickle in her hands several times.

I must have been mistaken about that, she thought. Perhaps it has nothing to do with healing after all. Perhaps it

113

means there is something wrong with me, some disease I have, or a forewarning of a disability to come.

Then suddenly the silence was broken by an excited voice: "I'm healed, I'm healed! Praise the Lord, I'm healed!" It was Aletha Cunningham, the epileptic fifteen-year-old daughter of Lanier's insurance man.

Brother Bennett rushed forward and drew Aletha to one side. Miss Mattie and Stella proceeded with the service.

The ice had been broken, and soon there was another healing. Mr. Bob Morrow, who at eighty-seven was the oldest active member of the Baptist Church, straightened his stooped back (although some later said they heard an ominous crack as he did so) and shouted, "Praise God! Hallelujah!" He threw down his two walking sticks and began to cavort about with wobbly, uncertain motions.

Many of the more conservative Baptists looked at each other in alarm. They were aware that Mr. Morrow had long been an advocate of what he called "the old-time religion," but shouting and dancing in church smacked too much of Holiness practices.

"He's got the Holy Ghost!" one of the Holiness men shouted. And others answered, "Amen, Brother. Praise the Lord!"

The church was in an uproar. The fat, feebleminded Kelly boy was prancing up and down the aisle with his father chasing him. Old Mrs. Johnson, whose stroke had left her with no damage other than exaggerated emotional reactions, was cackling gleefully. People were talking to each other, expressing joy or disapproval or simply saying, "I can't see. What's going on down there?"

At last Brother Bennett made himself heard over the babble. When the church was reasonably quiet, he said, "Truly our hearts are full and running over. We can only give thanks to God, whose goodness passeth understanding. My fellow Christians, let us pray."

At last the congregation ceased all murmurs and whispers. Brother Bennett began his prayer in a sonorous voice. A loud drumming sound interrupted him. Without lifting his head he opened his eyes to find the disturbance. The sight he saw struck him dumb in midsentence. With great presence of mind, however, he shut his eyes quickly and said, "To thee be the glory forever and ever, amen."

A few minutes later the entire congregation knew what had happened. Aletha Cunningham had been struck by an epileptic fit.

The congregation went out in great disorder. All of them were talking. Many were laughing. A few, largely those who had come to be healed, were crying. Irrespective of their reactions, they were uniformly agreed that the healing service had been a fiasco.

Stella did not care. She was so tired she could barely stand. Now and then her knees buckled as if they would let her fall, but so far she had managed to stiffen them again. She and Miss Mattie had remained standing for the prayer. Now people were going out. No one, it seemed, wanted to say anything to them, being too angry, contemptuous, amused, or disappointed to feel sympathetic. Stella did not care about that either, and she only half heard Miss Mattie's bitter recriminations.

Someone took her arm, and she heard Sam's voice say, "I'll take Stella home, Miss Mattie." Then she was being led toward the side door and, in a moment, shut into his car. She leaned her head back. She was too tired to move, too tired to speak, too tired even to think.

After a few minutes when she became aware that the car had stopped, she opened her eyes and saw that they were in front of the boarding house. She moved as if to get out, but he said in a rough voice, "No, wait a minute. I have something to say. You must never do that again, Stella. Keep on with the healing if you must, but not that way."

"Keep on with the healing! There wasn't any healing. I know that as well as you do. You don't have to rub it in."

"Don't be so touchy," he said brusquely. "I'm not commenting on the failure of your effort; I'm only saying the effort itself was too much for you. You're my patient, and that gives me a right to advise you. You're too exhausted. I don't want you to talk with anyone tonight—not Mrs. Overly or Valerie or anyone, even Grant."

"Grant. Now there's a likely possibility," she said bitterly.

"I take it you've quarreled. Well, don't think about that now. Go straight to bed. And come to see me tomorrow."

"Why? Do you think there's something wrong with me?" She thought vaguely of the "flu" and the strange tingling in her hands. But, somehow even her health didn't seem important at the moment.

He ignored her question. "Let me hear you repeat what I told you," he said, as if speaking to a recalcitrant school child.

"Go to bed and come to see you tomorrow," Stella repeated

115

in a lifeless voice. She paused, and when she spoke again, her words were slurred, "I haven't thanked you for rescuing me."

"Somebody had to do it," he said shortly. "Come on now. I'll go in and tell Mrs. Overly you're not to be disturbed. You'll probably feel better in the morning. But I want to see you after school tomorrow, regardless of how you feel."

The fog was closing in on her mind now, but through it she wondered vaguely why he was so insistent on that.

16

When Sam walked into his office the next morning, he was still angry. Every time he thought of how people had turned their backs and walked out laughing and talking, ridiculing Stella, his anger boiled up again. Didn't they realize the ordeal she had been through; couldn't they see how tired she was; didn't they know she had done it for them, in the hope of helping? What difference if she failed? They should appreciate the effort at least enough to show common courtesy.

He was angry with Grant too. Grant was engaged to the girl, supposedly in love with her, and no matter how much he disapproved of what she was doing, he should have realized she needed him last night. But he too had walked out without a backward look at her tired, white face.

But, most of all, Sam was angry with Stella. She had no business getting herself involved in a situation like that. She was intelligent—considerably more intelligent than he had realized when he first knew her—and old enough to have had some experience in dealing with people. She shouldn't have let Miss Mattie talk her into that healing service. He had told her what the previous healings were, and she seemed to accept his explanation, so why had she gone against that and humiliated herself before the whole town?

In his mind he saw her face again as it had been last night, her bloodless skin and dropping mouth and shadowed eyes, and he felt a return of uneasiness. It was only two weeks since her mysterious illness. He still didn't know what had been wrong, or what after-effects she might have. If she didn't seem all right this afternoon, he would send her to Tuscaloosa for some tests.

Nor was it only because of what she might have done to herself that he was angry with her. There was as yet no way to tell what effect the meeting had on other people, but he felt sure he'd be finding out before long. The excitement, the disappointed hopes, with their resulting anger, grief, and depression, the loss of religious faith—all those things would have an effect on health.

Fool girl, he thought, briefly summing up his feelings toward Stella Lidell.

She was pretty though. Even with weariness in every line of her face and figure, they were still some face and figure. That pale, gold-dusted hair, the curve of breast and hip—well, Grant was a lucky man. He and Stella should be happy—would be, Sam was sure, if only she would give up this faith healing business.

Sam sighed and rang the buzzer for Gaynell. He looked up as she came into the office. Suddenly he frowned as his eyes focused on her. "Are you all right?" he asked.

She blushed a little, as she always did when he made a personal remark to her. Gaynell, he had thought before, wasn't accustomed to being noticed.

She said, "I'm fine. A little tired after last night. We went to the healing service."

"Yes, I saw you across the church."

"It's a shame it didn't turn out better," she said. "I felt sorry for Miss Lidell. She looked like she was trying so hard."

"Yes, well . . ." He couldn't think of an appropriate comment. But he was glad to know somebody felt sympathetic. He said, "Any emergencies this morning?"

"No, I don't think so, just the usual complaints."

"Well, you can start sending them in."

Somehow she got back to her desk and sent in the first patient. Dr. Taylor was right though; she was not feeling well. She felt weak and dizzy, as if she might faint. She leaned her head forward, propping it in her hands, so it would seem she was studying the ledger in front of her. She must not faint. If she did, Dr. Taylor would find out what was wrong with her. No one must know, not until Warner came back. He would come. She must not lose faith in him.

But if he didn't?

She wouldn't think about that. He would come. He knew how much depended on it. No matter why he had gone away, he would return.

The ringing of the phone cut into her thoughts. Two minutes later Sam rushed out of the office. Eighty-seven-year-old Mr. Bob Morrow, the only person who had seemed to be healed last night, was dead. He had walked to breakfast as spryly as such an old man could and claimed he had never felt better in his life. His rheumatism, he said, was completely gone. Soon after breakfast, however, he lay down on the sofa, and by the time his granddaughter came with a quilt to cover him, he was dead.

Sam could only confirm his death and try to comfort his daughter and granddaughter by telling them that his attendance of the meeting last night had nothing to do with his death. "At his age we have to expect that death may come at any time," he said. "A heart can't beat forever, and his stopped as quickly and easily as a clock stops. A painless death is much to be thankful for."

What he told them was true, but still he had a faint feeling of unease, wondering if the excitement or some other effect of the healing service had hastened the old man's death.

Sam returned to the office and saw three patients. At ten o'clock he once again rushed out in response to a call, this time from Mrs. Farley's maid. Mrs. Farley was a diabetic, a nervous, unstable woman who was erratic in all her habits and had a history of both coma and shock. Sam had finally persuaded her to a fixed routine, and for about a year she had been in perfect balance. Now he supposed that she had got off her diet or her program of exercise. Or, he thought uneasily, the stress of the healing service might have done it.

She was in insulin shock. As soon as Sam had determined that and administered glucose, he turned to Mr. Farley. "How did this happen?" he asked.

Mr. Farley frowned. "I don't know. She didn't skip breakfast or sleep late or get off her schedule any way. I did suggest to her that she see you this morning, because she was at the service last night, and I thought possibly . . . But she said no, she wasn't healed and neither was anyone else. But if she *was* healed, her regular dose of insulin would throw her into shock, wouldn't it? Do you think that might have happened?"

Sam looked at him and thought of the sharp, logical mind that made Mr. Farley the best lawyer in the county. It was surprising that an intelligent man, trained to weigh evidence and detect discrepancies, would believe in something so unfounded in fact. Sam was beginning to think people would believe *anything* if they were desperate enough.

He said, "I don't have to tell you that diabetes is incurable. Mrs. Farley probably did something you aren't aware of. There's no evidence to make me believe there have been any faith healings in Lanier. But if you think it's a possibility, we can find out easily enough by doing some tests."

Mr. Farley looked a little embarrassed, but he said, "Yes, I think that would be a good idea." He hesitated. "I wish you wouldn't say anything about faith healing to her though, because she doesn't believe in it."

Sam was puzzled. "Then why did she go up to be healed last night?"

"Because I insisted. I wasn't sure whether I believed myself—and I'm still not—but I was ready to grasp at any straw. You'd think she would be too, wouldn't you? But she wasn't. I had to beg and coax and even threaten before she would agree to try it. Can you explain that to me?"

Sam shook his head. "Embarrassment? The thought that if she went up, people would laugh at her for being gullible?"

"Maybe." But he still looked dissatisfied. Nor was Sam satisfied with that explanation. He could understand why Mrs. Farley might not choose to go up if she felt it would do no good, but even if it didn't, it seemed a small thing to do to please her husband. Yet apparently she had been dead set against it. Because she was determined not to get well?

Some people had a stronger will to live than others, of course. Yet he had never thought that anyone might want to keep an illness or disability. Why would they? The pain and suffering—or the inconvenience and expense—should preclude it. Could there be advantages which outweighed the disadvantages for some patients? He considered. Sick people frequently get a lot of attention and sympathy. They have a built-in excuse for anything they don't want to do. And if an illness is long-standing, as Mrs. Farley's was, the patient builds a way of life around it. Thus, the sickness is established by habit and may be, in one sense, the most important thing in life.

No patient would admit to a reluctance to get well. But the question would never come up if it were an incurable disease like Mrs. Farley's. Could that have something to do with which diseases people had?

Did they choose, perhaps subconsciously?

Sam shook his head, feeling that he was getting way beyond the bounds of what the people around here called good ole horse sense. He could imagine the furor he'd cause if he expressed those thoughts. Still, some of them might be true.

Yet another unexpected event occurred in the early afternoon, but this time it was a pleasant one: Mrs. Ashford came to the office.

Mrs. Ashford was a widow in her early sixties, so crippled by arthritis that she could barely creep around with the help of two canes. She had not been to the office since Sam had taken it over, but he went by to see her once or twice a month. Although he could do nothing for her beyond advising aspirin and occasionally prescribing a mild sedative, it seemed to help both her and the daughter with whom she lived to feel that some effort was being made in her behalf.

And now here she was, walking without her canes and seemingly feeling no pain. It caused a sensation in the waiting room, and Gaynell came flying into the inner office in a state of excitement quite unlike her usual calm efficiency.

Sam saw Mrs. Ashford immediately—no question of making her wait her turn. Sure enough, she had a full range of movement, and even the Heberden's nodes which had so badly deformed her hands were gone.

He was astounded. Here was incontrovertible proof of the healings. There could be no question of remission or spontaneous cure. Mrs. Ashford had suffered from osteoarthritis, a degenerative joint disease characterized by mechanical erosion of the articular cartilages and overgrowth of bone at the joint margins. Such changes are not reversible by any means known to man. Now at last Stella Lidell had her miracle.

But Stella did not know that yet, although news traveled almost as fast in school as in town. By noon everyone knew that Mr. Bob Morrow was dead and Mrs. Farley had suffered the worst spell she'd had in a year or two. The healing service was not just a failure, Stella thought—it was a catastrophe. Sam had warned her she might do harm, but even he had not guessed how much. She was so upset she couldn't keep her mind on her teaching, and she finally set her classes to writing the answers to questions printed in the textbooks, something she rarely did.

Grant was right, she thought. I should have listened to him. What is he thinking now? I'll tell him I'm sorry. But being sorry is no good when one has done as much harm as I have.

The school day dragged to its close, and Stella walked as far as the boarding house with Valerie and then continued on to town, to Sam's office. She wondered why he wanted to see her and could only suppose that her fatigue last night had made him think she was sick.

It was nice of him to take her home after the meeting. "Somebody had to do it," he had said gruffly. But she thought that in spite of the curt way he talked, he was a kind man.

When she got to Sam's office, Gaynell said he was with a patient and asked if Stella would mind giving the information for her medical record while she waited.

As she complied, Stella noticed how thin and pale Gaynell was. She wondered if Gaynell was getting enough to eat. She knew the family was poor, but she'd never realized they were that poor. They lived on a farm, even though it was only rented, and surely they produced enough food for themselves.

She mentioned Gaynell's appearance to Sam when she got in his office.

He said, "I noticed it too, but she tells me she's all right. How are *you* feeling?"

"Fine. I'm only here because you asked me to come."

"Yes, well . . ." His voice trailed into silence, and he looked a bit perplexed, as if he wasn't sure what he wanted to say. Then he seemed to snap out of whatever reverie he had been in and said briskly, "The first thing is to check you over. You were too tired last night. I wondered if you are completely recovered from your illness."

"I'm sure I am. The fatigue last night was from emotional strain, I think. You probably know I've quarreled with Grant. Or rather he with me. Also, I was very nervous about whether the healing service would work, and, of course, tremendously disappointed when it didn't."

"But it did." He told her about Mrs. Ashford and watched her face change.

"You can't know how glad I am," she said when he finished. "It doesn't change the bad news about Mr. Morrow and Mrs. Farley, but it helps a little. Because even if there's some medical cause for the healing, I may have set it in motion. Or rather her faith in my power might have done it."

"As I got the story from her, she didn't have any faith," Sam said. "She went to the service only to please her daughter. And there isn't any medical cause for her recovery. Moreover, I'm wondering if Mrs. Farley isn't also healed, and if it wasn't taking her insulin without any need for it that caused her to go into shock. As for Mr. Morrow, the healing probably had nothing at all to do with his death. What I'm saying is that I've changed my mind, Stella. I think you really do have some strange power. . . . What's the matter? I thought you'd be glad."

"Nothing. I *am* glad. I have to be, don't I? How could anybody not be glad to be able to help people? And yet—I'm selfish enough to think of myself."

"You're right to think of yourself. There may be some effect on your own health. Remembering how tired you were last night, I've been wondering whether there's some release of power—some loss of energy . . . hell, I don't know what I'm talking about, how could I? But until you learn a little more about how it works, I hope you'll go slowly and not try to heal everyone all at once."

"All right." But her worried expression remained.

"Were you concerned about something else? Oh, of course, your job. I imagine you're pretty busy already, and this is going to take more of your time. But you'll just have to set some limits."

"Yes, but I wasn't thinking of any of those things. I was thinking about the effect on my personal life. On Grant."

"So, that's what your quarrel was about. I suspected it when I saw him leave without you last night."

"You didn't know? I thought he would have told you, since you are such good friends."

"I haven't seen much of him lately," Sam said evasively. He didn't want to tell her that he was deliberately cutting down on his intimacy with Grant because he didn't want to be the onlooker in his romance. He supposed he was a little jealous that Grant's happiness was already assured, while his was still somewhere in the unknown future.

"I was going to see him when I left here," Stella said. "I meant to tell him my healing efforts were all over. But now there's something different to tell him, and I don't know what to do."

"He'll have to know sooner or later, and it's probably better to tell him yourself. Remembering what he said about faith-healing that night we were all together, I'm sure he'll be surprised. But, as you said, how could anyone not be glad?"

"I hope so," she said vaguely. She got up, but she did not start toward the door. Instead, she stood motionless in a graceful pose, as if she were giving him a chance to look at her figure. Sam took it, his eyes moving from shapely legs across a flat stomach and small waist and lingering on high breasts under a clinging sweater. He thought, not for the first time, that she had the most beautiful body he'd ever seen. His eyes moved on to her face, but the self-conscious smile and inviting eyes the pose had led him to half-expect were not there, and the moment went suddenly flat as he realized she was completely unaware of his gaze.

"Was there anything else?" he asked. His voice sounded harsh. He was beginning to understand that his jealousy of Grant was not as generalized as he'd thought.

As he spoke, she seemed to make up her mind. "No," she said. "I've taken enough of your time today."

"A few more minutes won't matter. What is it?" The annoyance had gone out of his voice. It was toward himself anyway, but he couldn't tell her that.

She sat down again. "When a person loses his memory, how can he get it back?"

"You mean amnesia?"

She hesitated. "I don't know. I always thought amnesia was forgetting who you were and all about your previous life. This isn't like that. It's just one blank hour."

"Are you talking about yourself?" he asked bluntly. "Why don't you tell me the whole story?"

"Because you'd think I was crazy. I don't want to talk about it; I just wanted to know if there is any kind of drug to restore memory. But of course there isn't. It was a foolish question."

123

"No, it isn't foolish, and yes, there is a drug that might be said to restore memory. What it actually does is deaden the inhibitory areas of the brain, so that one loses the power to lie or to keep unpleasant experiences submerged. I've never used it, but I saw it used by a psychiatrist during the war."

"Does it have any aftereffect?" She laughed a little self-consciously. "I certainly wouldn't want to lose my inhibitions permanently."

"Do you have many?" he asked, and thought immediately that he shouldn't have asked that, at least not in that intimate, teasing voice. He said hastily, "You've nothing to worry about. It wears off in a short while."

"Would you give it to me?"

"I might," he said cautiously, "if I were convinced it was proper treatment. I'd have to know more than I know now."

She was silent, indecision written on her face.

He said dryly, "I'm hard to shock, Stella."

"All right," she said, "I'll tell you."

He didn't speak for several minutes after she finished. His expression was unreadable. At last he said, "Why don't we try hypnosis? Have you ever been hypnotized?"

"No. I've seen it done, of course."

"How do you feel about it?"

"I don't know. Would the doctor-patient confidentiality be the same if I were hypnotized instead of getting medical treatment?"

"Hypnotism *is* medical treatment in certain circumstances. Don't worry, Stella. I'll keep what you say confidential. I can promise you that both as a doctor and as a friend."

"Even if I had committed a crime?"

He thought that over. He was silent so long that she thought he wasn't going to answer. Then he looked up and said, "Yes."

"If you'd answered that quickly or with too many words, I wouldn't have believed you. All right then. When shall we do it?"

"How about tomorrow after I close the office? That way we'll have plenty of time."

"Will I remember what I said after I wake up, or will you have to tell me?"

"Do you have a recorder at school?"

"Yes, there's one in the library, and any of the teachers can check it out."

"Then we'll record what you say, and you can listen to it afterward."

She got up, and this time she left. Sam looked after her with an inscrutable expression. He realized he was looking forward to tomorrow with considerable eagerness. It was, he told himself, an interesting case.

Strange though. As J.T. Clayton's experience was strange. And the disappearance of Warner Fox. Everything seemed to have started on that Monday afternoon, now nearly three weeks ago.

He realized that Stella was afraid of what she would find out. "Even if I had committed a crime," she said. Of course she hadn't. He knew her well enough to be sure of that. All the same, his anticipation of tomorrow wasn't altogether pleasant; there was a bit of uneasiness in it.

Stella went to the drug store from Sam's office and fortunately found Grant unoccupied—or perhaps unfortunately as things turned out. She wished afterward that she had waited a while before trying to make up with him, because going by so soon may have seemed like saying, "I told you so." He wasn't pleased to hear about Mrs. Ashford.

His blue eyes regarded her coldly, and he snapped, "I know that—I saw her myself—but it doesn't change anything. The fact remains that you did something I asked you not to and made a laughingstock of both of us. I haven't changed my mind just because one old lady claims she's cured."

"But Sam said—"

"He must have said quite a lot to you. You were up there nearly an hour. And he took you home last night, didn't he?"

"Only because you wouldn't. Grant, Sam's a friend of yours. Surely you don't think—"

"I don't know what to think, Stella. I'm beginning to think I don't know a damn thing about you."

She was shocked by his use of the word "damn." Profanity was as common in Lanier as anywhere else, she supposed, but Grant did not use it in the presence of ladies. She could only suppose that either he no longer considered her a lady, or the force of his anger was so great he hadn't noticed.

She said, "You know I don't care for anyone else. And I can't bear for you to be angry. If we talked this out—"

"There's nothing to talk about until you promise to give it up."

She didn't answer that. Instead she said, "Will I see you tonight?"

The hard blue of his eyes seemed to soften a little. "I don't know," he said. "I may go to Caleb's Point on business. If I don't, I'll call you."

It wasn't much, but at least it told her he wasn't yet ready to call off their engagement. It was enough to make her cry because it wasn't more.

17

While Stella was talking with Sam, Sheriff Owen Perry was on his way to see J.T. Clayton. Owen was feeling a bit desperate about the Warner Fox case. Time was pressing in on him. Almost three weeks had gone by, and he was no nearer solving the case than he'd been the first day it happened. Fortunately all this faith-healing business had taken some of the heat off, but he knew that was only temporary. As soon as the healing was proved to be a hoax, people would be right back to talking about Warner again.

Thinking of the faith-healing, he frowned. He and Adelaide had gone to the meeting last night, and he had been sure it was a failure. His judgment seemed confirmed this morning when Mr. Bob Morrow died and Mrs. Farley had a bad spell, but then this afternoon Mrs. Ashford came to town apparently well of her arthritis, so now he didn't know what to think.

It seemed strange that it was Stella Lidell who was claiming to be a healer, because she was his most likely suspect if Warner had been killed, which he was beginning to look on as almost certain. He had even wondered if the healing hullabaloo was deliberately planned to take attention away from the case. If so, she didn't know him very well.

He didn't want to think Stella was guilty. She seemed like a nice girl. But who else could it be? J.T. Clayton was the only other person who could have been anywhere near the scene, and J.T. had neither motive nor, as far as the sheriff could learn, opportunity. Mrs. Clayton and the kids swore

126

he had been in the house all evening. Of course, they'd say that automatically if they thought he had been at his whiskey still.

Owen was sure J.T. hadn't done it though. The only kind of killing J.T. might ever be involved in would be over his wife or family honor; murder wasn't in his line. He was a moonshiner and a kind of all-round sorry man but too good-natured and easy-going to kill anybody. When he was drinking, he just got more and more friendly and agreeable. Besides, he was never drunk enough not to know what he was doing.

Still, he supposed it wouldn't hurt to talk to J.T. again. Owen was like a person who has lost something and keeps looking over and over in the same places, even though he knows it isn't there. But he couldn't think of any new places to look.

J.T. was nervous about talking to the sheriff, and he had an uneasy feeling that it showed. Ordinarily he was as relaxed as the loose end of a rope when the sheriff questioned him, but now that he couldn't trust himself to lie, he felt like the rope had been stretched tight and with a little pressure might break. He just hoped the sheriff's questions wouldn't hit on something he didn't want to tell.

But eventually they did. "Describe the car to me, exactly like it was when you found it," Sheriff Perry said.

J.T.'s heart began to beat faster, but he made a valiant effort. "The door was hanging open, and the keys were in the ignition."

"Anything on the seat?"

"Yeah, Warner's hat. And a pistol."

Owen had been leaning backward in the cane-bottomed chair, but now it came down with a thump. "There wasn't any hat or pistol when we got out here. Where are they?"

"On my closet shelf."

"You know better than to take away evidence," Owen said sharply. "How come you to do it?"

"I didn't want Miss Lidell to get in no trouble," J.T. said.

"I don't see—well, get them," Owen said impatiently.

J.T. went to the closet and came back with a felt hat and a gun. Owen examined them. The gun was a pearl-handled, short-barreled .32, and one bullet had been fired from it. The hat was a Stetson of a conservative gray, similar to the hats worn by most of the businessmen in Lanier. Owen ran his finger under the sweatband and pulled out a folded piece of paper.

"You've seen this?" he asked J.T.

"Yeah, I found it right away. And I wish now I'd tore it up. But I thought if I did, it might turn out Miss Lidell would need it later. It was hard to know what to do."

Owen looked down at the page in his hand. On one of the outside folds was a penciled note: "dress, 10; slip, 32; stockings, 9½." He unfolded the paper and read the letter inside: "Dear Warner, I can't make it until five-thirty. See you then. Love, Stella."

He folded the paper and put it back in the hat. "Is this all you found in the car, or have you got something else you didn't mention?" he asked J.T.

"No, Sheriff, that's all. I swear. I wouldn't've kept that from you if it hadn't been for Miss Lidell being so good to us. I hope she ain't gonna get in no trouble over this. I'm satisfied she didn't have nothing to do with it."

"What makes you think that?"

"Because a nice lady like she is wouldn't be mixed up in nothing underhanded."

Like J.T., Owen hoped Stella wasn't mixed up in anything underhanded. But that note was proof that she'd had an appointment with Warner. Her opportunity to kill him was now definitely established. And the motive could probably be found somewhere in the love affair they must have been carrying on. What a shock that was going to be to Grant Meadows, who had been courting her pretty regularly and, rumor said, was engaged to marry her.

Well, he'd have to talk with her again as soon as he got back to town.

Stella was at home, and she came to the living room to talk to him. Her eyes were a little red, as if she might have been crying, but her voice was steady as she answered his questions.

"I don't know anything about the gun," she said. "I never saw it before. . . . No, I don't know whether Warner owned a gun. He may have. It never came up in any conversations with him.

"As for the note, I wrote that months ago," she said. "We had planned to see a movie in the afternoon and then go to dinner and afterwards to his sister's to pay cards, but I found I had to stay after school to catalog the new library books, so I wrote the note. He must have made his list on the back of it and kept it because of that."

"What size dress do you wear, Miss Lidell?" Owen asked.

She flushed. "You think these are my sizes, that Warner bought clothes for me? No, Sheriff, even if Warner had wanted to give me gifts of clothes, which he didn't, I wouldn't have accepted them. Maybe that's a little old-fashioned nowadays, but it's the way I was brought up."

She wished she could tell him just how careful she'd been to follow the smaller conventions, much more careful than she would have been if he hadn't violated the larger ones. Not accepting intimate gifts was a small thing in comparison to the greater intimacies she had allowed, but behaving correctly in surface matters helped her self-respect a little. However, she couldn't tell the sheriff that even to convince him the clothes weren't hers.

She looked at the list again. "They *are* my sizes," she said, in evident surprise. "But I didn't give them to him. So they must be for someone else. Not his mother or his sisters though; they're all bigger. I don't know whose they could be."

"And you still say you didn't see Warner that afternoon?"

"Yes. I don't know why you keep asking me questions, Sheriff. I don't know anything about Warner's disappearance. If I did, I'd tell you. He was a friend of mine, and I'd like to see him found."

"Have you thought that he may not be found? That he's dead?"

She didn't flinch. "I guess everybody in town has thought of that. But if he were, it seems to me that you could find his body."

"I'd sure like to if he's dead. It would simplify matters a lot. But I want you to know this, Miss Lidell. To try someone for murder, it's not absolutely necessary to have a body."

"But I thought—I read a lot of murder mysteries, and they're always talking about corpus delicti. Isn't 'corpus' Latin for body?"

"Yeah, but the phrase means 'body of the evidence.' Generally the evidence includes a dead body, but it doesn't have to. The body might be burned up or on the bottom of the ocean, but if there's enough evidence to prove the crime, the law won't let the murderer get by with it."

"I see," she said slowly.

She did see. She saw that the sheriff was warning her, telling her not to feel secure just because he hadn't found Warner's body. He thought she had killed Warner. And she couldn't prove she hadn't because of that lost hour.

She hoped the hypnotism worked. At least, she guessed she did.

Grant did not call. She told herself that it meant nothing. He'd had to go to Caleb's Point on business, as he had said. He would call tomorrow.

18

Maureen Granger was not in despair about missing the healing service, because she still had hope. Her mother and father would not help her. Very well. She would help herself.

She believed she could do it. She was not as helpless as her parents thought. True, she could not speak or comb her hair or button her clothes. But she could walk after a fashion. Her movements were erratic; her gait was jerky and unsteady; and her forward progress was slow, but she *could* get from one place to another. To do what she planned, that was all that was required. She would not have to talk. Miss Lidell could look at her and know why she had come.

Maureen had not made the decision hastily. Until the last minute she hoped her father would change his mind and take her to the healing service. He seldom missed Wednesday night prayer meeting, and surely he would want to go to this one. When her mother put her to bed at her usual time and she realized that hope was gone, she felt as desperate a frustration as she had ever known. She would have torn down the house she lived in brick by brick with her own hands to be free. She would have beaten against the walls until they came tumbling down around her bloody hands. But she could not, and, even if she could, it would not free her, because the real prison was her own body. Her throat ached with the effort not to cry, but silent tears rolled down her face.

She hated her parents. She hated them for giving her birth, hated them for their shame that made them hide her away, and, most of all, she hated them for not taking the only chance she would ever have to be healed.

It was at that point that the idea came to her. Perhaps the service tonight was not her only chance. Miss Lidell would still be in Lanier tomorrow. She would still have her healing power. She didn't have to use it in a church. Miss Mattie and Mr. Howle and Wilma Jean Clayton were not healed at church. Wherever Miss Lidell was, she could heal people.

Maureen would go to her and be healed.

She would have to do it at night when her parents were asleep and couldn't stop her. That wouldn't be a problem, because they went to bed about eight o'clock most nights, so her father could get up at four-thirty.

She didn't know how long it would take to walk to town, or whether she could make it at all. It was over a mile to Mrs. Overly's boarding house. How would that compare to the distance she walked in the garden each day? In the garden, however, there were marble benches where she could sit down to rest when her legs got tired, as they frequently did. There would be no benches on the way to town, and she didn't think she could get up again if she sat down on the ground. She would have to keep going no matter how tired she got.

She didn't know whether she could do it. But she was going to try. With her decision she fell asleep immediately, and for the first time in her life, she dreamed of flying. First she ran, faster and faster, and then she flapped her arms and was suddenly airborne, swooping free as a bird over trees and rivers and cities. It was the most thrilling experience she had ever had, and she did it over and over. And then suddenly she lost it, and no matter how much she ran or how hard she flapped her arms, she could not rise into the air; she was bound to the earth. She awoke with tears on her face.

But with the return of consciousness being earthbound no longer seemed a sadness. Flying was only a dream, but running would soon be a reality, and it would be enough for her.

The next day seemed an endless age, even though she was so busy planning all the details of her venture that she hardly noticed what was going on around her. The trip seemed as fraught with peril as a polar expedition. It could go wrong at any point, and if it did, she was lost, because her mother would watch her twice as closely afterward.

Maureen anxiously went over and over her plans, trying to foresee every contingency and allow for every misfortune.

The day finally passed, and about seven-thirty Mrs. Granger had pushed Maureen's wheel chair into her bedroom and began preparations for getting her to bed. Maureen had not been able to figure out any way to avoid this, even though dressing again would take time she could not afford to spend.

As soon as her mother was gone, she began. Getting her loose nightgown off was not much problem; when she got it pushed off her shoulders, it fell to the floor. She had decided to wear as few garments as possible in order to save time, so she did not fool with underclothes or stockings but sat down on the bed and began struggling into the brown wool slacks she wore for her garden walks on cold days. The zipper was hard to get hold of; her hand kept jerking away, but finally she got it zipped. Then she put on the loose-fitting wool-jersey blouse she had selected because it was the only top she had which did not require buttoning. After two or three tries she got her bare feet stuck into her loafers. She knew her ankles would be cold, but that couldn't be helped.

She looked at the clock and noticed with despair that it had taken her thirty minutes, and she wasn't through yet; she still had to get into her coat and put the beret on her head. But the buttons on the coat were large enough to be easy compared to the zipper, and it was finally done.

She stopped at her door and listened. The house was quiet. She could hear no murmurs from her parents' room, so she thought they must be asleep. She waited a few minutes to be sure and then moved jerkily into the hall.

It was only a few steps to the stairway. She paused, holding to the railing, and looked down. She had never been on the stairs, but tonight she couldn't use the elevator, because the sound might wake her parents. Somehow she would have to get down the stairs. She had already thought about this problem, however, so, holding to the stair rail, she lowered herself to the floor and bumped down the stairs in a sitting position. At the bottom, still holding to the rail, she laboriously got to her feet again.

In the dimly lit lower hall she crossed to the front door, thankful for the carpet, which muffled the sound of her footsteps. Now came one of the tasks she had dreaded most—getting out the door. The lock was the push-button type which required only a turn of the knob to open, but there was a chance that her jerky motion would bang the door against the wall and wake her parents. She put her hand out, saw it jerk spasmodically, and pulled it back again. But it had to be done. She stood still a moment or two, willing herself not to be nervous. When she finally grasped the knob, it turned easily in her hand, and the door opened silently. She was outside! She had successfully completed the first stage of her journey.

And then she fell. It may have been that the relief at having got safely out of the house caused her to be overconfident, or it might have been a pebble or simply a misstep that caused her foot to slide and miss the second of the two concrete steps. As she fell forward, she put out her hands in a vain attempt to catch herself and felt them skin against the concrete walkway.

For a moment she lay there, hurting all over. Her hands were skinned; her knees were hurting; and on her cheek she could feel a wetness that must be blood. She had probably broken some bones too. Now she would be even more trouble to take care of. What a fool she was to think she could go all the way to Lanier. She couldn't even get out of her own front yard.

But gradually she began to think that perhaps her injuries were not so serious as she had first feared. She moved cautiously and heard no scraping bones. Perhaps she could even get up and go on—unless her fall had awakened her parents. Thank goodness, she had not cried out, but she had hit the sidewalk with an awful thump. It seemed to her that her parents must have heard it. She looked toward their window, but no light came on. The sound had not disturbed them. She could still go on. If she could get to her feet. If.

Slowly she turned herself around, sliding on the concrete, ignoring the discomfort, inching forward until she could grasp the ornamental iron railing down the side of the steps. Then she laboriously hoisted herself to her feet, stepped off the sidewalk to make her footsteps less audible, and walked toward the driveway. It was paved too, but she thought it was far enough from the house that her parents would not hear, and, in any case, she had to use it, because it had been graded to make a gradual descent to the road, whereas the lawn was too steep and had steps from one level to another.

At last she got to the road. Thank goodness, the moon was already up, so she would be able to see where she was going. The road was relatively smooth too. It had been graded recently but not graveled, so in the center it was hard-packed clay, fairly easy to walk on. She was still aching from her fall, but that was nothing. She would not fall again if the road was this good all the way.

She had been walking about fifteen minutes, she thought, but was not yet out of sight of her own house when she heard a car. Suddenly her heart was thumping wildly as she scrambled toward the edge of the road. Her efforts to hurry made her progress even slower, and she feared the car lights would be on her before she got off the road. If she were seen, the car would stop, and everything would be over.

It was getting closer; she could see the shine of its lights, but fortunately they were hitting on the other side of the road away from her. In another minute though, the car would round the curve, and then she would be in full view. She looked around desperately. There was not a tree, not a bush, not even a patch of weeds near enough to hide behind. There was only the embankment where she stood and below it an old field. If she were in the field below the road, the people in the car might not notice her. But she knew she could not move fast enough.

There was only one thing to do. She threw herself to the ground and rolled willy-nilly down the embankment until she lay at the bottom, totally spent and with her face stinging from the whipping of the dried weeds on the bank. The lights above swept by, and soon the sound of the car died away in the distance.

It seemed hours later that she was finally on her feet again, and even then she was not sure how she had done it. She had scrabbled at the bank, held to tufts of broomsedge and dead dewberry vines, cried and strained and prayed until she finally managed to stand upright again. But the bank was too high and steep to climb, so she could not get back to the road. She would have to make her way below it as best she could.

The footing here was more uneven than on the road above. There were weeds and holes and a log half-hidden in dead grass. Over and over she stumbled and fell, then crawled or slid to the nearest bush or fence post so she could get up again. She didn't know how far she had come or how long she had been on the way. She no longer felt the cold or the cuts and bruises, or if she felt them, it was only in some dull underlayer of her mind that did not reach her consciousness. She was no longer aware of any thought; she had even forgotten why she was doing this. She was not alert now, and when she came to the beginning of the paved street to town, she moved into it with no thought of traffic.

Fortunately there was none. It was eleven o'clock, and Lanier was asleep. The only cars that might pass now were those containing dating couples going home from a petting session at one of the favorite parking places. No one saw or heard her, and at last she reached Mrs. Overly's boarding house.

It was dark. Everyone had gone to bed. Maureen crawled up the steep steps to the porch and painfully hauled herself upright by holding to the bannister. She staggered across the porch and leaned against the doorbell. Then she slid to the floor.

A few minutes later Mrs. Overly knocked at Stella's door. "Get Valerie and y'all come help me move Maureen Granger," she said. "She's on the front porch, and she looks half-dead."

Mrs. Overly's face was white and frightened. Stella grabbed her robe and went to Valerie's door.

Somehow the three of them got her inside and put her on the sofa. "Call Dr. Taylor," Mrs. Overly said, "and then call her folks."

Stella turned to go to the telephone, but Maureen had come out of her faint. She caught hold of Stella's robe and began to utter unintelligible sounds in a guttural tone.

Stella looked at Mrs. Overly helplessly. "What is she saying?"

Mrs. Overly shook her head. "Nobody can understand her except her mother," she said. "Maybe she'll know when she gets here. What could Maureen be doing out by herself? And this time of night too. It looks like she's been beaten and rolled around in the dirt." Her eyes grew round with horror as she whispered, "Do you suppose she's been raped?"

Valerie had gone to make the calls, and she came back to report that Dr. Taylor would be here right away and that the Grangers were so shocked by the news that they wouldn't believe it until they looked in Maureen's room.

But Maureen was still making her grunting sounds, and now her face was contorted with the effort to make herself understood. Tears of frustration were running down her cheeks. She kept a tight hold on Stella's robe with one hand while with the other she made gestures that were utterly meaningless to Stella.

Suddenly Mrs. Overly said, "I believe she wants you to touch her, Stella. She must think you can heal her, poor child."

As soon as Mrs. Overly began speaking, Stella took Maureen's hand in hers. In the excitement she had forgotten about the healing power she presumably had. She waited for the now familiar tingle to start.

But nothing happened. She felt no prickly sensation in her hands. And it was quite evident that nothing had happened to Maureen, because she began to cry with great wrenching sobs.

19

Stella thought she would never forget the expression on Maureen's face when she realized that her incredible journey had been for nothing. Maureen and her parents were gone now, and the boarding house was once again dark and silent, but Stella could not sleep.

She had tried to comfort Maureen by telling her that the healing didn't occur immediately in the other cases but only after some time had passed. Maureen's crying quieted then, but Stella was not sure she had been wise to renew Maureen's hope. She was afraid Maureen had not been healed, because she had felt no tingle in her hands.

In no other case, not even for Wilma Jean, had Stella been so anxious for the healing to work. Maureen's need was greater; she had showed that by the effort she'd made. Surely she should be rewarded. And yet . . .

"Wait and see," Sam had said when, as he was leaving, she walked out on the porch to tell him her fears. "You touched her, and that's all you can do."

Remembering his words, Stella suddenly realized that she had touched Maureen before she requested it. She had helped Mrs. Overly and Valerie bring her into the house. Perhaps the tingling sensation had come into her hands then. In the excitement she wouldn't have noticed it, or if she did, it would have seemed the effect of lifting Maureen.

Sam was not in when Stella arrived at his office to be

hypnotized the following afternoon. Gaynell said he was at the Granger's. "He's been gone for quite a while, so I'm sure he'll be back soon," she said.

Stella's heart jerked. Surely nothing had happened to Maureen. She had been thinking about her as she walked to the office, thinking of how tragic Maureen's life had been and imagining the pleasurable excitement she might be experiencing at that moment. Yet perhaps even then some fresh tragedy was occurring. Stella thought of old Mr. Morrow, who had died after the emotional turmoil of the healing service. Maureen was younger, of course, but her stress had been far greater too. Stella couldn't even begin to imagine the fear and desperation and physical agony Maureen must have felt on that trip.

Stella sat down and picked up a magazine, but after a moment she felt as if she could not be still. She got up and paced about the room reading the diplomas on the wall, looking at the books in the bookcase, straightening the magazines, as if activity would somehow stave off disaster. She was aware that Gaynell was watching her, but she couldn't stop her restless pacing.

Gaynell said, "Have they heard anything more about Warner Fox? All the talk about him seems to have died down."

Stella turned. "People have something else to talk about now," she said wryly.

"Yes, but surely the case won't just be dropped?"

"Oh, no, I'm sure the sheriff is still working on it. Although I really don't know what more he can do. He seems to have done everything possible already."

"Yes, he even talked to me. I couldn't tell him anything, of course. Warner came in to see Dr. Taylor that afternoon, but we happened not to be busy, so he went straight in without stopping by to chat with me the way he did sometimes . . . The sheriff talked to you too, didn't he?"

Gaynell's voice was casual, but there was something in her face that made Stella wonder why she was so interested. Vicarious excitement probably—Gaynell's life must be very dull, circumscribed as it was by her family's poverty and the strict tenets of her church.

Stella answered, "I didn't know anything to tell the sheriff either. I was on the road to the Clayton's that afternoon, but I didn't see Warner."

"What did you think of Warner, Miss Lidell?"

"What do you mean?" Stella asked, puzzled.

137

Gaynell's face was pink. She was probably embarrassed at prying, Stella thought. Still, she didn't take the question back but instead said, "You dated him some last fall, didn't you? I just wondered what you thought of him, what type of person he was. I used to talk to him when he came in the office, but that isn't like . . . I just wondered."

"He was nice," Stella said. "Friendly, polite. Enthusiastic about his work. But of course you know all that. In fact, you probably know as much about him as I do. I only dated him a few times."

"He was an interesting talker," Gaynell said.

"Yes. He spent the war years in England, and he'd been to the places I teach about in English literature. We talked a lot about that. But he could talk on any subject; he seemed to be interested in everything. I suppose all good salesmen are like that."

Hearing footsteps in the hall, Stella turned toward the door as Sam came in.

He said, "Come on in, Stella. Sorry I'm late, but Mrs. Granger called. The miracle happened to Maureen. She's walking as normally as you do and is beside herself with joy. She can't speak clearly yet, but that will come in time."

"Thank God," Stella said as she followed him into his office. "I've been imagining—but never mind. How did it happen?"

"If you don't know, I'm sure no one does. She slept until noon today, and when she woke, she was normal. That's all I can tell you, except that this kind of improvement can't possibly happen with cerebral palsy. And yet it did."

They were both silent. After a moment he said, "Well, let's get started with the hypnotism. Are you nervous?"

"A little." She hadn't thought about it much with all the other things that had been happening, but now she realized that she was more than a little nervous. What if she found out something she didn't want to know?

"Don't be afraid," he said. "I'm going to regress you as an observer rather than a participant so you won't have any psychological damage."

"Why should I have psychological damage?"

"Well, we don't know what kind of experience you had, do we? If it's a horrible memory, it might be traumatic to experience it again. But this way you'll be seeing it, rather than living it."

Two hours later Sam removed the reel of tape from the

recorder and balanced it on his hand. "Well, you've heard it," he said. "It's an incredible story, isn't it?"

"Yes," Stella answered in a dazed voice. Then: "What are you going to do now?" She still looked stunned, and she sounded almost indifferent.

"First I'm going to put this in a safe place, and then we'll go to the café and eat."

She looked up at him and frowned. "Shouldn't we erase the tape?"

"No, I want to hear it again. And you will too after you've had a chance to get over the shock."

"I don't know whether I'll ever get over it. I can't believe what I said is true—and if it isn't, I must be crazy."

He sat down beside her on the sofa. "We've already been through all that. You aren't crazy."

She was silent for a moment, and then she suddenly seemed to lose some of her dazed shock. She said, "But it couldn't have happened! Just think of it, Sam, of what we're trying to believe—that strange, unearthly creatures came off that plane, or whatever it was, rendered me helpless in some way, took me aboard, and kept me there for an hour while they somehow gave me this healing power. Then they took that hour out of my memory and turned me loose. Who were they? Why did they do what they did? And how did they make sure I wouldn't remember?"

"I can answer the last question. They probably insured your loss of memory by the same method I used—hypnosis. You don't remember what went on while I had you hypnotized, do you?"

"No. I wouldn't even have known I'd been hypnotized except that we talked about it before and afterwards."

"You would have remembered everything though, if I hadn't made sure you wouldn't."

"Why did you do that?"

"For the same reason I explained before. It might have been something you wouldn't want to remember."

"Yes, well, I'm not sure I do want to remember it. In a way, I'm sorry I know about it. It frightens me. I'm sure I don't want you to take me through it as a participant."

"I don't think it's necessary. We got all the information this time—a description of the creatures and the interior of the craft and what they 'told' you. All we'd get by having you relive it would be your reaction, and I don't think you

139

had much reaction while it was going on. The reassurance they gave you seems to have allayed your fear at the time."

"I was frightened afterward though, when I realized I'd lost an hour. And I'm certainly frightened now. I don't understand any of it. How could they have told me anything without speaking?"

"Some sort of thought transference, I suppose. When you consider what we ourselves can do with hypnotism, it doesn't seem impossible that suggestion could be carried a lot further, perhaps imparted without the necessity for words."

She was silent a moment. Then she moved restlessly and said, "Who were they, Sam?"

He shrugged.

She went on. "If they weren't people like us, then they had to be something else, but what? Spirits? Angels? Men from Mars?"

He shrugged again. "Somehow I never thought of spirits and angels needing aircraft," he said. "These beings obviously have to travel by some means other than their own power. It was a strange vehicle, but a vehicle nonetheless."

"You're saying they *were* from Mars?"

"Or some other planet, maybe in another galaxy. Hell, Stella, you're out of my field now. I know a little about the mind but not the first thing about astronomy."

"I still think it may have all come from my mind. Maybe I have a lot of science fiction junk stored in my subconscious, and somehow it got through, and I went into some kind of trance during that hour . . .The only thing wrong with that theory is that I've never read science fiction, not even in the comics. I've never been interested in any kind of science."

"Yes, I remember you told me once that you didn't know anything about physiology."

"Or astronomy, or geology, or physics—it all leaves me cold. I'm interested in literature and art and human behavior, and that's what I read about and think about. So I can't believe I had a lot of stuff about strange flying machines and little men from another planet stored away."

He was staring at her thoughtfully. "What you said before though—there might be something in that."

"What did I say?"

"That you might have been in a trance during that hour. You're easy to hypnotize. I wonder if someone else knew that."

"You mean someone hypnotized me and put that story in

140

my mind—about seeing the plane and all the rest of it? Why would anyone do that?"

"For a joke maybe—or to make a fool of you. Is there anyone who might do that? What about Warner? Could this whole thing be some gigantic hoax?"

"You mean *Warner* hypnotized me and then disappeared? He'd have no reason to."

"Are you sure? You dated him back in the fall, and then you quit. Maybe he wasn't willing to quit."

"And wanted to get back at me? If he felt like that, he hid it well." She considered for a moment. "It's possible, I suppose. One has to know a person very well indeed to be certain how he is feeling and what he will do. Even when you know him well, you can be surprised. All I can say is, I *would* be surprised—shocked—if it happened like that. But I've thought all along that the two things might be connected."

As she stopped talking, her eyes widened. *"Sam, do you suppose they took Warner on board too—and didn't release him?"*

"My God, Stella!"

For a moment they stared at each other. Then he said, "We've talked too much. Let's give ourselves a rest. We're both hungry and tired. We need to eat, and then I suggest we go to the movie and forget all about this for the rest of the night. Tomorrow we'll have a fresh outlook."

"I'm sorry," she said. "About dinner and the movie, I mean. I'd like to, but—" She stopped, not wanting to say anything about Grant's jealousy.

He seemed to know what she was thinking. "Grant wouldn't like it?" he asked.

"I'm afraid not. After all, we are engaged."

"Are you? I haven't seen much evidence of it lately."

"That's because we've quarreled over the healing. He's still determined that I shan't do it."

"And you want to."

"No, I don't," she said with a flash of anger. "I wish I didn't have the power. It's complicated my life. I never thought much about illness before. Now it seems I have to feel for everyone, and it tears me apart. I'd like to go back to the way I was before, not uncaring, but not so involved either. Sam, I don't think I can bear everyone else's burdens on top of my own. No one can live like that."

"No, you're right. We're all in this world together, but we have to stay separate too. You mustn't let yourself feel other people's pain too much. . .Are you going to stop the healing then?"

"No, of course not. How can I? If I have the power, there's no way I can refuse to use it. Surely you can see that." Her voice was vehement.

"My dear girl, I'm convinced already," he said with a trace of amusement in his voice.

She looked confused. "Yes, of course. It's Grant I have to persuade."

He said slowly, "And what if you can't? Will it hurt you very much?"

"Yes. Yes, it will. He means everything to me. For the first time in my life I'm in love the way I always wanted to be. I was afraid I'd never feel anything real, that for me love would always be a physical attraction, but this is different; it's warm and comfortable and secure."

He wanted to say, so is a wool blanket. He wanted to say, it doesn't seem very secure to me, unless he's there when you need him.

He said, "It sounds as if you've found what you want."

"Yes, I have, and I don't want to lose it."

"Perhaps the movie isn't a good idea then, if you think Grant would mind. But surely you can go to dinner with me. You've missed it at the boarding house, and you have to eat somewhere."

He pulled her to her feet, reached for her coat, and held it for her. Suddenly her sight seemed inverted so that she was seeing Sam in a different way from ever before. His gray eyes had an unfamiliar light in them; his square face took on new planes and shadows; even his thick, dark hair looked different. It made her feel very strange. As if she were just meeting him for the first time. And simultaneously as if she'd known him forever. Bemused, she wondered if her vision would change again, if he would turn back into the Sam Taylor she knew, the familiar face she'd only half looked at all these months.

She turned and slipped her arms into the coat. His hands lingered a moment on her shoulder; they seemed to be burning through the cloth of her coat with a queer, electrifying heat. She wondered what his hands would feel like under the coat, under the sweater, against her bare skin. She turned and took a step toward him.

He saw the movement and the look on her face. His heart raced, and his hands tightened on her shoulders. There were

142

only inches between them, a small hateful space that wanted closing. He would pull her into his arms, kiss her parted lips, move his hands over that beautiful body, and she would respond. He was sure of it; every sign he knew told him so.

But he didn't think she would know why she was responding. She would not recognize that it was a part of what had gone before, the culmination of a relationship already established. He remembered how she had belittled physical love. Apparently, she thought it was unimportant, an insignificant accessory, perhaps something of which to be a little ashamed. He would not make love to her and have her be remorseful. Action must wait for understanding.

And so he stepped backward and turned around so she could not see his face. For excuse he reached for the reel of tape on the table, but his hands were shaking, and, for a moment or two he fumbled with it before he could pick it up. Then he turned around and said, "I'll put this in my desk and lock the drawer."

He was still avoiding her eyes, and so he did not see the look of despair and self-loathing on her face. She had thought herself finally free of the sexual desires that had already caused her so much anguish, but to her horror she found them still with her, like a poison for which there is no antidote. How could she want Sam when she was in love with Grant? And yet she had. She had wanted him so desperately it seemed she could not bear it if he didn't touch her, and when he turned away, she had felt it as a painful wrench and had to bite her lips to keep from protesting.

This was worse than anything she had done before. While Grant was controlling his desire out of love and respect for her, she would have betrayed him by going to bed with his friend. That she had not actually done it did not count. She had wanted to, and only Sam's lack of interest prevented it.

She wondered if Sam had guessed how she felt. If he had, she could never be at ease with him again. She thought back. She had done nothing except move toward him. He probably hadn't noticed that. Indeed, his turning away was proof of it. In her experience men did not refuse a convenient opportunity.

She was relieved to realize that Sam didn't know about her. And Grant needn't know either. She would take care to see that it didn't happen again.

* * *

143

Stella had already forgotten the conversation with Gaynell, but Gaynell was still mulling it over as she walked home from work. She was sure Miss Lidell had not realized her personal concern about Warner. To Miss Lidell it had been only a casual conversation such as she must have had with a lot of people since Warner disappeared. To Gaynell it was the chance to get the answers to some questions that plagued her night and day. Did Miss Lidell know something she hadn't told about Warner's disappearance? Had she seen him the afternoon he left? And even, had there been something more between Warner and Miss Lidell than he had admitted to her, Gaynell?

Now she knew that the answer to all those questions was "No." She had known it before, of course. She was wrong to doubt Warner even for a minute. She told herself that every day, but still the doubts came creeping back. How could she help it?

But at least she need not wonder about Miss Lidell again. She didn't know anything. She couldn't have talked in such an offhand way if she had. She hadn't hesitated or been evasive or looked guilty. Gaynell was sure Miss Lidell had no more interest in Warner than in any other man in town. Less than she had in Dr. Taylor. There was an electricity between them, although Gaynell wasn't sure either of them realized it.

Warner had told the truth about the relationship between him and Miss Lidell; it had been nothing more than a few casual dates during a time when he and Gaynell had quarreled.

Suddenly shock ripped into Gaynell's mind, and fright galloped along every nerve in her body. She and Miss Lidell had talked of Warner in the past tense—and it had seemed so natural she didn't even notice. It was as if she had already accepted his death.

But I haven't, she thought fiercely. I won't.

20

Gaynell was tired when she reached home, but she didn't think her fatigue was caused by the day's work or the two–mile walk. Those things had never tired her before. But now the worry which dragged at her mind every waking minute also weighed her body down so that it too seemed to ache constantly.

She went up the front steps and walked down the dogtrot toward the kitchen. Betty Lee and Lila were just entering it from the opposite end. Each of them carried a milk pail.

"You're milking tonight, Lila?" Gaynell asked in surprise. Then fear roughened her voice, "Is Mamma sick?"

Each of the Moore family had his own chores to do, and one of Mamma's was to milk Old Pied, the worst–tempered of the two milk cows.

"No, Mamma's not sick," Lila answered, "but everything is topsy–turvy around here today. Mr. Dal Edwards came and talked with Mamma and Papa the longest time. He hasn't been gone more'n thirty minutes. So that threw everything behind, and supper's not ready yet." She lowered her voice. "Something's up, Gaynell, but we don't know what it is yet."

A quick, sharp fear stabbed at Gaynell, making her heart gallop alarmingly. Had somebody found out about her and Warner?

Betty Lee said shortly, "Stop jawing, Lila, and get that milk in the kitchen. We've got to strain it before supper."

Betty Lee often spoke shortly. She was neither as pretty nor as outgoing as Gaynell and Lila, and, although she was only seventeen, life had already started to beat her down.

Gaynell said, "Didn't somebody hear at least part of what Mr. Edwards said?"

"Well, just as he was leaving, I heard him say to Papa, 'You can let me know,' " Lila answered.

Gaynell's hard–beating heart eased a little. That didn't sound as if Mr. Edwards had brought rumors about her. It was probably nothing more than some church business. Papa

145

wasn't a deacon or a heavy contributor, but there were only thirty-seven men in the church, so every one was important. But why had Mr. Edwards talked to Mamma too? Women had no voice in church affairs. They cooked for the all day meetings and sang in the choir, and they were rather frequent receivers of the Holy Ghost, but in church as elsewhere they followed Paul's counsel and submitted themselves to their husbands.

Gaynell had no use for the Apostle Paul.

"Is that you, Gaynell?" Mamma called, interrupting her thoughts. "Come make up the cornbread. I've got my hands so full, I don't know which way to turn."

Gaynell went into the lamplit kitchen, where Mamma was moving from the pots of black-eyed peas and canned green beans on the stove to the bacon she was slicing on the cook table. Gaynell looked at Mamma's face, but she saw no more than the usual amount of worry. Mamma never looked easy; she had a perpetual harried expression that had etched deep lines in her forehead and around her mouth. Now she was intent on getting supper done and served, but she didn't look as if she'd had any bad news. In fact, Gaynell thought, looking at her closely, she might even be pleased about something.

"Stop staring at me and get busy," Mamma snapped. "Your Papa's hungry, and he'll lose his patience if it takes us much longer."

After grace was said, the silence was broken only by the metallic clink of eating tools against the plates. Papa finished and rose from the table, but instead of leaving the room immediately, he looked toward Gaynell and said, "When you're done eating, you and your mamma come in the front room. The rest of you kids stay in the kitchen till we're through."

Gaynell's heart thumped so hard she thought it would jump out of her chest. Her eyes flew to her mother's face, but she could tell nothing from it. Mamma was dipping black-eyed peas onto her cornbread just as if nothing was wrong. Gaynell's breathing eased enough to speak. She said, "What does he want with me?"

Annabel Moore looked up. "Why, what's the matter, Gaynell? You're as white as a sheet. It's nothing to worry about. He just wants to talk to you."

Her words fell into silence. The usual after-supper chatter

146

did not start, and Gaynell knew why. It was because of her summons to the front room.

Silas and Annabel Moore were determined to bring their children up in the fear and admonition of the Lord, and Silas didn't mind if they feared him too. He whipped oftener, harder, and with less provocation than Annabel did. For such sessions he favored the privacy of the front room, although it was hard to determine why, since the event was advertised by screams and the procedure known from personal participation.

Thus, the children knew what this summons to the front room must mean, and they were shocked by it. After puberty the girls' whippings were administered by Mamma, although often at Papa's command. It had been five years since he decreed any punishment for Gaynell, longer than the memories of the younger children, so they had assumed she was immune.

Gaynell knew better. She was aware that she escaped the rod only by being careful to please Papa in most things and clever enough to hide it when she didn't. It was easier to please him now that she brought twenty-five dollars into the house every week, but even so, she knew he would not overlook a serious offense.

Dating without permission was serious. Dating a nonchurch member was worse. If Papa had learned that she was with Warner those nights she had told him she was working, he would have Mamma give her a whipping she could not forget. If he found out that Warner had bought her "sinful" clothes that showed her legs and bosom, he would whip her himself, and not just once either but every night after supper, until he was sure that all the "ways of a harlot" were beaten out of her.

And if he learned that she had committed fornication, he would kill her, or so near as made no difference. But he could not know that—yet. Even Dr. Taylor had not detected it.

She swallowed hard and asked again, "What does Papa want to see me about?"

Mamma looked up, and this time there was no mistaking it—there was the hint of a smile on her face. "He wants to tell you hisself," she said.

Mamma's casual tone of voice assuaged Gaynell's fear enough that she could breathe, but not sufficiently to re-

147

store her appetite. She put her fork down and said, "I'm finished. Are you?"

"Yes. I aimed to eat one of them fried apple pies left over from the school lunches this morning, but I see they're all gone, so I reckon I'm done."

She looked around the table. "Y'all turn to now and get the work done up. Lila, you wash dishes, and Clara Mae will dry. Betty Lee, you work on the mending. Me and Gaynell won't have time for it tonight. Andy, you can keep the fire going in the stove while y'all are studying. Seems like it's gonna freeze tonight."

Papa was sitting in a cane-bottomed chair by a fire that had burned down to red coals. A lighted kerosene lamp was on the dresser behind him, and he was reading the Bible in its dim glow. Gaynell knew he was selecting the scripture for family worship.

As she and her mother entered the room, he inserted the silk-ribbon marker at the place he was reading and laid the Bible aside. He leaned forward and put more wood on the fire. It blazed up, casting a flickering light on unpainted pine walls and a dark, old-fashioned bedroom suite, which was the best furniture in the house. It had been given to Annabel by her parents on her wedding day, and she kept the high bedstead and the enormous wardrobe polished to a fine glow with beeswax and the marble tops of the dresser and washstand scrubbed clean with baking soda.

This was Silas and Annabel's bedroom, and in the winter the family sitting room. (In summer they used the front porch.) The quilts under the white counterpane were Annabel's best, pieced in elaborate designs—Lights and Shades, Double Wedding Ring, Flower Garden, Log Cabin. Every three years she finished a new rag rug for the floor and relegated the old one to the older girls' bedroom. Annabel was proud of this room and never stopped to think what painful memories it held for her children, who never entered it without glancing quickly at the old razor strop hanging ever-ready on its nail by the mantel.

Gaynell sat down in one of the cane-bottomed straight chairs arranged in a semicircle around the fireplace, leaving the lone rocker for her mother. She looked across at Papa, trying to gauge his mood, and was surprised to see that, like Mamma, he looked pleased.

He said, "Gaynell, Mr. Dal Edwards was here this evening, and he told me something that concerns you. He wanted

148

me to talk to you about it. I told him there wasn't no use, that I could give him the answer myself, but nothing would do him except for me to wait and talk it over with you."

Gaynell didn't reply. She couldn't. This is it, she thought. Papa knows about Warner. Someone saw us together, and it's got back to Papa. Her head felt light and dizzy, as if she might faint. Papa's face began to recede and then jumped forward again as with an effort of will she refocused her eyes.

Papa continued, "You know Mr. Woodrow Lyle, of course."

Gaynell nodded, even more frightened. Did Mr. Lyle know too? Did *everybody* know? She wouldn't have thought Mr. Lyle would hear the gossip so soon. Mr. Lyle was the wealthiest member of the Heavenly Light Church, and the others stood a little in awe of him.

Papa said, and the note of triumph in his voice rang clear, "Mr. Lyle wants to court you."

For a moment Gaynell did not comprehend. Then she said in a weak, unbelieving voice, "Me?"

"I knew you'd be surprised. Me and your mamma couldn't hardly believe it either. Of course, it's been a whole year since he lost his wife, and it was to be expected that he'd marry again, but it never dawned on me that he'd want you. I just figgered when the proper mourning period was over, he'd settle on the Widow Crandall. She's young enough, and her land joins his, so it looked like a perfect match. I know everybody in the church expected it, the widow included. But Mr. Edwards said Woodrow—I might as well get used to calling him that if he's gonna be courting my daughter— Woodrow come over to his house yesterday and asked him to talk to us about you."

Gaynell felt relieved and astonished and confused. She grabbed one thought out of the multitude crowding her mind. "But Papa, Mr. Lyle is—he's *old*."

"Forty-two, according to Mr. Edwards. I'd of judged forty-five myself, but I reckon that bald head makes him look older. Forty-two ain't old. I'm forty-three, and I feel as hale and hearty as I did at twenty-three. A man in his forties has got a lot of good years yet. You're a mighty lucky girl, Gaynell, to interest a man that age who's already made his fortune."

Mr. Lyle had a big farm and a small sawmill, and between the two he'd made enough money to build himself a large six-room brick house which contained every modern convenience and the best furnishings the Sears catalog could offer. He had a fine car too, and last year he had presented the church with a new piano in addition to his regular offering. Mr. Lyle was rich all right, maybe richer than Warner, but that had nothing to do with her. She had already made her choice.

In the silence the fire popped and threw a spark onto the brick hearth. Papa stamped it out. Then he rocked his chair back on two legs and stretched his feet out to the fire. He said, "Well, I guess that's all I've got to say. I'll tell Mr. Edwards tomorrow that you'll be pleased to have Woodrow come calling."

He looked at Mamma for the first time. "Annabel, you'll have to make arrangements to have a fire built in the girls' bedroom for us to sit around, so Gaynell can have this room for courting. I figger Woodrow will want to get started right away; a man his age has got no time to waste."

"No, wait a minute, Papa. I don't—I haven't said—I don't want to date Mr. Lyle."

Papa's chair came to rest on all four feet with a thump. "What's that you're saying?"

Gaynell hastened to explain. "It seems odd for him to want to date *me*. You said yourself he's nearly as old as you are. What could we have to talk about? And if he did want a date, why didn't he just ask me? Why did he send Mr. Edwards over here to talk to you? I've been dating since I was sixteen, and nobody ever came to see you before."

Mamma spoke for the first time. "I don't guess you've ever had any cause to know how them things are done, Gaynell, so I better tell you now. When young boys court, they're just getting used to being grown-up and looking around to find somebody they might want to marry someday, but with a widower it's different. Like Papa says, a widower don't have much time to waste. He don't want to spend a lot of time on a girl and then find out she wasn't interested in nothing but a good time.

"So what he does is, he looks around and picks out a woman he likes and then gets a third party, a relative or friend, to go to her and ask if he can come calling. If she's agreeable, they court for a week or two or a month or two—however long it takes to be sure they can get along with each other—and then they get married. Once in a while something comes up in the courtship to make one or the other change their mind, but generally it works out as planned. So that's the way it's done, and folks would think it was mighty strange if a widower done it any other way."

She paused, glanced at Papa and then back at Gaynell, "You being so young, Mr. Lyle thought it best to ask us first, but he made it plain we was to talk it over with you before we give him an answer. So what it comes to is whether you're willing to have Mr. Lyle come courting with the idea of marrying him real soon."

"No, I wouldn't want to do that."

Papa jumped out of his chair. "What!"

Gaynell was so nervous she could hardly get the words out, but she knew she had to. She must convince Papa that what he considered already settled was impossible. She said, "I didn't understand what you were asking, but now that Mamma has explained it, I'll have to say no. I don't want to marry Mr. Lyle."

Papa stared at her for a moment, his dropped jaw and widened eyes indicating his shock. He sat down slowly. "Why not?" he asked.

"I—I don't love him."

"Oh, is that all? Well, that don't matter. The Bible commands a man to love his wife, but it don't say nothing about a woman loving her husband. She's got to submit to him that's all. Mamma will explain what that means before you get married. But the point is, it ain't necessary for you to love Woodrow to marry him."

"Doesn't Mamma love you?" Gaynell asked wonderingly. She had always assumed that there was some measure of affection between them. Otherwise, how could Mamma stand her hard life?

Mamma looked embarrassed. Papa said, "Yes, she does, but that come after we was wed. A woman will learn to love her husband if he treats her right. I'm satisfied Woodrow will be a good husband. He hasn't got a stingy bone in his body—just look at how nice his house is fixed and how much he gives to the church."

"But Papa—"

"You've got to be willing though," Papa went on as if he had not heard her. "I'd sure hate to say yes to Woodrow Lyle and then have you give him all them arguments about love and such. So you think it over tonight and get things worked out in your own mind. Then I'll go over right after breakfast and tell Mr. Edwards you're agreeable."

"I don't have to think it over," Gaynell said. "I couldn't ever love Mr. Lyle. I don't want to marry him."

Papa's eyes narrowed. "I don't believe you've heard a word I've said. I thought I made it clear that you'd have to *learn* to love him. There ain't nothing more to be said. You've always been a dutiful daughter, and you'll be a dutiful wife. Just keep your mind on that thought."

"Papa, I don't know how I can make you believe me. You'll have to say no. I won't marry Mr. Lyle."

He gave her a sharp look. "Don't tell me you've set your heart on somebody else. But no, that couldn't be. You ain't even walked to church with a boy in months. That doctor keeps you busy night and day, seems like."

"No, there's nobody else," Gaynell said hastily, realizing that a telltale blush was spreading into her face. She turned to the fire, hoping they would think she was pink from its heat.

"There better not be," Papa said flatly. "You ain't asked our permission, and you sure better not be slipping around. I'll take the hide off you if I ever catch you doing that."

"Now, Silas, don't get het up," Mamma said mildly. "It's natural for a young girl to be skittish about marriage. I'll talk to Gaynell before I go to bed. But if she don't want to marry Mr. Lyle, she oughtn't to have to. She'll have other chances."

"Yeah, that's what I'm afraid of. She'll turn Woodrow Lyle down and then marry some young whippersnapper who can't do nothing for her or us either."

He turned to Gaynell. "I didn't mention this before, because Woodrow sent word he didn't want you to know till later, but he said if everything worked out like he hoped, he'd deed me that five acres of bottom land that joins this farm on the north side. Then later on I could borrow the money from him to buy this place, and we'd be in good shape."

Emotionally fatigued, Gaynell forgot to be cautious. In anger and despair she cried, "So that's it. You sold me!"

Mamma gasped, and Papa jumped to his feet and in two strides was by Gaynell's chair. He jerked her to her feet and said, "I ain't never took such an insult from nobody. The money didn't have nothing to do with my decision, other than to show me what a good man Woodrow Lyle is. I don't know where you learned such impudence, but I'm gonna unlearn you right now. What you want is a good strapping."

152

He reached around her and took down the razor strop from its nail.

"Grab your knees, and pull that dress tight around you," he ordered.

Gaynell felt as if she would choke, but she did not bend over.

"No!" she cried. "I'm nineteen years old. I won't let you whip me."

"You won't *let* me!" Silas' voice was thick with rage. "We'll just see about that."

He jerked her under his left arm and forced her over so that her buttocks were in a convenient position for the descending strap.

Gaynell bit her lower lip and determined not to cry out. She could feel her body trembling in the dreadful anticipation of her childhood, but she was no longer a child to shed tears over a little pain. She would bear it silently no matter how bad it was, and when it was over, she would tell Papa the same thing she had said before; she would not marry Mr. Lyle. For that was what he was angry about; accusing her of impertinence was just an excuse to vent his anger over the other.

The first blow fell, and tears sprang to her eyes. She bit her lip harder and tasted the salt of blood. The second lick laid a wide stripe of fire over her backside, and she let out an involuntary yelp of pain. As the razor strop continued its inexorable rising and falling, the blistering pain became an agony from which there was no escape, twist and turn as she would. By this time her resolution for stoic acceptance had evaporated; she was sobbing as hard as ever she had as a child and pleading for mercy.

She got none. When he finally turned her loose, her thighs and buttocks were aflame, and her whole body ached from tensed muscles. She could not speak past the sobs still choking her throat, so, although her decision was not changed, its verbalization would have to wait for morning.

She turned and started out the door, but Papa reached out and pulled her back. "Time for family worship," he said, pushing her into a chair. The split-oak canes of its seat cut into the tender, blistered flesh of hers, and she wept afresh.

Mamma reached out and patted her hand. "I could cry too," she said. "That was a cruel, hard whipping. I don't know as I ever seen your papa give a harder one. But you deserved it, Gaynell. You spoke disrespectful to Papa, and

153

he'd not be doing his duty by you if he allowed that. You try to hush your sobbing now, and I'll doctor you with some of my herb salve soon as worship is over."

Gaynell appealed to her mother. "Let me miss worship tonight."

"Well, I guess—" Annabel began uncertainly.

"No," Silas said. "You've got a special need for worship tonight. The Scriptures lead to repentance. Call the other kids, Annabel."

The nine children entered the room quietly and took their accustomed places, casting at Gaynell quick little glances full of curiosity. The house was not soundproof, and every child was aware of what had happened. They were always outwardly reverent at family worship, but tonight they were even more subdued than usual. A whipping for one always reminded the others of their own vulnerability.

Gaynell kept her eyes lowered. Why is it, she thought, that a whipping is so humiliating, even when one is innocent of wrong? Or maybe especially when one is innocent. I can understand why they use the same word to mean defeat, because a whipping *is* defeat. One loses everything—pride, dignity, even personhood. One no longer acts, but is acted upon. I could do nothing either to stop the blows or keep from crying; I was no more than a whipped dog cringing before my master. Now I feel so degraded and ashamed I can't meet anyone's eyes.

And I hate Papa. The thought came calmly and without surprise, as if it had lain in her mind for a long time unrecognized.

Papa cast a stern eye around the gathering. " 'Children, obey your parents in the Lord: for this is right,' " he intoned, "Ephesians 6:1. 'Foolishness is bound in the heart of a child, but the rod of correction shall drive it far from him.' Proverbs 22:15."

Papa did not need to read from the Bible tonight, because he knew all the choice bits from Proverbs by heart. Gaynell did not raise her eyes as he went through his entire repertoire. He's justifying himself, she thought. Well, he could not justify himself to her. If the Bible proved Papa right—and she guessed it did, because those verses were in it—why then, she could do without the Bible. She wanted nothing to do with a God who was also a father.

She stole a glance at Silas, and, seeing his earnest, solemn face, she thought, I hate him. I hate him even more

154

because he believes what he is saying. I shall never call him Papa again, not if he lives to be a hundred. I don't hate Mamma. She believes what he is saying too, but she has some kindness in her heart. If she had married a different man and joined a different church, she might have been gentle and loving. I feel sorry for her, for what she's let him force her to become.

At the end of his Bible recitation, Silas said, "You all know Gaynell has been chastised tonight. If she's wise, she'll learn a lesson from it. If she don't, then I'll have to lay the strap on her again. Gaynell is a grown girl, but until a girl is married, she's subject to her father. Afterwards, she becomes subject to her husband. That's the way the Lord set it up, and that's the way it's gonna be as long as I'm head of this house. All of you better remember that. Now let us pray."

Gaynell's pain, both mental and physical, was still so great that she only half-heard the words, but her mind caught the sense of them: If she didn't agree to marry Woodrow Lyle, Silas would find more excuses to whip her.

Oh, Warner, she cried silently, please come back. I won't pray to God, but I'll pray to you. Wherever you are, please hear me and come back before it's too late.

21

At work the next day Gaynell greeted patients, answered the telephone, and typed medical records in a haze of pain. Sitting on her tender buttocks was torment. Yet when she moved, rough-textured cotton bloomers sandpapering raw skin was a greater torture. Underneath the physical pain her hopeless thoughts churned without ceasing. The dangers of tonight . . . and tomorrow . . . and, worst of all, the time when Silas learned the secret she could not keep much longer.

Already she was aware of changes in her body. She had always hated her ill-fitting cotton dresses, but now she was grateful for them, because they hid her heavier breasts and the faint bulge of her abdomen and insured a few more days of safety.

She would not think of that now. Warner would come back. She must keep her mind fixed on that thought, for without it she was lost. She must believe he was coming, and she must keep herself alive—and unmarried—until he got here.

That seemed hopeless with Silas so set on her marrying Mr. Lyle. What he said this morning foretold what was to come: "It pains me to hear that you're still of the same mind, Daughter. But I won't force you. You've got to make the decision yourself. However, the Bible says the rod is for correction, and not marrying Woodrow Lyle is a mistake that sure needs correcting."

Gaynell had been under Silas's strap often enough to know that in time she would promise anything to escape it. She thought her threshold of pain must be very low, and yet it was not so much the pain that conquered her as the dread—the feeling that she could stand no more but more would come. She despised herself for a coward, but she didn't think she could stand up to what Silas was planning.

Yet marrying Mr. Lyle was no way out. She wasn't married to Warner, but she *felt* married. She was as obligated to be faithful to him as if she had been through a wedding ceremony, and she would rather die than have another man touch her in that intimate way.

Mr. Lyle would if she married him, and when he put his hands on her body, he would know she was pregnant. She didn't know what would happen then. There was no precedent, for she couldn't remember a time when a Heavenly Light girl had been pregnant at marriage. They were all virgins (although few of them knew what virginity was or what would be done to take it away from them on their wedding nights). Mr. Lyle would expect her to be a virgin too, untouched and unaware. Finding her otherwise, what would he do? Send her back to Silas? Beat her? Force her to confess and repent publicly in church?

Certain it was that he would do something, because Heavenly Light men did not tolerate sexual sins in their women-folk. Mr. Edwards had switched Mrs. Edwards once for no more than looking too long at another man. Gaynell knew that if she married Mr. Lyle, he could do whatever he liked to her. She would have no protection, either from the church or the law. Brother Brown would cite Genesis 3:16 and various verses from Paul's Epistles and tell her she must bend to the rod. The Alabama law, she had heard, stipulated only that the rod be no thicker than a man's thumb.

A person could be beaten to death with a stick that size.

She might have two or three days grace before Silas started "correcting" her refusal of Mr. Lyle. She might have two or three weeks before her pregnancy was discovered. But sooner or later either Silas or Mr. Lyle would kill her.

At noon just as Dr. Taylor started out to lunch, she fainted. One moment she was entering the charges in the ledger for the last morning patient, who had just left, and the next minute she realized that the room was growing darker and her head felt strange.

When she came to, she was lying on the sofa across the room from her desk. Her feet were propped up, and her dress had slid above her knees. She sat up hurriedly, so alarmed that her hands trembled as they arranged the dress modestly over her legs.

Dr. Taylor said, "Come into the treatment room, Gaynell. I want to examine you."

"No, I'm all right," she said in a shaking voice.

He frowned. "You know you fainted?"

"Yes, but there's nothing wrong with me. I feel fine. It's just the—the time of the month, I expect."

"It's never happened before," he said. "I noticed a while back that you looked pale and thin. We'd better find out what the trouble is."

Her face remained resistant. He sighed. He had treated Heavenly Light women before, and he knew all about their excessive modesty. They wouldn't remove any part of their clothing for an examination, and even in childbirth they expected the doctor to work under the bedcovers without "exposing" them. He had thought Gaynell a little more enlightened, but apparently he was mistaken.

He said, "There are times when one ought to forget modesty, Gaynell. I have no interest in your body except in a medical sense. You can trust me. I won't ask you to undress completely, and I'll be as considerate as I can. How about it?"

She shook her head. "Honestly, Dr. Taylor, I'm all right. If I wasn't, I'd do what you say. It's not modesty. To tell you the truth, I don't believe like other people in my church. I wish I could get out of the church."

"Why don't you?" he asked, temporarily diverted by this

157

revelation. He had often wondered why anyone as bright as Gaynell continued to follow the primitive and ascetic customs of her church.

"My folks wouldn't let me."

"You're making your own living. Surely, you can do as you please?"

"I'm still a minor though. You wouldn't understand. You couldn't unless you'd been brought up like I was."

He had been observing her closely, and now he said, "Gaynell, are you pregnant?"

Her face flamed. She stammered: "No sir—no. No, of course not. I don't know why you should think that. If it was anybody but you, Dr. Taylor, I'd be angry. I'm not even married—how could I be pregnant?"

"It happens," he said dryly.

"Not to Heavenly Light girls," she flashed back. "You don't understand," she said again.

"It isn't the end of the world to have a baby before you're married. I can help you if you'll let me. If you think you might be pregnant, you should let me examine you. Then we can consider what to do."

But she persisted in her denials. He finally left her and started to lunch, but he was convinced that she was pregnant and scared to death someone would find out. He didn't know how she expected to keep it secret. However, the best he could judge through those awful clothes, she wasn't more than two months along; her breasts were heavier, but as yet her abdomen still looked flat. Nevertheless, she was pushing the limits of secrecy. Another two or three weeks—but maybe she expected to be married by then.

He wondered who the father was. One of the boys in her church, he guessed. Now that he thought of it, he knew very little about Gaynell's life. When she went home at five, she disappeared from his orbit. Heavenly Light people kept themselves set apart from the world, especially the women. Gaynell seemed to be the only one with a job. The others were seen in town very rarely, and then always accompanied by husband or father. He knew for a fact that there wasn't much premarital sex among them, but they usually married young and made up for it afterward.

Sam had not thought before how fond he was of Gaynell. When he hired her, he'd had some reservations, thinking a receptionist who dressed so oddly might be a disadvantage to him in his new practice, but he soon realized that the patients liked her. She was friendly and cheerful; she calmed the nervous, soothed the irate, and comforted the grieved. She kept him up to snuff too, without any unpleasant nagging. He was untidy in the office and careless about record-keeping, but Gaynell unobtrusively straightened his desk and treatment room, questioned him about the records, and somehow kept his irritation at a minimum.

Now she was in trouble, for having a baby out of wedlock was bad trouble for any girl in Lanier, and it was probably worse for one in Gaynell's church. Yet she wouldn't let him help her. He felt depressed and uneasy.

As he came out on the street, he hesitated. He and Grant always used to go to lunch together, but lately he had been making excuses. He had been conscious for some time that his feelings toward Grant had undergone a change. At first he attributed it to a feeling of envy at Grant's good fortune, but now he was aware that it was a bit more specific. He wanted Stella for himself.

But he didn't want to lose his friendship with Grant. Up to now it had been the most important relationship in his life. Of course, he had always known that sooner or later one or both of them would marry, but he had not foreseen any harm to their friendship from that. He should have guessed that men who had so many tastes in common and thought alike on so many subjects might also be attracted to the same woman. But this was something they could not share. One of them would have to lose.

Sam intended to win. He knew nine girls out of ten in Lanier would choose Grant with his good looks, his family background, and his inherited wealth, but he thought Stella might be the tenth if she faced her feelings honestly.

The problem was to get her to face them. He was a fool not to have taken the opportunity offered the other night in his office. If he had, she would at least have to consider how she felt about him. As it was, she had apparently dismissed the incident from her mind. She didn't refer to it afterward in the restaurant or on the way home. They had talked of school events and news in the town, and even talking about the developing romance between Charles Howle and Valerie had not brought the conversation around to her own feelings.

He was going to see her after school this afternoon, barring some emergency. He didn't know what pretext he would use, but he'd think of something.

He came to with a start and realized he had been standing

159

on the street several minutes. He looked toward the drug store. No, he wouldn't go by for Grant today. He would delay any extended conversation and hope for some development that would allow him to win Stella without losing Grant.

But when he got to the café, he saw Grant sitting at a table alone. He's avoiding me too, Sam realized with surprise. But now that we've met here, we can't ignore each other. He walked to Grant's table and said, "All right if I eat here?"

Grant looked up and said easily, "Sure, sit down. I wasn't certain you'd want to eat with me today."

"Why not?" Sam asked.

"I thought you might be feeling guilty. You should be."

The waitress came then, and Sam gave his order. When she left, he said, "I suppose you're talking about Stella."

"What else? You've been seeing a lot of her. You had her in your office two or three hours yesterday, and then afterward you went to dinner. You know it doesn't look right for an engaged girl to go out with somedoby else, even if he is her fiancé's friend."

Sam looked at Grant curiously. "Is that all you care about, how it looks?"

Grant's eyes narrowed. "Is there anything else to be angry about?"

Sam hesitated a moment. He could tell Grant the truth—and make him angry. Or he could delay and hope for favorable developments, as he'd decided earlier. He said, "I've never touched Stella. As a matter of fact, we spent most of that time talking about you. She's worried about your quarrel."

"Well, that's going to be over soon. Miss Mattie is right. It's up to me to make up with her, and I'm going to do it tonight."

"What does Miss Mattie have to do with it?"

"Oh, you know how she is, always sticking her nose into everything. She was in the drug store, and she said, 'I haven't seen you with Stella lately. Have y'all broke up?' I said no, we'd just had a misunderstanding, and she said, 'Send her one of those boxes of candy I see over there and tell her you're sorry.'

"Well, of course, I didn't say anything, but I didn't mean to do it. But the next thing I knew, I'd picked up a box of candy, written a note, and sent the delivery boy to the boarding house."

160

"Because Miss Mattie told you to?" Sam was frowning thoughtfully. He was remembering that Stella too had done what Miss Mattie said.

"It seemed that way," Grant admitted. "Although later on after it was done, I saw the sense to it, so maybe it was my own idea and Miss Mattie only provided the impetus. Anyhow, I'll see Stella tonight, and we'll get everything straightened out."

After a moment Sam turned the conversation to another channel, but he was even more determined to see Stella this afternoon.

After Miss Mattie's advice to Grant, she and Cousin Edith left the drug store and went down the street toward Bell's Dry Goods Store, where Miss Eunice worked. Miss Mattie had grown accustomed but not reconciled to having Cousin Edith with her wherever she went. It was like having a cocklebur in an intimate part of her clothing, a constant irritation that she could not politely remove. Of course, Cousin Edith didn't really bother her; she never said much and didn't interfere in any way. But she was always *there*, with her constantly shifting eyes, her high voice, and her unpleasant and inappropriate giggle. It was disconcerting to have someone constantly on hand watching and listening. Even at home Miss Mattie and her sister Eunice had no privacy. *I wonder when she's going home,* Miss Mattie thought.

"Tomorrow," Cousin Edith said, and Miss Mattie's startled eyes swung toward her. But she hadn't yet finished her sentence. "Tomorrow I thought I'd dye those faded dining room curtains, so you need to decide what color you want and buy the dye while we're in Bell's Store."

Miss Mattie was disappointed, but she tried not to show it. "Red," she said decisively. "I like good strong colors."

As she spoke, she saw Charles Howle step out of a car onto the sidewalk. She said, "Good morning, Charles. How does it feel to be a working man again?" Charles had once again taken over his desk in the office of the planer mill, of which his mother was half-owner.

"It feels wonderful to be back at work, Miss Mattie. Good morning, Mrs. Alexander."

"I see you've got a new car," Miss Mattie said, glancing toward the car he had just parked. "I hope you're giving the Lord his proper thanks for all this good fortune."

"Well—"

"Remember what Jesus said to a man who was healed, 'Sin no more lest a worse thing come unto thee.' You ought to get back to the church where you belong. The Lord will forgive you for straying, and you won't have to rejoin the church, because your name is still on the roll. So just march down the aisle next Sunday and rededicate your life."

"I'll give it some thought," Charles said. It was what he always said to Miss Mattie's exhortations.

"Don't just think about it, do it," Miss Mattie said, and she and Cousin Edith passed on.

Just before they reached Bell's Store, they met Adelaide Perry loaded down with packages.

"Let me carry those for you, Adelaide," Miss Mattie said, taking the bundles. "You ought not to be lifting anything in your condition. Looks like you bought out the store."

"It's the layette for the baby and some extra diapers and things," Adelaide said. "I guess it seems strange to wait until now to buy them, but I didn't want to do it too soon, because I thought it would make the waiting seem longer."

"Well, it can't be much longer now," Miss Mattie said. "I'm coming to be with you at your confinement, of course, but you'll need to ask a couple of others too. It takes several pairs of hands at a time like that."

She put the bundles in the back seat of Adelaide's car and said, "Now you go straight home. You've done enough for one morning. Leave the packages in the car for Owen to bring in when he comes to lunch."

Adelaide had intended to make a couple of other stops, but to her surprise she found herself driving toward home with her errands still undone. Well, she did feel a little tired. Maybe it would be better to leave the other things for tomorrow.

As Miss Mattie and her cousin wended their way home, Miss Mattie was well pleased with herself. She'd been doing the Lord's work this morning. Charles Howle hadn't actually promised to rededicate his life, but she thought he would before long. She'd noticed that lately people were easier to persuade than they used to be, and she knew why. God had healed her for a purpose, and so he gave her a little extra power to get the job done. Even Adelaide, who was pretty stubborn in some ways, had paid attention today and gone straight home. And Grant Meadows had actually thanked her for her advice. Of course, she hadn't given it to him just for his benefit. God had sent Stella to Lanier, and Miss Mattie had no doubt he intended her to stay, but she was practical enough to see that the only way that could happen was if Stella married somebody in Lanier. So settling the quarrel between her and Grant was a duty.

There was only one more thing bothering Miss Mattie; the question of what to do about Cousin Edith. Her visit had been long enough already to satisfy all requirements of kinship and hospitality, yet she showed no signs of leaving. So, it seemed Miss Mattie's duty to give her a hint to go. Not so much for my sake, Miss Mattie told herself virtuously, as for Eunice's. Of course the financial burden fell equally on them—extra heat, water, electricity, and company meals three times a day were wrecking the budget—but the annoyance of having someone always present was greater for Eunice. She worked in public all day and when she came home, she ought to be able to relax, but she couldn't with Cousin Edith constantly asking questions and having to be told every single thing that happened.

Miss Mattie and Miss Eunice were accustomed to gossiping, but they talked in a verbal shorthand which was perfectly comprehensible to anyone who knew the background and life history of everyone in town but impossible for Cousin Edith to understand. They were continually having to stop and explain to her, and so conversation which should be relaxing was often irritating. Miss Mattie had wondered once or twice why Cousin Edith wanted to know so many details about people she would never see again when her visit was over.

Then the suspicion crossed her mind that perhaps Cousin Edith didn't mean for it to be over, that she might intend to stay permanently. After all, she had told them she was a childless widow with no living relatives, so there was probably no reason for her to return to Texas.

But she couldn't stay here, and it was time to make her realize that. I'll give her another day or two, Miss Mattie thought, and then if she's still here, I'll tell her to leave.

22

At three-thirty Sam parked in front of the school, got out, and walked toward the one-story brick building. As he approached the steps, Stella came out the door, followed by Valerie and another teacher. His heart fell as he saw the others; somehow it hadn't occurred to him that Stella wouldn't be alone. With an effort he rallied from the disappointment and said, "May I give you girls a ride home?"

Valerie gave Stella a quick glance and said, "Charles is waiting for me." She turned to the other woman, "Come on, Anne. Stella can ride in Charles's new car another time."

Sam's spirits rose with Valerie's words. She had known instantly that he was here to see Stella, and that must mean Stella had talked about him. He asked her, "How did Valerie know it was you I wanted to see?"

Stella shrugged. "Feminine intuition, I guess." She glanced at his face, frowned, and said, "We haven't exchanged any girlish confidences, if that's what you're thinking. I don't talk to other women about my personal life—and even if I did, there would be no reason to mention you."

So she was going to ignore the moment of attraction between them. He said, "I came by to see if you'd like to ride out to the Granger's with me. I'm going to see Maureen, and I thought perhaps you'd like to come too."

"Oh, I would. How nice of you to ask me."

"I probably wouldn't have thought of it if I hadn't wanted to see you again anyway," he said honestly. Then seeing a look of alarm fly into her face, he added, "I thought we should talk more about your experience with the strange aircraft."

The apprehension in her face faded, and that told him it was not caused by what she had learned from the hypnotism, which had been frightening enough, but by some fear of what had happened afterward between them. He didn't understand it yet, but at least he knew she wasn't indifferent.

They went over the story she had told under hypnotism, but it was largely a rehash of what they had said before.

164

Just before they arrived at the Granger house, Sam said, "I've been wondering if we should tell the sheriff about this, since it might be the answer to what happened to Warner."

"Do you think he'd believe it? I can hardly believe it myself even though I saw it."

"I suppose you're right. If we knew that's what happened to Warner, it would be different, we'd have to tell. But it's just speculation, and, as you say, it strains credibility."

Maureen herself answered the doorbell, and she was overjoyed to see them. "Daddy was going to take me to town when he gets home this afternoon so I could thank you," she said to Stella. "I wanted to wait until I could talk properly. I've been practicing every minute."

"You're doing very well," Stella said.

"I've been learning to write too. Miss Lidell, I can't ever thank you enough if I live to be a hundred years old. You can't know . . ."

Mrs. Granger came in then and added her thanks to Maureen's, but hers were less effusive, almost perfunctory. She turned to Maureen. "Did you offer Dr. Taylor and Miss Lidell some refreshment? I declare, Maureen, you don't think of anything. What will you have, Miss Lidell? Tea? Coffee? Coca-Cola? I know Dr. Taylor drinks coffee."

"Coffee will be fine," Stella said. When Mrs. Granger left the room, Stella looked at Maureen. "It's hard to believe," she said. "When I think of how you were that night—and you hadn't improved at all when you left the boarding house. When did you first notice it? And how did you feel? Was there any sensation as you gained the use of your muscles?"

"I've already asked her all those questions," Sam said.

"And I can't answer them," Maureen added. "I was very discouraged that night. I'd had such a hard time getting to town, and then it seemed all for nothing. I felt hopeless, but I was so tired I went to sleep right away, and when I woke up, I was well. Whatever happened was in my sleep."

"Maureen didn't have to walk to town that night," Mrs. Granger said as she reentered the room and caught part of the conversation. "We'd have been glad to take her if we'd known she wanted to go."

Maureen flashed a look at her, but Mrs. Granger seemed not to notice it. "It was a dangerous thing to do. She might have been run over or injured some other way," she said.

"But I wasn't," Maureen said.

"No, but you could have been. And she's doing too much now," Mrs. Granger said, looking at Sam. "That's why I wanted you to come this afternoon. I think she's tiring herself out. If she's not in the library studying, she's outside running about or in the kitchen watching the cook and asking a million questions about everything. She hasn't been still a minute since she was healed. I think all this activity is too much for her."

"Well, I'll check her over before I leave," Sam said. "But I don't think it's going to hurt her to be active. As far as I can see, Maureen is as normal as if she hadn't ever had cerebral palsy. You and I are going to have to get used to treating her like a well person instead of an invalid."

"I guess so. But she couldn't have as much strength as the average person. She needs to have some rest periods and take care of herself."

"A short nap in the afternoon couldn't hurt," Sam conceded. "For a while anyway. But in general, I'd let her do as she pleases."

"I'm going to town tomorrow," Maureen said. "Daddy is going to send someone to drive me, and I can walk down the street and go in the stores, and if I want to buy something, I can tell the clerks. I'm going to start going to church too and to the movies and lots of places."

"You see what I mean, Doctor," Mrs. Granger said to Sam. "There's no end to what she wants to do."

On the way back to town Stella said, "Mrs. Granger doesn't seem as thrilled over Maureen's new activities and plans as Maureen is."

"It's a big change for Maureen's family," Sam said, "and no matter how pleasant a change is, it takes some adjustment. Her mother hasn't realized yet that Maureen is no longer her helpless child. But time should take care of those problems as Mrs. Granger begins to use her own new freedom."

"I hope so," Stella said. "I hate to see Maureen's good fortune cause contention between her and her mother ... Sam, what do you think happened to Maureen? I know she's well, but I can't help wondering what the process of getting well was like."

"I don't know either," Sam said. "Medically there's no explanation. Cerebral palsy victims don't improve. They may learn to manage better, to handle the handicap and have a normal life in spite of it—something that was denied to Maureen because of her parents' attitude—but the impairment of the motor function does not disappear. It's caused by some injury or damage before or during birth, and it's permanent. Yet in Maureen's case some sort of regenerative and restorative process seems to have occurred."

"If Grant could see Maureen, he'd have to approve of the healing," Stella said, as if to herself.

They were approaching the Holiness Church. Sam turned into the churchyard and cut of the engine. He said, "Are you still worried about that? Does Grant's opinion matter so much to you?"

"Of course it does. I told you before that I'm in love with him."

He said slowly, "Your mouth said that, but your body said something else."

He saw the blood move upward from her neck until it suffused her face in a fiery blush. She looked down at the floorboard, and her white-gold hair swung forward, shielding her face from his view. After a moment she said painfully, "I hoped you didn't notice that. I'm ashamed of it."

He put his hand under her chin and raised her face so that she had to meet his eyes. "Instead of being ashamed of your feeling, why don't you consider what it means?"

"Because it doesn't mean anything. A momentary physical attraction, that's all."

"Have you ever felt like that with Grant?"

"Of course not. That's entirely different."

"On a higher plane?" he asked with an undertone of laughter in his voice.

"Well, it is," she said defensively. "I don't think much about sex when I'm with him. I know it will come later in the right way, as an outgrowth of the love we have for each other."

"A sort of unimportant sideline," he suggested with that amusement still in his voice. "You don't know yourself very well, do you?"

"Too well," she said. Her voice was harsh and bitter. There was an angry defiance in her face, but he had a feeling that it was directed inward rather than toward him. She seemed to be facing some private enemy and remembering past wounds.

He said gently, "My dear child, don't look so stricken. It was nothing. Only one small impulse."

167

"Not so small," she said in a painful voice.

"Small enough to have no results, at any rate," he said lightly. "Not even so much as a kiss."

"That's right, it didn't," she said in a surprised voice. "You've made me feel much better."

"That's what doctors are for," he said, starting the car. He himself felt worse, because once more he had muffed a chance to make her aware of him, this time because he couldn't bear to see her unhappy. However, he talked cheerfully of this and that until he reached the boarding house. Then he said, "Stella, if you ever change your mind about Grant, will you tell me?"

"What does that mean?"

"Nothing much, just that I'd like to spend some time with you. The attraction wasn't all on your side, you know. So I thought if you're ever free, we might give it a whirl and see what develops. Will you promise?"

"All right. But that isn't going to happen."

As Sam drove away, he felt pessimistic. He had done nothing for his own cause. Stella was more convinced than ever that she was in love with Grant. Since Grant had already taken steps to make up their quarrel, they would probably be together tonight. That thought depressed him further.

However, it was still a long time until the end of school and Stella's wedding date. Anything could happen. Whatever did, he hoped next time he'd have sense enough to take advantage of it.

Stella entered the boarding house with her mind far from settled. She wished Sam had not told her he wanted to spend time with her.

"To see what develops," he said. She knew what would develop—and very quickly too. Because the minute he'd said that, she'd been conscious of the same excitement she had felt in his office that night. She loved Grant, but she wanted to go to bed with Sam. It was damnable.

She had controlled herself though; she had put down the feeling of excitement and answered him in a calm, cool voice. He had not guessed how she was feeling. Perhaps everyone had such moments of temptation. She wished she knew. She had not felt them for a long time now, not since that period immediately following Jim's death. But perhaps now that she had let herself feel again, she must expect them. Once she and Grant were married, they would probably cease. She hoped she would not have to be always on guard lest she react to every attractive man in sight.

Not that Sam was all that attractive. He had beautiful eyes—and a strong-looking face—and lovely muscles. But he was not nearly as good-looking as Grant. Not as courteous either. Grant would never have said some of the things Sam had said to her. Things that embarrassed and hurt—"Your mouth said that, but your body said something else." It was true, but it would have been kinder not to say it. Didn't he know she couldn't ever feel at ease with him again? Even after she conquered these disturbing feelings, she would always be aware that he knew about them.

Maybe that was why he did it. "The attraction wasn't all on your side," he said. He had felt it too. He wanted her. Not with any great urgency, she thought, just enough to say that if it was ever convenient. . . . Well, it wouldn't be. She would see to that. Even if the quarrel with Grant was never made up, she didn't want the kind of relationship Sam would offer her.

When she got to the upper hall, Valerie popped out of her room. "I have something to tell you, Stella. Will you come in a minute?"

The news—that Valerie and Charles were going to get married—was not surprising except that Stella had not expected it so soon. However, it brought a problem.

"At our age there's no point in a big wedding," Valerie said, "so we thought we'd go to Columbus a week from Saturday. Over there we can buy a license and get married all in one afternoon. But we'll have to have witnesses, and it's much nicer to have friends than strangers. So we want you and Grant—or you and Sam. I wasn't sure which one you'd want to ask. Lately, you've seemed to have both of them on the string."

"No," Stella said. "It's always been Grant. Sam and I are just friends. But I've quarreled with Grant, so . . . anyway, don't worry. The quarrel may be settled by that time."

Valerie chattered on about her plans, and Stella tried to enter into her happiness, but half her mind was on her own part in seeing Valerie married. She didn't want to go with Sam. She was having enough trouble overcoming the sexual attraction without adding the emotional impact of a wedding to it.

But she *was* happy for Valerie, and she had an extra

pleasure in thinking that she'd had a part in bringing this marriage about. Surely Grant would realize soon that the healing was a good thing. Perhaps he already did but was shy saying so or reluctant to admit he was wrong.

The first thing she saw when she walked into her own room was the package on her bed. She read the note once and went to call him, then with arrangements made for tonight, she came back to read it again. And again. It was just what it ought to be; never had anyone set pen to paper to such good purpose. The quarrel was over, and she was happier than she'd ever been before.

Later when they were eating dinner, she thought of how well Grant had managed the reconciliation, without the awkwardness of explanations and apologies and useless regrets. When she came down the stairs to meet him, he kissed her and said, "Let's don't talk about it. It's all over and forgotten. I have something for you."

It was the engagement ring he'd ordered. During dinner she could hardly take her eyes off it, not because of its one-and-a-half-carat size or perfect quality, which she would have expected from Grant, but because of its guarantee of happiness to come. As Grant's wife she would never again have to worry about slipping from the respectability she held so precariously. The sex drive which had plagued her all her life would be moderated by constant availability and the addition of family responsibilities. Grant knew how to keep sex in its place, not as an unimportant sideline, as Sam derisively suggested, but not the entire end and purpose of life either. With him she would be safe. Thinking of her own coming marriage reminded her of Valerie's, and she had just started to tell Grant about it when someone spoke at her elbow. She looked up. It was an elderly woman she had never seen before, a country woman from the look of her weathered skin and severe, old-fashioned hairstyle. Then her eyes moved to the man standing beside the woman, and she recoiled at the sight of his face. The lower right side of it was eaten away by what could only be cancer.

He said, "Excuse me for interrupting your supper, but we've got a long ways to go, all the way to the Hebron Community, so we couldn't wait till you finished. You're the lady that does the healing, ain't you?"

Stella said, "Yes," and, knowing what he wanted and anxious to get it over with, she reached out and touched his hand.

170

"Would you mind touching my face?" he said. "I know it ain't no pretty sight, but cancer ain't catching, and if you wouldn't mind—I feel like the cure would have a better chance to work if you'd put your hands right on the spot that needs healing."

Stella hesitated. The thought of touching that repulsive growth was abhorrent to her. She saw that Grant was shaking his head. She opened her mouth to explain to the man that the healing would work just as well from a touch on his hand. But she didn't actually know that. She didn't understand how it worked, and she didn't know how much the man's own faith might affect it. At any rate, he would go away with more peace of mind if she did as he asked. How awful it would be to have a thing like that on one's face. Surely if he could bear that, she could bear touching him.

She stood up and put her hand on the revolting growth. Grant made a sound, but she didn't look at him.

After they were gone, she went to the rest room and scrubbed her hands. She felt as if she could never get them clean.

When she got back to the table, Grant was sitting there smoking a cigarette, with his half-finished meal shoved aside.

She said, "Grant, I'm sorry. But what could I do?"

He took a final drag from his cigarette and stubbed it out in the ashtray. Then he looked up at her. His handsome face was both troubled and angry, and emotion dragged at his voice as he spoke. "I don't know," he said. "I honestly don't know. I guess you're doing a lot of good, and I see that since you've got the power, you can't quit using it. But I don't think I can take it, Stella. I don't like having people come up to you when we're out together. I don't like being the object of stares and whispers, and I don't like seeing you touch diseased people. It's nauseating to me. I couldn't eat another bite after that man left."

"It wasn't pleasant to me either," she said. "But it may never happen again. Don't let it spoil our evening."

"You don't understand what I'm trying to say . . . Let's get out of here and talk."

In the car he said once more. "You don't understand how I feel. I didn't realize it myself until I saw you touching that man. But that changed my feeling toward you. I'd always thought of you as clean and dainty, and now—"

"Are you trying to say that because I touched him you find me repulsive?" she asked.

"Yes. I'm sorry, but that's exactly how I feel. And I think I always would."

"Nurses and doctors touch sick people every day," she said. "Sam's your best friend. What about that? Grant, you're just reacting to a very unpleasant incident. You'll feel different later."

"No, I won't. Sam is my best friend, as you say. But that's different. He's a man, he's expected to deal with unpleasant things. Besides, I don't have to touch him. It's an entirely different sort of relationship from the one I expect with my wife. I've never been squeamish; I've seen a lot of worse sights than that man's face without feeling sick. It was your touching him that was so repulsive. . . . I guess I can't explain it, but I just suddenly realized I was wrong to patch things up between us. It won't work, and I should have left things as they were. If it hadn't been for Miss Mattie, I would have. I shouldn't have listened to her."

"Why, what did she say? . . . I see." But she didn't, not really. It seemed odd that Grant had listened to Miss Mattie, whom he considered a busybody.

Stella said, "You told me you loved me." She could hear the pleading sound in her voice, but she didn't care. Pride didn't seem worth much at the moment.

"When I said that, I did, or I thought I did. But whatever it was, is gone, for me at least."

"Then I guess there's nothing left to do but give your ring back."

"I feel like a heel," he muttered as he took the ring. "I hope you'll find someone else."

"I'm sure I shall," she said with a flash of spirit. "As a matter of fact, all I'll have to do is pick up the telephone. So don't feel sorry for me."

He looked at her in surprise, and after a moment he said, "Sam? . . . Well, I hope it works out for both of you."

There was no jealousy in his voice, and that, she realized, put the final seal on his rejection.

She said, "You might as well take me home."

"We could still see the movie if you'd like to."

She laughed a little wildly. What an anticlimax that would be. She knew he meant it kindly, but his rules of courtesy couldn't cover this situation. She said, "No, take me home."

As she went into the hall at the boarding house, she hesitated by the telephone. She wanted to call Sam and tell him what had happened. She could pour out all her hurt,

172

and he would listen. He would understand her resentment that the healing which had been a blessing to so many people had caused her, who had all the trouble of it, so much pain. And then afterward. . . .

Her mind stopped. That was why she couldn't call him, because of the afterward. She knew what he wanted from her, and it was what she wanted too on one level of her being. The lower level. That was why she must not do it. She wouldn't make the same mistake twice. She wouldn't let this loss drive her into a round of sexual activity which would leave her sickened and contemptuous.

She passed the telephone and went upstairs. Valerie was out with Charles and Mrs. Overly had gone to bed. There was no one to talk to, no way to escape her thoughts. She got a book and tried to read, but she couldn't keep her mind on the words. The house was too quiet. It was only nine o'clock, too early to go to bed. She doubted if she would sleep when she went.

She would have to call Sam eventually. She had promised him she would. Also, pride demanded that she carry through on what she said to Grant. She didn't want him, or anyone, to pity her. Going out with Sam would save her from that. One or two dates would be enough. She would call it off before anything happened.

How strange though to be thinking of pride when it was loss she felt. Strange too that she had not cried. But after a moment she realized that this was not the same as Jim's death. There was no grief. Grant was alive and doubtless would soon be happy with someone else. There was no need to feel sorry for him. Nor for herself. She still had her health and her work.

But she was alone.

Suddenly she knew she could not stay here in this room another minute. She had to do something. She would take a walk. It would cause comment and criticism if she were seen out unaccompained at night, but she'd have to risk that. Anything was better than staying in her room alone. She put on her coat and went quietly down the stairs so as not to wake Mrs. Overly.

Once again she paused by the telephone. Then she picked up the receiver and spoke softly to the operator. "Dr. Taylor's residence, please."

She was waiting on the sidewalk when he drove up. Her heart hammered as she got in the car. But, after all, she needn't have worried about what would happen, for nothing did. He listened to her story but offered few comments and made no advances.

Sam was suffering an attack of conscience. All his life he had gone after what he wanted with single-minded purpose. The world he lived in was organized on competitive lines. He had not organized it thus, but he had to live in it, and he would not be one of the losers. He had competed for grades, for entry into medical school, for jobs, for military rank, without a thought for those he left behind him. But at least he had always been fair; he had advanced by building himself up, rather than by tearing someone else down. He had never done anything dishonest or underhanded. This time he had, and although he couldn't really regret it, something prevented his claiming the prize made available by treachery.

So although they went several places together during the following week, his attitude toward Stella seemed to her impersonal, almost indifferent. She couldn't understand it.

She would have spent more time trying to, however, had not her attention been taken by several other things.

It now appeared that most of the people Stella touched at the healing service had been healed. Mr. Bob Morrow, of course, had not been. "Although," Sam said thoughtfully, "death is the only thing that will heal the infirmities of old age, so perhaps that was a kind of healing too."

Aletha Cunningham had suffered no more epileptic seizures, but whether she was truly healed was still a question. Sam said he would like to see an encephalograph but added that Dr. Marvin, whose patient Aletha was, wasn't likely to have one made. He hadn't even had Aletha on Dilantin.

There were two certain failures: Tim O'Mary, an amputee from the war, and the senile and helpless Mrs. Howle, mother of Charles and Miss Pauline. However, Stella, remembering that even the Bible contained no record of restored youth or replaced limbs, had not hoped for success in those cases.

Nevertheless, the rate of success was so high that Miss Mattie was well pleased and did not hesitate to scold those who disbelieved. For a different reason Stella too got a share of Miss Mattie's scolding.

"You're getting away from the religious side of the healings," Miss Mattie said, "and no good can come of that. I know they can't all be done in the church. Jesus himself healed people wherever he found them. But I don't think you'll find he ever did it without giving credit to God, and

174

you've got to do the same, Stella. If you don't, I won't be responsible for what happens."

Stella answered politely, but she wondered how Miss Mattie could be responsible in any case. Since Miss Mattie did not give her a direct order, she continued as she was doing.

Miss Mattie's admonition to Charles Howle was more fruitful. He walked down the aisle of the Baptist Church on Sunday morning and said he wanted to rejoin the church and be baptized again.

J.T. Clayton, apparently inspired by Charles' fervor, also walked down the aisle but was once more unable to give the proper responses and had to return to his seat red-faced and unshriven.

Miss Mattie had a talk with Owen Perry, and she told her sister and her cousin and everybody else who would listen what she had said to him: "Owen, you ask J.T. Clayton some more questions. If Warner was anywhere near his house that evening, I bet J.T. knows it. With all the moonshining he does, he keeps a sharp eye out for anybody wandering around his place. So just keep asking till he opens up and tells you."

Cousin Edith nodded. "I imagine we'll see some results from that soon," she piped.

You won't be here to see them, Miss Mattie thought. She had determined to speak to Cousin Edith tomorrow.

23

The following morning Miss Mattie's cousin in Caleb's Point called and asked to borrow twenty-five dollars. It was for groceries, she said. They'd been trying to pay off some doctor bills and overestimated the amount they could afford this month, so now she was out of grocery money until payday.

After a conference with Miss Eunice, Miss Mattie left immediately to take her the money. She invited Cousin Edith to go too, but Cousin Edith declined, saying she had some things to do at home and anyway she didn't feel much like going. Miss Mattie didn't press her; she welcomed the chance to make a visit without Cousin Edith's company. But she wondered a little. Having come so far to visit her relatives, Cousin Edith should want to meet all of them, yet she seemed interested only in those who lived in Lanier.

Miss Mattie returned at noon to find Cousin Edith dishing up the dinner. "Why, where's Arline?" Miss Mattie asked.

"She's quit her job," Cousin Edith answered. "She says she is going to live with her son in Birmingham.

"Well, I declare! I wonder why she didn't tell me her plans. It isn't like Arline to be so closemouthed. When did you find this out?"

"She came at her regular time this morning, but she didn't stay—just said for me to tell you."

"I sure hate to lose her. She's been with us so long she seems like a member of the family. I don't know where we'll find anyone else we like so well. I dread breaking the news to Eunice, but I guess she has to know."

But suddenly Miss Mattie's heart lifted a little as she saw a spot of silver in the dark cloud. She had meant to tell Cousin Edith to leave, and now she didn't have to worry about how to do it. This gave her a perfect excuse.

"Of course we can't accommodate company without help," she said. "It looks like you'll have to leave, Cousin Edith."

Cousin Edith giggled. "Why, I wouldn't think of going now, just when you need me," she said. "With Cousin Eunice working and you so busy with all your church activities, I can do the cooking and cleaning for a while, and maybe by the time I have to go, you'll have found a new maid. No, don't thank me," she said as Miss Mattie started to speak. "I'm glad to do it. It will work out fine for everyone. You won't have Arline's wages to pay, and I won't feel so bad about what my visit is costing you."

"But—"

"I won't hear another word about it," Cousin Edith said in a hearty manner which her high, thin voice was ill able to sustain. "It's all settled."

As accustomed as she was to having her own way, Miss Mattie couldn't find any way to insist on it without being totally inhospitable. So she said nothing. At least, she consoled herself, Cousin Edith had said, "By the time I have to go," so she didn't intend to stay permanently. That was some comfort.

Miss Eunice was as distressed as Miss Mattie over Arline's defection, and Cousin Edith's plan for taking over the work didn't seem to comfort her.

Miss Mattie said gruffly, "Well, don't worry about it yet, Sister. I'll go to see Arline this evening, and maybe I can get her to change her mind."

But Arline wouldn't. "You and Miss Eunice have been good to me, and I hates to leave, but Ray John has been wanting me to come up there and stay with him, and I think I better go," she said.

"But you don't like Birmingham," Miss Mattie protested. "You know how it is up there—so much smoke and soot in the air that white curtains are black in a week. I've heard you say that every time you visit, you can't wait to get back to fresh, clean air."

"Yes'm, and I don't like the noise and crowds either. But still, it's best to go."

"Why? If you need more money, maybe I could—"

"No'm, it ain't that. You pays me enough."

"Then what is it? I know you've been a little dissatisfied since Cousin Edith came, but she won't be here much longer, and—"

"You right certain about that?"

"Why, of course. She'll go back to Texas before long."

Arline shook her head. "Miss Mattie, it ain't my place to tell you this, I reckon, but we've knowed each other a long time, and I looks on you as my friend, so even if it makes you mad, I'm gonna tell you. That woman ain't up to no good. I ain't for certain what she aims to do, but I don't want to wait around to find out."

"But that's foolish. She isn't going to do anything except finish out her visit and then go back to Texas. Why don't you take a week off from work, Arline—I'll even pay you your wages while you're off—and by the time you're ready to come back, Cousin Edith will be gone."

Again Arline shook her head. "You ever notice how many clothes she's got with her? She come to stay a good long spell. I ain't sure she's ever gonna leave. She ain't got no kinfolks to go back to; I heard her say that myself. And when you think about it, that ain't natural."

"I don't see anything unnatural about it," Miss Mattie said sharply. "Older folks die out, and she's never had any children."

"You and Miss Eunice never had any kids neither," Arline retorted, "but you got plenty of kin. No'm, that woman ain't like ordinary folks."

"I remember that you said something like that before,"

Miss Mattie said slowly. "I admit she's a little strange, but—"

"More than a little," Arline said darkly. "You and Miss Eunice has so many things on yo' minds that you ain't noticed her as close as I has. One thing you've probably noticed though is that she don't eat hardly nothing. But did you know she takes about a hundred pills a day? I ain't never seen the like of pills she's got in her room. But she's in good health other than them coughing spells she has once in a while. She ain't taking them pills for sickness; she's getting her nourishment from them."

Miss Mattie started to say something, but Arline rushed on. "And something else—she's dumb about some things. Little things that anybody ought to know. Like one day I noticed the hem was coming out of her dress, and I handed her a safety pin and told her to pin it up and I'd sew it back later. She didn't even know how to work a safety pin! She just stood there looking at it, and after a minute when she thought I had my back turned, she slid the pin inside a book in the table and just ran her fingernail over that hem, and it stayed up. I couldn't believe my eyes, but sure enough, I looked in the book later, and there was the pin ... She don't know how to use scissors either, or a can opener," Arline added.

"But that's—that's ridiculous," Miss Mattie said.

"Yes'm, but it's the truth. You'd know it if you'd worked alongside her like I has. It's like she's learned all the hard things like reading and writing and driving a car but missed the simple ones she ought've learned at her mamma's knee. She's a strange one."

Miss Mattie couldn't deny that, but she said, "Everybody has their peculiarities. As long as a person believes in God and tries to do right, we ought to overlook the odd things they do. Cousin Edith has great faith. She believed in the healings before anybody else."

"Yes'm. Them healings has done a lot of good for both black and white, and I ain't saying nothing against them. But it's funny they didn't start till Miss Edith come here, even though Miss Lidell was here since fall. And it's funny how Miss Edith has got to know every single thing about every single one of them healings. It ain't so she can rejoice and praise God like you do, and it ain't so she can feel good about the people, 'cause she don't hardly know them. The best I can make out, she just likes to watch what's going on.

I tell you, it's just about run me crazy trying to figure out what she's up to, and I still don't know. But she gives me the heebie-jeebies, and I don't want to stay there with her no longer. So I'm leaving, and the only thing that could make me change my mind would be to hear that Miss Edith is done gone."

Miss Mattie sighed. "I wish you wouldn't go, but if you're determined, I want to give you a little going-away present."

"You don't have to do that," Arline protested, but her eyes lit up when Miss Mattie pressed a ten-dollar bill into her hands.

"Well, I guess I'd better get home," Miss Mattie said awkwardly. "If you ever want to come back to work, we'll be glad to have you."

Arline's gaze shifted. "Maybe someday," she said vaguely. Her eyes came sharply back to Miss Mattie. "You and Miss Eunice take care," she said urgently.

24

That same week Maureen Granger discovered in herself the quality that lies at the root of every advance the human race has made—a discontent with things as they are. Once she had thought that if she could walk like other people, she would be satisfied; she would never ask for anything more. Now, like her remote ancestors who built the wheel, she found that walking was not enough. Her life was still restricted; to make it less so, she would have to become more mobile, and since there was no public transportation in Lanier, that meant learning to drive. It was easy to arrive at the conclusion, but putting it into action would be difficult.

However, she hesitated only long enough to make her plans. After supper the following night when her parents were settled in the living room, Mr. Granger with the newspaper and Mrs. Granger with her knitting, Maureen broached the subject. "Daddy, I want to learn to drive."

Mr. Granger looked up from the paper. "To drive!" he said in a surprised voice.

Maureen said eagerly, "If I could drive, I'd be able to go

179

shopping when I wanted to and buy whatever I liked. You know I've never picked out a dress in a store; I've always had to take whatever they sent me. I could drive Mother wherever she wants to go too. Now that she isn't tied down with me, she'll want to get out more."

"Well, I guess it would be convenient," Mr. Granger said in an uncertain voice.

"There's no call for Maureen to learn to drive," Mrs. Granger said. "If we want to go somewhere, we can always arrange it with you beforehand, and you can send someone from the plant to drive us. Maureen is better now, but she isn't completely well yet. After being handicapped so long, she can't be as strong or have as good nerves as the average person. I don't want her to do too much too soon."

Mr. Granger looked at Maureen, and she knew he was going to agree with her mother as he always did. She said quickly, "My nerves are all right. I know I could drive as well as anyone else if you'd teach me. Please, Daddy."

Mr. Granger looked even more doubtful. Maureen rushed on, "I wish I could make you see how much this means to me. It will make it possible for me to do lots of things I've never been able to do before, and it will tell everyone that I'm normal. Lots of people don't believe that yet. They see me walking around, so they know I'm all right physically, but they still think I'm mentally deficient."

Maureen couldn't have found an argument more effective with her father. Always he had loved this only child of his, but always he had been ashamed of her. Now at last he could be proud, and he would allow nothing to stand in the way of that pride.

"I don't know how I can find time to teach you," he said. "Sunday is the only day I have off, and usually that's pretty well filled up."

With those words Maureen knew permission had been granted. All that remained was to settle the arrangements. She had her answer ready.

"What I really need is someone to give me a lesson every day," she said. "Someone who lives nearby and has a lot of free time."

After a few minutes of thought Mr. Granger made the suggestion she expected. "How about the oldest Clayton boy? I'd pay him, course, and he'd probably be glad to earn some money."

Mrs. Granger interrupted with an exclamation. "Why Calvin! The son of a moonshiner? How can you even consider such a thing? It's out of the question."

Mr. Granger's lips tightened. He was a small and mild-mannered man, but he was accustomed to ruling his household with the same unquestioned authority he exercised in his business, and although he frequently thought of his wife as a saint, it was never when she so forgot herself as to belittle his judgment.

His manner was still mild as he said, "The boy can't help what his daddy does. He's all right. I see him at church every Sunday, and I've never heard any harm of him."

"Like father, like son, I've always heard," Mrs. Granger said.

"Maybe so, but Mrs. Clayton is a good woman, and I'm satisfied she's brought her children up right."

"All the same, Junior has been around whiskey all his life. What if he shows up drunk? How do you think Maureen could cope with that?"

Mr. Granger eyed his daughter. "All right, I expect," he said dryly, surprising both Mrs. Granger and Maureen, who hadn't realized that her daddy knew how much like him she was.

He looked back at Mrs. Granger and said without the slightest change in his mild voice, "I've made up my mind, Inez, but I'll talk to the boy first if you're nervous about him drinking." He put his newspaper up before his face, a signal that the conversation was over.

Two days later Junior Clayton came after school to give Maureen her first driving lesson. As soon as she saw him, the anticipatory nervousness she had felt all day left her. Looking at his dark, handsome face with the startling blue eyes that could not find a place to rest, she thought, he's as nervous as I am. Perhaps more, because he doesn't know me as well as I know him.

Of course, she had never before seen Junior up close, or spoken to him or heard his voice. But she had watched him through her telescope. She knew his curiously graceful walk, so unlike the adolescent awkwardness described in books, his quick and frequent laughter, and his authoritative and protective attitude toward his brothers.

She wanted to know more about him, but her interest was more in the species than the individual. All her knowledge of young men came from books; she had never had a chance to observe one at first hand. It would have been nice, she thought, if Junior had been a little older, closer to her own age. But a practical person will use whatever material is at hand, and Maureen was intensely practical.

She said, "Come in a minute. I'll get my coat and be right with you."

Junior followed her into the living room, looking about with dazed eyes.

Maureen said awkwardly, "I'd introduce you to my mother, but she's lying down with a headache."

Junior made no reply. He seemed struck dumb. Maureen thought, I'm not saying the right things. I'm making him feel shy. But what should I say? I don't know how to talk to a boy.

"Would you like a Coke or something before we start?" she asked.

"What? Oh. No, I guess not. We better get on with the driving lesson. I ain't got but about two hours to spend."

His words hit Maureen with a little shock. Why, he doesn't use any better grammar than the servants, she thought. Yet his voice was deep and pleasant.

Once in the car Junior seemed more at ease. It was as if he'd at last found his own ground, and he launched enthusiastically into his explanations and demonstrations of clutch, brake, and gears.

After a while he said, "Well, I think you've got that. Now you need to get the feel of guiding the car. I ain't sure what's the best way to do that." He scratched his head.

"How did you learn?" Maureen asked.

"That ain't got much to do with it, because I started back when I was just a little shaver. I'd sit in my daddy's lap and guide the car while he worked the gears and all."

Maureen eyed the space under the steering wheel.

"I can't sit in your lap," she said in a matter-of-fact voice, "but if you'd move closer to the door, I could sit over next to you and be almost under the wheel."

Without a word he moved over, and Maureen slid closer to him. She could smell the faint odor to tobacco and feel the hard muscles of his legs against hers. She wasn't sure she liked being so close to him. But she shut her mind to everything except keeping the car in a straight path down the road.

182

She was doing fine until Junior decided it was time to turn around and go back. "Turn it at that road on the left just ahead," he said.

Maureen turned—and saw that they were headed straight for a deep ditch.

"God damn," Junior shouted. He grabbed the wheel and turned it hard to the left and then back to the right. They rocked to a stop on the side road, and for a moment Junior sat silent, white-faced, and motionless.

"I'm sorry," Maureen said in a shaking voice. "I guess I didn't turn soon enough. I don't blame you for being angry."

He looked at her in surprise. "I wasn't mad at you. I was scared. I thought sure Mr. Granger's car was gonna get busted up on our first day out. I was so scared I didn't know what I was saying. I guess you're mad at me for cussing at you."

"Why should I be? It was my fault."

"Naw, it was mine. I didn't tell you to turn soon enough; I forgot a new driver can't do things automatically. By the time you figured out where I wanted you to turn and how to move the wheel, it was too late. It was my fault, and I guess when you tell your daddy about it, he won't want me to teach you any more."

"Do you want to quit?"

"Gosh, no. Mr. Granger's paying me real good, and I don't get many chances to make money, especially doing something this easy."

"What kind of jobs do you usually have?"

"I ain't never had what you could call a real job. Once in a while I get a chance to help somebody load a truck or something like that, and I pick cotton in the fall. 'Course I do might near all the work at home when Daddy is off on a job."

"It must've been hard for you to be the man of the house so young." She tried to think what it would be like to have that kind of responsibility, but there was nothing in her experience to tell her.

"I'm almost seventeen," he said. "How old are you?"

"Nineteen."

"You sure don't look it. If anybody had asked me, I'd have said you was about my age. You're pretty too. I was surprised about that, you know. I don't hardly know what I was expecting, but it sure wasn't what I found."

183

Maureen knew what he meant. He had been afraid some sign of her affliction would remain, and just seeing her normal was enough to make him think her pretty. She wasn't really. Her mouth was too wide for her thin face, and her hair was plain brown and too heavy to curl. Her green eyes were attractive, but that was hardly enough to make up for the rest. Still, it was nice to hear a compliment, and she thanked him for it.

"Well, I guess we better go back," he said. "I'm sure sorry it turned out this way. I'd liked to go on teaching you."

"There's no reason you can't. I'm not going to tell Daddy what happened. It was nothing much anyhow, thanks to your quick reaction."

"Gosh, I sure appreciate that. I promise you I won't let it happen again. I think I was a little nervous this evening, it being the first time and all."

"So was I," Maureen said truthfully. "But I'm not any more, are you? And I have learned a lot. I think I can guide the car back into the road if you tell me how before we start."

That night when her father asked her how the driving lesson went, Maureen answered, "Fine."

Mrs. Granger looked up from her knitting and said, "I was worried sick the whole time she was gone. I had such a severe headache I had to lie down all evening. I just know something bad is going to happen."

"Now, Inez, I told you before that I'm satisfied Junior is a responsible kind of boy. You've just got to put the worry out of your mind." Mr. Granger picked up his newspaper.

Maureen began thinking over all Junior had taught her this afternoon. And she thought something else. As soon as her mother had grown accustomed to the driving lessons, she would bring up the matter of going to school.

She didn't mean to leave home. After all, one of the reasons she'd wanted to be healed was so she could be a comfort to her parents instead of a shame, so she could repay them for all the years they had devoted to her. But she also wanted to do something in the world; she wanted it for Daddy and Mother's sake and for her own too. She'd like to be a teacher like Miss Lidell. That shouldn't take more than five years, one at the high school right here in Lanier and four at the university in Tuscaloosa, which was so close she could come home every weekend and even at night if necessary. She could be company to her parents and go to school at the same time, and how proud they would be of her when she was a teacher.

But she'd have to move slowly with her new plans because it would take Mother a while to adjust to them.

25

Gaynell glanced around the office. All straight. She was ready to go home but reluctant to start, not only because it was raining but also because of what would happen when she got there.

As she had expected, Silas had given her a little time. Time, he said, to think over Mr. Lyle's offer and come to her senses. He did not, however, leave her to think it over alone but constantly talked about the advantages she—and the whole Moore family—would enjoy if she married Mr. Lyle. He admonished her for her stubborn nature and insisted she spend an hour each night praying for the Spirit's guidance, evidently having no doubt the Spirit would guide her into the path Silas had already chosen. He even had her mother talk to her, although he did not normally feel any need to call on Annabel to supplement his authority.

This morning after breakfast Annabel said, "Gaynell, your papa has got his heart set on this marriage, and I think myself it would be a good thing. I wish you could see it."

Gaynell shook her head.

Annabel sighed. "Well, I don't think you ought to be forced, and I told Papa that. But he looks at it different. He feels like you're being foolish and says it's up to him to drive the foolishness out of your heart with a rod. I have to admit that's scriptural, so I can't go against him, Gaynell. I'm mighty afraid if you don't come around to his way of thinking today, you're gonna get a whipping tonight. I heard him tell Andy to bring in three or four limber switches, and I think they're for you, because he don't ever use a switch except when somebody ain't yet healed from the strap. Gaynell, I wish you could see clear to marrying Mr. Lyle. I wouldn't ask you just on our account, but I really think

185

you'd have a nice, easy life. And so does Papa. He only wants what's best for you."

Goaded beyond endurance, Gaynell cried, "No, he doesn't. He wants that land Mr. Lyle promised him. He's selling me, just like I told him before. Silas Moore may think he's a Christian, but he's going to burn in hell for his meanness. I hate him. And every other child he's got will hate him just as soon as they start thinking for themselves."

Her mother was staring at her with her mouth open and shock on her face. "Gaynell, you hush right now, you hear me? I ain't never heard such awful talk in my whole life. If I didn't know the strain you're under, I'd wash your mouth out with lye soap. 'Honor thy father and mother,' the Bible says. I ain't gonna tell your papa how you've broke that commandment—he'd skin you alive if I did—but you better pray for forgiveness all the way to work."

So Gaynell knew there would be no help from her mother. Mamma wouldn't defy Silas. She didn't even want to defy him, because she had been brainwashed, just like those men in the prison camps during the war. Annabel believed that Silas was nearly always right, or always nearly right, and in either case wife and children must obey him. She prided herself on never having interfered with his discipline, and Gaynell knew she would not interfere now.

So as the time to leave the office approached, Gaynell was filled with fright and dread. She feared she couldn't take what Silas had in store for her. It was wrong to be so cowardly, but she knew the limits of her small endurance, and she knew she must not reach those limits.

She didn't want to die. But if she had to, she'd rather die painlessly. She walked into the inner office and opened the top right-hand drawer of Dr. Taylor's desk. This was where he kept the sample medicines the detail men gave him. She knew he had some sleeping pills, because she had already checked. The bottle wasn't full, but she thought there would be enough. She picked up the bottle and read the directions. Yes, there should be enough. Did she have the nerve?

She didn't ask herself whether it would be right. She had already been through all that, and she knew it wasn't right. But she didn't care. If she could defy Silas, it should be easy to defy God. Yes, she thought she had the nerve. She was going to do it. She unbuttoned the high neck of her dress and stuck the bottle in her homemade brassiere.

She hoped no one would blame Dr. Taylor. She didn't see

how they could though. Surely they'd know Dr. Taylor didn't give her the pills. But maybe he would blame himself for not being more careful with them. Or for not insisting on finding out what was wrong with her. Perhaps she should leave a note.

But that presented some difficulties. There was a possibility the note would be found prematurely, before she'd had a chance to do the deed. Also, a note would cause an investigation. She had thought this out carefully in the week since Silas whipped her, and it seemed possible she could do it in such a way that it would not require a medical examination to ascertain the cause of death. She wanted to avoid that. Except for Silas, she loved her family, and she would avoid disgrace for them if she could.

Maybe she could think how to write a note that would do that if she had time to think about it. But it was five o'clock; there was no time for lengthy planning. Oh, why hadn't she thought of the note before? If only she had more time, if only she could put it off a few days, if only Silas wasn't going to whip her tonight.

Maybe he wouldn't. It was Friday night, and they'd have to go to church, so maybe he wouldn't find time to whip her tonight.

But she knew that was a false hope. He would do it before church, probably as soon as she got home. Mamma had said he was going to. "If you don't come around to his way of thinking," she said. Gaynell couldn't do that.

But maybe she could make Silas believe she had. Or that she would if she had a little more time. Suddenly, as if it had been there all the time, the answer leapt out at her. She didn't have to write a note. She didn't even have to take the pills with her.

But caution intervened. Her new plan might not work. She'd better take the pills just in case it didn't. If she didn't have to use them, she could put them back Monday morning before Dr. Taylor got to the office.

When she got outside, it had started raining, a slow, cold drizzle that would thoroughly wet her before she got home. For a minute she was tempted to go back upstairs and wait for Dr. Taylor, who was out on a call. But then she thought he might discover the theft of the pills before she got away with them. She tied her scarf over her hair and walked out into the rain.

She still had the pills in her bosom when Silas met her

187

about a hundred yards from the house. She felt as if the outline of the bottle might be showing through her wet clothes, but a quick glance downward reassured her. The shapeless wool coat hid it. But she could feel it burning against her skin like the fires of hell, if there were any fires—or any hell for that matter, other than the one right here on earth. She guessed maybe she would find out about that soon if her new plan didn't work and she had to use the sleeping pills.

Silas said, "Well, Gaynell, you've had a week. What have you decided?" He took off his old felt hat and shook the raindrops off it as he spoke. She thought he was trying to be casual, but his willingness to walk out into the wet to meet her indicated his anxiety, and the set of his hard mouth told her what he was determined to do if she gave the wrong answer.

She spoke quickly, saying the hypocritical words she had rehearsed all the way home "I want to do the right thing, and I've prayed and prayed about it without getting an answer. So I wondered if the answer is in the Bible instead of in prayer? If I had a week or two to study, I believe I might find it."

She could see him turning her words over in his mind. Finally he said, "I can't fault the desire to search the Scriptures, Daughter. But I ain't sure what Woodrow Lyle will say. He's been mighty patient with you already, giving you a whole week to think it over. I hate to ask him for any more time."

"But surely he'd want me to know God's will before I say yes?"

"When you put it that way—"

She had put it that way on purpose. She wanted to suggest that her answer would be yes; otherwise, she hadn't a hope of getting Silas to agree.

But he shook his head. "I promised him an answer tonight at church, and I feel like I've got to give it to him. I've always been a man of my word."

"Then let me ask him for more time," she said. "You can see him at church and tell him that he can bring me home and stay a while. *I'll* ask him for some time to study the Scriptures, and I don't think he'll refuse. Not if he's the good Christian man I think he is."

And not if I can bring myself to play up to him in the right way. I've learned a thing or two about men that wasn't

188

taught to me in church, and I think I can whet Mr. Lyle's appetite enough that he'll be glad to wait another week or maybe even two. I'll have to remember to do it in a sanctimonious way though, casting my eyes down modestly and talking a lot about God and the church.

Silas was looking relieved. "Yeah, I think that might be all right," he said in his slow, deliberate way. "There ain't no doubt Woodrow wants to do the Lord's will, and besides, he'll see the benefit of having a wife who's up on all the Scriptures about marriage. I've heered tell he had to lay the strap to his first wife now and again for her willful ways, and there ain't no man who likes submission more than one who's had experience in the other direction."

He nodded his head in satisfaction and looked toward Gaynell. "I'm real pleased with you, Daughter. I was kinda afeared you was setting off on the wrong path, but I reckon that chastisement I give you the other night done its work, 'cause you seem like the sweet little gal you was before. I wouldn't say this to the others, but you always was my favorite. Being the first was one thing, I guess, but that wasn't all of it. It seemed like you always wanted to please."

Gaynell did not raise her eyes. She thought if she did, he'd be bound to see the hatred in them. Yes, I always wanted to please, she thought, because I knew if I didn't, you'd beat me half to death. As for that whipping doing its work, it just put the finishing touches on what you'd done a long time ago. It made me hate you so much I could watch you die with pleasure. But you're too mean to die.

She waited a minute to be sure she could control her voice, and then she said, "You won't whip me again then?" She had to make sure now, because the pills, if needed, would have to be taken at supper. She might not get a chance afterward.

"Course not. You know I ain't in the habit of thrashing a young'un that don't need it. Now that you've decided to do the right thing, I doubt you'll ever have to be whipped again."

You're righter than you know, she thought grimly. But then she relaxed. It was going to be all right. She had at least another week, maybe two, and surely Warner would come back before then. He must come back; he must.

She knew a lot of people thought he was dead. She heard all the gossip in town, not because she had any friends there—unless one counted Dr. Taylor, and he never gossiped—

but because she heard the conversations of the patients. She knew all the suspicions against Miss Lidell, but she didn't believe them.

She didn't know Miss Lidell well, but she seemed good and kind. And Dr. Taylor loved her. Anybody Dr. Taylor loved must be good, for, next to Warner, he was the best man who ever lived. Gaynell wasn't sure Miss Lidell was aware of Dr. Taylor's feelings, but she herself had seen the way he looked at her when he thought no one was noticing. It was the same hungry look Gaynell had often seen in Warner's eyes.

No, Miss Lidell had not killed Warner. All that talk of a lover's quarrel was absurd. Warner and Miss Lidell had never been lovers; he had dated her a few times during a spat with Gaynell, that was all. Afterward, he and Miss Lidell remained friends, and perhaps, if things had been different, Gaynell might have become friendly with her too, but Warner's friends could not be hers until it was safe for their interest in each other to be known.

Nobody had killed Warner. He wasn't dead. If he were, it would be as if she were cut in two, and that couldn't happen without awareness of the pain. Of course, it was painful to have him gone, but at least she knew he was still alive somewhere, and that helped.

But knowing he was alive, she wanted to stay alive too, and even more than that, she wanted to keep his baby alive. She knew men didn't much care for babies, but they were necessary, weren't they, to make the world go on? Kind men like Warner were the ones who ought to have children, not men like Silas. Warner would be a good father. And later when it was time for him to die, there would be something of him left. Yes, she had to keep the baby alive. If she could.

Warner would come back. He knew about the baby, and he knew how strict Silas was. In her first desperation she had thought perhaps that was why he left, that he was avoiding the difficulties. It was wrong to think like that. He had said they would be married, and he had never yet broken a promise to her. He wouldn't break that one. But he'd better hurry, because she couldn't hold out much longer.

One more week. Two at the most. That was all Silas and Mr. Lyle would give her. And it was all nature would give her too. If she had calculated right, she was about two and a half months along. In two more weeks the bulge of her abdomen would probably be detectable by any experienced eye.

26

After all, Stella went to Valerie's wedding with Sam. She could do nothing else since Valerie herself asked him. Anyway, she no longer felt as she once had about the danger of being with him in a romantic atmosphere, because as the days passed, she became more and more convinced that his interest in her was purely friendly with no overtones of either love or sex. Once or twice she had caught herself feeling a slight twinge of disappointment, but she knew that was only the residue of her old physical desires, which were almost conquered now.

She had no way of knowing how much of her confidence was due to Sam's control.

The wedding party left from the boarding house in two separate cars and rendezvoused at a service station on the outskirts of Columbus where, it being Saturday afternoon and the courthouse closed, they bought a marriage license presigned by all the proper authorities and were directed to a minister.

The minister took Charles and Valerie into his study for a talk, decided they were mature enough to know their own minds, and agreed to perform the ceremony. His church next door was decorated for a wedding at five o'clock, he said, and if they preferred, the ceremony could be held there.

The five of them went to the church, and the minister read a marriage service which included a promise to obey, one that Stella felt she would much rather omit if she ever got married. However, Valerie didn't seem disconcerted and made her responses in a firm little voice. In less than thirty minutes it was over, and the minister had pocketed his twenty dollars and gone back to his house.

Sam said, "Remembering that Mississippi is a dry state, I brought some champagne. Even a new church member ought to toast his own bride, Charles."

So they went to the hotel, drank some of the champagne, talked about how smoothly everything had worked out, how

191

lucky it was to find the church decorated, and what a nice ceremony it had been. After a while Sam said he'd better get back to Lanier, and he and Stella left.

In the car Stella said, "I hadn't thought about it before, but what do you do about your practice when you go out of town?"

"Hope to hell nobody gets sick," he said. "The telephone book and the sign on my office door give Grant's number. If it's not serious, he tells the patient to wait; if it is, he tries to find me or sends him to the hospital in Tuscaloosa. I refuse to be responsible for sending somebody to Dr. Marvin."

"It sounds as if you don't have much faith in him."

"I wouldn't send my dog to him, if I had a dog. I don't have much use for a doctor like Marvin, all personality and no knowledge. I doubt if he's opened a medical journal in twenty years."

"That's a pretty harsh judgment, isn't it?"

"I wouldn't say it to anybody but you. How did we get started on this anyway?"

"I was wondering how you managed your work and if it would be possible for us to stay and have dinner with Charles and Valerie."

"I thought they'd rather we didn't. It's at least three hours until dinner time. If Charles is as eager as I'd be, he'll spend that time in bed."

She felt a catch at her heart. Until now she'd kept a tight lock on her imagination, but his words opened it. How nice it would be to spend a honeymoon with a man one loved, she thought. One would be free to enjoy sex in a pleasant, moderate way. One would not be tormented by urgency, or doubt, or fear that sex would become a master.

She shifted on the seat and turned to face Sam. "I haven't thanked you for bringing me to Valerie's wedding," she said. "Or for helping me get through the last ten days. I don't know what I'd do without you."

"You don't have to do without me, ever."

He didn't say anything else. He was driving very fast, looking at the road.

She wondered if he'd meant that statement to be as meaningful as it sounded, but she was afraid to ask. He might think she was being flirtatious. He couldn't know she only wanted assurance that it didn't mean anything.

They rode on in silence.

After a time Sam broke it abruptly. "Stella, I have a confession to make. It may end our—our friendship, but I've got to tell you anyway. The man with the cancer on his face didn't find you in the restaurant by accident. I sent him."

She was too shocked for speech. Shocked and angry.

Sam said, "I could excuse myself a dozen ways. I didn't hunt the man up; he came to my office and asked about you. And I didn't force you and Grant to break up. Both of you were free to overcome the difficulty if you could. All I did was set up a situation that was bound to occur sooner or later, although perhaps in a less unpleasant form. But I'm not offering those excuses. The truth is that I did it hoping for just what happened."

"To break us up. But why? Grant is your friend, and I thought I was too. And you . . . you betrayed us."

"No. I set it up for Grant to betray you."

"That's despicable. You're mean. Cruel."

"I guess so. I do horrible things to people—probe and cut and cauterize, and I don't really think about the pain I'm causing. A man who feels for other people as he feels for himself couldn't do that. So yes, I am cruel. And ruthless. You might as well know it."

"But that's only to help people," she said. "You have to be unkind in the beginning to be kind in the end." She paused, surprised to find herself defending him. She said slowly. "I suppose it was the same thing with Grant and me. You did us a kindness. But I hope you'll forgive me if I don't thank you for it."

"Do you want Grant back?"

"No. Not now. It wouldn't be any good if I did. There's too wide a gulf between us."

"Then will you forgive me?"

"You didn't make Grant break up with me, so there's really nothing to forgive. But don't try to manipulate me again, Sam. I won't stand for it."

He realized that she didn't understand why he had done it—not because he thought she and Grant were mismatched, but because he wanted her himself. But he was so glad to have the secret revealed without losing her friendship that he decided not to push his luck. He said, "It's only five miles home, and still too early to eat. What shall we do?"

"You'll have to check with Grant, won't you? I suppose

you'd better drop me off at the boarding house on your way to the drug store."

"I'm not going to the drug store. I'll call Grant and let him know I'm back. I want to spend the time with you, but somehow I don't fancy sitting in the living room with Mrs. Overly, so I wondered if we could go to my house."

"Lanier wouldn't approve of that, even in 1947."

"Lanier won't know. And if it does, what's the difference? We're adults. You don't expect to live by public opinion, do you, like the father and son in the fable, who ended up carrying the donkey?"

"Of course not. But I only defy convention when it's important to do so."

He raised his eyebrows.

She said in a flat, emotionless voice. "I fell in love my freshman year at college. It lasted a year, until he got drafted. We planned to get married after the war, but he was killed. I've always been glad I didn't live that year by public opinion, as you expressed it. But I don't plan to do it again."

After a moment he said, "You didn't have to tell me that."

"I don't know why I did. It's not something I talk about much."

"Shall I take you to the boarding house then?"

"No, I'll go to your house. I just thought you should know it's not a consent to anything."

"I remember what you said about manipulating you, and I promise not to. How's that?"

"Reassuring," she said lightly.

Sam turned in the driveway at the side of a large ranch-style house and drove into an attached garage. Stella said, "Do you own this house?"

"Yes, I bought it last year. I was tired of living at the hotel, and owning my own home was a dream I'd had for a long time. My family moved a lot during my childhood, living in rented houses wherever my father found a job, when he *could* find one. I like having a permanent place of my own. It makes me feel I belong somewhere. Question: Who are you, Sam Taylor? Answer: I'm the guy who lives in the white house on the corner."

"Yes, I see. But how do you manage? Do you do your own work?"

"I eat at the café most of the time, but now and then I cook for myself. A maid comes twice a week to clean."

194

"So you don't need a wife," she said with a smile in her voice.

"Not to cook and clean," he answered, just as lightly.

They went into the kitchen from the garage. Stella noticed that it was tidy and immaculate—the maid's work, she supposed. She doubted that Sam was so neat. She hardly noticed the dining room, because she was staring toward the living room. It had cream-colored walls, several large multicolored woven rugs on the floor, a built-in bookcase, a brown sofa in front of the fireplace, and several comfortable-looking chairs upholstered in various shades of yellow and orange.

"What a beautiful room," she said. "Somehow one doesn't expect a man to—"

"To be interested in decorating? Why not? Home is as important to a man as to a woman."

"I guess so, but don't you worry about people thinking you're sissy?"

His voice sounded amused. "Is that what you think? No, my dear, you've hit on the one thing in the world I *don't* worry about. Would you like to look at the rest of the house while I build a fire?"

When she came back, the talked about the house a few minutes, and then she said, "The fire feels good. It's turning cold again. But wasn't it nice to have such a springlike day for the wedding? A few more weeks, and it will really be spring. . . . I'm chattering, and you don't like that."

"From you I do. You're right. Spring is almost here. How long until school is out?"

"A little over three months. They'll be busy ones. We'll have to start practicing the senior play soon, and I'll have to plan the graduation exercises. . . . I'm not coming back next year, Sam."

He gave a start. "Why not?"

"I won't be asked. Mr. Dennis told me yesterday that I caused too much disturbance in the school. And it's true. People are always coming in to see me, wanting to be healed. I thought at first that it would soon be over. Lanier is a small town, and there couldn't be so many disabled people in it. Once they were cured—but it isn't working out that way. It seems as if everyone has friends or relatives in other places. People are coming now from other towns in the county, and soon they may be coming from farther away. I don't see any end to it."

195

"Why doesn't Mr. Dennis just tell people you can't be disturbed while you're teaching?"

"Because he's always had a policy that teachers are available for conferences at any time, and he doesn't want to change that just for me. I think he's uncomfortable about the healing; he feels that I'm a freak or a charlatan or something. So it's best that I leave. But it will be the same wherever I go. I have to use the power I have, and if I do, it will ruin my career. I'm in a trap, Sam, and there's nothing I can do about it."

"I see that. How much does teaching mean to you?"

"It's all I have now," she said simply.

"But you'll fall in love again and get married someday. Will you quit then as Valerie is going to do?"

"If you got married, would you quit being a doctor? It's the same thing. Teaching is what I do, and I do it well. Anyway, I'm never going to get married. So what do I do about the healing?"

"The next thing. Take one day at a time and get through it. That's trite, but it's true."

"I suppose so. But sometimes I wish I'd never been given that power . . . although maybe 'given' is the wrong word, because I don't feel as if the power to heal belongs to me. It's something apart from myself. It's—how can I say this—it's something added on without my consent. It's as if somebody is using me for some purpose of his own. I'm just a—a transmitter."

"Maybe all of us are in a way. Certainly what we think has an effect on other people, and how do we know where our thoughts come from?"

"That's true. I've no idea whether I create my own or whether they come into my mind from somewhere else. But at least I have the option of whether to put them into speech or action. I have a choice. Or did before this healing power came along."

"You still do. You can touch people or not touch them. If you refuse, the power is inoperative. The reason you don't refuse is because you feel that the power is good, even if it does cause you some inconvenience."

"Yes. And thus we get back to the same old quandary. The power is good, so even though it's ruining my life, I have to use it. . . . I seem to be always crying on your shoulder over some problem. Let's talk about something else."

"All right. Did anyone ever tell you how beautiful you are?"

He realized he was moving to a path he'd promised not to enter, but her talk of being here only three more months had made him reckless. He had thought to wait until she recognized affection before he introduced passion, but what difference did it make which came first? And passion was the quickest route.

"No," she said promptly. "I'm not beautiful. Attractive is the most you could say, and that might be stretching it a bit. My teeth should have been straightened when I was a child, but my parents couldn't afford it, and so—"

"And so you have the most erotic mouth I've ever seen." He traced its shape with his finger. Then he pulled her into his arms and kissed her, taking his time about it. His hands moved, and she gave a little cry and pressed against him, lifting her face for another kiss. When it ended, he moved his mouth to the V of her neckline.

The telephone on the nearby table shrilled. "God damn it," he said under his breath.

"Don't answer it," Stella murmured.

"I've got to, Stella." But he kept one arm tight around her as he reached for the receiver.

He listened a minute, said, "I'll be right there," and hung up.

Without moving away from him, Stella asked, "Who was it?"

"Owen Perry. His wife is in labor, and Owen's scared to death. He says Dr. Marvin is too, and he must be to agree to Owen's calling me." He stood up and reached for his coat.

"But it can't be serious, can it? If it were, they'd have taken her to the hospital. Sheriff Perry is just nervous because it's his first child."

"Possibly."

"And it isn't your case anyway. You don't have to go."

"Yes, I do. I've never refused to go when someone needs me."

"Mrs. Perry doesn't need you. She has a doctor. Don't go, Sam. Stay here."

His frustration at the interruption exploded into anger toward her. He said, "Good God, Stella, don't make it any more difficult. I don't have time to argue with you. Get your coat and come on."

Affronted by his decision and infuriated by his anger

197

toward her, she picked up her coat and purse and started for the door.

He had got himself under control now. He said, "You won't mind if I don't take you home immediately? I'd like to find out what's happening first. It won't take more than a few minutes, and then I'll take you home. From what Owen said, I think it will be a while before she's ready to deliver."

"No, I don't mind," she said, aware that it was a lie. She did mind. She minded being dismissed so unceremoniously, and she minded not being taken straight home, where she could pound on something in silent fury.

In the car he glanced at her face and said, "Stella, this interruption is as disappointing to me as it is to you. You must know that."

She made no reply. It couldn't be, she thought, or you wouldn't have accepted it so readily. Almost as if you welcomed it.

"There'll be other times for us now that we know we—"

"Belong together" was the rest of his sentence, but she didn't let him finish it. "No," she said, "there won't be another time. You're assuming a great deal to suppose there would have been one time. Just because I let you kiss me doesn't mean anything. I've kissed a lot of men." She didn't care what she said, anything to salvage her pride.

"Then don't act like a child. You're a grown woman, you know that in another two minutes we'd have been in my bedroom. So for God's sake, don't cry sour grapes by denying your own responses."

"All right, I won't. You're a doctor, so no doubt you were observing them clinically." There were angry tears in her eyes, and her voice was hoarse with them.

"Clinical observation? My God, in the condition I was in?" His voice shook with laughter, and his amusement only angered her further. He said more soberly, "Stella, I suppose after what you've been through, this seems another rejection, but—"

"But I should be getting used to them by now?" she snapped.

It *was* a rejection; his willingness to be interrupted showed her that. But that wasn't what was really bothering her. She could forgive him for stopping; what she couldn't forgive was herself, for starting. Actually she was glad they had been interrupted. But she knew it was merely fortuitous, and it cut down little on her self-contempt.

"Stella, be reasonable. I didn't quit because I had second thoughts. I want you as much now as I did before. More."

"Well, don't worry, you'll get me," she said bitterly. "I'm available. Oh God, am I available!"

"But only to me. It's not right to feel guilty about that."

"Don't fool yourself, Sam Taylor. I can be had by anyone who wants me, especially if he catches me at the right time. I told you about Jim. I loved him. But the night after I heard he was dead, I went to a motel with another man, a lieutenant I hardly knew. And when he was transferred, someone else took his place. Before it was over, there were four. Four men whose faces I can't even remember."

He said, "Good God, Stella, what a time to tell me. We're almost to the Perrys'. We'll have to wait to talk."

"There's nothing to talk about. Facts are facts. I thought I'd conquered my—lust. But I haven't. There were men before you, and there'll be others after you."

"Don't threaten me, Stella. You've said enough. More than enough, by God. Be good enough to shut up until I have a chance to answer you."

27

As Sam drove into the Perry driveway, a scream came from the house.

"Mrs. Perry," Sam said. He reached for his bag. "Get out and come in, Stella. It's too cold to stay in the car."

As they walked toward the front door, he said, "Don't let the noise bother you. She may not be in as much pain as it sounds like. Some women make more noise than others."

His advice fell on unheeding ears. Stella could not believe those screams meant anything but the direst agony. She said, "Try not to be long. I don't want to stay here."

"I'll just have a quick look," he promised. Two minutes later he had forgotten everything but the emergency before him.

Besides the patient there were five people in the room. Dr. Marvin was hovering over the bed murmuring at intervals, "Now, now, Adelaide." Fanny Sue Langford, Adelaide's neighbor, was retying the long strips of cloth around the posts at the foot of the bed for Adelaide to pull on. Miss Mattie was standing by the bed murmuring a prayer, and Mrs. Alexander, her cousin, was standing back away from everyone else, her eyes darting from one person to another. A white-faced Owen was holding Adelaide's hand and looking as if he might faint at any minute.

"Get out," Sam said to him.

He stared stupidly, seeming not to comprehend.

"I said get out," Sam said impatiently. "And the rest of you stand back. I want to see what's going on here."

Dr. Marvin summoned a weak smile. "Nothing much," he said. "But she's only been in labor nine hours. It might take twice that long. I'm glad you're here though. Maybe it will calm Owen down a bit. He's giving us more trouble than Adelaide is."

Sam finished his examination and stepped back from the bed. "You ladies carry on for a while. Dr. Marvin and I need some coffee. Have you got some made?"

"Yes, on the stove," Miss Mattie answered. "I made it as soon as I heard you were coming." She turned to the bed and didn't notice that Cousin Edith followed the men out of the room.

In the kitchen Sam poured two cups of coffee and looked at the older doctor. "What do you plan to do?"

"Do? Why, nothing," Dr. Marvin said in a blustering voice. "She'll have the baby all right. It's just going to take a while."

"There's no way on God's earth she can deliver that baby alive, and you know it. Why in hell didn't you send her to Tuscaloosa?"

Dr. Marvin drew himself up to his impressive six-foot-two. His distinguished face under its shock of white hair was cold. "I've been delivering babies thirty years," he said, "and I've never yet had to call on a surgeon to help me."

Sam shrugged. There was no point in further recrimination. But Dr. Marvin was not finished. "I don't think we'll be able to work together, Dr. Taylor," he said, "and since Owen called you, I'm going home."

"No, by God, this is your case, and you're not going to turn it over to me after you've bungled it. I'll do the best I can, but you'll stay, or I'll tell Owen Perry what you've done."

At that point they both became conscious that someone

was choking and gasping just outside the kitchen door. Sam moved quickly in the direction of the sound, but by the time he got there, Cousin Edith had recovered her breath.

"I'm all right," she said. "I'll get a cup of coffee now." She passed on into the kitchen as the doctors went down the hall, but by the time they got to the door of the bedroom, she was close behind them again and followed them in.

Stella glimpsed the two doctors as they went through the hall. She started to get up and then sank back into her chair as she realized Sam wasn't even looking her way. He had forgotten her. She was glad he had. She didn't want him to think about anything right now except the woman in the bedroom who was screaming with monotonous regularity.

She looked at Sheriff Perry, but he didn't seem aware of her either. He was sitting in a chair with his face hidden in his hands. She thought he might be crying. She realized that her hands were clasped together so tightly they were hurting. She put them on the arms of the chair and tried to relax. But the next scream tightened her muscles again.

After a while she noticed that the intensity of the screams had diminished. In a few minutes Sam came into the living room. Owen stood up.

Sam said, "I've given her a shot to ease the pain. She's probably still going to scream, but I thought you'd feel better if you knew that she'll hardly be aware of what she's doing. Owen, I think I'd better be honest with you. We're in trouble. I think we can save Adelaide, but we'll probably lose the baby."

Owen nodded, and Sam turned to go back. Then he noticed Stella. "I'm sorry," he said. "Maybe Owen can take you home."

She shook her head, and he said vaguely, "Well, then . . ." and went back into the bedroom.

Her eyes had followed Sam, and when she looked back at Owen, she saw that he was staring at her, as if he had only this moment become aware of her presence. He said, "Miss Lidell, they say you have a healing touch. I don't know whether to believe it, but—would you touch Adelaide?"

"I don't think they'll let me go in," she said.

"Please."

She got up, walked down the hall to the bedroom door, and knocked. After a moment she pushed it open. Sam was bending over the bed and did not look up. Sweat was pouring down his face, and one of the women wiped it away with

201

a towel. Stella walked to the head of the bed. Timidly she reached out and touched Adelaide's hand. Adelaide did not seem to feel it, and nothing happened. Stella turned to leave. Sam said, "Don't go."

Startled, Stella stopped in her progress to the door. One of the women was crying quietly. Adelaide's screams were hoarse now, but they still went on and on with scarcely a pause between them. Stella thought they would go on forever, that there would be no end to this agony. And then she began to be afraid that they would stop, suddenly perhaps, and as each new cry began, she prayed that it would go on to the end. After a long time she noticed that Miss Mattie was moving toward the bedside with a white pad in her hands. Sam handed her a bloody, misshapened mass and said, "Give it to Stella."

Numbly Stella took the thing Miss Mattie handed her. She looked down at it, and nausea rose into her throat. Anger followed immediately. Sam had done this on purpose. He was getting revenge for their quarrel—or trying to teach her some kind of lesson that he in his great wisdom thought she needed. She could kill him for doing this to her. With a shudder she looked down again at what she held and suddenly it was not just a horrible mass of flesh. It was a little dead baby, with arms and legs and—but its face was flattened and inhuman. She picked up one of the tiny hands. It was perfect, not like the misshapened head. She began to cry.

Suddenly the small thing gasped and began to cry too, startling Stella so that she very nearly dropped it. Without looking around, Sam said, "You can clean him up now, Miss Mattie, and Stella, you go tell Owen he has a son and you to thank for it."

Miss Mattie took the baby, who was now crying angrily.

There was an exclamation from the bedside and Sam said, "She's hemorrhaging—Marvin! Get over here and help me. What's her blood type?"

Dr. Marvin shook his head helplessly. "Good God," Sam said. He turned to Fanny Sue. "Go get that boiling water and start cooling it. We'll keep her blood vessels from collapsing and buy a little time. Bring some more towels over here."

Stella stumbled out of the room.

Miss Mattie said sharply, "Get those towels, Cousin Edith, and help Dr. Taylor."

Cousin Edith didn't move or make any reply, and after a moment Miss Mattie hastily wrapped the baby, put him in the bassinet, and moved quickly to the bed. She could finish bathing the baby later. But why didn't Cousin Edith help?

Miss Mattie and Cousin Edith went home at eleven-thirty. Miss Mattie was so tired she could hardly move, but Cousin Edith seemed as fresh as she had this morning. Of course she didn't do anything except stand around while the rest of us worked, Miss Mattie thought. When Cousin Edith had insisted on going, Miss Mattie thought she might be useful, especially since Sarah Collins had canceled out at the last minute because of sickness in the family. But Cousin Edith hadn't been any help at all. You'd have thought it was the first baby she'd ever seen born for all she knew about what to do.

As they walked into the house, Miss Mattie said, "I'm going to have a cup of hot chocolate before I go to bed. Would you like some?"

"Yes, I would." Cousin Edith followed Miss Mattie into the kitchen and sat down at the table. "Everything turned out all right, didn't it?" she remarked.

"Yes, but you didn't help much," Miss Mattie said bluntly. "Hadn't you ever been at a confinement before?"

Cousin Edith didn't answer for a minute. Then she said, "No, to tell you the truth, I hadn't. That may seem strange to you, but somehow nobody ever asked me."

"I don't wait to be asked," Miss Mattie said. "I believe in going where you're needed. . . . Well, I can see how you might not know what to do the first time. Anyway, everything got done, and I believe Dr. Taylor will pull Adelaide through. It's funny that the healing power didn't help her at all. When Stella came in, I was mighty glad to see her, even though it's not suitable for an unmarried girl to be at a childbed. I thought sure after Stella touched her, Adelaide would perk up and have the baby without any trouble. Why do you suppose it didn't work?"

Cousin Edith giggled and shook her head.

"It can't be that she's lost the power," Miss Mattie went on in a puzzled tone, "because it was afterward that the baby was healed. If Stella hadn't been there, I don't think it would have ever drawn a breath, or if it did, it would have been deformed and feebleminded."

"Well, maybe that's an entry for the credit side of the

ledger," Cousin Edith said. "Though of course, one can't tell what may happen later."

"It's in the Lord's hands," Miss Mattie said. "But Dr. Taylor thinks he'll be all right."

"I meant whether his birth will be a blessing or a curse," Cousin Edith said.

Miss Mattie stared at her. "A baby is always a blessing," she said firmly. "I declare, Cousin Edith, sometimes I don't understand you at all."

28

Maureen's driving lessons were going well. She had graduated to the driver's seat, but Junior sat close beside her—so he could take the wheel if she got in any trouble, he said. Maureen wondered a little about that. He didn't have to sit *quite* so close to be able to reach the steering wheel. Once it had crossed her mind that he might be attracted to her in the boy-girl way, but, when she examined that thought, she could see that it was foolish. As handsome as Junior was, there would be lots of girls interested in him, girls who shared with him a background of experiences in school, church, and town, girls whose knowledge of boys was not all out of books, who knew how to talk and flirt.

Not that she ever had any problem talking with Junior in spite of the difference in their lives, and she wouldn't have wanted to flirt even if she had known how. She had no interest in Junior beyond the driving lessons and what she learned from him about boys in general. This knowledge she expected to be useful when she went to high school in the fall and later on in college. Boys would be a part of her life from now on, and probably someday she would even get married.

She hadn't mentioned to Mother and Daddy her plans for going to school. One thing at a time. Her mother couldn't seem to realize that she was completely normal now, and she hampered Maureen at every turn. Even the other day when the sheriff came to see her, Mother told him Maureen was resting and couldn't be disturbed. She was in her room because Mother insisted on an afternoon nap, but she heard the voices downstairs and went to see what was happening.

Of course, she couldn't tell the sheriff anything. That was exactly what she said: "I can't tell you anything, Sheriff Perry. Warner disappeared while I was still afflicted, before I could get around as I can now. I spent most of my time inside the house and didn't know much about what was going on outside."

She hadn't lied. Everything she told him was the truth. And he accepted it and didn't ask her any more questions. "I didn't really think you'd know anything," he said, "but you were the only person out this way that I hadn't already talked to, so I thought I'd better be sure."

Maureen hoped she had done the right thing. The others obviously had not told either, but of course they had not seen the whole thing from beginning to end as she had. She didn't want to cause anyone any trouble. Especially Miss Lidell. Fortunately the sheriff hadn't even mentioned Miss Lidell. If he had, Maureen knew she wouldn't even have worried about whether what she said was true. For Miss Lidell she would have lied herself blue in the face.

The third day after his son was born Owen Perry finally calmed down enough to get back to work. By then he had given cigars to every man in town and invited every woman to come to see the baby. By then too he had recovered from the periodic attacks of fear which sent him racing home at odd times to see once again that Adelaide and the baby were all right.

When Dr. Taylor had finally come out of the bedroom that night, he looked tired, and his explanations were brief: "We got the hemorrhage stopped, and I think she'll be all right. The baby is normal, as far as I can tell. He has a broken leg, but that's a result of my manipulation. I couldn't worry too much about him during delivery, I was trying to save your wife. You've still got her *and* a baby, and I call it a miracle."

Owen had never been more than conventionally religious, but he gave some fervent thanks to God and also to Sam Taylor and Stella Lidell, who he felt were more directly responsible. He knew that but for Sam, Adelaide would have died and but for Stella Lidell, the baby would never have lived. He and Adelaide named the baby Samuel Lidell and called him Sammy.

Sam said little Sammy's leg would heal without a limp. Already his features had lost their flatness, and his head had a better shape. Owen thought him handsome and had no doubt he was alert, because he seemed to know his parents already. Each night Adelaide reported on his feedings, his naps, and his bowel movements, and Owen listened entranced.

In short, Owen was as doting as a new father ought to be, and Adelaide correspondingly happy and content.

Thus, Owen was totally unprepared for Adelaide's attack on him when he went home to lunch that Tuesday. She began the minute he walked into her room. "Owen, what's this I hear?" she asked sharply. "Miss Mattie said you suspected Stella of murdering Warner Fox."

Owen felt a premonitory uneasiness, but his voice was casual as he said, "Miss Mattie talks too much about things she doesn't know anything about." He changed the subject. "Did you get up this morning?"

"Yes, I walked across the room and back again. I can't get used to the idea of getting up so soon though. I always thought new mothers had to stay in bed at least nine days."

"Dr. Taylor says this is something they learned in England during the war. He knows what he's doing, honey. I want you to follow his advice."

"Oh, I will, no matter how odd it seems. But you didn't answer me. Do you suspect Stella?"

"How could I?" he said evasively. "We don't even know that Warner is dead. Adelaide, I don't want you worrying about anything for a while. Just put all that gossip out of your mind, relax, and enjoy the baby."

"I will, after you tell me you're not going to arrest Stella."

"I'm not going to arrest anybody any time soon."

She looked at him closely. "I can see that you do suspect her. How could you? After what she did for us—have you forgot that so soon?"

"You think I *want* to arrest her? My God. If there's any way in the world to get around it—I don't think she's guilty. And yet—"

"I know she wouldn't kill anybody," Adelaide said. "If she did, it was because she had to. Self defense, or something like that. She's not guilty of murder. She couldn't be."

"I hope not."

"What kind of namby-pamby remark is that? I believe you are trying to prove she's guilty."

206

"No, but Adelaide, anybody can commit a murder. The most unlikely people. Doctors and lawyers and—and teachers. Just because we like Stella, just because she saved our baby's life—that doesn't mean she couldn't be angry enough or desperate enough or frightened enough to kill someone. I hope she didn't, but I'm sworn to unhold the law, honey. I can't let personal feelings enter into that."

"You'd better," she snapped. Then she said in a softer voice, "Owen, you *have* to judge by personal feelings. If you waited for all the evidence to be in, you'd never trust anybody. How do you think I trusted you enough to marry you? I didn't know much about you then. I only knew how I felt. And I was right. You are a good man, a just man. So that's how I know you won't be unfair to Stella. You'll try to find evidence for her instead of against her. Won't you?"

He nodded, but it was just to satisfy Adelaide temporarily. He knew that sooner or later he'd have to arrest Stella, because now he had overwhelming evidence that she was guilty. He had a witness.

But Miss Mattie couldn't possibly know that, because he himself had found out only this morning. One of the deputies must have talked about the earlier evidence, Warner's hat with the note from Stella in it and the gun. He had sworn them to secrecy, but they probably told their wives, and Jack Hall's wife was a second cousin of Miss Mattie's.

Miss Mattie was causing a lot of trouble one way and another. She was the one who had forced him to talk to J.T. Clayton again. Forced was a strong word but not too strong, because in spite of thinking it would do no good to question J.T. again, Owen couldn't rest until he did as Miss Mattie had ordered. He had gone to J.T.'s three times last week. But he didn't find out anything new, and he finally decided he was beating a dead horse and vowed he wouldn't waste his time again. And after all that, he'd felt impelled to go back again this morning, the very first day he was back at work.

He found J.T. plowing his garden, getting ready to plant spring greens. When J.T. got to the end of the row, he stopped the mule and came over to the fence. "Morning, Sheriff," he said politely enough but without any real cordiality. Owen couldn't blame him for that. He knew he'd been making a pest of himself lately.

Owen said, "Morning, J.T. I see you're busy."

"Yeah, but I'll take a few minutes off and have a smoke. Then I'll have to get back to work. The wife wants this job done this morning so the kids can get in here after school and rake up the rows."

"Well, I won't take much of your time. I just stopped by to ask you another couple of questions."

J.T. looked a little uneasy. Not meeting Owen's eyes, he made quite a business of getting his cigarette lit. Then he said, "Okay, but it seems like you've pretty well covered the ground by now."

"Yeah. You've told me you didn't see Warner, but it's come to me that nothing was said about whether you heard him. So that's what I want to ask you today. Did you hear Warner's voice or anything else that might have a bearing on this case?"

"Yeah," J.T. said.

Owen was so surprised he dropped his cigarette. He looked down and stamped it out with his foot and then looked back at J.T.

"What did you hear? Just tell it all from start to finish."

"I heard Warner holler, 'Stella! Wait!' What it sounded like was maybe they'd come out here together and he'd got fresh with her and she was walking home. And I was puzzled, because I just didn't think Warner would do that with a nice girl like Miss Lidell. Anyway, the next minute I knowed that wasn't it, because he hollered, 'Stella, don't.' And of course it's always the girl and not the guy that hollers 'don't' in a case like that. And then I heard a gunshot."

"What did you do then?"

"Well, I started in that direction, and—"

"What direction? Where were the sounds coming from?"

"From the road, I thought, about even with that cotton patch just before you get to the lane where his car was found."

"All right. Go on."

"As I say, I started in that direction, but when I got in sight of the road, I didn't see neither one of them."

And I hope to God he don't ask em what I did see, J.T. thought. He stopped as if that were the end of his story.

Owen said, "So what did you do then?"

"I just stood there a few minutes, and then I went to the house."

"How long was that before Miss Lidell got to your house?"

"About an hour. I wasn't in the room when she come in, but she got to feeling bad pretty soon, and my wife called me to take her home. That's all I know, Sheriff, every bit of it, and I wish to hell I hadn't had to tell you."

"Why didn't you tell me before? As many times as I've been out here, it looks like you might've thought to mention it." Owen's voice was sarcastic. He was angry, but his anger was more over what J.T. said than over his tardiness in divulging it. Owen didn't want Stella to be guilty. He wished he hadn't heard that story.

J.T. said, "I didn't aim to tell you at all if I could help it. Just the same way I didn't want to give you the hat and the gun. You know what I owe that girl. I hear you owe her a right smart yourself. Why can't we both just forget about this?"

Owen said slowly, "You know we can't do that, J.T. Unless I can learn something that cancels out what you've just told me, I'll have to arrest her, and you'll have to testify. But one thing we can do is keep this under our hats while I try to find some other evidence that might keep that from coming to pass."

"I'd pray you do if I was a praying man," J.T. said. "But Sheriff, I reckon I better tell you something, that is, if you'll promise not to take advantage of me by asking questions about whiskey stills."

"That's the last thing on my mind right now," Owen said.

"All right. What I wanted to say is that I ain't gonna be able to keep this under my hat if anybody asks me the right question like you done just now."

"What do you mean?"

J.T. looked embarrassed. "I've got to where I can't lie about nothing. I can keep my mouth shut if nobody don't ask, but when I answer a question, I've got to tell the truth."

"Oh, yeah, I forgot. You've got religion, haven't you? But this lie is in a good cause, J.T. If a man kind of avoids the truth to help somebody, it's not a sin."

"I ain't worried about it being a sin. What I'm telling you is that I can't do it. It don't matter what I want to say, the truth comes out. You ask Doc Taylor about it. I went to him when it first started, because I thought I must be losing my mind. He give me some pills, but they didn't do no good."

Owen almost laughed, thinking J.T. must be joking, but noticing J.T.'s expression, he didn't. "That's a mighty strange ailment," he said.

"You're durn tootin'," J.T. said fervently. "You ain't got no idy how much trouble it's caused me. And now it's caused trouble for Miss Lidell too, and that's the last thing in the world I wanted to do."

On his way back to town Owen thought about what J.T. had told him. He'd have to confront Stella with it and make her tell him where Warner's body was. Then the case against her would be complete. Because what J.T. heard must mean Stella had shot him. It couldn't mean anything else. If J.T. was telling the truth, Stella was guilty.

And he'd said he couldn't lie. That was a laugh though. Anybody could lie. J.T.'s word was pretty good, especially considering his reputation otherwise, but it was ridiculous to think he *couldn't* lie. Ask Doc Taylor, he said. He probably didn't think I'd do it, Owen thought. Maybe J.T. has a reason for lying about Stella. Maybe he's guilty of something himself. All that talk about truth-telling might just be a coverup. Well, I'll fool J.T. I will ask Sam.

However, his talk with Sam was no comfort. At first Sam said brusquely, "You know better than to ask me about something a patient told me."

After Owen explained that J.T. had sent him, Sam said, "Well, all right. He did come in to see me about his trouble, and I gave him some pills, placebos, for the psychological effect."

"What's the matter with him? Is he crazy?"

"No, I'd say it's just what he told you. He can't lie."

"Good God, Sam, anybody can lie."

"J.T. can't . . . Why are you asking me this?"

"I can't tell you that." But he realized Sam would find out, that is, if his relationship with Stella was what Owen thought it was. He said, "Sam, have you thought about how many odd things have happened in Lanier lately? Warner's disappearance, and all the healing, and this thing that's happened to J.T."

"Don't forget Miss Mattie," Sam said.

"Yeah, now that you mention it, that's funny too. She's always been bossy, but we didn't use to pay much attention to her. Now every time she tells somebody to do something, they do it. Like Charles Howle joining the church, and Adelaide staying home before the baby was born, and me going out to talk to J.T."

"And me changing my office procedure," Sam said. "I

never sent out a bill in my life until she told me to. Then I found myself telling Gaynell to do it and afterwards saw several reasons it should be done."

"What's going on here?" Owen asked.

"I don't know," Sam said.

After Owen left, Sam reflected that if he'd told Owen what he thought was going on, he'd have convinced him that J.T. wasn't the only crazy one. He wondered what J.T. had told Owen about Warner. It must have been startling enough to cause Owen to accuse him of lying, otherwise he wouldn't have had to defend himself by telling about his affliction. Sam hoped it had nothing to do with Stella.

He hadn't seen Stella since Saturday night, and it was his own damn fault, most of it. If he hadn't been so abrupt . . .

They had left the Perry's at twelve-thirty, and after six hours of bending over a bed while he fought for two lives, Sam was so tired that all he wanted to do was sleep ten hours. But Stella apparently wanted to talk. She started out by saying she was sorry she'd tried to keep him from going to the Perry's and then she said, "I'm sorry for some other things I said too."

He said, "Stella, let's not go into that tonight, I'm too tired to think about it, and I'd probably say all the wrong things. Let's leave it until tomorrow."

She said, "All right," in a quiet voice, and he had gone to bed without any worries. Because he knew that when he did have a chance to think about what she'd told him, he'd see the reason for it, and besides, when it came to how he felt about her, he wasn't going to give her up if she'd slept with the whole damn army.

And why in hell hadn't he told her that, instead of saying he was too tired to talk? By the time he called her Sunday morning, all set to take her to church and spend the rest of the day with her, she said stiffly that she thought it would be best if they didn't see each other again. And, knowing the operator was probably listening in, he couldn't think of any way to persuade her. So finally he said, "All right, I'll be here all day. If you change your mind, call me."

About nine o'clock that night, she did. And heard another woman answer the phone. So now he didn't know how he was going to get the mess straightened out. He had gone by the boarding house a couple of times, but first she was out and next she was lying down with a headache.

But she couldn't avoid him forever in a town the size of Lanier. Somehow he would talk to her and make her listen.

He wished he knew what she was thinking and feeling now. He thought he knew how she had felt Saturday night. First she was angry with him over the interruption, and then she was angry with herself for being angry. She hated her strong sexual desire; it made her ashamed and self-contemptuous. That's why she flayed herself by telling him about her past.

But he couldn't understand why, having told him, she didn't want to know his reaction.

Stella thought she knew it. It was plain enough when he said, "I'm too tired to think about it, and I'd probably say all the wrong things." If he had still wanted her, he wouldn't have had to think about it, and he wouldn't have been worried about saying the wrong thing. So she knew his feeling had changed. It hadn't been much to start with, only physical attraction, and now it wasn't even that. If she'd needed any proof of it, she'd got it when she called him Sunday night.

A woman answered. It was a husky voice Stella did not recognize, not a young voice but old either. Stella was so astonished she almost dropped the phone. Before she could say anything, Sam's voice came on the line.

"Who was that?" Stella asked.

After a moment's hesitation he said, "I can't tell you. I'm tied up right now. Can I call you back?"

"No, don't bother," she said stiffly. "It wasn't important."

Nevertheless, about thirty minutes later he did call her back. "Stella, I'm sorry. There was someone here, and—"

"A patient?"

His voice sounded reluctant. "No. Just a visitor. I can't tell you who it was."

She didn't say anything, and after a minute he said, "Would it be all right if I came over there for a while? It's only a little after nine."

"No, there's no use. I wanted—" She paused and searched her mind for an excuse for calling, something besides the real one, which was that she had such a longing to see him that she had finally convinced herself she might be mistaken about his attitude. Suddenly she thought of something she had meant to ask him last night but didn't after he cut her off so abruptly. She said, "I wanted to ask you why the healing power didn't work for Adelaide Perry."

"I told you before that I think what you have is some kind of force that regenerates and rebuilds. So it wouldn't help in childbirth, which is a natural process rather than a disease. That's why I didn't ask you to touch Adelaide. I didn't think it would help ... Stella, don't hang up. I have to talk to you, and I can't do it over the phone. When can I see you?"

"I expect we'll run into each other sooner or later," she said.

And put the receiver back on the hook.

I shouldn't be surprised about the woman, she told herself. I'm not naive enough to think he's celibate at his age. Even if I were, his lovemaking told me different. No, I shouldn't be surprised. But I am.

It was only last night that he wanted me. How can he turn to somebody else so soon? Even though it was only a sex thing between us, it deserved some kind of commitment, some loyalty and exclusiveness. I may have done a lot of sleeping around, but even I wouldn't go to the arms of another man until the relationship with the present one was ended.

But of course that was it. The aborted lovemaking last night was all there was to be between her and Sam. He no longer wanted her. She couldn't blame him after what she had told him about herself. She tried to believe she was not disappointed. She had decided during her sleepless night that she must not see him again, because she didn't want to start another sickening round of sexual activity. Perhaps it would not have been sickening with Sam though. Perhaps with him she could have satisfied the demands of her body without losing the respect of her mind.

Well, she'd never have a chance to find out. He didn't want her now.

29

On Thursday Miss Mattie visited Mrs. Granger, taking Cousin Edith with her. She would have preferred to go alone, but when she picked up her car keys, Cousin Edith asked where she was going, so of course she had to invite her to go too.

Mrs. Granger seemed a little disconcerted to see them, but Miss Mattie scarcely noticed it, because, as she would have said, she was used to Inez's ways. But she did think her friend looked tired, and with her usual tactlessness she said so.

"I declare, Inez, you look more worn-out than you did back when you were tied down with Maureen, before she was healed. You're not sick, are you?"

"No," Mrs. Granger said in an apathetic voice. "I've been having a few headaches, but other than that, I'm fine."

"You need to get out more," Miss Mattie said briskly. "That's one reason I came. I've been expecting to see you about town or at some of our meetings, and when I didn't, I decided you might just need a little urging. I know it's hard to get back into the swing of things after staying at home as long as you have, but it's time you got started."

"That's what Calvin says," Mrs. Granger replied, "but I never seem to have much time. Maureen isn't really strong, even is she is well, and—"

"Nonsense," Miss Mattie said. "There's not a thing wrong with Maureen. She's well able to take care of herself, and you couldn't have much to do with all the conveniences you have and a houseful of servants besides. I was thinking yesterday that you could take over the Girl Scouts. Valerie Howle has had them two years, and she wants to quit now that she's got married. So right away I thought about you."

A look of alarm came into Mrs. Granger's face. "I couldn't do that," she said. "I wouldn't have any idea what to do."

"Valerie can tell you. There's nothing hard about it. Little girls are easy to manage and ready to learn. All that's needed is someone who has the time and will take an interest."

"I'm sure I wouldn't be any good at it. I wouldn't even know how to talk to them. After being out of things so long, I've almost forgotten how to talk to adults, much less children." She sounded panicky. Miss Mattie was relatively insensitive, but she couldn't help noticing the frightened voice and the nervously twisting hands.

"Well, maybe it is too big a job to ask you to take on right at first," she conceded reluctantly. "But, anyway, you need to get back to Sunday school and church and missionary society. Our next circle meeting will be at Mrs. Dennis's house on Wednesday. I'll come by for you."

"I don't know Mrs. Dennis," Mrs. Granger protested desperately.

"No, I guess you wouldn't, because it can't be more than three of four years since Mr. Dennis came here as principal. She'll probably be the only person you don't know though. Lanier doesn't change much."

Cousin Edith tittered. It was the first sound she'd made since she told Mrs. Granger she was glad to meet her, and both women looked at her. But she said nothing.

After a moment Mrs. Granger looked away, and Miss Mattie said, "Everybody will be glad to see you again. We start at ten, so I'll come by at a quarter till."

"No, wait a minute. I—"

She broke off as Maureen came into the room. She greeted Miss Mattie and was introduced to her cousin.

Miss Mattie said, "Maureen, it's just wonderful to see you walking and talking like anybody else. How do you spend your time now that you can be active?"

"I'm doing the things I always wanted to do," Maureen said. "Just now I'm learning to drive. In fact"—she looked as her watch—"I'm having a driving lesson in a few minutes."

"Oh Maureen, not again today," Mrs. Granger said.

Maureen turned to her. "Now, Mother, you know Daddy said I'd learn more quickly if I got regular practice."

"That doesn't mean you have to go every day. You know how I worry about you."

"You shouldn't. Junior is as careful as you could want. He's teaching me all the safety rules."

"You mean Junior Clayton?" Miss Mattie asked.

But neither Maureen nor her mother seemed to hear her question. They were arguing about whether Maureen should have the driving lesson, although perhaps arguing was not quite the right word, Miss Mattie thought, because Mrs.

Granger was largely complaining and pleading, while Maureen was answering in a reasonable but slightly impatient tone.

At the height of the discussion Cousin Edith began to cough and gasp. Maureen and her mother stopped talking, and Miss Mattie pounded her cousin on the back. After a moment or two the coughing stopped, and Cousin Edith said apologetically, "Something went down the wrong way."

"Nonsense," Miss Mattie said, "it's your old trouble. She has these choking spells ever now and then," she said to Mrs. Granger.

"I've been trying to get her to let Dr. Taylor have a look at her throat, but she won't hear to it."

"Doctors can't do much for allergies," Cousin Edith said.

"If you're allergic, it must be to arguments," Miss Mattie retorted, "because that's when you always start gasping. Whoever heard of being allergic to talk?"

Just then the doorbell rang, and Maureen said, "There's Junior now. I've got to go, Mother. You'll be all right. Just don't worry about me." She went out.

"How can I help worrying?" Mrs. Granger said half-apologetically to her guests. "I didn't want Maureen to learn to drive, at least not yet. I certainly didn't want Junior Clayton to teach her. But she and Calvin wouldn't pay any attention to me. So I not only have to worry about Maureen overtaxing her strength or having a wreck or something dreadful like that, I also have to worry whether Junior Clayton might be drinking. You know what his daddy has always been."

"Yes, but I don't think Junior drinks," Miss Mattie said. "He's come to church all his life, and he seems like a pretty nice boy. No, I think you're worrying about the wrong thing."

"What do you mean?"

"They might get too fond of each other," Miss Mattie said bluntly.

"Oh, there's no danger of that. Maureen is nineteen, but she's still a little girl in lots of ways. She isn't interested in boys, and even if she were, it wouldn't be a member of the Clayton family. She'd look among her own kind. As for Junior, I'm sure he would never think of himself as Maureen's equal."

In that, Mrs. Granger was only partly right. Before he met Maureen, Junior knew that her family was wealthier than his, and the first afternoon they spent together he

216

knew she was far above him in character, which translated into specific terms meant simply that she had no experience in smoking, drinking, or sex. But it had never occurred to Junior that wealth was a social barrier, and, like most Southern males, he expected to marry a girl superior to himself in character. Thus the question of equality did not enter his mind. What he wondered was whether Maureen liked him. He couldn't tell from the way she acted. She never teased or flirted or found double meanings in what he said—she didn't behave at all like the high school girls he knew. So he couldn't put his arm around her or ask her for a date or anything like that, because he didn't know how she would take it. He would have liked to though. She was the prettiest, sweetest girl he'd ever seen.

Maureen was subliminally conscious of his feelings, but she didn't think about them because she instinctively wanted to avoid complications. She liked Junior, but she recognized the difference in their backgrounds, interests, and goals in a way that he, not having an analytical mind, never would. That there might be danger in spending too much time with a boy so different from herself, however, did not occur to her.

What Maureen was thinking about this afternoon was the conference her daddy was going to have—or probably had already had sometime earlier in the day—with Mr. Dennis, the high school prinicpal. Her mother knew nothing about it, because since the struggle over the driving lessons Maureen did not want to cause a premature argument. For some reason her mother objected to every new move she made, so she would wait until Daddy got Mr. Dennis's answer before she mentioned going to school.

After Miss Mattie and her cousin left, Mrs. Granger dragged herself upstairs to her room and lay down. Her head was pounding dreadfully, and she had an all-gone feeling in the pit of her stomach. It wasn't all because of the worry over the driving lesson. When Mattie said as she went out the door, "Now Inez, you be ready to go at a quarter till ten Wednesday," Mrs. Granger knew she would have to go to the circle meeting.

Maybe something would happen before Wednesday. Maybe she would be sick. If she had a headache like this, she certainly couldn't go. Yet she didn't think even being sick would be enough. Mattie would say getting out in company was the very thing she needed to get rid of her headache. Mattie wouldn't take no for an answer. She'd make her go.

But that was silly. Mattie Shepard had no authority over her. Mattie had always been bossy, of course, even when they were schoolgirls, but no one ever did what she said unless it was something they wanted to do anyway. Yet for some reason she felt she had to obey Mattie in this.

Maybe it was because she knew Calvin and Maureen would agree with Mattie. They expected her to go places and talk to people and work in the church and do all sorts of things she didn't want to do. She was satisfied with her life the way it was. She liked having her own routine and knowing what each day would be like. All she wanted was to take care of her family and know it was appreciated.

Only lately it didn't seem to be. All those years she had suffered the sadness of having a handicapped child, all those years she had worked so hard without complaint, were forgotten now. Everything had changed. Calvin and Maureen made all kinds of reckless decisions without regard to her judgement or wishes.

She wasn't important to them anymore. She was just in their way. Perhaps she had always been in their way and was only now realizing it. After all, what had she ever done for either of them? She had wanted to give Calvin a son, but all she could produce was an afflicted daughter. She tried to make up for that by devoting her life to the child, but what was that worth? Calvin was a rich man; he could have hired someone to care for Maureen. In fact, he kept the house so fully staffed with servants that everything she had ever done for Maureen could as well have been done by someone else. She was no use to anyone.

After a while she heard Maureen come in, but she did not get up. She lay wide-eyed and sleepless on her bed with her head pounding unmercifully.

30

Earlier that same Thursday afternoon the grandparents of one of Stella's ninth-grade English students came to get him out of class.

"Daniel's daddy has been taken bad sick," they said, "and Dr. Taylor rushed him to the hospital in Tuscaloosa. We're on our way there now, and we thought we'd better take Daniel if he's ever to see his daddy alive again."

Stella knew Daniel Morgan's father. He was one of the people who had been healed at the church service. "What's wrong with him?" she asked in alarm.

"Internal bleeding, Dr. Taylor said. He wasn't sure what was causing it."

Fear was already in Stella's mind. Could it be something connected with the healing? She knew so little about it— and she couldn't forget that Mr. Bob Morrow had died. Her heart was pounding, and she was too upset to go on with her lesson. Fortunately by the time she had answered the students' questions, the bell rang, signaling the end of the school day.

Instead of going home Stella went to Sam's office. She had to find out what was wrong with Mr. Morgan. He'd had bronchial asthma before, but both he and his wife insisted he was completely cured. There was no reason to disbelieve it, because he hadn't had an attack since. But of course asthma attacks came only periodically, so maybe he'd had one now. Could asthma cause internal bleeding? She had never heard of that.

There were several patients in the office, so she had to wait her turn. Too upset to talk to anyone, she sat down apart from the others and picked up a magazine. She had been there only a few minutes when Sheriff Perry came out of the inner office. He stopped to speak to her, and she asked about Adelaide and little Sammy. Owen said they were both doing well except that Sammy seemed hungry all the time, so he had come by to talk to Sam about his formula.

"I'd like to talk to you again about the Warner Fox case," Owen said in a low voice. "Would tomorrow after school be all right?"

Stella was puzzled. "Yes, but I don't know what I can tell you that I haven't already said several times."

"Well, it won't hurt to go over it again. By doing that, people sometimes mention some little detail that throws an entirely new light on the matter."

He left, and finally Stella's name was called. As she walked into the office, Sam looked up in surprise. "I didn't know you were out there," he said. "Is something wrong with you?"

"No, I just came to find out about Mr. Morgan. His in-laws got Daniel out of school. It sounded serious."

"I talked to one of the doctors at the hospital a few minutes ago, and he said it was what I suspected—a bleeding ulcer. He came through the surgery all right."

"Sam, do you suppose this could have anything to do with the healing?"

"I don't see how. Bronchial asthma and duodenal ulcers are two entirely separate diseases. Although," he said thoughtfully, "they might have similar causes."

"What do you mean?"

"There's no doubt in my mind that they're both caused by emotional stress. Possibly anger turned inward. You've heard people say that something was eating on them? Well, that's exactly what a duodenal ulcer does; it eats on the duodenum. And someone said asthma was a substitute for crying. Instead of wracking sobs, you get wracked breathing."

"But he was cured of his asthma."

"But maybe not of his anger, so it found a different target."

She was silent a minute, then she said, "Could that be what Jesus meant when he told a man he'd healed to sin no more lest a worse thing come upon him?"

"Exactly. At least, that's what I think."

"But what's the good of the healing if something worse is going to happen? Mr. Morgan is a nice man. Maybe he's angry inside, but he doesn't show it on the outside. It doesn't hurt other people, so how could it be a sin?"

"It hurts him. It's a sin against his own body. Of course, it may not be anger. I may be frustration at his lot in life or an undue dependency on someone who disappoints him. Or it could be something else. But whatever it is will probably make him sick one way or another until he gets rid of it."

"Maybe he can't get rid of it, and if that's so, he'd be better off with asthma than ulcers. At least the asthma wouldn't kill him, would it?"

"No."

"Then I shouldn't have healed him."

"You can't pick and choose whom you'll heal, Stella. Even Jesus didn't do that; he healed everyone who asked. What happened afterward was up to them. Don't worry so about this healing. You seemed determined to lay blame on yourself."

"That's not true. I don't blame myself enough for some things. It's easy to make excuses."

"Not for you apparently. If it were, you'd have realized why you slept around after your fiancé died."

She looked at him with a startled expression. "Why?"

"Because in the midst of death you were looking for life."

She was staring at him with rounded eyes. "Yes, I think that's what it was. But how could you know?"

"Because I know you, Stella."

She continued to stare at him, but he thought she was not seeing him; she was thinking about what he had said and trying to fit it into her knowledge of herself. At last she shook her head, "You're only partly right. If that were all it was, I wouldn't still—"

"Still what?" he prompted.

"Still be having lustful thoughts about every man I meet."

"*Is* it every man? Or is it only me?"

"Well, you're the only one on the scene right now, aren't you?" she flashed back. "But I don't have to worry about you anymore."

Since you're so well occupied with another woman, she was thinking.

The hell you don't, he thought angrily. Damn her stubborn thick-headedness. He could pull her out of that chair and kiss her until she had no resistance left and would go willingly to the sofa in the waiting room. He had half a mind to do it. But that would only complicate matters. He must let her come to her own understanding.

He said, "You don't seem to realize that there's a sex consciousness in most men-women relationships. It doesn't have to erupt into overt behavior. So if you're worried about that, forget it. I don't want your body."

Your body only, he amended silently.

221

She said stiffly, "That's plainly spoken."

"I thought it was time to be plain. Now will you stop saying you don't want to see me anymore?"

"Of course. After all you've done for me, I owe you my friendship."

"You don't owe me a damn thing. But I accept it anyway. Will you go to dinner with me tonight?"

At dinner they talked of food first. Sam complained that eating out in a small town was pretty monotonous. Everything was Southern-fried, or if not fried, than at least boiled with salt meat. He liked Southern cooking up to a point, he said, but sometimes he thought he'd sell his soul to go to a Chinese or French restaurant for a change. Stella said if he had to eat at a boarding house, he wouldn't be so blasé about the restaurant, which at least gave him the choice between—she looked at the menu—steak, ham, or fish, even if they were all fried.

Then they talked of books. Sam asked what she taught in her literature classes and wondered aloud how she could persuade adolescents to read *Silas Marner,* which he considered the dullest book in the English language. Stella jumped to George Eliot's defense but finally confessed that she liked Jane Austen and the Brontës better. He asked which of the books written in recent years would become classics. Stella voted for *Gone With the Wind* and *The Yearling,* and he accused her of being prejudiced in favor of women and the South and ignoring the best American writers.

Movies, they both agreed, were deteriorating. When one compared *The Best Years of Our Lives,* the Academy Award winner for last year, to its predecessors, one could see how lean the year had been. Sam disliked the movie because it was based on the problems of returning servicemen, which, he said, loomed larger to writers and moviemakers than to the men themselves. Stella disliked it because it had given her neither entertainment nor insight.

They went to their separate beds that night, both pleased at getting through the evening without letting the other see any signs of physical desire and each with a few qualms about how long it could be kept up. Sam thought savagely that expecting him to spend five hours without touching her was asking too much, and Stella thought in despair that it was easy enough for him because he had another woman and didn't want her, but what was she to do about wanting him?

222

On Friday afternoon, as promised, the sheriff came by the boarding house to talk with her, but the talk was so far from what she had expected that she stuttered and stammered her way through it. When he left, she was shaking.

That story of shouts and a gunshot seemed to be proof that she killed Warner. Yet everything in her cried out that it wasn't so.

Still, how could she know? If someone had heard Warner pleading for his life, calling her by name, it must be true. Even though she had no reason to kill him, even though she couldn't imagine doing it, she must have.

Had she been under some awful compulsion imposed on her by those beings in the aircraft?

Where had she got the gun? And where was it now? Who was the witness who had overheard?

The sheriff wouldn't tell her who it was. She had seen no one that night until she got to the Clayton's. But perhaps that too was hidden in her mind.

She looked at her watch. It was five o'clock. Sam would pick her up at seven. She must get him to hypnotize her tonight and try to find out if the story the witness told was true. She had denied it to the sheriff, but she didn't *know*. All she knew of what happened during that missing hour was what she had learned through hypnotism. Perhaps she had not told the whole story. Perhaps even under hypnosis one protected oneself by conveniently forgetting anything harmful. But this time Sam would know what questions to ask. He could make her tell.

And if she were guilty?

Hastily she thrust that thought out of her mind. It could not be true. She wouldn't even allow herself to think of the possibility.

But she had thought of it. She went on shaking. If she had to wait two hours for Sam to come, by the time he arrived she wouldn't be able to tell him what had happened. She went to the telephone, picked up the receiver, and dropped it with a clatter. Finally she managed to give the operator his number.

Gaynell answered. She said that Sam was busy with an emergency case but she would have him call back as soon as he was finished. Stella hung up the phone, but she did not leave the hall. She paced up and down waiting for his call.

It did not come. Thirty minutes later Gaynell called back.

"Dr. Taylor asked me to tell you he'd had another emergency, Miss Lidell. He doesn't know what time he'll get back to town, but he'll call you when he does."

"All right," Stella said. After a moment she remembered to thank Gaynell. But she stood with the receiver in her hand for several minutes before she realized she should hang it up.

The bell rang for supper, but Stella didn't go. She knew she wouldn't be able to swallow, and her upset would be visible to everyone.

She went back to her room. In the hope that Sam might yet be there by seven she took a bath and dressed. Finishing her makeup, she straightened the top of the dresser. After that she started on the drawers. Seven o'clock came and went. She straightened her desk and turned to the closet. The clock in the downstairs hall struck eight. She let down the hems in two skirts.

At nine-thirty the phone rang, and she raced downstairs to answer it. Ten minutes later she was seated beside Sam on the sofa in the boarding house living room telling him what the sheriff said to her.

"My God, who could be doing this to you?" he said.

"You think it isn't true?"

"Of course it's not true. Somebody is lying. I don't see why though. Surely it wouldn't be Owen, so it must be the witness, whoever he is. Do you have an enemy who hates you that much? It couldn't be Grant, could it? If it is, I'll—"

"It isn't Grant," she said. "He doesn't hate me. I don't think he has any feelings at all toward me except maybe pity. I do have enemies here, I guess; I know some people still think I'm perpetrating some kind of hoax. But I can't think of anyone who feels strongly enough to tell that kind of lie . . . Sam, perhaps it's true."

"Don't be a fool, Stella," he said curtly.

"I want you to find out," she said steadily. "I want you to hypnotize me again. I know I wouldn't have done it in my right mind. But how can I know what was done to me aboard that aircraft?"

"My God," he said in a wrenched voice.

"Are you too tired to do it tonight? I didn't even ask you what your emergency was. It was in the country, wasn't it? A farm accident?"

"No. This is just for your ears, Stella, because they don't

want it to get out—you know how the Grangers are about keeping things secret. Mrs. Granger cut her throat."

Seeing her alarm, he said hastily, "She's not dead. But she made a pretty good job of it, and if it hadn't been for Maureen, she'd have died. Maureen told the maid to call me, and she held that jugular vein together with her hands until I got there. I still can't believe it ... Anyway, I think Mrs. Granger will make it. I patched her up the best I could and sent her to Tuscaloosa by ambulance."

"Why did she do it?" Stella asked. "I know she had some conflicting emotions, but that hardly seems enough to make her try to kill herself. After what she must have gone through during the years Maureen was handicapped, and then just when things were better—it's hard to understand. She wasn't needed any more though," she said slowly.

"Oh no, she's needed," Sam said. "If you could have been there—but perhaps she didn't know how important she was to them. All she saw was that Maureen didn't need her in the same way. She didn't realize Maureen might need her just as much in other ways."

"How can people be so blind?" Stella said.

"I've often wondered," he said dryly. She cast him a quick look, but his face told her nothing. After a moment he said, "The precipitating factor was probably Maureen's plan to go to the university this summer."

"To the university? I saw Mr. Granger at school yesterday, and I thought he was talking to Mr. Dennis about entering Maureen in high school next year."

"Yes, but Mr. Dennis said they'd give her a test, and if she did well enough on it, she could probably get in college instead. Maureen didn't seem to have much doubt she'd be able to go in June."

"Sam, do you think my healing power would help Mrs. Granger?"

"I don't think it has any effect on injuries, Stella. It doesn't reduce fractures; we know that because I had to set the Perry baby's leg. I don't think it would have mended Mrs. Granger's throat either, but it might speed up the healing process. We can go visit her in the hospital if you like. But now, we'd better do the hypnotism if we're going to."

"Are you sure you aren't too tired?"

"No. Anyway, I'll have some time off tomorrow. I've decided to close the office early on Saturday. Three hours should be enough to see the country folks who come to town only on Saturday, and the town people can get used to coming during the week. I need some time to live my own life. Let's go to my office to do the hypnotism. We'll be sure of not being overheard there."

"I just thought of something. We don't have the tape recorder. Can you do it so I'll remember what I say?"

"I think it would be better if I told you. Don't worry. I'm not likely to forget any of it."

An hour later he wished he could forget it. He sat looking at Stella. She was still in the trance, and he was in a panic. He couldn't tell her what she had said, and yet he didn't think he could lie to her when she asked him.

He said, "Stella, we're going back to the boarding house. You'll go in and sit on the sofa in the living room. When I say your name, you will awaken, but you will not remember any of this. You will not know you have been hypnotized. It will all be wiped out of your mind. But you will know you didn't kill Warner Fox."

Ten minutes later when he called her name, she looked at him and said, "Hadn't we better get started with the hypnotism?"

"I've decided I'm too tired tonight," he said. "Let's put it off until tomorrow."

"All right. I don't feel so frightened anyway since I've talked to you. I know I didn't kill Warner."

He wished he were sure of that, but the fact was that the hypnotism session seemed to confirm the story the sheriff had. Stella had not actually admitted anything, but. . . .

The questions and answers ran through his mind once more. After he had put Stella on the scene with the strange aircraft, he said, "Is Warner there?"

"Yes, he's calling to me. He's saying, 'Stella! Wait! It's Warner!' "

"Is that all?" he asked.

"No, he's saying, 'Stella, don't.' But I don't listen, and soon he stops talking."

"Why did he stop?"

Stella answered with a frown, "I don't know. Perhaps he had to."

"What do you mean?" he asked.

She said irritably, "Not able—impossible. He couldn't talk any more."

226

"Where is he now?" he asked.

At that Stella became very upset. She twisted her hands together and began to cry. "I don't know. Gone. I don't want to talk about it."

He had got her calmed down without bringing her out of the trance, but he knew he'd gone as far as he could with her. That was when he'd thought of taking her back to the boarding house before he woke her.

So now he didn't know. He managed to hide his fear from Stella until he left soon afterward, but as he drove home, it rose to torment him again.

She had been compelled to heal. The power had been imposed on her without her consent. Would the same beings who had done that also force her to kill? And if they had, could it be proved against her?

He was afraid it could. If Owen had found a witness to add to the circumstantial evidence he already had . . . Of course, Stella had a lot of friends, and that would be a help in a trial by jury. He had friends too. But even with a friendly jury, the evidence would weigh.

His only hope was to keep her from being tried. Owen Perry was the answer to that. He would go to see Owen the first thing in the morning.

31

Troubled by dreams in which courtroom scenes figured prominently, Sam slept poorly, and awoke early. Immediately he began thinking of what he would say to Owen Perry about Stella. He went on thinking while he doggedly did his customary morning exercises, cooked and ate breakfast, and counted out his maid's weekly pay and left it on the counter. Then he dressed and went to town.

His anxiety had made him early. Clerks were still sweeping sidewalks in front of stores, and Owen had not yet arrived at his office. When he came, he didn't seem surprised to find Sam waiting. "I guess I know why you're here," he said. "Stella?"

Sam nodded. "I understand you've got a witness, some-body who claims to have overheard Warner pleading with her for his life. Who is it?"

Owen looked undecided for a moment. "Come on in the office. There's no sense talking about this on the sidewalk for the whole town to hear. I'm trying to keep it quiet. Even the deputies don't know."

Some of the anger that had built up in Sam against Owen faded. He said, "Why?"

"Hell, you ought to know why," Owen said with irritation edging his normally placid voice. "If I can keep it quiet, I may have a chance to refute the evidence. Though, God knows, I don't see how."

"Who's your witness?" Sam asked again.

Owen cast a glance at Sam and said, "J.T. Clayton. Remember the day I asked you about him? He had just told me the story. I was trying to believe he was lying, but you assured me he couldn't lie."

"Even if he's telling the truth, there's another explanation."

"I hope so," Owen said. "I'll be honest with you though. I don't know how long it will be before the news gets out, and when it does, I'll have to arrest her."

"You can't do that," Sam said desperately. "Once she's arrested, it will follow her all her life. You know what small towns are like."

Owen's homely face remained set. Sam said, in a hard voice, "Look, Owen, I never thought I'd say this to you, but I have to. I saved your wife's life so you owe me. Stella means as much to me as Adelaide does to you. I'm calling in the debt."

"I know what I owe you—and her too," Owen said, still with that irritable sound in his voice. "Why do you think I haven't arrested her already? But when the news gets out, if I don't make the arrest, somebody else will, one of the deputies or the town marshall. All I can promise is that I'll do the best I can to keep it from happening."

Sam left the sherrif's office even more troubled than when he came. He saw now how powerless even Owen was to hold back the catastrophe threatening Stella.

He could tell Owen about the hypnotism and let him listen to the tape. But even if he believed it, which seemed unlikely, evidence obtained under hypnotism wasn't allow-able in court. The tape didn't answer the question of where

Warner was anyway. It merely suggested where he might be—and that only to an imaginative mind.

Well, he'd see Stella this afternoon, and he'd ask her to go over what she consciously remembered. And suddenly he thought of something else. J.T. had that curious compulsion to tell the truth, so he must have got it from the same place Stella got her healing power. But Miss Mattie had a strange power, too, the power to command, *so Miss Mattie must have also been a witness to whatever happened.*

Sam parked his car in front of his office, and walked back down the street to see Owen again

Stella too was still worried about the evidence against her, but she was no longer in the panic she'd been in last night. She knew she was innocent, so she'd have to trust that somehow the sheriff would find more evidence. In any case, there was nothing she could do about it now, today, and there were other things she must do. She had three sets of papers to grade, and the roles in the senior play must be assigned so the students could start memorizing their parts. With only twenty-nine students to choose from it was not easy. Some of those who had histrionic ability would be unwilling or unable to memorize; others who could learn the parts would be too shy or too frightened to perform.

It was two o'clock when she finished. She put down her pencil and got up from the desk. What she wanted now was exercise.

It was a soft, warm day, the kind that sometimes comes to the Deep South in February to tantalize people with a promise of spring. On such a day it was a shame to stay inside. She decided to walk to the post office. She wasn't expecting any mail, but in Lanier one could not walk alone with no destination without being considered mentally deficient.

She had just turned away from her post office box, which was empty as expected, when through the plate-glass windows she saw Wilma Jean Clayton coming out of the drug store into the bright sunshine. She had an ice cream cone in her hand and a big smile on her face. Stella smiled too. That's one good thing that happened because of me, she thought. Maybe I've made a mess of my personal life, and I guess my career here in Lanier is going down the drain, but I've done a little good. Wilma Jean will have a normal life, and—

Before she finished the thought, Wilma Jean darted into the street. "No, go back!" Stella shouted, and started to run. Brakes screeched, and tires slid shrilly on the black-topped street surface. There was a dull, sickening thud, and Stella watched in horror as Wilma Jean's body rose into the air and then bounced along the pavement.

Stella ran into the street. Other people were running too, and some of them were screaming as she was. Wilma Jean was lying motionless. A man got out of a car and began directing traffic. A voice said, "How bad is she hurt?"

And then another voice said, "Stand back." It was Sam, and people did as he asked. He bent over Wilma Jean's body. In a few minutes he looked up. "She's dead," he said. "Grant, you go call the funeral home, and somebody find her parents. They'll be in a store somewhere." His eyes stopped on Stella. "Sit on the curb and put your head between your knees," he said sharply. "You're going to faint. Somebody help her."

Time ceased to have any meaning. Dimly, as from a distance, Stella could hear the voices and activity in the street. After a while she raised her head. Some men were putting a covered stretcher into the ambulance, and the sheriff's deputies were circulating in the crowd, asking questions. The sheriff himself was talking to Mrs. Ashford, the driver of the car. Stella knew her; she was the widow who had been healed of her arthritis at the church service. Mrs. Ashford was crying hysterically.

Stella stood up. She supposed the deputies would want to get her statement too, since she had seen the accident. She started toward them. She was trembling so hard she could barely walk. A hand on her arm stopped her. "That can wait a while," Sam said. "I told Owen you saw it and he could talk to you later. Come in the drug store."

He led her to the back of the store and had her sit down at a desk behind the prescription counter. Then he rummaged in one of the desk drawers, pulled out a bottle, and poured something into a glass. "Brandy," he said briefly. "Drink it."

It burned her throat, but soon the worst of the shaking stopped, and she felt a little better. Sam said, "It wasn't Mrs. Ashford's fault. Wilma Jean ran directly in front of her. There was no way she could stop."

"Did you see it?"

"Yes, I was standing at my window looking down. As a

matter of fact, I was watching you and wondering . . . Anyway, I saw it all. Several people did, so I doubt if the sheriff will get around to you today."

"She was so *happy*," Stella cried. "She had an ice cream cone. I could see her face, Sam. And then the car hit her, and she bounced—"

He put his arm around her shoulder. "Don't think about it right now," he said. "You'll be able to take it better later, when some of your shock has worn off. Is Valerie at home?"

"No, she and Charles have gone to Tuscaloosa for the day."

"Well, you don't need to be alone. I'm through for the day. Let's go to my house for a while."

There Sam made her another drink, but he himself didn't have one.

"I never do except once in a while at night," he said. "People would be horrified to smell alcohol on my breath, and I wouldn't really blame them. A doctor has no business drinking."

"A teacher doesn't either," Stella said. "But I think this one will be good for me." She took a sip of her drink and said, "Sam, I can't stop thinking."

"Then think about something else. Think about Owen and Adelaide's new baby. Did you know they named him after us?"

She nodded. "I went to see Adelaide one afternoon. She had called and asked me to. She wanted to thank me, but I told her she should be thanking you. I didn't do anything."

"Stella, that baby was born dead. Something in you brought him back to life."

"I know. Something in me healed Wilma Jean too, but she'd have been better off if it hadn't happened."

"You can't know that. You don't know that she wouldn't have died just the same. You have no way to measure her previous pain or the relief of being free of it, and you don't know how much it was worth to have a few weeks of normal childhood."

She continued as if she hadn't heard him. "And if I hadn't healed Mrs. Ashford, there wouldn't have been a car to hit her. Mrs. Ashford started driving again after she got rid of her arthritis. Did you see her face? She—"

"It wasn't your fault."

"Whose then? I was so sure I was helping people, but I was harming them instead. Wilma Jean and Mrs. Ashford. Mr. Morgan. Mrs. Granger too."

"If you're determined to flay yourself, you might as well complete the list," Sam said in a harsh voice. "If you hadn't healed Mrs. Farley, her husband wouldn't have left her."

"I didn't know he had. But surely the healing didn't have anything to do with that."

"It did though. He told her he had been in love with someone else for five years and now that she was well of her diabetes, he was going to divorce her and marry the other woman."

She looked out the window and then back at him. "Miss Mattie told me this would happen. She said, 'Stella, you're leaving God out of the healing, and no good can come of that.' And she's right. It is turning out wrong, and maybe that's why. But the power was given to me in that aircraft, wasn't it? So God had nothing to do with it."

"Are you so sure how he works?"

She stared at him. At last she said, "What are you saying?"

"I'm just thinking aloud. How can you know God has nothing to do with the healing? You believe he works through people, don't you? Are you so sure he deals exclusively with those of us who live on earth?"

"You mean he might have other people, other places? Yes, I suppose so. Is Miss Mattie right then? Should I be doing the healings in the church or preaching a sermon to everybody I touch?"

He laughed. "I doubt if you have a gift for preaching, any more than I do. What kind of results do you think I'd get if I tried to preach to my patients?"

"They'd think you were crazy."

"Exactly. And soon I wouldn't have any patients. By trying to do more than heal, I'd make it impossible to do that. The way you are doing right now with all your questions."

"But I'm only trying to understand. I don't want to harm people. If I could know how and why the healing happens I could use it better. For good instead of ill."

"Stella, I can't tell you how or why any healing happens. Nobody can. We see what goes on, and that's all. We know that bleeding stops, wounds close, and nerves quit carrying a message of pain, and we can help the process along a little by certain procedures, but how and why it happens is a mystery. Benjamin Franklin said that God does the healing and the doctor collects the fee, and I think that's true. What I'm trying to say is that I don't think we can find the answer to your questions."

"But surely it isn't wrong to try. How else would we ever learn anything?"

"That's true. But if you wait for perfect understanding, you won't ever do anything. You'll limit yourself—and maybe you'll limit God too."

"You think I should go on with the healing in spite of all the disastrous results?"

"You'll have to answer that for yourself. Maybe it would help you to know that you aren't the only person who's had to face that question."

"You?" she asked in a disbelieving voice.

He nodded. "I had a patient, a middle-aged woman, who was having headaches. She was a hypertensive type and at a difficult age. So I thought it was just the usual nervous complaint. I gave her aspirin and placebos and sympathy without paying much attention to her. She called one afternoon when I was setting a broken arm and had an office full of patients waiting, so I told her to take aspirin and lie down and I'd be there as soon as I could. When I got there, she was in a diabetic coma, and she died. Afterwards I found out that she'd had the classic symptoms—increased urination and excessive hunger and thirst, which she hadn't mentioned to me because she didn't connect them to the pain she felt."

"But it was her fault. She should have told you all her symptoms."

"If I'd been alert, if I hadn't depended on my own preconceived ideas, I'd have asked her. It was criminal carelessness. I was guilty, or partly guilty, of her death, Stella. There's no way I can get around that."

"What did you do?"

"I went through a week of hell. It happened at Christmas time—the extra sweets she ate probably contributed—and I'd already planned to take off a few days to visit relatives. When I left, I didn't mean to come back. I was going to give up medicine."

"For one mistake?"

"I wasn't thinking of it as a mistake. I was thinking of it more as murder. I'd always known I would make mistakes,

233

but I thought they'd be unavoidable errors, without any guilt on my part, and I didn't really think they'd be very serious. I had a pretty good opinion of myself in those days. I'd been a brilliant medical student, and I thought I was a good doctor."

"You are."

"But fallible. I had to learn that. It didn't make me any more tolerant of mistakes, either my own or others, but it did keep me from quitting. I balanced my fallibility against the good I could do and decided I'd have to keep trying."

"That's exactly what I'm doing."

"Yes, but your balance is lopsided. You aren't just weighing the healings against the failures—people like Maureen against people like Mrs. Howle whom you couldn't help. You're demanding more than cures. You think healing is more than it is."

"I don't know what you mean."

"When you heal someone, that's all you've done—healed his body. You haven't changed his personality or made him more careful or guaranteed him long life and happiness. You haven't obligated yourself to watch over him the rest of his life either. Stella, you're trying to take too much responsibility and blaming yourself for things you couldn't help."

"But if the healing does no good—"

"It relieves pain and restores movement and makes it possible for the person to solve his own problems. But that's all, and to expect more is to insure yourself disappointment. How long do you think I'd have practiced medicine if I had expected all my patients to live in perfect peace and harmony afterwards? Or even if I expected all of them to live? I just do what I can for them and hope God will take care of the rest."

They were silent for a few minutes, and then Stella stirred and said, "I'd better go now. Thank you for talking to me. You're a real friend, Sam."

He let that pass. "I'm going out to the Clayton's," he said. "I talked to them for a few minutes right after it happened, but I'd better see them again. They'll need to talk about it a lot to make it seem real. Also, I want to take Mrs. Clayton some sleeping pills."

"I need to go to see them to," Stella said.

"All right. We'll go together."

When they went out of the house, Stella shivered and

said, "It's turning cold again. And getting cloudy. The spring weather is gone."

On their way to the Clayton's it began to rain, a dreary winter rain, gray and hopeless. Sam said, "It's going to be a cold, wet night. Why don't we cook at home and then sit by the fire?"

"Alone?" she asked sarcastically, and could have bitten her tongue.

"What's that supposed to mean?" he asked in an irritated voice. Then comprehension came into his face. "Oh, you're talking about the woman who answered my telephone that night. Stella, don't you know who that was?"

"No," she said in a puzzled voice. "But you don't have to tell me. It's none of my business, and I'm sorry I brought it up."

"I couldn't tell you that night, because the operator listens in on all my calls to find out who's sick. But you have a right to know. It was Miss Pauline Howle."

"Well, why didn't you say so? I asked you if it was a patient, and you said no."

"I've made a big point of not seeing patients at my home, so I couldn't afford to say yes. Besides, Miss Pauline isn't really a patient when she comes to see me at night."

For a minute she looked confused, and then her eyes widened. "You mean you and Miss Pauline—but she's too—" She stopped. She had been about to say "too old," but she suddenly realized that Sam must be well past thirty, and Miss Pauline was not yet forty.

Sam said, "Let me explain. Miss Pauline is a spinster and, I daresay, a virgin, and because of her situation, she isn't likely ever to be anything else. I think she sees life passing her by and frequently feels lonely and somewhat desperate. Maiden ladies in that circumstance often turn for masculine attention to a doctor, minister, or lawyer—someone they have a legitimate reason to contact. Miss Pauline's house is in sight of mine; she can see my lights at night. So sometimes she comes to see me with a minor medical problem—a cut finger, a speck in her eye, insomnia—some excuse to talk and give me a few coquettish glances."

Stella looked up. "And you don't—"

"My God, no!" His voice was explosive. He paused and when he spoke again, the vehemence was gone. He said, "Sex doesn't come into it. I think she'd run like a hare if I

235

made any advances. I just chat casually and treat whatever ailment she's thought up and ease her out of the house as soon as I can. I don't know why she answered the phone that night. She's never done that before. I'd turned around to get something out of my medical bag, and she reached for the phone at the first ring."

"She changed her voice," Stella said. "I didn't recognize it. Yet now that you tell me who it was, I can realize that it sounded a little like her. I suppose she felt daring . . . Sam, that's pitiful."

He nodded. "Yes, it is. That's why I try to be understanding, why I've never told anyone until now."

Stella said slowly, "I wonder if I'll ever be like that."

Maybe she was like that now. Miss Pauline was seeking a romantic adventure, whereas she was looking for sexual satisfaction, but it amounted to the same thing. They were both hounded by guilt and fear, wanting something and yet not wanting it.

And they both found Sam kind and understanding, and so they kept selfishly infringing on his time, not asking themselves what he wanted.

She said that to him. "Sam, both Miss Pauline and I have been selfish. We've been thinking only of what we want. What do you want?"

"From Miss Pauline? Nothing." The familiar undertone of laughter was in his voice. But it went out as he said, "From you I want whatever you'll give me."

"You said you didn't want my body."

"Yes, so I did. Is that all you have to offer?"

She thought he was amused again, and it made her angry. "Some people haven't thought that so little," she snapped.

"Sometimes I wonder if you're confessing or boasting," he said curtly. Then quickly, "I'm sorry. But don't keep throwing those other men in my face."

"Why should you mind?"

"I don't, but you've told me once; you don't have to keep reminding me. Forget it yourself. You're only twenty-three years old; you've got a whole life before you, but you can't live it if you keep holding to the past. Let it go, Stella."

"It's not a matter of that," she said in a hopeless voice. "It won't let me go. . . . I'd better not go to your house tonight. I appreciate being there this afternoon. I can't tell you how much you helped me. But I should go home when we get back to town."

"Because you're afraid of what might happen? There was a time I would have made love to you, I admit it. But we've come past that point, Stella. You have nothing to worry about tonight, I promise."

He wants my company, she thought. He's facing an evening alone, and I'll be someone to talk with, someone to help him hold back the loneliness. I owe him that. Surely I can keep down my contemptible sex drive through one more evening. I won't bother him with my problems as I've done this afternoon. I'll talk only about impersonal subjects. I'll be as prim and dignified as a spinster school teacher ought to be.

And then I won't see him anymore. I don't honestly think I can without humiliating myself and embarrassing him. He has said he doesn't want my body. I can't change that, and I mustn't try. But I will if I keep seeing him, I know I will. So this must be the last time. It's only three months until school is out. I can avoid him that long, and I won't be back here next year.

She felt a queer wrench at the thought of never seeing him again. What a shame they couldn't have fallen in love. Perhaps they would have if it hadn't been for Grant. But no, not even then, because from the first time she was alone with Sam, there had been that sex thing between them. Sexual attraction was not love. Thank God, she had never made that mistake.

When Sam and Stella came out of the Clayton house, it was raining harder. Sam's car was parked a considerable distance from the house. He said, "There's no way to get the car closer, Stella, with all these others parked near the door. We'll just have to make a run for it."

They got wet, of course, but Sam was wearing a wool suit, whereas Stella had on a skirt with a long-sleeved silk blouse, suitable dress for the warm day it had been but not much protection against the chill rain. When they got to the car, he was merely damp, but she was soaked, and the silk blouse clung coldly to her skin. He said, "I should have given you my coat, but I didn't think. I'm a boor, Stella. Why didn't you ask for it?"

"I didn't think either. I'll be all right as soon as the heater gets warmed up."

237

They were both silent for a time. Then Stella asked, "Did you see Maureen? I talked to her for a few minutes."

"I saw her, but I didn't get a chance to talk to her. Did she say anything about her mother?"

"Yes. I wasn't sure I should ask, because you said they didn't want anyone to know, but Maureen brought it up herself. She said they were keeping it quiet, but she didn't mind telling me. Mrs. Granger is doing fine. Maureen's been staying with her and was going back tonight. She said every time she left the room, her mother caught her hand and wouldn't let her go until she promised to come back."

"That sounds as if we were right about why she did it."

"Yes. I think Maureen understands that too, because when I mentioned college to her, she said she had decided not to go."

Sam said, "She's an extraordinary girl. I'm sorry to see her waste her life."

"I said something of the kind to her," Stella said, "but she just smiled and said it wouldn't be wasted."

"It's still a shock to me to see Maureen out in public," Sam said, "and I was particularly surprised to see her tonight. She must have come back to town just for that purpose, and it seems odd. The Grangers and the Claytons may be neighbors, but socially they're a long way apart."

"Yes, but Mr. Granger hired Junior to teach Maureen to drive, so I suppose it was noblesse oblige . . . Did you see Miss Mattie?"

"Yes, and that cousin of hers. I'd like to know what's wrong with her eyes. It isn't nystagmus. It's something I've never seen before."

"She seems strange to me," Stella said. "I overheard her saying to Miss Mattie that Wilma Jean's death was a debit for the ledger. What do you suppose she could have meant?"

"I don't know. What did Miss Mattie say?"

"She said, 'Cousin Edith, you talk like you're keeping books on the Lord's work. It isn't for us to criticize him.'"

"Depend on Miss Mattie to take up for God," Sam said as he turned into his driveway.

Stella was still cold when they got inside. She walked through the living room into the hall to stand on the floor furnace and feel the hot air creeping up her clammy body.

Sam said, "You'll get warm more quickly if you pull off

those wet clothes and take a hot shower. You can put on my robe and hang your clothes over the floor furnace. They'll be dry in time to wear them home."

His voice was brisk and impersonal, but the gray eyes looking at her were warm; there was a flame behind them. As he finished speaking, he clamped his square jaws together as if he were resisting the desire to say more.

He stooped quickly to hold a match to the wood already laid in the fireplace. He had thrown off his coat, and his white shirt stretched tautly across his shoulders as he bent forward. As she watched him, she remembered how those muscles had felt under her hands, and she wanted to touch him again, to have him touch her. . . . But she'd promised herself to be dignified.

He got up from the fireplace and said, "I'll get the robe for you."

She thought, I want him. I want him to kiss me and touch me and not stop. But he doesn't want me. I could make him want me though. I know I could. He's a man, and his body will react no matter how he feels in his mind. I'll never get another chance like this. But I mustn't. I'd wake up tomorrow nauseated by self-contempt. Still, I'm what I am. God knows I've tried to change, but it's no good. If I could have married Grant—but I couldn't. Sex is all that's left, so why not enjoy it? It isn't just for me. He'll enjoy it too. Even though he doesn't want me now, once he starts, he'll forget about the other men. Until tomorrow. And tomorrow doesn't matter, because I wasn't going to see him again anyway. She shivered. No, I can't. But she knew she was going to.

He came back with the robe and abruptly stopped stock still. Stella had moved off the floor furnace and was unbuttoning her blouse. She acted as if she did not know he was there, but when she finished and slid it from her shoulder, she handed it to him, looking him full in the face. Hers was pink, but she did not drop her eyes. Then, still with that look of defiant and half-amused embarrassment, she unzipped her skirt, let it drop to her feet, and stepped out of it.

Sam gasped. Somehow at the moment he could imagine nothing more intimate than that white satin slip, and yet he could not wait for her to pull it off. Slowly she slid the straps over her arms and wriggled her hips out of the slip, letting it too fall to the floor.

His breath was coming very fast now. He wanted to tear the remaining clothes off her and—but he did not move. He watched as she got out of the rest of her clothes slowly and gracefully. Even then he stood motionless for a moment gazing at her before he said, "Oh, God," in a strangled voice and reached for her.

Afterward, lying beside her in his bed, he said, "Stella, that striptease you did was absolutely the most beautiful, the most exciting, the most—well, the most everything. I could no more have kept from making love to you than I can keep from breathing. You must have known that. Is that why you did it?"

"Yes, I thought since you wouldn't seduce me, I'd seduce you."

He gave her a playful whack on the bottom. "Shameless hussy." Then he said more soberly. "As for seducing you, I was getting around to it in my bumbling way."

"I don't believe you *could* bumble with sex. I was pretty good with the striptease though, wasn't I?" she said with a complacent little giggle.

"Incredibly good. You moved so seductively, and at the same time you were blushing all over."

"I was embarrassed. I didn't know how you would take it. I thought you might gruffly tell me to undress in the bathroom."

"Fat chance. . . . But that reminds me, your clothes are still lying on the floor where we left them. Why don't you hang them up while I cook? Then after dinner it's back to bed for you, young lady."

"You're a demanding brute, Sam Taylor. But I love it."

"And me? Do you love me?"

"Why do you ask that?" she said in a startled voice.

"It seems logical, considering what we just did," he said dryly.

"That hadn't anything to do with love. Don't be idealistic about me, Sam. I'm not in love with you any more than you are with me."

He said slowly, "I do love you, Stella. I have for quite a while."

"Oh, no!" she said involuntarily. "I had no idea, I thought it was a physical compulsion with you, as it was with me. I thought we could have fun. If I'd known, I wouldn't have—"

"No! I won't have you anything but glad for this," he said

harshly. Then in a softer tone he said again, "I love you. And whether you know it or not, you love me. Your response told me that."

"Your technique is superb," she said in a flat voice. "I responded to that. Not to love."

"Is it Grant? Are you still in love with him?"

"I don't think so. If I were, it would hurt more. I hardly ever think of him now."

He said slowly, "Then there's no reason we can't be married, even if you don't love me. Because we're damn sure going on with this, and in Lanier it would be more convenient to be married."

She did not answer immediately, but when she did, she said, "That's very tempting, but I don't want to make any vows I'm not sure I could keep."

"I'll take my chances on that, sweetheart."

"You're still fooling yourself that I'm in love with you. But what I feel for you is physical; I could feel that for anybody, and in fact have. Right now I can't imagine ever wanting anybody but you, but tomorrow or next week . . . If you didn't love me, it wouldn't matter; I'd marry you in a minute. But I can't—it wouldn't be fair."

"My dear girl, I'm thirty-three years old. Please allow me to decide for myself what's fair. Will you marry me?"

"No. But you can have me any other way you want."

"All right. There's no use turning down good coin because it isn't hundred-dollar bills. I'll play by your rules, Stella. But if you're ever sorry, please remember that you're the one who made them."

32

Owen Perry was having a restless night, a rare occurrence for him. Partly, he guessed, it had to do with being without Adelaide so long—three months before the baby was born, and it looked like another three months to go, because he certainly didn't want to hurt her, and he figured she'd need about twice as much time as other women, having had twice as hard a time. He wasn't complaining; doing without was a mighty small price to pay for having a son, but all the same, it did make a man restless. Nothing else under the sun could smooth out a man's troubles so well and leave him feeling at peace with himself and the world.

It had been a bad day. J.T. Clayton's little girl—now there was one of the worst things that had ever happened in this town. And completely unavoidable, he'd satisfied himself as to that. Mrs. Ashford was as cut up about it as the Claytons were. She'd even said she wished she had never been healed, because then she wouldn't have been driving. But, as he told her, there was no use in thinking like that. Even the Claytons didn't blame her. It was just one of those terrible accidents for which no one can find a reason, and to try was to attempt to outguess God.

Losing a child must be the worst thing that could happen— no, losing a wife would be the worst. A man expected his children to grow up and leave him, but he hoped to keep his wife all his life. She was a part of him in a way no one else could ever be; at least, that's how he felt about Adelaide. He hadn't even given the baby a thought when Adelaide was in labor, because his terror for her hadn't left room for anything else. If he hadn't known what "forsaking all others" meant before, he did now.

No, losing a child wasn't the worst, but it would have to be the second worst, and Owen had ached all over when he went to talk to the Claytons and tell them how it happened.

He turned over in bed and pulled the covers up around his shoulders. There was no use thinking about the Clayton child. It had happened, and there was no way to make it unhappen, no matter how bad everybody wanted to. Some things a person just had to accept.

He got out of bed and straightened the sheet and quilts. The bare floors felt cold to hes feet. He missed the wool rugs of his childhood, but it was all the style now to have polished hardwood floors with no rugs. He went into the hall and turned the thermostat higher. Couldn't have Adelaide and Sammy getting cold. Then, padding down the hall, he opened the bedroom door softly. They were both sleeping peacefully now, but Sammy would be awake at two for his bottle, and Owen hoped he could get a few hours sleep before then.

But after he returned to bed, his mind resumed its grinding, and the fragments of his day spewed forth. There were other problems more worrisome than the traffic accident, because they required not just resigning himself but making a decision and taking action. That he knew already what the decision had to be only made his situation more distressing.

Actually, the other problems were all part of one big question: Should he arrest Stella Lidell for Warner Fox's murder? Considering the story J.T. Clayton had told, he thought he'd have to.

But how could he? Stella had given him his son's life. Was he now to take away her own? Because that's what it amounted to, no matter how he looked at it. He doubted that the prosecutor would ask for the death penalty, but Stella would lose her life just the same. She would go into prison a beautiful girl and come out a middle-aged woman with no life behind her and none before. Or if that did not happen, if she were acquitted, she'd still lose her life—or everything she valued in it. She couldn't live in Lanier afterward, and she probably couldn't get another teaching job anywhere. She would lose Sam Taylor, for how could a man in his position marry a girl who had been tried for murder—even worse, one who had been cheapened by having her intimacy with Warner laid out to public view? Not many men could take that.

Sam said Stella meant as much to him as Adelaide did to Owen. Of course that wasn't so and couldn't be until he'd lived with her and had a baby, but all the same Sam loved her. So maybe he'd stick by her. But anyway, he was going to be angry, and he was goint to feel that after all he'd done, Owen had knifed him in the back.

How could he possibly arrest Stella? Yet how could he not arrest her? He'd have to hide the evidence, lie and cheat and connive. He'd have to go against his sacred oath, and he'd be a different man then, not one he could respect. He would hate himself, and he thought someday Adelaide would hate him too.

And even if he could bring himself to do all that, it still might not help Stella. Because J.T. Clayton might not be able to keep quiet. And now the evidence was so overwhelming that it would roll on of its own momentum and crush Stella in spite of all Owen could do.

He rolled over again, trying to escape that painful thought, and the bedclothes moved with him, exposing his back. He

243

straightened the covers once more. It sure had turned cold in a hurry. Warm enough for short sleeves this afternoon and now almost freezing again. The whole winter had been cold, the coldest since 1941, when they'd had the biggest snow in the history of the town and the temperature went below zero. But he guessed Lanier was lucky at that. It never had more than two snows a year and some winters not any. Even this year when the papers were full of pictures of snow in England and Belgium and Germany, Lanier had so far escaped with less than three inches total.

But Owen's mind had a will of its own. Before he was aware of what was happening, it left the weather and went back to his problem. The evidence against Stella had been piling up bit by bit ever since Warner disappeared. Of course, Warner's body still hadn't been found. But what Owen had told Stella was true. A body wasn't absolutely essential if there was good enough reason to think a murder had been committed. And in this case it looked like there was incontrovertible proof.

He had clutched at every straw only to find them breaking in his hand. When Sam came back this morning and suggested that Miss Mattie might be a witness too, Owen went to see her right away. But Miss Mattie wasn't any help at all. True enough, she had been on the road by the Clayton's that evening, but she'd got off into telling him about some religious vision she'd seen right after she passed the Clayton's house. Owen didn't pay much attention to that, because everybody knew how fanatical Miss Mattie was on the subject of religion, even though she was pretty hard-headed and practical when it came to business. Now that he thought of it, Miss Mattie wasn't really the type to see visions, even religious ones, and it was funny she'd seen it right around the same time J.T. claimed to have heard the shooting.

And if Sam was right, J.T. and Miss Mattie both had some strange powers. And so did Stella.

Owen shivered again, but this time not from the cold. As he'd told Sam earlier, something funny was going on in Lanier. But, in the name of all the saints, what could it be?

He shouldn't have told Adelaide what J.T. said or about Sam coming to see him this morning. He didn't know why he had, except that he was accustomed to telling her everything. He could depend on her not to gossip, and it was a help to talk over his problems. Sometimes Adelaide surprised him by her insight, but even when she had no answers, he felt better for having told her.

Today, however, instead of listening quietly and then offering some comment, as she usually did, Adelaide had flown at him like a hen protecting her chicks, blaming him for everything and accusing him of deliberately searching for evidence against Stella. She wouldn't listen to any of his explanations; she said she was not concerned with his sworn duty to uphold and enforce the law. All she wanted was for him to promise not to arrest Stella. And that he couldn't do.

It was the worst quarrel they'd ever had, and it looked as if it would last a long time. Unless he found some way to avoid arresting Stella—and he didn't think he could—Adelaide was going to stay mad. Of course, eventually he'd be able to love her out of it, but he couldn't start that for another three months.

The anger was all on her side. He wasn't mad at her, because he felt the same as she did about this arrest. He just didn't have anybody to blame it on.

He twisted and turned, trying to get comfortable, but the discomfort was in his mind and couldn't be eased by a change in position.

He was going to have to arrest Stella Lidell.

He'd as soon cut off his right arm.

Thank God, tomorrow was Sunday. That would give him one more day. But no later than Monday morning—or maybe he'd wait until school was out in the afternoon. If anyone asked him about it—and of course someone would, because news always traveled—he could say he was waiting until he checked out some other leads.

His mind stopped, and then began to race. Why couldn't he say that all week? If he could wait a week, he might be able to find *something* that would help. He couldn't believe Stella had done it, and somewhere there must be something to refute J.T. Clayton's story. He would find it. Or kill himself trying.

At last he dropped off to sleep. And of course ten minutes later a lusty wail brought him to his feet. Two o'clock. Time for the baby's bottle.

33

Except for the trip back home to make a condolence call to the Claytons, Maureen had been with her mother ever since Friday afternoon. Mr. Granger had arranged for private nurses, of course, so there wasn't much for Maureen to do, but Mrs. Granger didn't want her to leave. At Mr. Granger's insistence authorities at the hospital set up another bed in the room so that Maureen could stay both day and night.

With her mother sleeping most of the time, Maureen had hour upon hour to think, but it took scarcely one hour to come to her decision—she could never leave her mother.

She realized now what she should have known before, what she would have seen if she hadn't been so carried away with thinking of her own life and making her own plans. Her mother couldn't accept the new situation. Of course, it was plain from the beginning that both her parents were disconcerted by the sudden change. They were thankful for her healing, but having an active, energetic daughter instead of a handicapped one took some getting used to. That hadn't seemed terribly important at first. Time, she thought, would take care of it. It would be like a couple with their first baby; after a while it would seem entirely natural. And to Daddy it had. Very soon he was treating her as if she'd never been handicapped and was entering into her new plans enthusiastically. But Mother hung back, reluctant to admit that Maureen was entirely normal, still trying to hold her to some of her former dependence.

That was easy to understand too, once one really thought about it. Daddy had his business to run, the church and Rotary Club activities to participate in, people to talk with all day. He loved his family, but he had a life apart from them. Mother didn't. For nineteen years—twenty if one counted her pregnancy—her family had been the sum of her existence. Every waking minute was devoted to their welfare, especially Maureen's. She was a mother first, a wife second, a housekeeper third—and nothing else. She went nowhere and had no hobbies or intellectual interests. She was interested in the news of the town her husband brought home, but as an onlooker rather than a participant.

Maureen had always assumed that her mother's life was a matter of necessity. One of the reasons she'd been so anxious to be healed was to relieve her mother of the burden of her care, to free her to live her own life. But now she saw that was not possible. She wasn't sure whether her mother was held to the kind of life she'd always lived by inclination, habit, or fear of something new, but held she was. She could accept nothing else. So there was only one answer—Maureen must continue to be dependent on her, or at least make her mother feel that she was dependent. If her mother couldn't loose her, then she must stay bound.

When she got to that point in her thinking, she felt desperate. To have her wings clipped just as she was finally learning to fly seemed an injury too great to be borne. She'd had great plans—college, a career, travel—and eventually marriage and a family of her own. All of that, she had thought, could be accomplished without leaving Lanier permanently or depriving her parents of her devoted attention. They would be proud of her career, ready to travel with her, fond of her husband and the children she would have.

But she might give up the dreams. She must content herself with staying at home, with being only her parents' child to the end of their lives. And then what? Then it would be too late. She would spend the rest of her life a lonely spinster without a career, family, or friends.

Well, perhaps not without friends. There was no reason she had to stay at home all the time. She could go to town, to church, to club meetings. She would get to know people, and surely someone would want to be friends with her. After all, Junior Clayton like her; probably other people would too.

Junior Clayton . . . She thought about him for a long time, and when she was through, she had made another decision and a plan to carry it out. She wasn't sure it would work, but she would try it. Right away, while she still had the opportunity provided by the driving lessons.

34

Sunday morning, Sam and Stella went to church together for the first time and had the dubious pleasure of overhearing some whispers about themselves.

"Miss Lidell and Dr. Taylor! Well, that's news."

"Seems funny for a doctor to take up with a healer. You'd think he'd see through her."

"She's pretty though."

"All the same, he'd better be careful. She's crazy in more ways than one. They say she killed Warner Fox."

"Sh-h, they'll hear you."

The whispers were on the bench behind them. Sam glanced at Stella, but she was looking straight ahead, stony faced. Unease tugged at his mind. Had J.T.'s story already got out? He didn't see how. Owen wouldn't have told, and surely no one would ask J.T. any questions while he was mourning for his little girl. Sam's mind stopped on a fact he hadn't thought of for some time. He hoped to God J.T. never found out about that. He was pretty sure no one else knew it though.

His mind flicked past J.T.'s problems and came back to his own. If the whispers had been just about him and Stella, he wouldn't have been disturbed. Everybody was interested in the romantic affairs of the town. But this talk of murder . . . Still, everyone knew Stella was on the scene that night. And that she had dated Warner for a short while. There was bound to be some speculation.

Driving away after the service, he said, "You heard what those gossips were saying, of course."

"Yes. Sam, I hadn't thought before about the effect on you, but I think it would be best if we weren't seen together again. I'll come to your house at night when you want me."

"You mean I can call you on the telephone and say, 'Please come to see me tonight,' and you'll come?"

"Of course."

"And how much shall I pay you?"

"Sam!"

"Sorry, Stella, but that's what it sounded like. Did you honestly think I'd agree to that? No, my love, this you'll have to do my way. We'll be together everywhere, or nowhere. Today we're going to the café to eat and then to that fund-raising tea at the public library. I *want* to be seen with you, sweetheart. I'd like everyone to know you've chosen me. Even—" there was an undertone of amusement in his voice—"if it is only for my body."

She laughed. "Well, you do have quite a body, sir. And, if I may say so, you use it very effectively."

His voice was suddenly serious. "Stella, all this vicious talk about you and Warner—we need to get it stopped. Should we play the tape for Owen Perry? Do you think that would help?"

"I don't see how. He'd only think I was crazy. No, Sam. No, no, a thousand times no. Too many people already think there's something strange or wrong about me because of the healing. That would make everybody certain. The tape wouldn't prove anything to anyone. They'd just say I killed Warner in a fit of insanity . . . You haven't hypnotized me again yet," she said. "You should do it today. That might tell us something."

"We've got today planned already, but we can do it tonight."

And if it turned out the same as it did before, he'd keep the knowledge from her again. Because if she ever found out that she had confirmed J.T.'s story, she would be sure she was guilty of killing Warner. She wasn't, and he wouldn't have her burdened with thinking so. Even if she had pulled a trigger, she wasn't guilty. She would have done it only under some outside compulsion, and she wasn't going to be punished for it; he'd spend the last breath in his body to prevent that.

But she hadn't shot Warner. Sam thought he knew what had happened, the only thing that answered the problem without making Stella guilty. Warner had seen the flying machine as Stella had and, unlike her, had known it was no earthly craft. So when he saw her walking toward it, he had called to try to stop her. Perhaps he had shot the gun at one of the strange creatures. And now when Stella tried to tell about it under hypnotism, she became too upset to talk, because Warner too had been taken aboard and had not come out again.

And try to tell *that* in a courtroom. Testimony obtained under hypnotism wasn't admissable, but even if it had been, no one would believe such a fantastic story. He couldn't expect them to. Even Owen, as much as he wanted to exonerate Stella, wouldn't believe it. Still, Sam might have to try to convince him. Because it was all they had.

He would save it for the last resort though. Owen had promised not to do anything unless he was forced to by J.T.'s story becoming known. J.T. wouldn't tell unless someone asked questions, and no one would, Sam thought again, until a decent mourning period had passed. The funeral was tomorrow; it should be at least a week before anyone talked to J.T. about it.

Gaynell Moore awakened the following Friday morning to the heavy knowledge that this was the last day. Her time was up. Up with Silas, up with nature. She'd had a two week respite, and tonight it would have passed. The time was past too when she could hide her condition.

Last night Mamma had said, "Gaynell, I don't want to see you in that dress again till you've let it out across the front. Your bosoms are showing as plain as they did the day you was baptized . . ."

A faraway look came into Annabel's eyes. "I'll never forget the way that white dress was plastered to you when you come up out of the water and how you come wading out to the creek bank before I could throw your coat on to you. Everybody said it was understandable you'd forget your modesty at a time like that, but Papa had me whip you anyhow soon as we got home. And I reckon he was right. You oughtn't to have forgot your modesty even at your baptizing. And you specially ought not to forget it now, when you're fixing to be wed. We better squeeze the money for some dress material out of your pay this week."

Gaynell was grateful for Mamma's reminiscing; it had saved her from closer scrutiny. But the time was up. Mamma would buy the dress material in town tomorrow morning and probably get the first dress finished in the afternoon so Gaynell could wear it to church the next day. She would be sure to know what was wrong as soon as she started fitting the dress. Only her constant busyness and natural lack of suspicion had kept her from noticing already.

The time was up.

It had been a pleasant two weeks though with the burden of decision-making gone and nothing to do but wait. Gaynell felt fatalistic. All her plans were made. What would happen, would happen. There was peace in that thought. Peace at home too, where she was now treated with the deference and respect due the maker of the family fortune.

As Silas told Annabel, "We'll sure be taking a big step up with land of our own and Woodrow Lyle for a son-in-law. I reckon we'll miss Gaynell's wages at first, but I don't doubt she'll find some way to slip you a bit of change now and again, with Woodrow so rich and openhanded.

"Besides, I figure either Betty Lee or Lila can get that job with the doctor when Gaynell gives it up. They're both as old as Gaynell was when she started working out, and we won't have to worry about them succumbing to temptation any more than we did her. 'Train up a child in the way he should go, and when he is old, he will not depart from it.' That's what the Scripture says, and I reckon we've proved it to be so.

"We've got a fine bunch of young'uns, Annabel. Never any trouble with any of them—at least none that couldn't be cured by a good strapping. Yessir, them young'uns is gonna be the comfort of our old age. Gaynell is just the first, and look what she's bringing us."

Being so pleased with Gaynell, Silas made no demands on her except the hour of Bible study and the recitation of those verses he deemed particularly pertinent. She had two or three hours each day to spend with her brothers and sisters, and at night after she went to bed, she thought about Warner and relived every moment they'd had together. There was much to smile over and little to regret—nothing really except that silly quarrel back in the fall, and even that had only showed her how much she loved him.

But now it was Friday morning; the two weeks were up, and Warner had not come. He might come tomorrow or the next day or a week from now, but it would be too late. An ineffable sadness settled over her. She got out of bed slowly, like an old woman, and began to dress.

The sadness stayed with her at work. Usually in the office she could throw off her troubles, at least enough to smile and chat with the patients, but today she couldn't. She kept thinking, "This is the last time I shall do this," and it made her heavy and dull. It was strange how she felt on this, her last day. Unbearably sad, and yet at the same time a little numb, as if she were already partly gone, as if she were not altogether present in this time and place. Perhaps last times were always like that. She was glad she had not known when her last time with Warner was until afterward.

Her heart lifted in one glorious moment of hope. Perhaps Warner would come today, before she got home, before—There was still time. In imagination she began to live the scene.

But soon she stopped. He would not come. She wouldn't hope any more. It had taken a long time to get to this resignation, this feeling of peace, and she must not lose it now.

A little after four Dr. Taylor was called to an outlying farm where a man had fallen off a barn roof. He told the patients in the office where he was going and said he didn't know when he'd be back but if he was going to be long, he'd send word after he got there.

It was his customary procedure. Emergencies took precedence. Usually when they had one, the people who weren't very sick went home to return another day, and the others either stayed or left their names for Dr. Taylor to visit them at home later.

Gaynell hoped they would all go home today. Not knowing whether she would have another chance, she had got the pills from Dr. Taylor's desk when he was out to lunch, but she had thought perhaps she would have a few minutes alone to bid farewell to this place, which was more home to her than the old farmhouse where she slept. She had been treated kindly here; she had felt important and needed. Besides, it was where she had met Warner and where, one afternoon when Dr. Taylor was out and the office empty, he had talked to her and ended up asking her for a date. She thought she might cry when she left the office, and she wanted to be alone.

However, Miss Pauline Howle stayed. Gaynell tried to hide her disappointment. She chatted with Miss Pauline a moment and then finished typing the last medical record. After that she cleaned out her desk, a matter of only a few minutes work, because Gaynell had no personal possessions, and her office supplies were kept in good order at all times.

Dr. Taylor came in shortly before five, looking cross and irritable. Toby Elliott had a wrenched back that might heal if he took care of it, which he wasn't likely to do with the

252

busy farming season about to start. Ordinarily Gaynell would have felt the tragedy as Dr. Taylor did, but today she had no time for other people's troubles. She thought it was perhaps as well, after all, that she had not been alone in the office. Her life here was over now. All that remained was to leave quickly and with little thought. She put on her coat, gave a final look around, and went, not looking back.

As Gaynell left, Dr. Taylor was seating Miss Pauline in his office.

"Well, Miss Howle, what's the problem?" Sam had never called Miss Pauline by her first name, although she had once asked him to. It was wiser, he thought, to keep the relationship as formal as possible.

He felt impatient. He had hoped to get away early tonight and take Stella somewhere out of town for dinner and maybe some dancing or a movie. With all the stress she had been under this week, she needed some diversion. Besides, it might be the last chance they would have. J.T.'s story was not known yet, but the other evidence was being talked about everywhere. Sam hadn't even known about the gun and the note from Stella until he'd overheard a conversation in the drug store and got the information from Grant.

Grant was reluctant to tell him. "I don't want to pass on any gossip about Stella to you," he said. "You'd think I was jealous or had some hard feelings."

"I know how you and Stella broke up," Sam said impatiently, "and I know you aren't jealous. I've got no hard feelings toward you either. We've been friends a long time, and we're still friends. So for God's sake, if you know anything I ought to know, tell me."

When he'd heard what was being said, he realized how much pressure Owen must be under and knew the time had come to let him hear the tape and to tell him his conclusions.

But it hadn't helped at all.

Owen said, "Yeah, I believe it. Knowing what I do about Stella, I'd believe her if she said she'd been to the moon and back. But you can be pretty damn sure you won't get twelve men on a jury who will believe it. Once she tells that story, she's sunk—unless she pleads insanity."

Sam was in a hurry to see Stella. All week he'd felt an urgency that was almost panic, and several times he'd been tempted to shut down his practice and spend every minute with her for as long as he could. Now here was Miss Pauline taking time away from him with some trivial complaint.

But looking at her, Sam noticed that she was pale and worn, with puffy dark circles under her prominent blue eyes. Menopause, he supposed. Maiden laides often had a bad time of it, possibly because they saw it as the end of hope.

"I'm having trouble sleeping, Doctor," she said.

"Again?" He thought of the several times Miss Pauline had appeared at his house at night with that complaint.

"It's worse than before," she said. "Then it was just some restlessness in the early part of the night, but now I find myself tossing and turning all night long. I'm having headaches during the day, and I know it's from sleeplessness, but I just can't go to sleep."

"When did this start?"

"I don't know. About the time Charles got married, I think. That would be two weeks ago. I don't think I can go on much longer."

He asked her several questions and then said, "Well, I think we can rule out anything serious. It's just nervous tension. Take a sleeping pill for a couple of nights to catch up on the sleep you've lost, and then don't worry about losing more. The human body usually gets the sleep it needs if nothing interferes. You may be sleeping more than you realize, even with all the tossing and turning."

He opened his desk drawer. "I'll just give you a couple of pills to get you through the next two nights."

But the pills were not there. He searched for a moment or two, and then he said, "On second thought, I believe I'll write you a prescription this time. But I don't want you to take them every night, just when you feel you have to. I won't give you many, because I don't think you'll need them often."

As he was writing the prescription, he said, "How are Charles and Valerie? I haven't seen them for several days."

"Fine," Miss Pauline said. "Valerie is a sweet girl, so much help with Mamma. She's fixing up the house too."

And not leaving you much to do, Sam thought shrewdly. Aloud he said, "That must be nice for you, after being tied down so many years. The first thing we know, you'll be over at the university getting a Ph.D."

"Oh, I don't know," Miss Pauline said, blushing at the

implied compliment. "I'm not sure I'm that smart. I was offered a teaching fellowship two years ago when I got my master's though. Of course I couldn't leave Lanier then. I suppose I might still get the fellowship," she said thoughtfully.

Maybe I will, she thought, with the first stirrings of enthusiasm she'd felt in some time.

As soon as she left, Sam went through his desk drawer again, but the sleeping pills had not miraculously appeared. He thought back. He had given Mrs. Clayton four pills last week, but he hadn't used any since. He was sure the bottle was in the drawer yesterday when he gave Mrs. Weems those new diuretics to try. Someone had taken it today.

But who? He hadn't left anyone alone in the office. Suddenly the answer came to him: Gaynell. She was the only person who'd had an opportunity. But what would someone as young as Gaynell need with sleeping pills? Unless—of course, that was it. Even as he galloped down the stairs, he was cursing himself for a blind fool. He had known she was in trouble, and he should have seen this coming. He'd been too busy with his own affairs to think of Gaynell. But that was no excuse.

35

He met Stella on the sidewalk below. "Were you going to the office?" he asked. "I'm on my way somewhere. Come on, you can go with me."

As she got in the car, Stella said, "Sam, I have something to tell you."

"Can it wait? I think Gaynell is committing suicide, and I've got to stop her." He glanced at his watch. "It's five-forty-five. She'll be home by now. I don't know when she'll take the pills—they're sleeping pills, so she may wait until bedtime. Or she may be taking them right now."

He went on talking, trying to figure out what Gaynell would do and castigating himself for not foreseeing this. Stella listened quietly, and overshadowed by this, her news faded from her mind.

Sam drove recklessly fast, not slowing even after he left the pavement at the edge of town. Since last week's rain the dirt road was badly washed, but Sam jounced over the ridges as if they were not there. The frame of the car rattled in protest, and Stella put her hand on the dashboard to brace herself against the sickening jolts. Concentrating on the narrow road, Sam did not appear to notice. As they approached a curve, he blew his horn and then skidded around it without decelerating.

The rushing air screamed against the car. Splitting the darkness, the car lights picked up the shining eyes of some small animal, but they sped by, leaving it unidentified. They dipped down a sharp little hill, slid around a final curve, and were there. Sam jumped out of the car, leaving the engine running and the door open. Stella closed the door and shut off the engine. Then she got out and followed him up the brick walkway to the porch.

When Stella got to the steps, Silas Moore was standing in the open hallway with a kerosene lamp in his hand. Evidently some conversation had already taken place, because Mr. Moore was in the middle of a sentence. "—dressing for a beau," he said. "I'll have my wife get her. Won't y'all come in?"

"No," Sam said. "If you don't mind, we'll wait here on the porch. I wanted to talk to her privately—office business, you know."

"Well, Doc, if you're wanting her to work tonight, I can tell you myself she can't do it. I don't mind her working late once in a while. There ain't no harm in it with you such a well-respected man, and Gaynell a good girl, and your office being public thataway. But tonight she just can't go. This is a mighty important man coming to see her tonight, and I wouldn't want her to spoil her chances with him, even for you."

In the dim lamplight Stella could see Sam's face, and she knew him well enough to see that he was puzzled. But she didn't think Mr. Moore had noticed, and Sam's voice was casual as he said, "It isn't that. It's about one of the medical records. I can't find it, and I thought she might tell me where it is. I'm not very neat, and—"

"I don't reckon it's a man's business to be neat," Silas said. "Womenfolks is supposed to pick up after them. You wait here then if you want to, while I send for Gaynell."

They waited about fifteen minutes before Gaynell came. She was carrying a lamp too, but she set it down on one of the chairs in the hall out of the wind. Then she came out on the porch and sat down to talk to them. She was dressed neatly as always in the same style clothes she wore to the office: a high-necked, long-sleeved, cotton-print dress of dull gray, a navy-blue, coat-style sweater, black cotton stockings, and sturdy black oxfords. Even in such garb she managed to look attractive, like a pretty Dutch girl with golden braids of hair wound around her head and the delicate bloom of peach blossoms in her cheeks.

She said in answer to Sam's question, "No, Dr. Taylor, I don't know anything about a bottle of sleeping pills. Are you sure you put them back in the drawer? Sometimes you misplace things, you know."

They talked about the lost pills at some length, Gaynell suggesting places to look and Sam assuring her in each case that he already had.

Finally she said, "I don't know, Dr. Taylor, unless one of the patients took them. I don't know who would though. I never send anyone in unless you're there. But of course somebody could have gone in without me knowing. I can't watch every minute."

At last Sam gave up. Obviously Gaynell had not swallowed the pills yet, but if she intended to, he didn't know how he could stop her.

He was perplexed. He couldn't understand why Gaynell had found it necessary to lie to her father about working nights when it was so obvious that he approved her boy friend. And he couldn't see any reason for her to be desperate enough to steal the sleeping pills, if she was going to get married, as Silas Moore had implied. Unless, he thought slowly, this man tonight is a different one, not the father of her child but someone Silas has picked out. . . . Yes, that could be it.

He said, "Gaynell, what time is your date? Could you come back to the office with us and help search for the pills? You're always good at finding things."

He rather expected her to refuse, but her voice was almost eager as she said, "Of course, just let me get my coat. It's cold out here."

As Gaynell rose from her chair, Mrs. Moore came into the hall. "Good evening," she said. "I hate to interrupt y'all

257

while you're talking, but Mr. Lyle is due any minute, Gaynell, and your papa has gone to sleep on the bed in the front room."

Gaynell made some small noise, and Mrs. Moore continued, "I can't make him get up. You'll have to help me get him moved. We can't have him piled up on the bed thataway while you're entertaining company. I can't think what's got into Silas. He never goes to sleep before eight-thirty. That's been his bedtime summer and winter ever since we married. And here it is not much past seven and him asleep already. You'll excuse me, Doctor, Miss Lidell, but I'm a mite upset with so much depending on Gaynell making a good impression tonight."

Before she finished, Sam was striding toward the front room on the right where the lamplight was, flinging some words back over his shoulder: "I'll move him, Mrs. Moore."

Like a flash Gaynell was barring his way. "No, Dr. Taylor, I'm sorry, but you can't go in."

He shoved her aside, not gently, and went into the room. Gaynell started to cry. Mrs. Moore said, "Why, what—"

Stella said, "Why don't you go see if you can help Dr. Taylor, Mrs. Moore? Gaynell and I will go to the kitchen and make some coffee." She took Gaynell's arm and propelled her down the hall, picking up the lamp as she went.

In the kitchen she surveyed the wood-burning stove and said, "Well, thank goodness, the fire is already built. But you'll have to make the coffee, Gaynell. I don't know where to find things."

Later when everything had been done that could be done and Sam was ready to go, he said, "Whatever happened to your date, Gaynell?"

"I sent him home," she replied. "I told him we had sickness here."

"Mr. Moore will be all right," Sam said to Annabel. "Don't be surprised if he sleeps a lot tomorrow though."

"What was it, Doctor?" Annabel asked. "Sleeping sickness?"

Sam glanced at Gaynell's white face. "A new kind of flu," he said. He turned to Gaynell. "We still need you at the office, and it's late now. It might be best if you spent the night with Miss Lidell."

It was only nine o'clock, but he supposed that would be late at the Moores. "That's all right, isn't it, Mrs. Moore?"

Annabel looked around, as if searching for Silas to ask. She answered in an uncertain voice, "I guess so."

258

In the car as they drove away from the house, Sam said, "Why did you do it, Gaynell?"

She had cried at first, but she got over that now. Her voice was dull but tearless as she answered, "I had to."

"Because you're pregnant? Couldn't you go to the boy? Who is he anyway?"

But she wouldn't tell him that. She wouldn't say any more, no matter how many questions they asked. Finally she said in a leaden voice, "It didn't work out the way I planned it."

"How's that?" Sam asked.

"I thought maybe nobody would ever know. He'd die in his sleep, and everyone would think he'd had a heart attack. We'd be better off without him."

"But he's your father!" Stella protested.

"You don't understand," Gaynell said.

"But you must have known you might be caught," Sam said.

"I thought if I was, they'd let me have the baby anyhow before they executed me. That's why I killed Silas. Because he would have killed me, and I couldn't stand the way he'd do it. I had to kill either him or myself, and if I died, the baby would too."

"Is the baby so important to you then?" Sam asked gently.

"His daddy is," Gaynell answered.

"Then why the hell didn't he help you? What kind of a man would leave you to face this alone, to be driven to the point of killing your own father to save his baby? Never mind. I can see by your face you won't answer. God, what a mess."

Sam stopped the car. Gaynell looked around and said, "What are we doing here?"

"Where did you think we were going?"

"To jail, of course."

"No, first I'm going to examine you, as I should have weeks ago. We'll make sure you really are pregnant and see what shape you're both in after enough stess to kill a dozen women."

Stella waited in Sam's office while he was doing the examination. After a while he came out, rolling down his sleeves. He looked at Stella and said in answer to her unspoken question, "About thirteen weeks, I'd say, and everything seems all right. . . . I found out the way she

259

thought Silas would kill her—by beating her to death. He gave her a sample two or three weeks ago. After hearing what she says, I can't say I blame her for trying to kill him."

"Then I don't see why we have to tell anybody."

"You know that makes us accessories after the fact?"

"Legally maybe. But morally . . . Besides, the legal procedure would just be a formality anyway, so all we'll be doing is avoiding some unpleasantness for her."

"All right, that's settled."

"She can't live at home any longer though. Valerie's room at the boarding house? And somebody will have to tell her folks."

"I'll do that tomorrow," Sam said. "I'm looking forward to telling Silas Moore a few facts."

He glanced at his watch and said impatiently, "I wish Gaynell would hurry. Dammit, our time is getting away from us. I meant for us to go out of town tonight, but now it looks as if we'll be lucky to have even a couple of hours at home."

And there may not be a tomorrow, he thought.

Stella started to say something, but Gaynell came out just then, and Sam rapidly told her what they had decided. She dropped her eyes, but not before they saw the surprise that was turning into hope.

"My baby's father is Warner Fox," she said.

As Sam said later, "A non sequitur, if I ever heard one."

"No," Stella replied. "It followed directly after she learned she wouldn't go to jail. It was then that she decided she could trust us completely. Also, you'd said some harsh things about her lover, and she wanted to exonerate him. You couldn't blame him for deserting her once you knew it was Warner."

But that was later. At the time neither of them was thinking of Gaynell's motives, because both were gripped by powerful emotions of their own.

It was Sam who voiced the sudden suspicion in both their minds. His face darkened ominously, and he asked in an ugly voice, "Did you kill him, Gaynell? Did you kill him and let Stella take the blame?"

"Me kill Warner?" The shock on her face was too genuine to doubt. Then the implication of the question seemed to hit her, and she slid quietly to the floor.

260

"It was the shock of hearing us say he's been killed," Stella said as Sam was bringing Gaynell back to consciousness. "She hasn't accepted it. Neither have I. But what I do believe wouldn't be much comfort to her."

After they settled Gaynell at the boarding house, there was, as Sam predicted, little time left to spend together. And soon there might be none at all, he thought again. Inside his house Stella came into his arms immediately, as if she too felt the urgency of time.

Later he raised himself on his elbow and said, "Sweetheart, why did you cry? I didn't hurt you, did I?"

"No. Don't ask me why, Sam."

"I want to know." But he could see that she wasn't going to tell him, and he thought, she knows too. She will be arrested very soon, maybe tomorrow, and she knows that this could be our last night together.

And I can't stand it.

"Stella, get up and dress."

She glanced at the clock on the bedside table. "We've a few minutes more," she said. "There's no hurry."

"Stella. Get up." He was already out of bed, pulling on his clothes. "We've got to leave right away, because I'll have to be back here by ten o'clock in the morning."

"Back here? I don't understand."

"I'm going to take you to Atlanta and put you on a plane for—oh, I don't know, somewhere a thousand miles from here. You can decide where you want to go before we get there. And what name you want to use. After a while, when the fuss has died down, I'll join you. If you stay here, you're going to be tried for murder, and you've no defense. I let Owen listen to the tape today, and he said . . . Well, never mind that now. Get dressed, and let's go."

"It's impossible, Sam."

"No, it's not. Get up, Stella. You can't teach under a false name, I guess, but I'll give you some money. We'll work out the details on the way. God damn it, do I have to drag you out of that bed?"

"Sam, listen to me. I'm not going anywhere."

"Yes, you are. I won't let you be sent to prison. I love you. Can't you get that through your thick, stubborn head?"

"You're panicking. It isn't as bad as you say. They can't prove me guilty if I'm not. I've got to stay here and fight it out. I have a right to decide that for myself. You can't make me go."

"Can't I?" He caught her ankles and pulled her across the bed like a sack of meal. Then he grabbed her arm roughly and hauled her to her feet.

She said quietly, "All right, you're proving that you're stronger than I am, but you're not proving you love me. If you did, you'd listen to me. You'd consider what I want."

Abruptly he let go of her upper arms, which he had been holding so tightly that she could still feel the separate pressure points of his fingers. Tomorrow those finger marks would be blue, but she didn't care; she was only thinking of how to make him feel better.

She said, "You haven't hypnotized me again yet. That may help. You can do it tomorrow. And we could talk to the Claytons. . . . Oh, I almost forgot. I had something to tell you. Junior Clayton and Maureen Granger are married."

"You're trying to distract me. Stella, please . . ."

But after a while he had to give up. And after a while longer he even began to catch some of the optimism Stella was so determinedly showing. By the time they left for the boarding house, he had hope again. He also still had his plan for her to run if the danger appeared imminent, but it was useless to try to persuade her now.

He said, "So Junior and Maureen are married. He's not more than sixteen, is he?"

"Nearly seventeen, and looks twenty. I have him in Junior English. He's a good-looking boy in a flashy sort of way."

"Yes, like his daddy . . . I'm surprised though."

"So am I, but we shouldn't be. He's been teaching her to drive, and at that age proximity is a powerful spur. I don't think they've told Mrs. Granger yet, and Mr. Granger was threatening to have it annulled so she wouldn't have to know. Maureen is over the age of consent, but Junior isn't. However, all that came to nothing."

"I take it the marriage had already been consummated."

Stella laughed. "Yes, they went straight to a hotel. At eleven-thirty in the morning, I understand."

"Good for Junior."

"You sound as if you approve."

"I don't see why it shouldn't work. Mr. Granger will see that Junior finishes school and then give him a job at the Coca-Cola plant. That should be a good occupation for him, because his family has always been in the beverage business; it's in his blood. As for the rest," he said, "I'm betting on Maureen to make it work."

"Sam?"

"What is it, sweetheart?"

"Nothing. I like you better than anybody I know."

It wasn't nothing, he thought. But neither was it what he wanted to hear.

36

J.T. was well pleased with Junior's marriage. The boy was a little young, he guessed, but he'd been only a year older when he married Esther, and he'd never regretted it a minute. J.T. didn't see any reason for Junior to have regrets either. Maureen seemed like a sweet little girl, and anybody could see she was crazy about Junior.

At first it had looked like her daddy might cause some problems, but he calmed down when he found out they'd went to a hotel as soon as the preacher got done. Mr. Granger seen then that there wasn't no way to annul the marriage, and also that his little girl might already be pregnant. After that it seemed like he couldn't do enough for Junior. So the upshot of it was that Junior and Maureen would live with the Grangers, and Mr. Granger would help Junior get started in a job as soon as he finished school. It looked like Junior was set for life, though of course the boy didn't realize any of his good luck yet except in getting the girl he wanted. He just watched Maureen the whole time, and J.T. could see as plain as day what was on his mind.

But Junior's good fortune wasn't the only reason J.T. was pleased about the marriage. He thought maybe having a daughter-in-law would take Esther's attention away from losing Wilma Jean. If something didn't come along to get her mind off it, she was going to grieve herself to death. She wasn't sleeping or eating, and she cried all the time. She tried to hide the tears when he came into the room, but her red, swollen eyes gave her away. She wouldn't talk to him about Wilma Jean though. When he tried to talk to her, she

263

just listened with a set face and then pretty soon walked out of the room.

J.T. was feeding the mules as he meditated on these matters. As he started to the house, he saw two of the boys taking in stovewood. The other one was milking, and he'd have both cows to milk tonight. With Junior gone there'd have to be some changes in the chores.

He said that to Esther when he walked into the kitchen, but she didn't reply. She was standing at the stove, and she looked as if she had forgotten what she started to do.

He tried again. "Well, sugar, what do you think of your new daughter-in-law?"

She didn't answer. He took her by the shoulders and turned her around, and the glassy expression in her eyes set his heart to galloping. She wasn't even seeing him; she was a long way off. This wasn't the first time he'd seen that expression in her eyes, and it scared him every time because he thought, what if she don't come back?

He said, "Sugar, you oughtn't to grieve by yourself. Talk to me. We can help each other."

She didn't look at him. Her unseeing eyes were fixed on a point beyond his shoulder.

"Look at me. You're acting like I'm not even here, like you're the only one that misses Wilma Jean. She was my child too, wasn't she?"

"No," Esther said. "No, she wasn't." A startled look came over her face, and her eyes flew to his. She started to cry and pulled away from his hands and walked out of the kitchen.

He let her go. He was too shocked to do anything else. The boys came into the room with their loads of stovewood, looked around in surprise, and said, "When are we gonna eat?"

"After while," he said. "If y'all are hungry, you can eat whatever is left from dinner. Just leave your mamma alone."

He walked out to the front porch and stood there a long time, looking into the lowering darkness. Finally he went into the front bedroom where Esther was. She was lying across the bed. He said, "You'll get cold back there without any covers. Come to the fire."

But she didn't move, so after a minute he went to the closet and got a quilt to put over her. He asked, "Was that true what you said?"

But he knew it was. He'd already worked that out. He had asked her a question, not even meaning for it to be a question, and she'd had to answer it truthfully.

She said, "Yeah, it's true. But I didn't aim to tell you. I've kept it to myself all these years, and I wasn't ever gonna tell you no different. But the Lord wouldn't let me get by with it."

"The Lord didn't have nothing to do with it," he said roughly. "It was—" But he stopped, knowing the impossibility of explaining something he didn't understand himself.

He said in a voice he didn't recognize. "Who was the man?"

"Nobody you know," she said.

"Who?"

"His name was Ben Jenkins. He ran a rolling store by here for a while, but he sold out before you come home from your job. It was that time you was away so long and didn't write much or send me any money, so I was lonesome and mad and—well, it just happened. And when it did, I was scared to death you'd find out and kill somebody, him or me or both of us. But the way it worked out was that he went away without knowing I was pregnant, and you come home and figured it had happened your first night back. So I thought I'd got by with it. Of course, Wilma Jean didn't favor neither one of us, but you didn't seem to question where she got them brown eyes, when everybody on both sides of the family has got blue eyes."

She started crying again. He said, "Shut up," in an angry voice, and she stopped, only she couldn't stop altogether but kept snuffling, like a spanked child.

But after a while that too stopped and she said dully, "What are you gonna do?"

He didn't answer that. Instead he said, "What I want to know is how come you acted so high and mighty over what I'd did when you ain't a damn bit better yourself."

"I reckon that was why. Because God had punished me so hard for what I done, making Wilma Jean sick and all, and it didn't seem fair that you could do the same thing or worse and not suffer a bit for it. And once I'd started being so hateful to you, it seemed to go on by itself."

"Looks like you would've stopped after Wilma Jean got well though."

"I wanted to, but seemed like every time I tried to make

265

up with you, you'd say something to hurt me. And then after she got killed, I knowed it was no use. I knowed the punishment wasn't over. It's gonna go on till the day I die. So I ain't scared any more that you'll kill me. I wish you would."

"Well, I ain't going to," J.T. said. "But I'm gonna do something else." He went and thumb-bolted the door and came back to the bed and said, "I want to get one thing straight first. It don't matter a damn who you lay with the night you got Wilma Jean; she was my little girl, and I don't want to hear nothing else about it. Now, move over."

Life was funny, he thought lying in bed drowsily listening to Esther rattling around in the kitchen getting supper ready. If he'd found out about Wilma Jean when it happened, he probably would've killed somebody. He'd changed a lot since them days. He'd changed a lot today. Up till now he'd kept Esther somewhere way up above him. Now he saw that she was just human, the same as him. He didn't love her no less, but it was different. He didn't think she was right about everyting the way he used to. He even thought she was wrong about God. And suddenly he wanted to tell her.

He got up and dressed and went into the kitchen. The boys were sitting at the table waiting for supper. He said, "You kids go out on the porch a minute. I want to talk to your mamma."

"Esther, you're wrong about God," he said. "If he's anything, he's good, and he wouldn't punish Wilma Jean for something you done. I wouldn't do that myself, and I don't lay no claim to being good. What happened to Wilma Jean was accidental."

She looked up at him and said, "You are good though."

"No, I ain't. I've did just about every sin you can think of and caused you all kinds of misery. I'm sorry for it now, even the moonshining. Did you hear what I just said? You reckon I've repented? I believe I have. It musta slipped up on me somehow. But anyway, if I've repented, there ain't no reason I can't join the church. And when I do, I'll tell people what wrong ideas they've got about God."

"You're gonna start preaching?" she asked with big, shocked eyes.

"That wasn't what I meant." He thought about it a minute. "I might if I had enough education, though. But I ain't."

266

"There's lots of country churches where it ain't needed."

"You're right," he said after considering this. "And something does seem to be telling me to go out and tell folks. You reckon that's a call?"

"It sounds like it to me."

He started laughing. "Now wouldn't it be something if J.T. Clayton started preaching?"

But he thought it wouldn't be no stranger than the things that had already happened. He put his arms around his wife and kissed her. Then he called the kids to supper.

37

Sam closed his office at one o'clock and walked to the boarding house to get Stella. They would eat lunch and then go talk to the Claytons and see if they could come up with something—anything—to help Stella. After that if she insisted, he would hypnotize her again, but he rather hoped she wouldn't insist, because he'd done it twice already, even though she wasn't aware of it. He had little hope that a third time would be more successful.

She did insist, however, and as he expected, the results were the same as before. She corroborated J.T.'s story but did not explain it. He couldn't tell her that and hand her a guilt she didn't deserve. And having promised to hypnotize her, he couldn't this time take away the memory of it. So when she was awake, he forced himself to lie and tell her she had denied J.T.'s story. She didn't question what he said but remarked that they were no better off than before.

Later he would remember every word they said, but at the time the hypnotism did not seem important except for the discouragement it produced, and Sam would have sworn that hit him harder that it did Stella.

They were at his house and he assumed Stella would stay until midnight, but at four-thirty, soon after the hypnotism session, she told him she wanted to go home and change. He said he didn't see why, because he planned to get her clothes off later anyhow. But she insisted, so he took her to the boarding house. He was to pick her up in an hour.

He was there five minutes ahead of time. He went into the hall and pressed Stella's buzzer. She did not come. Perhaps she was not finished dressing. He waited a few minutes and pressed the buzzer again. As he removed his hand and stepped back, he noticed an envelope on the table beside him. It had his name on it. He tore it open and took out a single sheet of paper with a few sentences written on it: "Sam, this is goodbye. Thank you for all you did, but don't try to do any more. It's too late. I haven't time to explain, but you'll understand later. All my love, Stella."

His heart slammed against his chest, and he felt as if he couldn't breathe. He took the stairs two at a time and crashed into her room.

There was no one there. He looked into the bathroom, but it was empty too. His heart eased a little, and he went back into the hall and knocked on Gaynell's door. "Where's Stella?" he asked without taking time for preliminaries, because the fright was coming back.

It was a suicide note. It had to be. This is goodbye.... It's too late.... But why? Why would she refuse to go away last night and then do this today? Just an hour ago she had seemed happy. Seemed was the key word though. How could he know what she was feeling? He thought of all the emotional stress she had lived through recently—Wilma Jean's death, Mrs. Granger's attempted suicide, Gaynell's venture into murder. All things for which she could blame herself. And her own problems: doubts about the healing, which was all too often followed by tragedy; worry over being accused of murder; fear of being arrested. Even her affair with him might be traumatic, since she could not believe in love and despised her own desires.

But none of those things was a fresh pain. She had surely already adjusted to their burden. So why today, now? He thought back over the afternoon, trying to find a reason. She had not seemed unduly depressed by the failure of the visit to the Claytons and the hypnotism.

His darting mind caught at one thought and hung there. The suggestion must have failed. She must have remembered what she said. She thought she was guilty of murder.

With difficulty he brought his attention back to Gaynell. "Where's Stella?" he asked again.

"Isn't she in her room?" Gaynell asked. "I haven't seen her. I just got back from town." Behind her on the bed he could see shopping parcels.

He said, "She left me a note.... I haven't time to explain, Gaynell, but will you call Valerie Howle and Adelaide Perry and Miss Mattie Shepard and anybody else you can think of who might have seen her? I'm going to drive around and look for her, and then I'll be back to hear what you've found out. Oh, and be sure the sheriff knows she's disappeared."

His own words were comforting. Disappearance was better than death. I was panicking again as I did last night, he told himself as he sped toward town. Last night.... I was going to take her away, but she wouldn't go. Was it because she wanted to wait and go alone? It would be like her not to want to trouble me. But she should know I'd be twice as troubled not knowing.

If she has gone away, though, I may have ruined it by telling Owen.

But when I first read the note, I didn't think of disappearance. I thought it was a suicide note. It can't be though. She wasn't in her room.

Of course she wasn't in her room. She knew I would look there. "Don't try to do any more," she said. But she must have known I would. Where would she go to kill herself? There aren't that many places to go. The restaurant, the library, the bus and train stations.

He checked them all. It took only a minute or two at each place. Where else? Oh Lord, help me think.

My office. I gave her a key to it at the same time I gave her a key to the house. It was a little thrill to give them to her, like saying, "All I have is yours." Of course, she's never used them. Until maybe now. But there's everything a suicide might need in that office. Drug samples, disinfectants, cleaning fluids, scapels.

He slammed on the brakes, jumped out of the car, and raced upstairs, cursing the time it took to get the door opened. He knew she wasn't there even before he turned on the lights, because he had no sense of her presence. But he made sure all the same.

Then back to the car. Where to now?

Back to the boarding house. Maybe Gaynell had some news. Maybe Stella had told somebody she was leaving. If she was giving up her job, she'd have notified someone in the school. She wouldn't go away without a word. Valerie might know.

Perhaps he was wrong. All this panic might be for nothing. Perhaps she was not leaving the town but only him. She could be visiting some friend now, unaware of how he had interpreted her letter and satisfied that she had made it clear she did not want to see him again.

But he did not believe it.

He skidded to a stop in front of the boarding house and ran up the walk. Gaynell was in the hall, just hanging up the phone. "Nobody knows anything, Dr. Taylor," she said. "I've called everyone I can think of. Mrs. Perry said the sheriff would look, too. He wants you to take the south side of town while he takes the north."

"All right," Sam said. "Keep trying, Gaynell."

He turned his lights to bright and began driving down the streets of the town, forcing himself to go slowly enough to check both sides of the street and even, as far as possible, the yards. He felt desperate. He knew he was wasting time. She would not be walking down any of these residential streets.

But what was that? On a lawn in front of him was a shapeless huddle that could be a body. He slammed on his brakes, but, even before the car stopped rolling, the huddle disentangled itself and turned out to be two little boys wrestling. He put his foot on the accelerator again and went on.

He glanced at his watch and saw that only thirty minutes had passed. It seemed hours. But it didn't take long to cover all the streets in Lanier. So maybe there was still time. Stella had no car. She would be walking. She couldn't get far in thirty minutes.

Walking where though? Where would she go if she wanted to kill herself and not be found until it was done?

Suddenly he thought of the river, and immediately he made a U-turn and headed for the river road, not bothering to go slowly now, because he had covered these streets already. Street lights flashed by so rapidly that there seemed no space between; they were like beads on a string. In five minutes he had left them behind, and the car was slicing through darkness, whipping around the none-too-gentle curves of the blacktopped road at an incredible speed and held to the pavement only by the skill of its driver.

It was six miles from the edge of town to the river bridge, and he made it in four minutes. There was no one on the bridge. He drove across it, parked on the shoulder of the road, and scrambled down the bank with his flashlight. The water made a soft, sighing sound as it flowed under the bridge, slapping gently at the concrete pilings. But Sam knew its tranquil murmurings were deceptive. It was deep here—some said forty feet—and strong enough to carry a body miles in one night.

The flashlight was inadequate to light the dark water, but he turned its beams here and there straining to see. His blood froze as the light picked up a dark object caught against one of the pilings, but the next minute it worked loose, and he saw it was only the dead limb of a tree.

There was nothing here, thank God. It was foolish anyway to think she would have walked so far. He hurried as fast as he could back up the sloping bank to the road and got in the car. A hundred yards farther the land leveled out on each side of the road, and a driveway turned into the yard of the bridgetender's house. He turned around there and headed back to town as if the fires of hell were licking at his heels. Another idea more frightening than any he'd had before had struck him.

Halfway back to town he met the sheriff's car. Owen was driving at a moderate speed and sweeping the woods with his searchlight.

Owen did not expect to find Stella. Unlike Sam, he was familiar with the bus and train schedules, and he knew that a bus to Birmingham had left at five-ten, just minutes before Gaynell called his house. He thought Stella was probably on that bus. Cecil Payne, the station manager and ticket seller, had not sold her a ticket, but he pointed out that the driver could have taken her aboard anyway and let her buy her ticket at the next stop. Owen had asked Adelaide to call the police in Tuscaloosa and have Stella taken off the bus there.

He hadn't meant to arrest her so soon. He'd hoped for a few more days to find a miracle. If she had not run away, he might have had it. Or if Sam hadn't been so quick on the trigger to inform him, it might have taken a few days to locate her. But they themselves had precipitated her arrest.

He couldn't expect to hear from Tuscaloosa for another hour, however, so he might as well spend that time searching Lanier for her. After all, he thought uneasily, it was possible that Stella had not run away but had now disappeared in the same way as Warner.

Possibly even at the same place.

He stepped down on the accelerator, and the car jumped ahead. Although he did not turn the searchlight off, he was now traveling so fast that it was unlikely he would see anything in its light. He did not stop at the river but sped across the bridge and turned into the same graveled driveway Sam had used. Pebbles hit the underside of the car as he backed out and headed back toward town.

Stella had not been quite honest with Sam when she told him she wanted to go home to dress. She knew that Sam did not care what she wore. But she had told him she was going home to change, and so she would do that first. Her real reason for leaving was that she suddenly thought of how to find out what had happened on that fatal night. She didn't want to tell Sam her idea until she had checked it out. He had been disappointed too many times before. If this worked, she could surprise him with it. If it didn't, he would have no letdown.

It was surprising that she hadn't thought of it before. After all, she had first noticed Miss Mattie's power over people about the same time that she became aware of her healing power. But she had paid little attention at first. Miss Mattie had always been bossy, and the difference—that she was now being obeyed—did not immediately catch one's attention. Even after Stella noticed it, she was merely puzzled and did not see any connection with her own power of healing.

But now suddenly it occurred to her that if Miss Mattie had a new power too, it had probably come from the same source as her own. That meant Miss Mattie must have been on the scene and might know something about Warner, or might at least have an explanation for the words J.T. Clayton claimed to have heard.

Stella slipped on her best dress, the aqua-colored silk shantung she had bought for Valerie's wedding. Sam might

272

not notice, but she wanted to dress up for him. If she had good news, she would be dressed for a celebration. If not, at least he'd have a better memory of her. Hurriedly she put on her makeup and then started downstairs to call Miss Mattie.

She was halfway down when the front door opened and Miss Mattie came in, followed by her cousin, Mrs. Alexander. Stella ran down the remaining steps. She would have preferred to talk to Miss Mattie alone. Mrs. Alexander gave her an uncomfortable feeling. Her high voice and strange amber-colored eyes which darted ceaselessly made her seem oddly restless and unsettled. One could not feel at ease with her.

Miss Mattie said, "I'm glad we found you at home, Stella. We're on our way to the Clayton place, and we want you to go with us. Cousin Edith thinks she knows where Warner's body can be found."

Stella stared at them openmouthed. When she found her voice, she said, "Then shouldn't you be talking to the sheriff?"

Mrs. Alexander laughed in a flustered way, a curiously inappropriate reaction, Stella thought. Miss Mattie said, "No, Owen wouldn't pay any attention to us. We don't even know ourselves whether we're right. But Cousin Edith took a nap this afternoon and had a dream of where Warner's body is, so we thought it was our duty to find out if it was true, and we wanted you to come because . . . because . . ." Miss Mattie floundered and came to a stop.

"Because we didn't want to go out there by ourselves, just two women alone, and we knew you had an interest in solving the crime," Mrs. Alexander said in her high, piping voice.

"Yes," Miss Mattie said, taking over again. "You must know there's been some gossip about you killing Warner, but Cousin Edith thinks finding his body with the position of the gunshot wound and everything will prove he must've shot himself. So come on. We need to hurry, because it isn't long until dark."

When Miss Mattie said, "Come on," Stella knew she had to go, and she said, "All right. But you'll have to excuse me just for a moment, so I can leave a note for somebody."

"Well, don't tell whoever it is where we're going or what

273

we're going to do, because if we do find the body, we don't want a crowd out there before the sheriff gets a chance to examine the evidence."

Prevented by Miss Mattie's restriction from telling Sam the facts, Stella tried to think hastily what she *could* say to him. Of course everything between them must come to an end now. Immediately. Before he was tainted by being connected to a murderess. He couldn't escape some gossip, she supposed—she wished he hadn't been so insistent about appearing in public with her—but the gossip wouldn't be so bad if he disconnected himself now.

Of course this might turn out to be nothing more than the hysterical imaginings of two middle-aged women. But somehow Stella was sure it wouldn't, because she knew something Miss Mattie did not know. She knew about J.T. Clayton's story. And she also knew that the minute Warner was found dead of a gunshot wound she was as good as convicted of murder.

She felt strangely peaceful though, as she laid the letter on the hall table and followed Miss Mattie and Mrs. Alexander to Miss Mattie's car. Everything was out of her hands. What is to be, will be, she thought fatalistically. She settled back on the cushions of the rear seat and closed her eyes. She closed her ears too, shutting out the sound of the conversation between Miss Mattie and her cousin.

Stella was thinking about Sam. She hoped he would take her at her word and not try to do anything else for her. If he tried to see her in jail, she must find a way to prevent it. It was hard to force him into anything, but somehow she would do it. She could find words more cruel than those in the note. In fact, now that she thought of it, that note was entirely wrong. "Thank you," she said, and, "All my love." It sounded sad and regretful. That was how she had been feeling, but she should not have let him know. She should have been cool and uncaring.

It was too late to worry about that now though. And, in any case, she had been cool and uncaring up to now. She had been completely honest with him, insofar as she understood her own emotions. She had not pretended to love him just because she was sleeping with him, and she had demanded nothing from him. He thought he was in love with her, but he would get over that when he learned that she really had killed Warner. Perhaps he would know she hadn't meant to. She hoped he would. But she was guilty just the same, and she could not expect him to forgive her.

He was a forgiving person though. Understanding. Sometimes she thought he understood her better than she understood herself. He had been right about why she went with those other men after Jim died. She still regretted that, but she no longer felt the terrible guilt or worried that she would react the same way again. He was right too about getting married. They should have, even if only for the pleasure of having more hours together. But no, it was a good thing they didn't, because now. . . .

The car had stopped. She opened her eyes. They were parked in J.T. Clayton's yard behind his battered pickup. Miss Mattie was getting out of the car and going toward the house.

Mrs. Alexander said, "We thought we shouldn't go on Mr. Clayton's land without asking him to come with us."

Stella closed her eyes again and went back to her thoughts about Sam. She smiled a little as she relived some of their moments together, and she was completely unaware that Mrs. Alexander's darting eyes had fixed on something to Stella's left.

Miss Mattie came back with Mr. Clayton in tow. He said, "I'd better get a shovel," but Mrs. Alexander said, "No, there's no need of that." Her voice was still high and thin, but somehow it had a different note in it, sure and authoritative. And ominous. Stella sat up in sudden alarm, but before she could say or do anything—and afterwards she was not sure what she had meant to say or do—Miss Mattie had started the car and turned it around.

"Back toward town," Mrs. Alexander said crisply.

They went down a little hill and around a curve, and there before them was the cotton patch by the road—bathed once more in a strange red glow which seemed to emanate from the flying craft Stella had seen before. Beside her J.T. gave an exclamation, and Miss Mattie slammed on the brakes so hard the sudden stop sent Stella hurtling toward the front seat. She caught herself in time to hear Mrs. Alexander say, "All of you get out."

As soon as her feet touched the ground, Stella felt herself begin to move toward the aircraft. But this time she thought of Warner and of the strange powers she was convinced were in the craft—power to heal, power to command, power to lift her unwilling feet and make her glide toward the machine—and she did not want to go. She did not want to disappear as Warner had. She wanted to stay with Sam. Even if everything ended between them, she wanted to stay in the same town, the same country, the same world. She did not want to go away. And she did not want to be given some further power. She could live with the one she had, although she was not sure even yet that it was altogether good, but how could she know that the next one would not be entirely evil?

She would not go. Human will must be worth something. If God had given man a choice—and in spite of her fatalistic thoughts a few moments ago she really believed he had—then surely man could choose not to obey a will outside his own. She would not go.

Sam and Owen had come to identical conclusions, and not many minutes apart. But Sam drove much faster, because he had more to lose by being slow and less to lose by going fast. He had no wife and baby at home to be grieved by an automobile accident; he had only Stella who might even now be going aboard a ship that would carry her out of his reach.

He ripped through town not heeding the speed laws, but watching the curbs to be sure there were no pedestrians to step unexpectedly into his path. Once out of town he pressed the gas pedal to the floor and watched the speedometer needle swing toward its highest mark.

A curve, a hill, another curve—he took them all without decelerating, knowing that if he saw the lights of another car, he would have to leave the narrow road, and would probably be killed. But there would be nothing else to do, because he would not kill someone else, and he could not hug his side of the road at this speed. He took a calculated risk because unless he found Stella, he did not care.

His car raced down the dark road as if it had a will of its own, as if it wanted to reach Stella as desperately as he did, and he let it go. The wind set up by its motion roared past the closed windows and rippled the broomsedge along the edge of the road. Loose bits of gravel spattered against the car, and one hit the windshield and left a round mark on the shatterproof glass.

There was the Granger house and there up the road beyond it, a cotton patch, which Sam recognized only because he remembered it and not from any look of familiarity about it now. It was filled with a strange red light, and in the center of it . . .

The tires skidded and gravel sprayed out as he threw on the brakes. For a moment the car rocked dangerously, but then it righted itself and rolled to a stop. He jumped out and ran toward the light.

But at its edge he was thrown backward, as if he had hit a concrete wall.

After a few moments he got his wind back and picked himself up. He tried again to go into the light, only to be stopped by that invisible barrier. Again and again he hurled himself against it, but each time he was thrown back.

He was still trying when the sheriff's car parked behind his. For a moment Owen sat in the car, staring with dazed, unbelieving eyes at the scene before him. What Stella said was all true, he thought, every last word of it. He had tried to believe it; he had told Sam he did believe it, but he hadn't until now. Hearing someone else tell about it, even Stella, whom he wanted to believe, was not like seeing it himself.

He got out of his car and went to where Sam was still vainly trying to move into the red light. Owen put out his hand and touched what seemed to be a smooth wall, like a glass window. Except that there was no window, no glass, nothing but the red light.

Owen said, "Sam, it's no use. Nobody can get through."

Sam turned a ravaged face on him. "You don't understand," he cried. "Stella is in there!"

At that moment as if in response to her name she came out of the saucer-shaped aircraft, and behind her were two other people, Miss Mattie Shepard and J.T. Clayton.

"Godalmighty," Owen breathed.

Sam was calling on God too but in a different way. "Please, God," he was saying over and over.

And before anyone could have walked across that cotton patch, the three had moved over it as a skier moves with a sliding, gliding motion. And then they stood in the road with Owen and Sam, watching the red glow fade. A blue light illuminated the craft, and with a humming sound

277

it rose straight up into the air and disappeared into the east.

After that the scene was somewhat confused. Sam had Stella in his arms, and he was laughing, but she felt his wet face against hers and said in a voice of wonder, "Sam, you've been crying! What are you doing here?"

Miss Mattie said, "Praise God! I've seen another vision!"

J.T. looked at her with dazed eyes and muttered, "So that's what it was! The Lord is sure enough calling me to preach."

Miss Mattie said, "Cousin Edith, this has happened to me before . . . why, where is Cousin Edith?"

Sam went to Owen, taking Stella with him, as if he were afraid to turn her loose. He said, "Owen, these people probably don't remember being aboard that thing. Do you, Stella? No, I thought not. And maybe it's best if we don't tell them. What do you think?"

"I sure hate to get the town riled up," Owen said, "but how are we gonna explain Mrs. Alexander disappearing unless we tell them the truth?"

"And who will believe it if we tell it?" Sam asked.

"But you and me—"

"How would you feel if it were two other respected citizens?" Sam asked. "Say Mr. Farley and Judge Penbury."

"Yeah, I see what you mean . . . This sure puts me on the spot. Warner and Mrs. Alexander—two people who've disappeared."

"Miss Mattie and J.T. think they've had a religious vision," Sam said. "Couldn't we say Mrs. Alexander was told to go home and you carried her to the bus station? We'd be lying, but no one is going to ask so many questions about a stranger, a visitor from . . . Texas, wasn't it?"

"No, not Texas," Stella said. "She was one of them. Well, she was, whether you believe it or not. I knew that before we started toward that red light. They talk to you without making any sound. She did that."

Sam said, "Are you sure?" He considered a moment and then answered his own question. "Yes, I expect so. I kept trying to tell myself her eyes were brown, but they weren't; they were yellow. And her voice . . ."

"She never used it again after we got here," Stella said. "She just put the thoughts in our heads somehow."

"What thoughts?"

278

"I don't know what she told the others," Stella said slowly, "but to me she said she'd promised to tell where Warner's body was and that it was in town."

"It can't be," Owen said, and then, "I'd better go see." He got in his car and left.

"Where is Cousin Edith?" Miss Mattie was still asking. "The sheriff shouldn't have left before we find her."

Sam took a deep breath and plunged into the story he and Owen had agreed on. ". . . so the sheriff took her to town and put her on the bus," he finished.

"Well, she could've waited to say goodbye," Miss Mattie said. "However, if she had a message from the Lord . . ." Now that the mystery was solved and her anxiety dissipated, she couldn't help drawing a big sigh of relief over Cousin Edith's departure. It would be nice for her and Eunice to have the house to themselves again, nice not to have Cousin Edith always around her neck like a millstone, nice to have Arline back again. God surely knew what he was doing to send her home, Miss Mattie thought approvingly.

Her thoughts turned back to her experience. "Eunice talked me out of telling it before, but now that it's happened again, I'm sure the Lord means for it to be known. I'll make the arrangements with Brother Bennett for us to give our testimony tomorrow night. Stella, you're the youngest, so you talk first, and then Mr. Clayton, and I'll be last."

Stella and J.T. spoke together, both refusing.

Stella said, "I'd rather not."

J.T. said, "No, ma'am, there's some things too sacred to talk about in public thataway. I ain't sure I'm ever gonna tell anybody about this night, even though I reckon I'll start preaching like the Lord has called me to do."

Miss Mattie sounded surprised, but she said, "Maybe you're right. I'll have to pray about it."

"Well, I guess we'd better get home," Sam said. "Stella will ride with me, Miss Mattie. Can we give you a lift, J.T.?"

"Much obliged, but I think I'll walk. I've got considerable to think about."

A quarter of a mile away J.T.'s new daughter-in-law also felt that there was much to consider. Her breath was coming very fast, and it was not just because of what she and Junior had been doing, because that was an hour ago, and he was still sleeping the sleep of slaked passion in the bedroom

279

behind the balcony where she sat. No, her quickened breath was caused by what she had seen through her telescope.

It was very similar to what she had seen before. Then she had not been able to tell anyone, but now she could. She jumped up out of her chair and started inside to wake Junior. If she hurried, he could get here in time to see the aircraft take off.

She stopped at the door. It wasn't her story to tell, and maybe the people concerned didn't want it told. Except for Miss Mattie, they were all people she did not want to offend. Stella, Dr. Taylor, Mr. Clayton. Stella she loved, almost worshipped, first out of gratitude, but now also because she had discovered an affinity she felt sure would make them the closest of friends. Dr. Taylor was her oldest friend, had once been her only friend. Mr. Clayton was family. She was obliged to love him for Junior's sake, but she would have anyway, because he had the same kindness and good humor she appreciated in his son. No, she wouldn't do anything Stella or Dr. Taylor or Mr. Clayton might not approve, not for the world.

So, she wouldn't tell Junior. He wouldn't be able to keep the secret. Poor baby, he was still immature in some ways, she thought tenderly.

She wondered what this meant though. Was it the second in what was to be a series of visits? Would it be followed by another strange occurrence like the healing? Or was it the end of something?

She didn't know. But she thought she wouldn't give the telescope to Junior's brothers as she had intended. Not just yet.

She didn't use the telescope much any more and, in fact, had only decided to take a last look through it because she had nothing else to do until Junior woke up hungry for dinner. Her parents were visiting relatives this weekend, and she and Junior had the house to themselves. He was making good use of the freedom. They had been in bed a good part of the day.

But she was glad to do what he wanted. Perhaps she didn't enjoy it quite as much as he did, but she expected that would come in time.

Maureen was surprised that people didn't immediately see how suitable her marriage was. But perhpas it was better if everyone, especially Junior, thought her overwhelmed

280

by love and passion. They did not have to know that she loved her husband because she had chosen to love him. Had chosen it with her eyes open and every faculty alert.

Marrying Junior Clayton was the perfect answer to her conflicting needs to have an independent life of her own while ostensibly remaining dependent on her parents. Junior was good-natured and easy-going. He didn't mind living with his in-laws or going into the Coca-Cola business at the low level Daddy thought appropriate. Indeed, as far as Marueen could see, the outward circumstances of his life did not concern Junior overmuch. He would work hard out of custom and duty, but he had no great ambitions for fame, fortune, or material possessions. His real pleasure came from fishing, hunting, and making love, although not necessarily in that order of importance.

She would see that he got what he wanted. So the arrangement was perfect for Junior too. Because of his marriage he would even have the financial success he would never have attained for himself. And love too, for she did love him, and if it was because she willed it, that took nothing away from Junior. Being practical didn't preclude being happy too. In fact, she was pretty sure it was an additional guarantee.

Certainly she was happy now, and she owed it all to Stella and to whatever or whoever had given her the power to heal. So instead of going to wake her husband, Maureen Clayton sat down in her chair and with a secret smile on her face watched the blue glow of the strange, saucer-shaped aircraft fade into the distance.

38

On the way back to town Sam asked Stella twice if she felt all right.

"I'm thinking of how sick you were before," he said. "Of course, I don't know what caused it, or whether any precautions would be effective, but anyhow let's stop by the boarding house so you can shower and change clothes."

So she and Sam were there when Warner Fox arrived.

Somewhat later, as they drove toward Sam's, Stella said, "What Shakespearean turns of phrase leapt to mind when Gaynell and Warner met. 'Do not impute this yielding to light love . . . I'll follow thee, my lord, throughout the world.' "

"Juliet? But he's done more, I think. He's followed her throughout the universe."

"He doesn't know it though, does he?" Stella asked. "What exactly did he say? I missed some of it while I was upstairs getting dressed."

Sam answered, "He said when he came to himself on the road near the Clayton's, he immediately started looking for his car, with his mind on going to Birmingham and coming back next week to get married. But he didn't find the car, of course, so he walked to town and went home to call Owen. Now he knows it's three months later, but he doesn't know where he's been or what's happened. So apparently they did the same thing to him that they did to you, erased his memory."

"At least he's alive. I was so afraid . . . I wonder why Mrs. Alexander—although I guess that isn't her name—I wonder why she told me Warner's *body* was in town?"

"Well, it was, wasn't it?" Sam said with a smile. "It strikes me that she had a sense of humor. Peculiar maybe, but who knows what cosmic humor is like? I wouldn't be surprised if this whole thing was some kind of tremendous joke. The laughter of the gods, or something like that."

"Or maybe an experiment that's now ended," Stella said slowly. "Maybe that's why Mrs. Alexander was here—to observe it. She went everywhere with Miss Mattie, but she never said much or took any part in what was going on. She was just there, watching. I wonder why though. Why would those—those beings—want to experiment with us?"

"To help us?" Sam suggested.

Stella frowned. "Maybe, but Mrs. Alexander didn't strike me as having any great compassion. I'd say that whatever she did was for her own benefit—or for some larger, impersonal good."

"It wasn't impersonal, though," Sam objected. "Look at the powers they bestowed—healing and truth and authority. They had results on a limited and purely human level."

"Yes," Stella agreed. "But maybe the experiment was supposed to have a wider application. If it worked with us here in Lanier, it might work with everyone."

"And make the world a better place to live? If they're as indifferent as you say, why should they care?"

"Because it affects them in some way." Her eyes widened. "The only thing I ever saw affect Mrs. Alexander was an argument. She couldn't stand dissension. Remember how she used to get a coughing spell every time the discussion got heated? Could that be it? Are they trying to find a way to make us live together in peace so we won't destroy ourselves—and perhaps upset the balance of the universe?"

They stared at each other. Finally Sam said slowly, "I suppose it's possible. Maybe that's why it happened at this time. We didn't have the power to destroy ourselves until we built the atomic bomb. . . . If that was the purpose, let's hope it worked."

Stella's expression was thoughtful. "I wonder," she said. "Did you notice that Miss Mattie ordered J.T. and me to participate in a church service and we refused? I couldn't have done that a month ago, or even yesterday. She has lost the power to command . . . Sam, I wonder if I still have the healing power?"

"I don't know, sweetheart. We'll just have to wait and see."

"When do you think we'll know?"

He shrugged. "Who can tell? Maybe they've left it with you or if not, maybe they'll give it back someday. Perhaps they have to evaluate the results first. And of course, their time may not be like ours."

"It's strange how I feel about the healing," she said. "A month ago I wouldn't have wanted to keep it, but now . . . I've learned a lot from you . . . If I've lost the healing power, will it change your feeling for me?"

His heart began beating faster, but he answered lightly, "Of course not. It wasn't based on an interest in your healing."

She didn't say any more, and his disappointed heart slowed down.

He drove into the driveway, and they went into the house. As soon as they were inside, he put his arms around her. She leaned back and said, "Sam, do you remember what I said in that note?"

He laughed. "Lord, what a question. Shall I recite it for you?"

"No. I just wanted you to know I meant it all. No, wait, let me say it. I love you. That's why I cried that night, but I

283

couldn't tell you then with arrest hanging over me. But I can tell you now. I love you with all my heart, and with all my mind, and with all my soul—yes, and with my body too. There's a line in a marriage service—Church of England, I think—that says how I feel about you: 'With my body I thee worship.' "

"My God, Stella. My God. I hope you know what you've done ... Shall we have those same words in *our* marriage service?"

"And shock Lanier out of ten years growth? But yes, let's do."

And after that silence reigned in the Taylor house for a very long while.

ABOUT THE AUTHOR

Elna Stone was born in Mississippi and has lived in the South all her life, mostly in Pensacola, Florida. She is married and has four children. Her first novel was the highly praised *The Visions of Esmaree*.

NEW FROM POPULAR LIBRARY

CURRENT POPULAR LIBRARY BESTSELLERS

☐ **DUST DEVIL**   04667 $2.95
  by Parris Afton Bonds
  A saga of love and survival of the early settlers of the untamed
  southwestern plains.

☐ **MURDER IN THE WHITE HOUSE**   04661 $2.95
  by Margaret Truman
  A gripping novel of an unprecedented crime in the cloistered pre-
  cincts of the highest office of the land.

☐ **FALLING IN PLACE**   04650 $2.95
  by Ann Beattie
  This is a novel about missed connections and accidental collisions—
  about couples who can never say what they mean, and more often
  say what they shouldn't.

☐ **INNOCENT BLOOD**   04630 $3.50
  by P.D. James
  A novel which explores the themes of the growth of love and the
  search for identity. An adopted girl finds herself in terrifying danger
  when she learns the truth about her biological mother.

☐ **THE FATHER OF FIRES**   04640 $2.95
  by Kenneth M. Cameron
  A monumental saga of the Morse family, owners of a munitions empire, whose lives and loves lead them from Europe to the New
  World.

Buy them at your local bookstore or use this handy coupon for ordering.

COLUMBIA BOOK SERVICE
32275 Mally Road, P.O. Box FB, Madison Heights, MI 48071

Please send me the books I have checked above. Orders for less than 5 books
must include 75¢ for the first book and 25¢ for each additional book to cover
postage and handling. Orders for 5 books or more postage is FREE. Send check
or money order only. Allow 3-4 weeks for delivery.

Cost $_____	Name_____
Sales tax*_____	Address_____
Postage _____	City_____
Total $_____	State_____ Zip_____

*The government requires us to collect sales tax in all states except AK, DE,
MT, NH and OR.*

Prices and availability subject to change without notice.   **8214**

CURRENT CREST BESTSELLERS

☐ **BORN WITH THE CENTURY**   24295 $3.50
by William Kinsolving
A gripping chronicle of a man who creates an empire for his family, and how they engineer its destruction.

☐ **SINS OF THE FATHERS**   24417 $3.95
by Susan Howatch
The tale of a family divided from generation to generation by great wealth and the consequences of a terrible secret.

☐ **THE NINJA**   24367 $3.50
by Eric Van Lustbader
They were merciless assassins, skilled in the ways of love and the deadliest of martial arts. An exotic thriller spanning postwar Japan and present-day New York.

☐ **KANE & ABEL**   24376 $3.75
by Jeffrey Archer
A saga spanning 60 years, this is the story of two ruthless, powerful businessmen whose ultimate confrontation rocks the financial community as well as their own lives.

☐ **GREEN MONDAY**   24400 $3.50
by Michael M. Thomas
An all-too-plausible thriller in which the clandestine manipulation of world oil prices results in the most fantastic bull market the world has ever known.